"The woman in red will be your friend," the High Lama had said, *"and through her will come the one to fear, who will be your enemy, the Silver Man . . . ."*

I knew he stood before me now. Bloodless he was, for while Eleanor had a slight tan from the sun, Vernon Quayle's face was unnaturally white, as if from lack of pigment rather than ill-health.

One part of my mind kept telling me that I was being stupid and over imaginative, that because Eleanor's husband was silver-haired there was no reason to believe he fulfilled some strange prediction made by a dull-witted girl and an old monk, six years ago and half a world away. But somewhere deep in my being, I felt that I was looking at the one the Oracle had called the Eater of Souls.

I stared, with horror creeping through me, remembering the other words, *". . . within the bounds of earth and incarnation, I had never thought to feel such power."*

Who was this terrifying stranger? And what did he want with me?

MERLIN'S KEEP

a novel by

Madeleine Brent

FAWCETT CREST • NEW YORK

MERLIN'S KEEP

THIS BOOK CONTAINS THE COMPLETE TEXT OF
THE ORIGINAL HARDCOVER EDITION.

Published by Fawcett Crest Books, a unit of CBS Publications,
the Consumer Publishing Division of CBS Inc., by arrangement with Doubleday and Company, Inc.

Copyright © 1977 by Souvenir Press Ltd.

ISBN: 0-449-23810-5

Selection of the Doubleday Book Club.
Selection of the Literary Guild.

Printed in the United States of America

10 9 8 7 6 5 4 3 2 1

MERLIN'S
KEEP

CHAPTER ONE

Even before we reached the top of the Chak Pass, I saw the tall figure of Sembur begin to sway in the saddle, and knew that his heart was laboring badly in the thin air. A chill deeper than the coldness of the mountain winds touched my own heart, for Sembur was all I had.

My place was at the rear of the straggling caravan, but none of the men said anything to stop me as I touched heels to my pony and urged her forward. The wind was keen, and we all had our heads down and our hoods drawn closely round our faces, so perhaps nobody even noticed me as I moved past the long line of yaks plodding tirelessly under the burden of big leather panniers loaded with salt.

When I came up beside Sembur I reached out to grasp his arm and spoke in the tongue that only he and I knew, the tongue he had taught me from the beginning. In time to come I was to discover that I spoke it with a very bad accent, but at this time, when I was in my thirteenth year, I had never heard it on the lips of anyone but Sembur, and so I spoke the strange tongue just as he did. Sembur called it Hinglish, and was himself a Hinglishman, which meant that he came from a country on the other side of the world.

"You all right, Sembur?" I asked anxiously.

He turned his muffled head, and two bloodshot blue eyes looked down at me from his weatherworn face. I saw that his color was bad, his lips bluish, and even the sharp points of his mustache were drooping. A shiver touched me. This was Sembur, who had always walked or ridden with a back as straight as the golden spires of Galdong, and who had always seemed to me as strong and ageless as the mountains them-

7

selves. But of late I had realized that he was no more than human, and now I saw that he looked old.

"You don't 'alf look rotten," I said. "Put your 'and on my shoulder."

He pulled himself together with an effort, and glared down at me. "What's this? What's this, hey? 'Oo told you to leave your post with the rear guard, young lady?"

"Ah, don't go and get cross with me, Sembur. I saw you sorter swaying about and I got ever so worried. Go on, 'ang on to me a bit, till you feel better. You'll be all right, soon as we get over the top an' down a bit lower."

Sembur spoke through stiff lips, panting a little, and pitching his voice just loud enough to carry above the hissing of the wind. "Don't want this lot to see I'm not meself, Jani." He twitched his fair bushy eyebrows and turned his eyes to one side, then the other, indicating the score of men from Namkhara who had ridden with us on the month-long caravan.

I said, "Listen, you gimme your rifle to carry, Sembur, then you can lean on me an' pretend you're telling me 'ow it works while we go along." When he hesitated I added urgently, "Come on, we're not going to 'ave any trouble with them Khamba tribesmen now. They never attack in the pass, and we'll be in Smon T'ang soon." This was the name of the country where we lived. The people were known as Lo-bas, and we were returning now after a trading journey into the land of Bod, or Tibet as Sembur always called it.

He nodded, and slipped the rifle from his shoulder. I knew that this was the finest rifle in the whole country, for it was a Hinglish one, with a narrow metal box called a magazine, so that the cartridges did not have to be put in one by one. I took the rifle, made sure the safety catch was on, as Sembur had always taught me, and sat holding it in front of me with both hands, guiding my pony, Pulki, with my knees. Sembur rested his hand on my shoulder. I was too small to give him much support, but I knew I was strong enough to steady him, so he could sit more restfully in the saddle.

After a few moments I heard him give a little sigh, then he said, "Thanks, lovey. I'm getting a bit old for these 'igh halti-tudes. We must 'ave a little chat about it when we get 'ome."

"All right, but don't talk now. You need your breath."

He gave a feeble chuckle. "Sounded just like your ma, you did just then, Jani."

I did not answer, for I was too busy reproaching myself

8

for not setting a demon trap outside our tent each night, to keep the mountain demons away. They were even worse than the plain demons, and I had no doubt that one of them had got into Sembur and was plaguing his heart and lungs. The trouble was that Sembur himself had forbidden me to make or set demon traps.

I remembered how shocked he had been the first time he found me busily making one, with part of a ram's horn, plaited straw, some small pictures I had scratched on little pieces of bark, and some spells I had persuaded Lahna the Witch to draw for me on strips of leather. Everybody in Smon T'ang knew that there were over four hundred demons of earth and air, fire and water, and that these evil spirits could cause a thousand or more diseases, as well as bring violent death to a victim in five different ways.

Sembur did not believe any of this, and said no Hinglish person would believe such nonsense. In a way I knew he was right, but in another way I was quite sure there were many demons in this part of the world even if there were none in Hingland. It was sometimes difficult to make Sembur understand the people we lived with, because although we had lived for ten years in Smon T'ang, or Mustang as he called it in Hinglish, he still spoke only a few words of the language, and was always making mistakes. He had never grasped that there were two ways of speaking, an ordinary way when speaking to ordinary people and a special way when speaking to a higher person.

"They're all a bunch of 'eathens, this lot, Jani," he had said to me many times. "Good-'earted, mind you. They been very nice to us most of the time, I must say. But they're hignorant, see? Never been taught proper."

"Taught what, Sembur?" I had once asked.

"Eh? God bless my soul, just about *heverything*, girl! I mean, they don't even wash regular an' keep themselves clean an' well turned out like we do, for a start." That was true, and in the past I had often envied the other children, who were bathed only for festivals, while I had to stand stripped in a small wooden tub every day to be washed from head to foot. Three summers ago Sembur had said I was becoming too big a girl for him to bathe me, and that I must do it myself in future. At first I had cheated, pulling the yak-hair curtain across the doorway of the little room where I slept, and only pretending to bathe myself. But then to my dismay I discovered that I felt miserable if my body and clothes were not

9

clean, and I went back to the washing habits I had known all my life.

On another occasion when Sembur was on the same subject, reminding me of the differences between the Lo-bas and ourselves, he said, "It's not just that they're hignorant about keeping clean an' smart, Jani. They're not heducated neither. None of 'em can read or write, except for the monks. But you can, because I've taught you to read an' write as good as me, so there's no excuse for you be'aving like these 'eathens."

I had had lessons almost every day for as long as I could remember, and I had read a book called *The Holy Bible* three times. We had only two books, and the other was called *Tales of Jessica*. This one had pictures in it, and was about a girl who wore a long dress and sometimes rode on a bicycle, an amazing machine with two wheels. Jessica was always doing exciting things like going to school, or to a place called the seaside, and she was very good at helping people. The picture I liked best was of Jessica waving a flag to stop a huge engine with big wheels going along a railway line, because a gentleman had got his foot caught in one of the lines. I often hoped I would grow up to be like Jessica and save people from getting run over by big engines.

Sembur said there were hundreds of different books, all telling different stories. This was hard to believe, but it had to be true, for I knew Sembur never told me lies. There were some very strange stories in the other book, *The Holy Bible*, and I found it difficult to understand many of the words, but I could read them out loud, and this was good enough for Sembur.

Once I said, "There are lots and lots of scrolls in the Galdong monastery, Sembur, an' scrolls are like books. Ghenling told me about them, he's seen 'em. I wouldn't 'alf like to read something different."

Sembur had laughed his sharp throaty laugh that sounded like a dog barking. "You can't read *them*, Jani. They're all written in foreign, not Hinglish."

"Why can we only read an' write Hinglish then?"

He had given me his fierce stare, which he used a great deal on the Lo-bas. "Gawd's strewth, Jani, because we *are* Hinglish, that's why! And you better be proud of it, my girl."

"I dunno, Sembur. Sometimes I wish I wasn't. I mean, when the other children don't like me and act rotten to me because of being different. Grown-ups too, sometimes."

Sembur had sighed. "I know, lovey, I know," he said in the

gentle voice he sometimes used. "Mostly they're all right, these people, but sometimes I don't like to turn me back in case they stick a knife in it. Still, you got to make allowances for 'em. It's just hignorance. They're always seeing omens everywhere. Only needs a yak to fall down a crevasse, and they'll see 'alf a dozen omens to say it's all because of two foreigners living in the village." He shrugged. "Still, all we 'ave to do when they turn funny is clear off for a few days, an' they soon forget about it."

What Sembur said was quite true. I had seldom felt really frightened in Namkhara. I played with the other children, and worked with them in the fields round the village, or in the sheds where the women spun goat's wool or yak hair, and cured hides. Without Sembur, I might almost have been accepted as one of them, for though my skin was pale I had eyes as dark and hair as black as any of the people of Smon T'ang. But though Sembur was respected by the Lo-bas, he could never have become one of them, for he was unable to change his Hinglish ways, and would never dream of trying to.

When I thought about it, I realized that he was exactly the same as he had always been, going right back to that other world at the very beginning of my memory, the world that was like a half-remembered dream. I always assumed, without quite knowing why, that my parents had died in that other world. I did not remember them, and I suppose I had given little thought to the past until my tenth year, when for a short time I became intensely curious, pestering Sembur to tell me about my mother and father, where we had lived, and what had happened to them. For the most part Sembur managed to avoid my questions or to put me off in some way, but when at last I pinned him down he frowned, rubbed a hand over his bristly short-cropped hair, then twisted the right-hand point of his mustache rather savagely, as he always did when troubled.

"Well, I dunno, Jani. You're a bit young still, to understand."

"At least you can tell me what 'appened, even if I don't understand."

"What makes you think *I'm* not your pa? That's what all the Lo-bas reckon."

"I know, but it just . . . it just doesn't seem like that, some'ow."

"Oh? I'm not good enough, hey?"

"Don't talk daft. Are you really my pa, honest?"

"I'll tell you one day. When it's safe."

"What's that mean?"

"It means if I'm not careful you might be in danger."

"Coo! Like Jessica stopping the train?"

Sembur made a grimace. "I'm not saying any more."

"All right, but what about my ma? Is she dead, Sembur?"

He nodded, and I saw him swallow hard. "Yes. I'll explain everything when you're a bit older, lovey, I promise."

"How much older?"

"Now don't you start nagging, young lady. I got enough to think about, trying to bring you up proper. It's very 'ard for a man 'oo's got no experience of little girls."

I had sulked for a while, but then my curiosity had waned, perhaps because Sembur took me on my first trip with a salt caravan into Bod, the land he called Tibet, and this excitement drove everything else from my mind. I forgot about my past for the time being, but sometimes, half waking from a dream of great rooms and silken rugs and soft arms holding me, I would remember Sembur's promise, and feel impatient for the time when I would know all that was hidden from me.

By the time we had descended from the top of the pass to ten thousand feet, Sembur looked better. His breathing was easier, and there was no longer that frightening blue tinge to his lips. He took the rifle from me, slung it on his shoulder, and turned in the saddle to look back along the straggling column of yaks and ponies. The walls of the pass were high here, protecting us for a while from the harsh mountain winds which made this last caravan before winter such an exhausting journey for men and beasts alike.

Ghenling called out from the rear, and Sembur muttered sharply, "What's 'e saying, Jani?"

"Just a silly joke, asking 'ow many Khambas I was going to shoot with your gun."

"Gun?" Sembur rolled up his eyes and gave a snort of contempt. "Tell 'im a Lee Metford three-o-three isn't a *gun*, it's a rifle."

"They 'aven't got separate words, Sembur. Anything that goes bang, they call it a gun."

"I thought you were always telling me they 'ad three words

12

for everything, one 'igh-class word, one low-class word, and another for writing."

"Well, they do in a way. But it's not so much different words. It's more like a different way of saying the same thing."

Sembur sniffed again, and I giggled to myself. He had taken care of me all my life, and I loved him very much, but I still thought him in many ways the strangest and funniest man I had ever known. The Lo-bas would have treated him as a fool if it had not been that they respected him as a powerful warrior. It was not just that he possessed the finest gun in the world, while they owned only a few muzzle-loading weapons. He was also a man of strong spirit, forceful and unafraid.

Before Sembur's time, at least two caravans each year had been set upon by the fierce Khamba tribesmen of Bod, who had seized many packs, panniers, and animals. When Sembur began to ride with the caravans, carrying his deadly rifle, it was different. The robbers were driven off, and nothing was lost. Sometimes a group of Khambas would appear at a distance, watching and following for a few days, but as long as they saw Sembur's tall figure standing out among the Lo-bas, they never dared to attack.

I often felt very proud and superior because I was the only girl who ever rode with the salt caravans. The boys were not allowed to make the journey into Bod until they were eighteen, and no females at all were allowed, except for me. There were two reasons why I was allowed to go. Earlier, when I was small and Sembur went away on a caravan, he always left me in the care of a woman called Chela, who was married to two brothers but had no children. I did not like her because she used to tell terrible stories about demons, which frightened me and gave me bad dreams.

Then Chela died, when I was in my tenth year. Sembur said it was something called a busted appendix, but what had really happened was that a demon had entered her and made her belly swell up very painfully until her spirit was driven out and she died.

When the next caravan was due to go, I begged Sembur to take me with him. I had started riding ponies almost as soon as I could walk, and promised I would be no trouble. Sembur was taken aback, but at last he gave that brisk nod which meant he had made up his mind. In the morning, when the caravan assembled, I was there with him. And when Old

13

Tashi, the leader, waved his arms and protested, Sembur said very loudly in Hinglish that either we both went or we both stayed in Namkhara. Nobody understood him, of course, and he said to me in the sharp voice he used most of the time: "You tell 'em, Jani. If they want me and my rifle to see 'em safe to Magyari and back, then it's hessential they let you come along."

When I translated this into polite phrases for Tashi, the Lo-bas were dismayed. Over the past few years they had stopped being resigned to the occasional loss of a caravan of salt, or of the grain and silver coins we carried to Magyari for barter. They had become used to traveling in safety under Sembur's protection, and this was why they were never unfriendly towards us as foreigners for long, even when the omens said we brought bad fortune. They knew well enough that Sembur had brought good fortune with the caravans. They also knew that in his last life he had been a snow leopard, which was why the Khambas were so afraid of him.

Sembur himself did not know he had once been a snow leopard, and I had never told him because I knew it would make him cross.

Old Tashi scratched his head and held a long discussion with the other men. At last we all set off, but halted for many hours at Galdong, some miles to the north, while Tashi went into the great monastery to seek the advice of the monks. I never knew what they told him, but when at last he emerged I began my first trip out of Smon T'ang and into the land of Bod.

The second reason I was allowed to go with the salt caravans, or rather the reason I was welcomed on them after that first journey, was because it was discovered that I had what the Lo-bas considered a truly magical gift with the yaks. They were slow-moving creatures, always bad-tempered, and sometimes a yak would decide to stand still and gaze at nothing for many hours without moving, like a monk in meditation. It was too heavy to drag, and nobody dared to use any painful method of goading, for fear that the creature might be the reincarnation of some dead relative, with a heavy karma to discharge before it could be reborn in human form.

When one yak stopped, the caravan had to halt, and this meant endless delays. My gift was that I could persuade a yak to move, just by rubbing its nose and talking to it. I had no idea how I did this, I only knew that it happened. Sembur said it was because I liked yaks when almost everybody else became annoyed with their slowness and stupidity.

It was true I liked yaks. We used them for plowing and as beasts of burden, we spun their hair to make our clothes, and twisted it into thick strands to make our boots. We drank their milk, burned their dung for warmth, and bled them once a year to eat their dried blood. They were too precious to slaughter when young, but in time they gave us meat and bone.

I was grateful to yaks. Sembur said they did not exist in most of the world, and this amazed me. I could not see how people could survive without yaks. Of course, he may have been wrong in thinking that they obeyed me because I liked them. Perhaps the truth was, as Lahna the Witch once told me, that I had been a herd leader in an earlier life, and the creatures recognized me as one of them. Whatever the real reason, I had been welcome on the salt caravans for the past three years, and was now completing my ninth journey.

Behind us the peaks were gray and white. Before us the trail wound steeply down to a high narrow valley, then on beyond, dropping at an easier gradient through brown foothills scarred by thin ragged gullies which snaked down toward the patchwork of green fields covering the flat plain. From where we moved on the winding track above, the small river was a thread of silver twisting through the fields. Beside it was the road to Namkhara, and at the point where the river widened into a moon-shaped lake stood the monastery of Galdong, six great oblong terraces of dull red stone rising one upon the other, topped by four needle-like gold spires. Each tier was pierced by many long windows edged in white stone, and along the roof of the highest tier stood a row of huge prayer flags in the five colors which represented the five different aspects of life.

The monastery stood in a great courtyard surrounded by a high wall with an arched gateway. Outside the wall which faced the river was a line of squat, heavily carved and ocher-painted chortens, with short conical spires. These were shrines where the ashes of lamas had been placed, and it was well known that it was a good thing to go and pray by these shrines if you wanted to acquire merit and make your next life easier, as everybody in Smon T'ang did, except Sembur.

In the courtyard I could see little red dots moving about. These were the lamas in their tall red hats. I was always rather afraid of the lamas, but Sembur called them an idle lot.

He thought it a disgrace that they sent the holy women out to work in the fields while they did nothing but spin prayer wheels and meditate and write in huge silk-bound books which were kept in a place called a library.

The High Lama of Galdong was very important, but not as important as some other High Lamas in other monasteries, because Galdong was one of the smallest. I had met him three times to speak to, on occasions when he had sent for Sembur and had needed me to translate. His name was Rild, and he had a very quiet face, as if his thoughts were always somewhere else, but I liked him, because although he gazed through me or past me he always smiled and spoke gently to me.

He only sent for Sembur if the omens were bad and it seemed wise for the two of us to go away alone into the hills for a while. I remembered the last time he had spoken to me in his thin high voice as we stood before him in a lofty chamber with butter lamps flickering along the walls.

"You will inform Sembur that in the past days all omens and auguries declare that those who are strangers among us are opening the way for new demons to descend upon us."

"I will say this to him now, Highborn."

When I did so, Sembur growled, "Ask 'im why all these hextra demons turn up in winter, when there aren't any caravans that need guarding."

"I can't say that to 'im, Sembur! He can't 'elp what the omens show."

"What omens?"

"Well, the way clouds move, and the way a bird flies, and 'ow the stars lie, and whether the goats move left or right when they're going to the river—oh, there's 'undreds of omens."

"Tommyrot, the lot of it."

I turned to Rild, "Forgive me, Highborn. He is slow of wit, like a yak, and there is need for me to explain as to a small child. I have told him, and he understands now."

The High Lama went on, "No Lo-bas will harm you, for that is against the Law, and would cost a man much merit in his journeying on the Wheel of Life. But then it must be said that if the people of Namkhara were to drive you out of their village, they might expect to gain much merit by diverting the influx of bad spirits and demons, who will otherwise be drawn to Namkhara by your presence, according to the omens. Do you understand, child?"

I understood only too well. If Sembur and I did not leave Namkhara of our own accord for a while, and live alone in the hills, then we would be driven out of the village. It had happened before, but only once, because Sembur had learned his lesson after that first time. He had been ready to break one or two heads with a cudgel when the men came to drive us out, but they did not come. Instead, a dozen or more women descended upon us, waving sticks, calling him a foreigner, and threatening to beat him without ceasing until he fled. Sembur was aghast and furious, but quite unable to stand firm against the women. Within a few minutes he had packed our tent of black yak hair and our few belongings, had set me on my pony, and we were gone.

Since then we had been sent away from Namkhara three times, but we had always gone without argument or fuss. Our exile never lasted longer than a few weeks, for in the world of demons all things changed with the new moon, and it was very rare for them to be hostile to us for two months at a time. When we returned to Namkhara we were always welcomed in the most friendly fashion. The people did not dislike us. They only drove us away at those times when our presence opened the door to demons who would bring sickness and misfortune.

I often felt lonely when we had to go away into the hills by ourselves, because I missed having the other children to play with. Sembur tried to make the time pass by giving me lessons, because he wanted me to be heducated. I quite liked to practice reading and writing, but some things he taught me were very strange, such as the world being round like a ball, and a place called London, where engines on wheels moved about on rails all the time, just like in *Tales of Jessica*, and other engines moved about on roads, with no horses to pull them.

There was also a lesson called Istory, in which the Hinglish people kept moving about the world on enormous lakes known as the sea. They traveled in ships, which were big iron boats with steam inside. These ships belonged to a lady called Queen Victoria, and they took soldiers to all different parts of the world to heducate people in other countries and teach them how to do things.

I found Sembur's lessons very confusing, and was always glad when we could return from the hills to our home in Namkhara again, for it was cold living in a tent in winter. Last year we had been fortunate, for the omens were kind, but the one before had been very bad. Our exile had lasted through seven weeks of bitter weather, and for three of those weeks I had had to nurse Sembur when a disease demon settled in his chest.

We had not been summoned to the presence of the High Lama of Galdong since our return from that exile, and now, as we rode down into the valley with our slow-moving caravan, I hoped fervently that we would not be sent away in the winter months to come.

Beside me, Sembur said briskly, "Shoulders back, Jani. Sit up straight in the saddle, there's a good girl."

I stretched to ease my aching muscles, and with an effort drew myself up. "Sorry . . . I'm 'alf asleep."

"I know, lovey, I know. But I told you before, you got to 'ide it. Never let this lot see that you're tired or scared or worried."

"Why not, Sembur?" I had never asked that before.

"Hey? Well, because you're Hinglish, that's why, so you've always got to be'ave calm an' quiet. And another thing, it 'elps to give you hauthority, see? If people see you got the wind up, or you're all fagged out, they're not going to 'ave any respect."

Sometimes, when I felt tired, I wished I had somebody besides Sembur to look after me, and I would have especially liked to have had a mother, but whenever these thoughts came to me I felt very guilty, for I was old enough now to realize that all my life I had been Sembur's sole concern, because it was a matter of duty to him. I did not know why he believed it to be his duty to look after me, unless he was my father, for certainly he was not well fitted to bring up a little girl from babyhood, but he had done it as well as he could, hiding all doubt and anxieties behind an air of brisk confidence.

And now, when I straightened my back and rode on between the fields of barley stubble as if I felt fresh and unweary, I did not do it because it would gain me respect from the Lo-bas, but simply because it was important to Sembur.

Some of the fields were being plowed before winter turned the ground to iron, but the plowmen halted their yaks to wave and greet the caravan as we passed. Some of the hundred holy women of Galdong were working in the fields, gathering stones in big baskets and carrying them away on mules. Old Tashi remembered the holy women clearing the ground of stones in his childhood, just as they did today. It seemed that however many were carried away, more would always appear. The holy women were not supposed to look at the men as the caravan came by, but they always did. They had hair cropped very close to their heads, and wore long russet skirts decorated with small turquoises which matched the color of their tunics.

This was the last caravan of the season. It was to be the last ever for Sembur and for me, but we did not know that then. We were all in a cheerful mood, despite the long day's journey, because we had come back from Magyari well laden this time. Apart from the usual load of salt, we had some bales of beautiful silks and rich brocades which had been traded in Magyari by the yellow men who came from beyond the land of Bod.

We also had some sacks of their tea, which the noble families of Smon T'ang liked very much. The ordinary people preferred the tea that came from the south, from the land of India, beyond Pokhara, where we bartered our salt for silver and grain. Some of the silks would be traded in Pokhara, with the salt, but some would be kept by the lamas and nobles, for making their robes and fine clothes.

We never went with the southbound caravans, Sembur and I. Old Tashi had asked us to go, for although the Lo-bas did not need Sembur's protection there, they were always glad of my gift for handling the yaks. But Sembur would never take me south. I knew that in the ten years since we had come to Namkhara he had gone south only twice, and then he had gone alone. When I asked why, he had told me that he would explain one day when I was older.

Because I was pretending not to be tired, I quickly began to feel less tired, and I dropped back to chat with Ghenling, the young man who was our neighbor in Namkhara. He liked to tease me and make silly jokes, and the more I pretended to be cross the more he enjoyed it. We were drawing close to the monastery now, where we would halt in the great court-yard while the monks came to examine the merchandise we had brought from Magyari, to decide how much we must leave for the tax gatherer when he came to our district. Beside me, Ghenling said, "When we stop in Galdong, I will make *tsampa*, and we will eat six bowls between us, you and I, Jani."

Tasmpa was the main food in Smon T'ang, and in Bod also. It was made by heating barleycorns on very hot sand in an iron pan until they popped, then sieving the sand away and grinding the corn very finely. This fine corn we carried with us, to mix into a paste with sour milk or with butter tea made with rancid butter, and the final paste was called *tsampa*. I liked it because I had always eaten it, but Sembur had never grown used to the taste, though he had eaten *tsampa* for so many years now.

When Ghenling said we would eat six bowls between us I pretended he had never played this joke on me before, and said, "Six bowls? Good! I am very hungry. That is three bowls for each of us."

"No. That is six bowls for me and none for you!" Ghenling rocked in the saddle with laughter.

I made an angry face, glared at him, and raised my voice as I said, "You're mean, Ghenling! You're greedy! I want some *tsampa*, too!"

Ghenling was delighted. "No, you cannot have *tsampa*. It is bad for little foreign girls."

"I'm not foreign! And I'm not a little girl any more, I'm quite grown up. I'm *twelve*."

"If you are not foreign, why do you have a funny white face?"

I tried to hit him on the arm, for this always amused him greatly, and said, "It isn't white, it's just not so dark as yours."

Ghenling clutched at his arm and rode forward, giving out loud groans of pretended agony and calling, "Sembur! Save me from Jani! She has broken my arm again! You should keep her on a chain like a bear!"

Sembur twisted in his saddle and called to me, "What's all the 'ollering about, Jani?"

"Nothing, Sembur. Just Ghenling 'aving one of 'is barmy jokes."

"Good. Good lad." Sembur nodded at Ghenling, and gave one of his rather fierce smiles. He approved of people who were cheerful and uncomplaining.

Ten minutes later our caravan trailed through the wide gates of the monastery's outer wall and into the courtyard. Lamas and monks were assembled there, waiting for us. The lamas wore tall pointed red hats. The monks were bare-headed, some of them very young, for boys could be entered into the order of the Galdong monastery when they were only nine. There were also a number of demons, who were really some of the monks and holy women dressed in brightly striped robes and wearing big masks over their heads in the shape of fierce monsters with sharp fangs, scales, and bulging eyes.

Three of the lamas had very long trumpets, longer than the height of a man. They were made of copper decorated with silver, coral, and turquoise. The bell of each trumpet rested on the shoulder of one of the boy monks, and the lamas were now blowing the trumpets while other lamas and monks beat on drums and cymbals.

All this was done to drive away any demons we might have brought in from Bod with the caravan. As the noise grew, the pretended demons in their horrible masks began to run about as if in fear, and at last fled out of the courtyard, to set an example to the real demons in the hope that they would do the same.

I always enjoyed the demon-chasing, especially at big festivals, when the lamas and monks paraded in their hundreds and there were scores of pretend demons. Sembur thought it was all very stupid. He watched coldly now, giving an occasional sniff, and said, "They got no more sense than a bunch of kids. Look at 'em."

I took his hand and held it, watching the drum-beating monks advance on the demons. "Oh, I dunno, Sembur. It's a bit of fun."

"Ah, fun—yes, that's different. I got nothing against a bit of a carnival an' suchlike, but they reckon they're doing it for *religion*, an' that's daft."

"Why's it daft?"

"Why? Well, because religion's what's in the 'Oly Bible, that's why. It's not dressing up and 'opping about like clowns in a circus."

"What are clowns in a circus, Sembur?"

He looked down at me and sighed. "It's very 'ard explaining things to you, Jani. Not your fault, but you 'ardly know anything about anything. All you know is what I've been able to tell you, and you get that all twisted round most of the time. Look, a circus is a big tent where 'undreds of people come to watch other people do acrobatics and put their 'ead in a lion's mouth an' suchlike. Sometimes they walk on long wires, right up in the roof. Well, clowns are men 'oo dress up funny and paint their noses red, then they do daft things to make you laugh."

I could not imagine a tent so huge. There would be scarcely enough yak hair in the whole world to make it. But then everything else Sembur had just described was quite beyond my imagining, too.

As the demons fled and the noise faded, three lamas bearing blank scrolls and quills began to examine our load, with Old Tashi in attendance. Sembur and I would be paid for our work according to the value of the caravan, and I thought that if we were lucky we would get at least fifty rupees for this trip.

I had once found it hard to understand why we were not among the very poorest of our village, for we earned almost nothing except what we were paid for "escort duty," as Sembur called it. Because we were foreigners, the nobleman who owned all the land round Namkhara would never rent us a field for growing or grazing, and Sembur had no trade to follow. Now that I was grown up, I was able to earn enough barley flour and vegetables to feed us by helping a farmer called Bhola, who owned some yaks. Sembur sometimes earned a little by helping the blacksmith or the slaughterer, but he could never stick at it for long, for both these trades were considered the lowest of the low, and the men lived like outcasts on the very edge of the town. We would never have had meat to eat if we had been living only on our earnings.

It was three years now since I had realized that Sembur had some secret source of money. At that time we had seemed to be getting steadily poorer, living mainly on *tsampa* and beans. Then Sembur put me into the care of Chela and her two husbands, and traveled south with a caravan, down into Nepal. But he did not return with it. He came back alone, three weeks after the caravan. To the Lo-bas he gave the impression that he had gone on down into India to get more cartridges for his wonderful rifle, and indeed he returned with more than forty clips of eight rounds each in his pack. But he also brought back a whole bag of silver coins, which he hid in the secret place in our home, in a hollow dug out beneath a big stone beside the hearth.

This hoard was enough to keep us for several years, and I guessed then that Sembur had brought back money in the same way the last time he had made the journey south, when I was just a little girl. In time it had been spent, and now he had brought back some more. I said, a little awed as I stared at the bag of silver, "Gawd, Sembur! How d'you get 'old of it all?"

"Don't say 'Gawd,' young lady. I'll 'ave no bad language, thank you."

"You say it."

"That's different. And anyway, I didn't ought to."

"All right, I'll try to remember. But where d'you get all that money? I mean, we got nothing to sell, 'ave we?"

Sembur finished setting the stone in place above the secret hollow, then rose to his feet. "When we first came 'ere, I brought one or two things that belonged to your ma. Bits of jewelry, see? They're yours by rights, but I've 'ad to sell a couple of bits to keep us going."

"Coo! Is there much left?"

"Enough for a nice little nest egg when you grow up."

"Can I 'ave a look, Sembur?"

"When you're a bit older, and if you're a good girl. That means you got to keep it dead quiet, Jani. Never say a word to anyone. Anyone at all. Understand?"

"Yes, all right, Sembur. I promise. Cross my 'eart."

I had kept my promise, and was sure that nobody knew of Sembur's secret hoard, for he was very careful never to be extravagant in any way. I had not thought about the money or the jewelry for a long time now, but they came to my mind as we stood in the courtyard of Galdong, waiting for the lamas to value the caravan. I was talking to my pony, Pulki, telling her that she had been a good girl, and that I would give her a big feed as soon as we were home, when I saw that her saddle, much mended, was almost beyond repair now, and I began to wonder if I could persuade Sembur to buy me a new one from Hauki the Tanner.

I decided to ask him about it tomorrow, when he was not tired, and went on talking with Pulki. I had been riding her for as long as I could remember, and loved her very much, but she had not been young when Sembur first bought her, and was quite old now. I hoped she had acquired a lot of merit in this life, and that in her next one she would be born a little girl, so that if I found her I would have somebody special to play with. I had trained Pulki to look in the pocket of my cloak for a little buckwheat cake sweetened with honey, and when she died I planned always to carry one in my pocket, and to look out for a girl-child who knew where to seek for the tasty morsel.

I was explaining this to Pulki, whispering in her ear, when I heard Sembur say in a low voice, " 'Allo. Look what turned up 'ere."

I turned my head and saw a plump, round-faced young lama making his way toward us. This was Mudok, the chief

23

secretary to Rild, the High Lama of Galdong, and I felt my heart sink. It seemed that we were to be summoned to Rild's presence, and this would surely mean that the omens were against us once more. When I glanced up at Sembur I saw that his face was drawn and his eyes weary. He had been ill coming through the pass, and ill during our last winter exile. I knew how he must dread the thought of two or three winter weeks in the hills, living in a tent, and I could have cried for him at this moment.

Mudok halted in front of us, glanced at Sembur, then looked at me and said, "The High Lama will speak with Sembur."

"I will tell him, Reverend One. At what hour will the Highborn be pleased to receive us?"

"Now." He turned to lead the way across the courtyard and into the monastery.

I said quickly, "Is it that the omens speak ill of us?"

Mudok stopped, half turned, and looked down at me, the tall red hat bobbing a little as he tilted his head to one side. "It is not as before," he said, frowning as if puzzled. "It is another matter, arising from a vision of the Oracle."

I was startled, and hastily explained to Sembur as we followed Mudok up the broad steps and through the great doorway.

"Oracle?" Sembur muttered.

"Well, I dunno if that's the right word in Hinglish, but it's a sort of fortune-telling by a special 'oly woman, an' when I asked you what Oracles meant in the 'Oly Bible you said it was like telling someone's fortune."

"What's she saying about us?"

"Mudok didn't tell me. I expect we'll 'ave to wait till we see Rild."

CHAPTER TWO

We had once been summoned to the monastery and then waited four hours to see Rild. But today Mudok had said "now," so I hoped we would not have long to wait. Little daylight entered the monastery, for most of the windows were shuttered. Every hall and corridor was lit with scores of butter lamps, the little flames dancing and flickering as we passed. There were chapels where silvery statues of gods and goddesses sat cross-legged on plinths round the walls. There were passages where the masks of a hundred devils glared down upon us. Somewhere a big gong was booming faintly to a steady rhythm. We passed through a passage lined with silk screens on which many different animals and birds were painted, then up a narrow curving stairway and through another hall of wooden pillars draped with red silk. Here, in a great niche at the end, squatted an enormous demon with a single green eye in its brow and long red horns. Two monks stood before the demon, each drumming on a ram's skull with slender black ebony batons.

In all the corridors there were small shrines, each with a stick of incense smoldering above, and the air was sickly with the scented fumes. We came at last to the anteroom, where we had waited for audience before. This time there were no others waiting. Mudok took two khabtas from a number which hung in a big iron ring on the wall, and handed one to each of us. It was impossible for us to enter the presence of the High Lama without these narrow white scarves, for no ceremonial greeting could take place without the offering of a khabta from the lower-born to the higher-born.

Mudok paused with his hand on the big door, and glanced at us rather irritably. I did not like Mudok. It was true we

25

were dirty, dusty, and ill-dressed to be received by the High Lama, but that was no fault of ours. I said softly to Sembur, "Don't try an' talk their language while we're in there. Please, Sembur. Please do it through me." I remembered the last occasion, when Sembur had tried to string together the few words he had picked up. He had used the crude form of speech suitable for speaking to a peasant, and I had gone crimson with embarrassment.

Now he muttered testily, "All right, all right. I know when to keep me mouth shut." Next moment Mudok had thrown open the door and beckoned us forward.

Daylight poured into the High Lama's room from a huge arched window. The walls were hung with gold brocade, and white goatskin rugs covered the floor. There was a very large wooden desk to one side of the window, with inkpots, quills, scrolls, and many papers. A great golden Buddha towered against the eastern wall. Rild himself sat with his back to the window, cross-legged like the Buddha, on a low platform which was painted with strange beasts in green and gold. He wore no hat, and his head was smooth and domed above the quiet eyes.

We halted in front of him, holding out the white scarves in a token offering, and bowed, saying nothing, for it was the High Lama's place to speak first. He waved a slender hand in acknowledgment, looked at a point somewhere between the two of us, smiled faintly, and said, "I greet you with a blessing."

I said, "May your blessing aid our release from the wheel of rebirth, Highborn."

I nudged Sembur, who drew himself up very straight, hands by his sides, heels together, and said loudly and rapidly, "Very 'appy to see you in good 'ealth, sir."

"He says he is most grateful for your blessing, Highborn."

Rild nodded absently. Slowly his eyes focused on me, then looked through me. "It is hard to know where merit lies," he said in a singsong voice. "To speak is to act, and all action must lead to suffering, for this is the law of Karma. Yet if I speak, and tell what the Oracle has seen, I may avert the destruction of a human creature"—his eyes flickered to Sembur—"and thereby acquire merit."

I waited, my heart pounding. It seemed that Rild had warning of some danger which threatened Sembur, but I dared not urge him to speak. Five minutes passed, and no word was spoken. Rild gazed into space. Sembur also gazed into space, staring over Rild's head. I stood trying to hide the anxiety that gnawed within me.

At last the High Lama said simply, "The Oracle has seen a demon who has put on human form. The demon is coming from the south, to take Sembur and destroy him."

I felt the blood drain from my face. Beside me, Sembur said sharply, "What's up, Jani? What's 'e say? Are you all right?"

"It . . . it was just a bit of a shock, what 'e said." I turned to look at Sembur, and translated Rild's words. Sembur did not believe in Oracles, except those of long ago in the Holy Bible, but to my astonishment he stared down at me from narrowed eyes for long seconds, then said slowly, "Does 'is nibs know what this demon looks like, Jani?"

I said to Rild, "He begs to ask if it was given to the Oracle to see a likeness of this demon, Highborn."

Rild stared at nothing for a while, then closed his eyes. There was silence. I heard Sembur stir beside me, drawing breath to speak, and I turned my head quickly, putting a finger to my lips and frowning him to silence. He did not understand that the High Lama was answering my question in his own way. There was nothing for us to do but wait.

Several minutes passed, then the door to our right opened and a young woman with a shaven head and wearing a white robe entered the chamber, followed by Mudok, who carried a silver tray with a plain glass bowl and flask on it. The flask was almost full of some inky black liquid. The girl moved to stand before Rild, and bowed. Her mouth hung open a little, and her face was dull, with no animation.

Rild opened his eyes and said, "I have summoned you to look again into the darkness, child, for the likeness of the demon who comes from the south."

I realized then that this girl was the Oracle, or at least one of the monastery's Oracles. It seemed to take several seconds before Rild's words sank in, then the girl said, "I will look, Highborn." She turned towards Mudok, who was pouring the black liquid into the bowl. When he had finished, he moved toward the girl and stood holding the bowl in front of her. She bowed her head slightly, staring down upon the shiny black surface of the liquid. After a few moments her eyes began to blink rapidly, then they opened very wide, and her whole body seemed to grow stiff. When she spoke, it was in a voice quite different from the voice we had heard her use before, higher-pitched, sharper, and more alert.

"He rides a black horse. He has taken the form of a man from a foreign land. The same land as the foreign man from Namkhara, who is called Sembur. The demon comes to take Sembur and destroy him. It is . . ." The girl's voice faded for a moment as she hesitated, then, "It is a warrior who comes, sent by a greater warrior, because . . . because Sembur has done an evil thing."

There was a silence. Rild said very softly, "Tell me the look of this demon, child."

She stared down at the liquid blackness, and I felt a shiver of awe touch my spine. "Long boots, made in a far country," she said musingly. "White fur to cover his body, and a gun that rests in a case tied to the saddle." Her lips curved in a strange smile. "He is young, this demon. Black hair, tight-twisted, and eyes like a clear sky at dusk. Proud . . . too proud. But his pride will be broken." She began to speak more quickly, and her breathing became labored. "He is born of the eagle and the snow leopard, yet he is feared by both. He will go down into blackness, and then will come the bloodless one, the Silver Man, the Eater of Souls . . ." She was panting now, and gabbling in a shrill voice so that her words were hard to follow. "And there is the debt to pay, and in the Year of the Wood Dragon they will come to the land of Bod, to seize the teardrop that fell from the eye of the Enlightened One—"

Her voice rose to a shriek, then ceased abruptly. Her body quivered like a plucked bowstring, and flecks of foam appeared on her lips. Then her lungs emptied with a long sigh, her body loosened, and the life went out of her face, transforming her to the slow, rather dull-witted girl she had been before looking into the bowl of darkness.

Rild moved a hand. The girl bowed and turned to plod her way out of the room, followed by Mudok with the tray, bowl, and flask. I found it difficult to keep my teeth from chattering, and felt suddenly cold, though the room was warm. Much of what the girl had said was meaningless to me, but it was clear enough that somebody very dangerous was seeking Sembur to do him harm, and I was frightened. Until two years ago I would not have feared for Sembur, for he had always seemed bigger, stronger, more confident than any man I had known, but now it was different. There was less spring in his step, more gray in his hair, and a mottling of veins in his cheeks.

Rild was speaking. "You will inform Sembur that it is not

28

sufficient for him to leave Namkhara. He must leave Smon T'ang, so that our land is not tainted with the disputes of those who are not of our kind—"

At the same time Sembur was muttering to me urgently, "What did she say? What about this demon, Jani? Come on, girl, don't just stand there like a goat with the gout! What's she been saying?"

I pressed my hands to my head and whispered frantically, "For Gawd's sake, shut up, Sembur! I'll tell you *later*. I'm trying to 'ear what the 'Igh Lama says!" I think Sembur was shocked into silence, for I had never spoken to him in such a way before. I bowed to Rild, and said, "Forgive me, Highborn."

For the first time he looked directly at me, and I saw amusement in his eyes. Then his gaze became remote again and he went on, "It is a full month now since the Oracle spoke. I have sent messages to my master, the Abbot of Lo Mantang, and to the king himself. All monasteries have studied the auguries, and it is beyond doubt that Sembur must go from Smon T'ang, or catastrophe will befall us. It is seven nights now since a star fell in the south, and the Oracle at Lo Mantang has declared that this heralds the coming of the foreign demon before the moon is full."

With shock I realized this meant the demon could appear at any moment now. In a shaky voice I said, "Where are we to go, Highborn?"

"That is a question for Sembur." Again the pale eyes focused on me for a moment, studying me, and Rild said slowly, "It is permitted that you remain, child. You may become a novice here, and study the True Way."

I said nervously, "No, Highborn, I must go with Sembur."

The High Lama gazed at me in silence for two minutes, then gave a faint shrug. "Each one must acquire whatsoever karmic burden he wills. Go with my blessing, child." Again his hand moved slightly, then his eyes closed, and it was as if Sembur and I were alone in the chamber. The door opened and Mudok appeared. He did not speak. When he turned we followed him out, walking behind him through the maze of halls, stairs, and corridors until at least we emerged into the wintry sunshine again.

I must have begun to weep without knowing it, for there were tears on my cheeks. As I rubbed them away I said, "I'm sorry, Sembur. I mean, I'm sorry I said 'for Gawd's sake' an' told you to shut up. I 'ardly knew what I was doing."

"Never mind, lovey," Sembur said in a very gentle voice, and rested his hand on my shoulder as we made our way to where we had left our ponies. "The 'Igh Lama was saying I've got to clear off, wasn't 'e?"

I nodded. "The king 'imself says so. An' that chief Abbot at Lo Mantang, where they 'ave the big festival. It's because they don't want that foreign demon 'ere, causing a lot of trouble."

Sembur nodded bleakly. "Tell me all about it when we get 'ome, Jani. I'll just go an' get our pay from Old Tashi."

The lamas had completed their estimate of the caravan's value, and put aside the portions to be given to the monastery. I saw Old Tashi make a fuss about paying over the little handful of silver coins before we had even reached Namkhara, but Sembur just stood there grimly with outthrust hand until the old man delved in his money bag.

Ten minutes later we were on our way once more, traveling the last few miles to Namkhara, the village which had been my home for as long as I could remember, but which would be my home no longer. Sembur was thoughtful as we rode. I knew he would question me closely once we were home, and I was trying to remember every word the Oracle had said in her prophetic trance as she gazed into the blackness. I was also trying to find the best way of translating what she had said into Hinglish, for the two languages were so different in so many ways that it was never easy to translate from one to the other.

The shadows were growing long as we came into Namkhara. To the south, the great peaks of Annapurna and Dhaulagiri took fire from the dying sun, and the wall of the Himalayas stretched away to the west, towering so high that it seemed like solid cloud in the sky. One of the things I had always loved most was to stand on the little bridge where the river curled about Namkhara, and watch the sun go down behind the huge stone battlements of the mountains. Or if I was herding at dawn, bringing the yaks in for milking, I was always touched by joy to watch the mountains in the east turn to gold as the sun woke the world to life again. But I did not think about such things that day of our last caravan, as we came into Namkhara, for I was too troubled and afraid.

Old Tashi led the caravan towards the stables and storehouse in the middle of the village. Sembur and I, after a brief exchange of goodbyes with Ghenling and one or two others, turned off toward the two-story house of rough stone and rammed earth, where we rented rooms on the ground floor from the two brothers who had been Chela's husbands. They owned the house, and they had now married another woman, called Kachke, a widow with two children by her first husband.

The stalls and booths, their festoons of butter lamps twinkling in the dusk, were busy as we rode slowly along the twisting lane which led to the house. There were jewelers with trays of turquoises, fortune-tellers, cloth merchants, tailors, and men and women with stalls bearing sugar and rice, bricks of tea, butter, grain, and many vegetables.

On other stalls there was meat for sale, goat and pig, sheep and chicken, while the craftsmen were offering scroll paintings, religious images, and ornaments in gold or silver filigree. Everybody in Namkhara knew us, for we were foreigners. If I lived there for the rest of my life I would still be a foreigner to them. But we had some friends among the Lobas, mainly the parents of children I worked with or played with, and so we were greeted cheerfully several times as we made our way home. It was a relief to find that the foreign demon from the south had not yet arrived here in Namkhara. I knew this without having to ask a direct question, for if any foreigner had entered the town everybody would have been talking about it.

So we were safe from him until tomorrow, at least, for there was a high wall round Namkhara, and only one gate in that wall, which had been closed for the night after our caravan had come in. The watchmen would let no stranger in before sunrise.

After what the High Lama had said, I was certain we would have to go away to another country, and I wondered where Sembur would decide to go. The demon would come from the south, so perhaps we would go north into the land of Bod, or beyond, to where the yellow men lived. I wondered, too, what the girl had meant when she spoke of some evil thing Sembur had done, which was the reason that the foreign demon had been sent to destroy him. Whatever vision she had seen in the gleaming black liquid, I knew she must have seen it amiss in some way, for there was no evil in Sembur.

The first thing we did on reaching the house was to take our ponies into the small stable across the street, feed and water them and give them a good rubdown with handfuls of straw. This was not the way of the Lo-bas, but it was a habit ingrained in me by Sembur. "There's a right way of doing things, Jani. Don't matter 'ow tired you are, first you take care of your 'orse, your rifle, your subordinates, then yourself."

At times when I was very weary, but had to see to Pulki before I could rest or eat, I had found it was only difficult if I let myself believe it possible to act in any other way, and now I was able to scrub away at Pulki's coat, and groom and feed her, without thinking about how tired I was. Even on this day when there seemed so much to think of, my mind was blank while we were attending to our ponies.

Afterward we walked across the street, exchanged a greeting with Kachke, who was nursing a new baby, and went into our home. It was a very nice home, for Sembur had worked hard to make many improvements over the years. There was a living room, a small kitchen with an iron stove, and a bedroom which Sembur had divided in two with a wooden partition three years ago, because I was growing up, he said. Rugs covered the stone floors, and Sembur had hung some pieces of painted paper on the walls of my bedroom, to make it pretty. We had beds, two tables, and four chairs, all made by Timoo the Carpenter, as well as some big cushions and several boxes for keeping our spare clothes and other belongings. There was a window in every room, each one with a cover of yak hide stretched across a wooden frame which fitted exactly. Few rooms in Namkhara had windows as good as ours.

As soon as we entered, Sembur spread an old blanket on the table and began to clean his rifle carefully. I opened all the windows for a few minutes to air the rooms, then took out my flint bag. On top of the ironstone I put some of the dry fiber made by rubbing the leaves of a mountain plant we called murghim. This always lit at a single blow with a flint, and I soon had a nice fire of dried yak dung burning in our big fireplace in the living room. I lit another in the stove in the kitchen, closed the windows, lit some butter lamps, then went out with a leather bucket to fetch water from the stone cistern Sembur had built.

While the water was heating in a big iron pot on the stove, I took some silver coins from the money Sembur had been paid, and ran to the market to buy some food for our dinner. On the way back I met little Armin, the three-year-old son of Kachke. Instead of playing with the other children he was sitting on his own looking very miserable, and seemed glad when I picked him up and carried him home. I thought nothing of the incident then, but I was to remember it later.

By the time I returned, Sembur had finished cleaning his rifle, unpacked our saddlebags, set aside all our soiled clothes ready for washing, and put everything else neatly away. He had taken the big pot of warm water, put another on the stove in its place, and was now in his bedroom with the curtain drawn, having his bath. I could hear much splashing of water and puffing as he stood in the little tub and scooped up water in a jug to pour over himself again and again. When he had finished, he would carefully strop his razor, then shave, with particular attention to his mustache. Finally he would wax the ends of it, put on a clean tunic, trousers, and woolen jacket, and at last be ready for dinner.

I went into the kitchen, cut up the piece of mutton I had bought into small squares, then skewered them on the long thin spit in the living room, where the fire was glowing hotly now. I washed and prepared some onions, turnips, and cabbage, made a big bowl of *tsampa*, and put out some bricks of the tea Sembur liked best, ready for the making.

By this time the water was hot enough for me to take my bath. I lifted the pot from the stove, carried it into my room, filled the tub on the floor, then stripped off my clothes and began to make a nice lather with a piece of the yellow soap we made from yak fat and wood ash. I washed my hair first, glad that it was no more than three inches long and would dry quickly, then rinsed it well with some water I had left in the pot, and stepped into the tub.

Sembur called through the partition. "Did you carry that 'ot water through yourself?"

"Yes, but I managed, easy."

"It's too 'eavy, Jani. You call me next time."

"All right, Sembur. But I'm ever so careful, honest."

I dried myself on my big gray towel, put on a clean vest and drawers of thick wool, then my red tunic, quilted trousers, and indoor shoes which Sembur called slippers. Less than an hour later we were sitting at the table near the fire, and in front of each of us was a well-piled plate of food that smelled wonderful. I pressed my palms together, closed my eyes tightly, and tried not to be impatient as Sembur said solemnly, "For what we are about to receive may the Lord make us truly thankful."

We both said "Amen," then began to eat, and almost five minutes passed before either of us could spare time and attention to talk. Then Sembur looked across the table at me, gave a sad little smile, and said, "You're a good girl, Jani. I wish I could 'ave done better for you, lovey."

I looked up in surprise, remembered to finish chewing and swallow the food in my mouth before speaking, as Sembur had taught me, and said, "I don't see 'ow we could've done better. We've got a nice place to live, and I reckon we eat better than most of the Lo-bas."

"Well, that part's not too bad, I suppose. But you're growing up now, and . . . well, I dunno what's going to 'appen, Jani. I mean, I ought to 'ave done something about your future, except I've never been able to think what to do." He shook his head, troubled. "That's where heducation comes in. If I was a heducated man, I'd know what to do."

"Ah, go on. You're heducated better than anyone 'ere in Namkhara."

"Only by comparison. I 'ad a bit of schooling as a boy-soldier, that's all, but after that there was just the Army." He looked at me sharply. "Nothing wrong with the Army, mind you. Teaches a man to be disciplined an' self-reliant." He grimaced. "But it don't teach a man 'ow to bring up a little girl." His plate was clear now, and he put his knife and fork together. We were the only people in Namkhara who used forks. "Still, I done me best, Jani. Someday, when you might feel a bit sadly toward old Sembur, just try an' remember I done me best."

I slipped down from my chair, went to him, put my arms round his neck, and pressed my cheek against his. Suddenly I felt sad and afraid, more for him than for myself, though I was not sure why. I said, "Don't talk daft. I'm ever so lucky the way you've always been kind an' looked after me. I wouldn't ever think bad of you."

He patted my shoulder, and gave a strange little laugh. "Lord, when you make your eyes go all big an' wide like you did just now, you don't 'alf remind me of your ma. Come on, let's 'ave the *tsampa*, Jani. We got a lot to talk about to-night."

I fetched two bowls of *tsampa* from the kitchen, and two mugs of strong tea, which I set down on the brick hob by the fire to keep warm. We said little during the rest of the meal or while we were washing up together in the little kitchen. When Sembur was settled in his fireside chair with a fresh mug of tea, and I was sitting in my favorite position on a cushion beside the hob, he said, "Right, then. Let's 'ave it, Jani. What did that Oracle girl say?"

I had been refreshing my memory of that time in the High Lama's chamber ever since we had left the monastery, and although I could not repeat what the Oracle had said word for word, I was certain I could give Sembur the exact sense of it, with nothing missed out. He listened carefully, tapping his teeth with the stem of his empty pipe, and continued frowning into space for a long time after I had finished.

I said, "D'you believe it then, Sembur? You always say it's rubbish, all these things they believe about demons an' magic an' omens."

"I never said it's *all* rubbish. I've seen some funny things down in India. Very peculiar. Just because I say it's barmy to bury an 'orse's skull near your front door to deep demons away, that don't mean *everything* they say is nonsense."

"So you reckon this foreign demon might really be coming 'ere from the south?"

"Not a demon," Sembur said slowly. "But somebody. Somebody looking for me."

There was a tight feeling in my chest as I said, "She spoke about 'im coming to take you away an' kill you for doing something wicked."

Sembur stared into the fire. "D'you trust me, Jani?"

"Course I do."

"I never did this bad thing they say I did, but nobody's going to believe me, except you."

"I don't care what 'appened, anyway. If this feller comes 'ere to take you away an' kill you, I'll get your rifle and I'll kill 'im first."

"You can stop that kind of silly talk this minute, young lady. I won't 'ave it."

I gave him a scowl. After a little while, thinking back to what the Oracle had prophesied, I said, "What d'you think she meant about 'im being too proud, and 'is pride would be broken?"

Sembur shrugged. "Sounds more like this other bloke's trouble than mine, so I'm not going to worry about it. Tell me that last bit again, Jani."

"Well . . . it was a bit confused. There was something about 'im going down into blackness, and then she talked about someone without any blood, a silver man, called the Eater of Souls, and they were going to come to Bod in the Year of the Wood Dragon to take the teardrop that fell from

35

the eye of the Enlightened One." I had closed my eyes, remembering, and now I opened them. "Sembur, that's what they sometimes call the Buddha 'ere, because he sat under a tree and suddenly got enlightened. Sort of ever so heducated."

Sembur gave one of his sniffs. "When's the Year of the Wood Dragon?"

"Um . . . let's see." I counted on my fingers. "It's the Year of the Fire Bird now, so the Wood Dragon's another seven years off. That's nineteen 'undred and four, the way you count in Hinglish."

"Right, then we can forget about it, lovey. Now let's tackle this in a soldierly fashion, eh? First, information. It's expected that a young man, a soldier, probably an officer, is on 'is way to Mustang, looking for me to take me back. We 'ave a rough description of said young man. Now, if said young man succeeds, I'm a goner. They'll 'ang me or shoot me."

I jumped, and a chill touched my bones. What kind of mad people could there be in India who would do such a thing to Sembur? He rubbed the bowl of his empty pipe against his nose, then went on. "Intention. To be gone from 'ere before said young man reaches Namkhara, and to settle somewhere in another country, where nobody can find me."

Sembur looked at me. "Now we come to method," he said slowly, a hint of tiredness in his voice. "No way to go but north. Get right across Tibet and into China."

It was hard to think of leaving our home and starting a journey of more than five hundred miles to the far side of Bod, there to make a new home as best we could in the strange land of the yellow men. I smiled and tried to make my voice sound cheerful as I said, "Sooner we go, the better, Sembur. It's nearly winter. Another week or two an' we'll never get through the passes into Bod." An idea came to me. "I tell you what. We ought to buy a couple of yaks. I know they're expensive, but we've got the money." I glanced toward the big stone which hid our secret hoard. "And I know they're slow, but they could carry a lot more of our things, and we wouldn't 'ave to load the ponies 'ardly at all."

Sembur looked away from me. "I can't take you with me, Jani. It's not fair. They'll let you stay all right, as long as I clear off."

"No!" I was on my feet, my lower lip trembling so much that I found it hard to speak clearly. "No, Sembur, I'm not 'aving that!"

He straightened in his chair, and gave me his wide-eyed,

shocked stare. "Eh? Can I believe my ears? You'll do what you're told, young lady, an' that's an end of it!"

"No! No, not this time, Sembur, I _can't._" I was half angry, half despairing, my hands clenched into fists and pressed under my heart. "I'm not stopping 'ome while you go off on a journey like that. You'll never get there alone, Sembur. You . . . you'll die!"

He gave a sudden grin, a cheerful grin I had not seen from him throughout the weeks of our recent caravan. "I've 'ad me time now, Jani, so it wouldn't be anything to cry over, even if I did peg out somewhere up there in the mountains. I'll 'ave me boots on and I'll be going forward, an' there's no better way for a soldier to make an end."

I went to him, knelt on the rug beside his chair, and took his hand. The moment of fright had passed now, and I felt calm, but I was very determined. "Sembur, I told you what Rild said about me being taken into the monastery. That's what they'll do if you leave me 'ere. They'll shave all my 'air off, an' stick me in a robe, and I'll spend all me time burning incense in front of idols an' whatever else the nuns do. I'll be miserable all me life, Sembur."

He chewed on his pipe stem, and rubbed a hand fiercely back and forth across his short-cropped gray hair. "That's all very well, Jani, but I'm right up a gum tree. Whatever I do, it's going to be bad for you one way or another. I'm at me wits' end trying to think what's least bad."

"Tell you what," I said quickly. "I got a good idea. If we leave in the next couple of days, we'll get through the passes an' make for Magyari. We know one or two merchants there, so we won't be complete strangers. Now, p'raps this foreign demon will find out that the Lo-bas trade with Magyari, and guess we've gone there, but 'e can't chase us for another four or five months, because of winter! So we'll 'ave all that time to think where it's best to go. And if this foreign demon comes after us _next_ year, we'll be gone!"

I went on talking urgently, reminding Sembur that the people of Bod were enormously secretive. A stranger trying to track us down in that country would have a hopeless task. And we could move from place to place along the great Tsangpo River between La-tzu and Lhasa with no difficulty, for on that long stretch of water the people of Bod used coracles of hide and bamboo.

By the time I had run out of good reasons for my plan I was breathless. Sembur looked down at me, and I was glad to

37

see a twinkle in his eye. "You're a caution, you are, Jani. And a chip off the old block. That took me back a few years, listening to you just now."

I did not know what he meant, and did not care, but with a huge inward relief I knew I had won him over, and that he would not leave me behind. I said, "When d'you think we'd better leave, Sembur?"

He rubbed his chin. "We 'ave to balance the advantages, Jani. This feller might not arrive for a couple of weeks, or 'e might turn up tomorrow. Then there's the weather. Sooner we get through the pass, the better, but the more time we take to prepare, the easier it'll be in the long run. So let's give ourselves three days. That ought to be plenty of time for buying a couple of yaks and whatever else we need."

He gave my hand a little squeeze, then got up, moved to the hearth, picked up the long iron poker with its chisel-shaped end, and used it to lever up the stone which hid our secret place, an oblong hole, four hands wide and eight long. In it were some special papers of Sembur's in an oilskin wallet, the remaining ammunition for his rifle, about one hundred rounds, a leather bag with a drawstring neck containing all our money, and an old tobacco tin.

We counted the money, added our earnings from the caravan to it, put aside what I thought we would need for buying two yaks, and returned the rest to the bag. Sembur opened the old tobacco tin, and we stared down at it as we knelt side by side. I knew that at last I was looking at my mother's jewelry. There were two earrings, each made of a large red stone set in a droplet-shaped piece of gold, a ring with three square green stones, and a gold brooch shaped like a peacock's tail, set with six diamonds. There were two empty settings on the brooch, and I guessed that these had once held diamonds to match the others, until Sembur had sold them on the two occasions he had traveled south into India when we needed money.

"Quite a fortune there when you live simple like we do," Sembur said quietly. "Wicked to break up that brooch, but I didn't dare try an' sell it complete." He shivered suddenly, as if somebody had walked over his grave, and began to fit the lid back on the box.

I said, "Was all that my ma's jewelry, Sembur?"

"That was only a bit of it. A few pieces."

"She must've looked nice wearing it."

"She was the most beautiful lady I ever saw, Jani."

"Do you always shiver when you look in that box?"

"Do I? Yes, I suppose I do. It's just . . . memories."

"They must be bad ones. I wish you'd tell me about 'em."

"P'raps I will soon. You're very grown up for your age." He was packing the money bag, ammunition, and jewelry back into the hole. When he had finished he set the stone in place and rose to his feet, dusting the knees of his trousers. "Now then, suppose you go and get the 'Oly Bible and read to me for 'alf an hour before you go to bed."

While I was in my bedroom, getting the Holy Bible from the small cupboard beside my bed, a thought came to me. It was beautifully warm in our home now, and I called out, "Just a minute, Sembur." Next moment I had whisked off my tunic and trousers. From the place where I kept my clothes, on a rail behind a little curtain, I took the sari Sembur had bought me as a present three years ago, on his last trip south. It was a broad strip of red-and-gold silk, and the most wonderful thing I had ever owned.

I wound it round me now, in the way Sembur had shown me, tucked in the end, then picked up the Holy Bible and went back into our living room. Sembur was gazing absently into the fire, and did not notice me until I sat myself down on a cushion opposite him. His eyes widened and he started, then let out his breath in a long sigh. "Lord, you gave me a turn then," he said. "Just like a miniature of your ma you looked, sitting there with a book in your 'and."

"Coo, then I must be beautiful! You said *she* was."

"Don't get big-'eaded, young lady. Remember that story I've told you about the ugly duckling. Well, that's what you are, and *maybe* you might turn into a swan, but don't be too sure."

I giggled. I had long since given up hope of changing from an ugly duckling. A year ago, on a caravan to Magyari, I had haggled for a looking glass I had seen in a booth there. It was half as big as I was, and had been a great nuisance to carry home, but now it hung in my bedroom. At that time I had studied myself carefully in the looking glass and had felt quite downcast. My hair was thick and black and bowl-shaped, and my face was a strange color, not strange like Sembur's, whose face was white and pink, but much paler than any other face in Namkhara. Also my eyes were too low down on my face, and a funny shape, while my nose was narrow instead of being broad and flat.

I had felt quite miserable for a while, but then I became

used to looking the way I did, and stopped worrying about it. I knew that when Sembur said I looked like a miniature of my mother it was only because I was wearing a sari.

The book I liked best in the Holy Bible was the one called Ecclesiastes. I could hardly understand any of it, but the words seemed to be full of magic. When I read them out loud it was like listening to the distant sound of the great trumpets of Galdong, and I would shiver, feeling my throat grow tight and my eyes prickle. Tonight I felt too tired to bear this strong word magic, and said, "What d'you want me to read, Sembur?"

"Just a few bits from 'ere and there. Whatever you fancy, Jani."

I turned to Zechariah. This book always mystified me, and also seemed rather comical in places, though I did not dare say so to Sembur. It was about an angel who kept coming and talking to Zechariah, and showing him strange things, like four carpenters. Then when Zechariah asked why, the angel said they had come to fray the horns of the Gentiles. I had asked Sembur about all this, but he did not understand it either.

A new thought struck me, and I said, "Sembur, why are there some words that don't 'ave a haitch in front, but we say it just the same, like 'hangel'?"

Sembur sucked at his empty pipe, frowning and nodding slowly. "Well, that's a very 'ard question to answer, Jani. Tell you the truth, it really needs someone with more book learning than me. But *reading* is different to *saying*, if you follow me, so I think what really 'appens is that you get certain words like hangel and Hinglish and—er—heducation, where you put in a haitch when you're saying it, for what they call hemphasis, see?"

"Well . . . that's all right, I suppose, but 'ow do you know which words to do it with?"

"It's like a lot of things, Jani." Sembur waved his pipe airily. "You just learn it as you grow up. Comes with experience, see?"

"Not really, but I'll 'ave a think about it later." I turned to Chapter Five, where the angel had come to talk to Zechariah again, and began:

"Then I turned, and lifted up mine eyes, and looked, and be'old a flying roll. And he said unto me, What seest thou? And I answered, I see a flying roll; the length thereof is twenty cubits, and the breadth thereof of ten cubits . . ."

Sembur sat holding his pipe in his mouth, eyes closed, head a little on one side, listening carefully a giving a little nod of approval every now and then. I read from the Bible for fifteen minutes, choosing different pieces I liked, then fetched my other book from the bedroom, *Tales of Jessica*, and read my favorite story from it. This was the one about Jessica on holiday at the seaside, where she sees a lady and gentleman cut off by the tide, and rescues them in a sailing boat. Afterward she is scolded for being late home, but she says nothing of what happened because she doesn't want to boast.

Sembur always said Jessica was enough to make you sick, but I thought she was very brave. By the time I had finished he was dozing in his chair. I put my books away, washed up the tea mugs, then stood close to Sembur and whispered sharply, "Atten-*shun!*" He gave a great start and came out of his chair before realizing where he was. This was an old joke I had played on him before, saying the word that was a magic one for soldiers.

"I caught you that time, Sembur!" I crowed.

"Hah! You know what you are?" He twisted both ends of his mustache. "You're an 'orrible little girl, that's what! I wouldn't be surprised if one of those fire demons didn't sneak in 'ere tonight an' nibble your toes!"

"Eh!" I looked uneasily at the hide-covered window. "They couldn't, could they?"

Sembur threw back his head and gave one of his big laughs. "Bless my soul, Jani, I was only pulling your leg. Don't you believe all that rubbish. No demon's going to get in 'ere tonight, I promise you. So off you go to bed, and 'ave a good sleep. Oh, and don't forget your prayers."

I kissed him good night, but fell asleep when I was only halfway through my prayers. Perhaps that was the reason a demon did get in during the night, to torment Sembur. It had happened several times over the years, and at first I had been frightened but I was used to it now. As usual I woke up to the sound of Sembur crying out, and knew that the demon had cast a nightmare upon him. I could hear the gasping, the ragged breathing, and the creak of his bed as he twitched and turned upon it. Sometimes he muttered, sometimes spoke in his cool brisk voice, and sometimes seemed to be speaking to himself.

"*Yes. I'll 'ave to take the jewels . . . need money.*" A pause, then a terrible whisper. "*I can't do it . . . can't touch her.*" The ragged breathing grew harsh, then steadied. In a

41

flat voice Sembur said, *"Yes, sir. Beg pardon. It was just . . . 'aving to do what I just done. I'd 'ave sooner been crucified . . ."*

Another wordless time of tortured breathing. I was out of bed now, trying to keep my hands steady as I struck flint on ironstone to light a butter lamp. He spoke again, half sobbing. *"Oh, God . . . oh, dear God, 'ave mercy . . . poor girl, poor girl . . ."* Again his voice became calm, as if with a huge effort. *"Yes, sir. I've got 'em . . . all the jewels she was wearing. Yes, I can trust Parvati . . ."*

I had a flame now, and was moving out of my bedroom and through the curtain into Sembur's room. As the tiny light drove back the darkness I saw that he was propped on an elbow, staring with blank, sightless eyes, sweat running from his face. *"You can . . . rely on me, sir . . ."* he said, and in his voice was a horror that made my blood run colder within me than the snow-fed mountain streams. His hand moved to his hip, came away as if holding something, then lunged suddenly down. He fell back with a terrible sound in his throat and began whispering, *"Steady . . . steady now . . . don't cry, lovely, don't make any noise . . . old Sembur's got you . . ."*

I think he was talking to me in his dream, but paid little attention to his words, for I was too concerned with trying to wake him from the nightmare without getting hurt. The time before last he had lashed out at me in the moment before waking, catching me on the shoulder so hard that I was knocked across the room.

I stood near the foot of the low bed, pulled up my woolen nightdress, and kicked at his legs with one bare foot. "Sembur! Wake up! Come on, stop all that 'ollering an' wake up!" I kicked him again, and jumped away as he jerked upright in bed, blue eyes glaring, one hand thrust out in front of him as if holding a sword ready to lunge. Then the fury and menace faded from his eyes, his shoulders slumped, and he drew one forearm unsteadily across his forehead. "Jani? Ahhh . . . it's you. Sorry . . . been 'aving a bad dream. Did I wake you?"

"Course you woke me, yelling an' groaning like that." I put the lamp on the low cupboard. In my mind I was saying some special magic words in the tongue of Smon T'ang, taught me by Lahna the Witch, to drive the sleep demon out of the house now that I had driven it out of Sembur by waking him. I moved to the bed. "Coo, just look at the tangle you've made of the blankets." I began to straighten them.

"Come on, lie down an' I'll tuck you in. Would you like me to fetch you some warm milk and 'oney?"

"Some *what?*" Sembur blinked at me in horror. "Don't talk daft—" He stopped, and dragged a hand down his face. "Sorry, Jani. No, thanks, I'm all right. Sorry I woke you." He was trying to sound cheerful now, but his voice was tired. "My word, fancy 'aving nightmares at my age, eh? Now you stop fussing and 'op back in bed before you get cold, lovey."

"All right." While tucking in the blankets I had finished saying in my head the mantra, as Lahna called it, for driving away the demon, and I felt sure Sembur would not be troubled again that night. I took the lamp and went back to my own bed, thinking as I snuggled down into the warmth that it was a pity Sembur would not let me set demon traps to protect our home. They might even have averted the coming of the foreign demon, prophesied by the Oracle.

But this was a foolish thought, as I was to learn. It would have taken more than skull bone, horn, and enchantments on strips of leather to stay the Hinglish demon I was so soon to meet.

CHAPTER THREE

It was little more than twelve hours later, on the road between Namkhara and the village of Yamun, that I came face to face with him. Sembur and I had risen early, for there was much to be done. We had to sort through our belongings, decide what to take and what to leave, buy stores for the journey, and pay the rent owing.

Throughout the morning we were busy with preparations at home. When the sun had passed its high point I set off on Pulki for Yamun, with a bag of money tied to my waist under my jacket, to buy two yaks. They would be cheaper in Yamun, for the people there would not yet know that we had to leave Smon T'ang, as almost everyone in Namkhara knew now, and so it would be easier to make a good bargain.

I was thankful I had persuaded Sembur that he could not spare the time to come with me, for he was not good at haggling and seemed unable to grasp the way of doing it. The fact that he knew so little of the language made it hard for him, of course, but he always made things worse by losing his temper. Then he would return to speaking Hinglish ever more loudly, as if the Lo-bas would understand if only he shouted hard enough.

I knew that I would pay for the yaks about half what I would first be asked, but this would take at least half the afternoon, and two or three times I would have to pretend to the farmer that I had lost interest and was going home. Given two days, I would have paid only a third of the first asking price.

There were a few people on the road that afternoon. Some were traveling between Namkhara and Yamun, as I was, and some were turning east where two trails joined, making for the more distant village of Gemdring. Pulki was moving at a steady walk, and I was lost in my thoughts when I heard a voice behind me calling, a man's voice.

He was speaking in the tongue called Gurkhali, used by the small men from Nepal. Sembur could speak it a little, because many of these men became soldiers with the Hinglish Army, and Sembur had been in charge of almost a thousand of them for many years. During the long evenings he had taught me some Gurkhali, and I found that much of it was like the tongue of Smon T'ang. This made it all the more surprising that Sembur spoke our language so poorly, but the accent was different, and I suppose he had a poor ear for it.

The voice I heard now was saying, "Wait, boy. I wish to speak with you."

Pulki stopped and turned at my touch. It was then I saw the man on a great black horse riding easily towards me, and I knew that this was the foreign demon whose coming had been seen by the Oracle in the monastery of Galdong. The shock was as if Pulki had thrown me on hard ground, and all the wind had been driven from my lungs. For a moment I saw only a black-and-white blur, then swiftly the picture took shape for me.

He wore a short coat, very well made, of white fur which I recognized as Indian lamb, and breeches of a heavy brown cloth, finely ribbed, tucked into tall leather boots. His hands were gloved in soft brown kid, and he wore a cap of thick felt with earflaps which were buttoned across the top. Both saddlebags were bulging, and behind the saddle was strapped a large canvas-covered roll which would hold his tent, bedding, and whatever else he might need on his journey. In front of his right leg was a long holster with a rifle in it. The butt was like the butt of Sembur's rifle, but this weapon was shorter by almost three hands.

All this I remembered later, but at the moment of first staring up at the demon from the south I was aware only of his face. It was a face that sun and weather had made darker than my own. The eyes were blue, but deeper blue than Sembur's, the nose as thin and ugly as mine, jutting above a long tight mouth. The eyes, beneath two hooks of eyebrows, looked upon me as if from an immense distance, as cold and haughty as the eyes of a snow leopard.

He said in Hinglish, but not the proper Hinglish that Sembur and I spoke: "Good God, it's a girl. I thought she was a boy." Then, in slow Gurkhali: "Can you understand me?"

My heart seemed to be trying to climb into my throat. I had thought of this man as a foreign demon, because that was how the Oracle had spoken of him when we stood before the High Lama, but I knew I was looking upon a real person, not a demon who had taken on human form. Yet I could not have been more frightened if a true dragon demon with a tongue of fire had appeared before me.

Even so, it was a strange kind of fear, with an almost painful excitement in it. Perhaps this was because he was the first Hinglish person I had ever seen, apart from Sembur. There was no scrap of warmth in his face, yet I felt an impulse to reach out and touch him, to hold his hand and lead him to our home, and talk and talk about a thousand things to do with the world he knew and I did not, things I had scarcely wondered about before.

With an effort I tried to gather my confused wits. This man was a soldier, come to take Sembur away to be hanged or shot. He was a mortal enemy, to be deceived and sent on a wild-goose chase, if I could manage it, and he was still looking down his thin nose at me, waiting for an answer. It was hard to believe that this was a man alone in a strange land, for he was completely sure of himself. There was careless arrogance even in the way he sat his horse.

I said slowly, in Gurkhali, "I speak this tongue a little, honored sir."

He took off the cap and began to unbutton the earflaps. "I seek a foreign man," he said, "A white man, of my people. He has lived many years in Smon T'ang."

I saw with surprise that the stranger was younger than I had first thought, perhaps twenty-two or -three, but with the confidence of a man ten years older. His hair was as black as mine, but clung to his head in short tight curls, making him look very like the fire demon carved over the entrance to the small shrine by the gatehouse of Namkhara, except for the two double fangs and the horns.

He continued slowly in Gurkhali, "I have spoken to men in the hills to the south. They say such a man has passed through their village. Two, three times. He carries a fine rifle." The stranger touched his own rifle. I did not look at him but pretended to be more interested in the beautiful black horse than in what he was asking. A touch of impatience came into his voice as he went on, "They have told me that the one I seek dwells in Smon T'ang. They believe he is

46

from the town of Namkhara. Do you know of such a one, girl?"

I said idly, "There is a foreign man who has lived here many years, sir. A big man, who was a soldier, it is said."

"Yes. The one I seek was a soldier. Where shall I find him?"

Still looking at the horse, I said, "I am from Namkhara. Once the foreign man you speak of lived near to me. But in the winter that is past, he went away to live in a small village."

"Where?"

"To Gemdring." I pointed to where the trail forked away from the road between Namkhara and Yamun, and tried to make my mind blank so he would not see I was frightened.

"How do you know he still lives there?"

"I do not know. It is half a year since I saw the foreign man."

"How is he called?"

I pretended to think for a moment. "It was . . . yes, I remember now. He was called Sembur."

"Sembur . . . ?" the stranger echoed softly. "Sembur?" His voice sharpened. "Ah, yes!" He repeated the name once more, but in a strange way, so that it sounded more like Ahressembur. There was a little silence, and then he said, "Look at me, girl."

Trying to appear willing, though I felt the opposite, I obeyed. It was not easy. I felt at this moment that he was a man who had a nose for the truth, who half suspected that I was lying, and who might very quickly have the truth out of me before I knew what I was saying.

"You have told me Sembur dwells in Gemdring?" he said, a question in his voice.

"No, honored sir. I say only that he went to live there."

He gave a little nod. I felt relief, then jumped as his black eyebrows came together and he said suddenly, "Are you telling the truth, girl?"

Panic touched me, and for something to do I reached out my hand toward the big black horse as I began an answer which I knew would sound halting. "Sir, I—"

He cut in sharply. "Get your hand away from his muzzle! He'll have it off if you're not careful."

That changed everything for me. I could not hold back a giggle as I put my hand firmly on the cold damp nose and said, "We are friends, sir. He will never hurt me." The black

47

horse edged forward half a pace, nudging and butting my hand. I could feel the strong spirit of him, and knew he would be dangerous to any but his master, and to the few who felt true love and respect for him. I said to him in the language of Smon T'ang, laughing with him, "You have a demon in your heart and another on your back, I think, my handsome one."

The man on his back said in Hinglish, "Good God, what on earth's got into you, Flint? Has the child bewitched you?"

That made me laugh again, but inwardly, so the man would not know I had understood. I said, "We give you welcome, Flint, and we will carry your name in our hearts, Pulki and I. May your grazing ever be good, my little one." I called all creatures "little" as an endearment, even the great lumbering yaks. Flint had pulled my glove off, and I held it in my hand as I rubbed his chin groove with my knuckles. To the stranger I said in Gurkhali, "It is you who have not spoken truly, honored sir, not I."

He looked baffled, and a little angry. "What do you mean?"

"You have told me that your horse would bite my hand off. That was an untruth."

His lips drew into a tight line, and he looked down at me with dislike. "How far is Gemdring?"

I pointed along the trail. "You will come there before sunset, sir."

"Good. I hope I shall not meet any more little girls who are too clever." He clapped the cap on his head, gathered the reins, touched heels to the great horse, and wheeled away. I watched him for a long time as he moved down the trail to Gemdring. He rode straight-backed, a hand resting on his thigh, as if he were lord of every village in the valley. Somewhere in my whirling thoughts I decided that he was a good horseman and that Flint would be happy with such a master.

When he passed out of my sight beyond a shallow fold of ground, I turned Pulki and started back toward Namkhara at a fast trot. There would be no going to Yamun to buy yaks for our journey. The foreign demon was here already. If I had not paid Lahna the Witch to cast a spell for our good fortune that morning, I would surely never have met him on the road, and he would have been in Namkhara within an hour.

As it was, I had won us a good advantage. Sembur and I could be well into the foothills by nightfall, and making camp in the upper valley of the pass by sunset next day. My foreign demon had yet to reach Gemdring and discover I had deceived him. It would take time for him to learn the truth, return to Namkhara, and discover at last that we had gone north to Bod. We would have a lead of two days at least, and surely no stranger would dare to venture the Chak Pass alone, with the snows of winter so close.

So I thought. But I knew too little about my demon then.

We camped at sunset in a broad gully at the foot of the pass, where the thin earth had not yet given way to rock, and there was some scanty grazing. I had been on the verge of tears for hours, because we had been forced to leave Pulki behind, exchanging her for a younger and stronger pony who could carry more. I had not thought of a name for my new pony yet, but I had talked to him a great deal because I was afraid my sorrow over losing Pulki would make him feel unwanted.

While we heated some *tsampa* and ate a few pieces of the yak meat I had cooked before leaving, Sembur and I spoke hardly at all. I knew that having to leave in haste had distressed him. He liked to think carefully and take his time in all he did. As it was, we had left Namkhara less than two hours after I had arrived home. Even before we started I felt tired, for Sembur, quite unlike his usual self, seemed to find it hard to make up his mind about anything, and in the end all decisions were left to me.

As we sat by our small fire he looked up after a long silence, pushed back his hood a little, and said, "Did he say what 'is name was, this feller?"

"No. All he did was ask questions. Once he said something in Hinglish, to the horse, but it was a funny sort of Hinglish."

"I expect it was posh. He'd be an officer, see, a heducated person. What was he like, Jani?"

"I told you."

"No, I mean did he seem a decent sort of fellow or what?"

"I dunno. He didn't like *me* much, and he was very proud, like the Oracle said. But I didn't mind that. In a way I sort of liked 'im, really."

Later, as we lay in the little black tent, warm in the thick woolen sleeping bags, Sembur said, "Talk about proud, I'm proud of *you*, Jani. You got initiative, an' you got a lot of moral fiber."

"What's that?" I said sleepily.

"Doesn't matter. Just something we used to look for in a man."

"I'm a girl, Sembur."

"I know, lovey." I heard him sigh. "And that doesn't make it any easier for you. But all the more credit to you, I suppose." I was vaguely wondering what he meant when I fell asleep a few seconds later.

At first light we rose, ate a good hot breakfast to help us through the day's climb, and struck camp. We had done this so often when on caravans that it was automatic now, and as the rising sun touched the golden spires of Galdong, we set off up the pass, leading our heavily laden ponies.

It was a journey we knew well now. There was a lower ridge at about ten thousand feet. We hoped to get beyond this today and drop down into a high but sheltered valley where we would camp for the night. Next morning we would start the climb to the true crest of the pass, a hard climb, for the air was thin and gave little nourishment to the blood. There we would follow the twisting trail for over a mile across the great wall of the Himalayas before starting the descent into the land of Bod.

Once we were launched on our way to the top there could be no stopping until we were well down the northern slope on the far side, for the weather could turn against us overnight, and we would be trapped by snow.

We hardly spoke at all that day, for we were saving our strength. Toward the end of the afternoon I became worried about Sembur, for his color was not good and he seemed unable to get enough air. I made him lie down while I lifted the panniers and bedroll from his pony, called Bugler, and strapped them on my new pony. This took a little while because I had to half empty the panniers before I could lift them. When it was done I made Sembur mount Bugler and ride until we had passed the first ridge and were dropping down into the high valley beyond. Sembur was in a difficult mood because the thin air made him confused in his mind, and he felt he ought not to ride, but when I got very cross and shouted at him he did as I wanted.

I slept uneasily that night, wondering how we would manage the next day's journey, which would be harder and would take us another five thousand feet higher. My fears were not calmed when I woke to find that the sky was heavy with the threat of snow, while a wind had risen to whip flurries of snow from the great peaks above us, so that they seemed to be smoking.

I was fretting to be on the move, but forced myself to be patient while we made breakfast and fed the ponies from the sacks of mixed buckwheat and crushed barley we had brought with us. To my alarm I was feeling very peculiar, as if my mind was becoming more and more separate from my body. My head felt hot, my throat sore, and it seemed certain that I had fallen victim to a disease demon.

All that day, as we moved steadily up the ever-winding pass, I was chanting mantras to myself to drive out the demon. I dared not think what would become of us if I fell badly ill, for I knew it would be all Sembur could do to get himself through the pass unaided. At midday we reached a point a mile short of the true crest, where the trail turned to pass across the great ridge. From here it was possible to look down across the valley below, where we had spent the night. White peaks thrust skyward to east and west, and beyond the valley lay the long descent to Galdong. I stood for a moment gazing down, saying a silent goodbye to the land where I had grown up.

Something moved. Far, far away on the small slope which ran down from the lower ridge into the valley, a black and white dot moved along the trail. I stared stupidly. Where had I seen that strong contrast of black and white before?

Black horse. White fur. I narrowed my eyes, trying to see more clearly, but there was no need. With sinking heart, and a feeling that every demon of plain and hill and mountain was fighting against us, I knew that Sembur's pursuer was no more than half a day's march behind. It frightened me to think that he could have allowed himself and his horse no more than two hours' rest in Gemdring before setting out for Namkhara by night. The watchman at the gates of Namkhara would never have let him enter before dawn, but might have shouted an answer to the foreign demon's questions, just to be rid of him. Whatever had happened, he was following us now.

I did not tell Sembur what I had seen, for it would only have made him feel hopeless, and this would drain his strength. I said, "We're doin' ever so well, Sembur. Soon be going across the top, and after that it's easy."

He paused, leaned on his pony, and peered at me closely. "You all right, Jani?" he said raggedly, his chest heaving. "You look . . . a bit queer."

"No, I'm all right. Come on."

But I was not all right. During the next hour several strange things seemed to happen to me. Sometimes I walked a few inches above the ground, sometimes I flew away up the towering slope beside us, and looked down at the figures of Sembur and Jani trudging slowly up the pass, leading their heavily burdened ponies. Once I went away completely to a place where the sun was very hot. There was a white-walled garden with mellow brick paths and flowers of fierce bright colors. In the center lay a round pool where a fountain played. I heard voices, a man's voice and a woman's, speaking Hinglish, but in the same strange way that I had heard the foreign demon speak it.

Something cold touched my cheek, then my brow, my chin. I was in the pass, trudging with painful slowness up the last few hundred yards of the climb. Sembur was gasping and croaking beside me. The cold I had felt was from great flakes of falling snow.

"Keep . . . going, Jani!" It was a rasping whisper from Sembur. "Get through . . . 'fore it's too late."

We took half an hour to reach the top, and by then the snow was halfway to my knees. The wind was from the north, buffeting us as it funneled between the sloping walls that hemmed the pass through this high rampart of the Himalayas. The huge soft flakes were like icy butterflies flung into our faces, and it was impossible to see more than a few yards ahead.

Sembur was staggering, and even above the wind I could hear the awful sound as he struggled to drag enough air into his lungs. Terror struck into me, for I knew now he could never stay on his feet for that long mile across the top. Yet if we did not do it within the next hour we would die, for the snow would soon be thigh-deep.

I took my knife from its sheath on my belt, looped the reins over my arm, and called, "Sembur! 'Ang on a minute!" Head down against the wind, I pushed through the snow toward him and began to cut the ropes and straps which held Bugler's load. Sacks and panniers fell to the snow. The tent and bedrolls were on my pony. As long as we had those, we might live long enough to find some way of surviving. For the moment nothing else mattered.

"Get up on 'im, Sembur!" I called. "Up on Bugler. Oh, for Gawd's sake don't argue now! Get up!" Somehow Sembur dragged himself into the saddle, slumping forward. I took

52

Bugler's reins in one hand, my own pony's in the other, and started to plod forward into the driving snow once again.

The disease demon was still with me. At every step he kept tightening a band of fire across my throat. Sometime later, it was hard to judge how long, there came a moment when I knew it was hopeless, that we could never get through the pass against this blizzard. And in the same moment I remembered the cave.

It lay on the east side of the pass, about a hundred paces from the trail and up a slope which ended in a great upthrust of cliff. Here there was an overhang, with the entrance to the cave beneath it. Sembur and I had explored the cave once, during a summer caravan. The Lo-bas would not go near it as we passed, except to throw in an offering, because they knew that wood demons lived there. I had been a little afraid of the wood demons myself, but now I did not care if a thousand of them lived in the cave. It was better to face them than to fall down and die.

I was peering through the swirling snow, trying to pick out the overhang, when a figure loomed through the heavy yellow light that encompassed us. At first I thought it was a strange squat horse, and then saw it was a bear. I did not feel afraid, for I knew the bear was simply making its way down the pass to a more comfortable place for the night, but I heard Sembur give a sudden shout.

I turned and saw that he was sitting up, dragging his rifle from the saddle holster. I cried, "No, Sembur, it's all right!" But I was too late. Startled by the shout, the bear stood upright and lumbered curiously toward us. Bugler gave a whinny of terror, I felt a sudden painful wrench, then the reins were torn from my hand. The pony lunged sideways, Sembur was flung from the saddle, and next instant Bugler was gone, away past the bear, vanishing into the blizzard with a muffled sound of hooves, going north along the pass.

I stood knee-deep in the snow, close to sobbing with panic. The bear shuffled past me, still on its hind legs, with an air of apology. Then it dropped to all fours and went lumbering on its way.

Keeping tight hold of my pony's reins, I moved to Sembur, bent over him, and shouted, "Come on, we'll just 'ave to get to the cave and 'ope the snow don't last! Might be just a little snowstorm before winter." He did not stir. Crouching, I saw that his eyes were closed and his face twisted as if in pain. I knew he could not have hurt himself falling into the snow,

53

yet he was unconscious, and did not respond even when I gave his face a hard slap.

I think I cried with despair then, but I remember nothing more until I found myself moving slowly up the slope toward the overhang. I was leading my pony. When I looked back I saw that I had taken the coil of rope from the saddle, tied it round Sembur's shoulders, and fastened the other end to the pommel. Sembur was on his back, sliding along through the snow. When we reached the overhang I urged the pony on, and supported Sembur's head as he was dragged across the short stretch of bare rock.

There were three holes giving entrance to the cave, two barely large enough for a man to crawl through, the third more like a rough doorway, and high enough for a horse to pass. Inside, the cave was perhaps fifteen paces across, but ran back twice that distance into the cliff. The roof was low, only a few inches above my pony's head.

It was a huge relief to be out of the wind and the driving snow, but my problems were far from over. First I needed light, and it was several minutes before I had managed to unpack the leather bag containing what Sembur called our basic kit, and get two butter lamps lit. I unrolled Sembur's groundsheet, laid out his bedding, then heaved and struggled to roll his limp body on top.

Over the years, travelers had thrown hundreds of offerings into the cave to please the wood demons who lived here. There were roughly carved wooden statuettes, bundles of long sticks tied together, strings of big wooden beads, and effigies of straw, paper, and twigs. There was also much dried animal dung, and a carpet of tiny bones from small creatures, which showed that many a snow leopard had made the cave his home through centuries gone by.

I lit a fire near the entrance, in case the bear we had met decided to seek shelter here, and then at last I was able to attend to Sembur. It was hard to see his color in the dim light, but his breathing was very uneven and he was still unconscious. The mountain demons had sunk their talons in both of us, for my throat was on fire now, and my head ached so much that I felt my brain had stopped working. I was almost glad of this, for I knew that if I started to think I would be even more terrified than I was already.

I went out and gathered snow in a pan until I had enough water, then returned and started to make some *tsampa* on the fire. The play of the wind was sucking any smoke out through one of the small holes, and I was grateful for this. While the *tsampa* was heating I hobbled my pony, took off his saddle, then set out all we had left of our possessions.

There was our bedding, our tent, and our basic kit, with food for nine or ten days. I must have picked up Sembur's rifle in its oilskin case and taken the pack from his back before tying him behind the pony to be dragged up to the cave. In his pack there were some clips of ammunition, spare socks and underclothes, a towel and toilet bag, his special papers in a big oilskin wallet, and his pipe in an old pouch. There was also our small bag of silver coins, the tobacco tin containing the pieces of jewelry, and our two books, *The Holy Bible* and *Tales of Jessica*, wrapped in another piece of oilskin.

In my own pack I had spare clothes and my toilet things, an earthenware jar of butter and some dried goat meat, cut in strips and wrapped in cheesecloth. My mind working very slowly, I decided that if the snow stopped before it became too deep, and if Sembur recovered a little after a day or two of rest, and if only the demons of ill-fortune would leave us alone, then we might live to make the long journey to Magyari.

I spent a little while talking to my pony, saying how good he had been and telling him I would call him Job, because there was a man in the Holy Bible of that name who had a lot to put up with. Then I sat beside Sembur while I waited for the *tsampa* to be ready. His breathing was still harsh, but seemed not quite as bad as before. I loosened his clothes, and kept rubbing his hands while I talked to him.

After a few minutes he gave a long sigh and said in a thick voice, "Jani? Where are we? What's 'appened, lovey?" He spoke very slowly, with long gaps, as if he found it hard to remember the right words.

"We're right at the top of the pass," I said. "In that cave. We lost Bugler when a bear frightened 'im, and 'e bolted, but we've got enough to manage with. I'll 'ave something 'ot for you to eat soon."

"Your . . . pony?"

"In 'ere with us. He's been ever so good."

"Go back . . . down to Galdong. Take what you need, Jani. But 'urry . . . 'fore it's too late. I'm a goner."

"No!" I stared at him in fear. "No, you'll be all right, Sembur, you got to be!"

"Go on, Jani. Do . . . like I say. Be . . . good girl."

My spirit broke then and I hunched forward as I knelt

55

beside him, putting my hands over my face and bending till they rested on my knees. "Sembur, I *can't*." I sobbed. "I can't leave you 'ere . . . an' even if I could, I . . . I'm too tired. I feel ever so rotten, Sembur, like 'aving a bad fever."

I felt his hand touch my knee. Through my tears, I saw when I lifted my head that he had closed his eyes as if in pain. Head tilted back, chin jutting, he whispered, "Ah, sweet Jesus, 'elp 'er now." I heard the hiss of the *tsampa* boiling over, and scrambled up, wiping my eyes on my sleeve as I ran to take the pan from the fire. Adding some butter and salt, I poured the *tsampa* into our two bowls and carried them to where Sembur lay.

He could not sit up, but by supporting his head I was able very slowly to give him a few spoonfuls before he became too exhausted to take any more. I left my own bowl of *tsampa* until it was almost cold, because my throat hurt so. When I had eaten, I took Sembur's boots off and spread his sleeping bag over him, then went out to look at the weather.

I should have been relieved to find that the snow had stopped, for this could well mean the difference between life and death to us, but somehow I felt too far away to care. Above the western wall of the pass I could see the gold-and-pink glow in the sky from the setting sun. It was as I turned to go back into the cave that I glimpsed movement from the corner of my eye. At first I thought the bear had returned, but as I stared down the shallow slope which rose from the pass to the cave, I saw a man in white fur leading a black horse, lifting his booted feet high as he pushed through the deep snow.

The foreign demon. I had forgotten him entirely during these past hours, and now he had caught up with us. I saw that the snow which had fallen since we reached the cave had only half filled the deep groove made by Job when he dragged Sembur up the slope. The man in white fur was following that sign. As I watched he lifted his head and saw me standing under the overhang.

I suppose there was no room left in me for fear or despair. I stood still, and he came on steadily, passing from the deep snow to the thin scattering under the overhang. His eyes showed neither strain nor triumph, and when he pulled down the scarf he had wrapped across the lower part of his face I saw that his wide mouth was set hard. He stamped snow from his boots and trousers, put a gloved hand under my chin, and tilted my head to look at my face.

"You're a convincing little liar, aren't you?" he said in Hinglish. He seemed to expect me to understand, and I knew that at Namkhara he must in some way have learned I was foreign, like Sembur, and spoke the same tongue.

I said tiredly, "I couldn't 'elp it, Mister. Sembur said you'd take 'im away to be 'anged. Sembur's the one 'oo looks after me. I got nobody else."

He took his hand away and looked past me. "Is he in there?"

I nodded, and put a hand to my throat. "Yes, Mister. But he's sick. Being 'igh up made 'is 'eart go funny. Then it snowed a blizzard, an' a bear came along. Sembur got thrown, an' we lost 'is pony an' a lot of stuff. Everything went wrong."

"So it seems." He moved past me and into the cave, leaving his horse, Flint. I touched the wet nose and whispered a greeting before turning to follow him. He paused for his eyes to grow used to the dim light, then walked to where Sembur lay. When he spoke, he said Sembur's name strangely, as I had heard him say it before.

"Ahressembur?"

Sembur opened his eyes. For a moment or two he stared blankly, then I saw his body gradually stiffen beneath the blankets until he lay rigid. He said, "Sir?"

"Captain Gascoyne, Third Battalion, 2nd Queen Victoria's Own Gurkha Rifles, detached on special duty. I have orders to place you under arrest and take you to First Battalion Headquarters at Gorakhpur. From there you will be taken under escort to Delhi, to stand trial for theft and murder."

"Yes, sir. I beg to report . . . unable to move . . . for the moment, sir."

"Heart?"

"I believe so, sir."

"I know of no way to ease your condition except by getting you to a lower altitude."

"Perhaps . . . tomorrow, sir. After I've 'ad a rest."

"Very well. And don't lie at attention, it doesn't impress me. You're a disgrace to your calling."

That woke me from my stupor. I kicked the stranger on his booted leg as hard as I could, and shouted, "You leave 'im alone!" He looked at me tight-lipped, turned, and went out of the cave, limping slightly.

Sembur said painfully. "Be'ave yourself, Jani. Please. Nobody can do me any 'arm now. But I want 'im to look after

57

you . . . get you back safe. Be polite to 'im, lovey . . . please, for my sake." I dropped to my knees, put my head on his shoulder, and hugged him, crying silently, for I knew what he meant. Sembur had just told me that he was going to die.

"None of that now." A little strength came into his voice. "No tears. Don't make it 'ard for me, Jani. I got to do a bit of thinking, so you just get on with whatever needs doing."

There came another strange time of going away from myself, so that I remembered nothing. When I came back I was sitting on my bedding, staring at a little light which proved to be a spirit stove. Flint was now in the cave beside Job. Sembur seemed to be dozing. The stranger had taken off his cap and fur jacket and was heating something which smelled very good in a small round pan.

I remembered Sembur's words, and said, "I'm sorry I kicked you, Mister."

He looked at me, unsmiling. "I thought you were still sulking."

"No, I was just sort of asleep."

"Have you eaten?"

"I 'ad a bit of *tsampa*. Sember couldn't eat much, though."

"Fetch your bowl and have some of this."

I shook my head. "Thanks, Mister, but I'm not 'ungry." That was true, and my throat seemed to be growing smaller, making it hard for me to swallow. The stranger shrugged. I said, "Can I try giving a bit to Sembur? Even if 'e can only take a few spoonfuls it'll 'elp."

"I wasn't proposing to let him go without. Fetch the bowl."

"Thanks, Mister."

There was some kind of hot stew in the pan, taken from a tin the stranger had cut open with a special tool. I roused Sembur, and he made a big effort to eat, as if trying to gain a little strength. When he had finished the stranger said to me, "Have you been through this pass before?"

"Yes, Mister."

"In winter?"

I shook my head. "Can't get through in winter. If it starts snowing steady now, we'll be stuck 'ere."

"Do you expect more snow soon?"

I went out of the cave. Night had fallen, but the sky was clear. That meant nothing. It could be solid with snow in only a few hours. I sniffed the air, and listened to the wind, then went back into the cave. "It won't snow tonight, Mister, p'raps not tomorrow either. I can't tell after that."

"Thank you." The words were polite, but the way they were spoken made me feel like a ghost, as if he scarcely knew I was there.

I laid out my groundsheet and sleeping bag, then got wearily to my feet and picked up our canvas bucket. The stranger's brown face under the tight black curly hair turned toward me. "What are you doing?"

"Going to get some water. I got to see to my pony before I go to bed." The cave swam suddenly, and I rubbed a hand across my eyes. "We lost all the feed we were carrying, so I got nothing for 'im to eat."

The stranger studied me, and for the first time a tiny hint of warmth came into his eyes. "I found the stuff you dropped to lighten the other horse, and I picked up one of the bags of grain. It's over there, behind Flint."

"Coo, thanks, Mister. I'll feed 'im in the morning, though. Just give 'im a drink for now."

"I'll see to both horses. Go to bed, girl."

"I 'ave to see Job meself, Mister. Sembur always says—"

"Don't argue. Go to bed."

I took off my boots, wrapped my spare blanket about me, wriggled into my sleeping bag, and rested my head thankfully on the spare clothes in my pack. I felt beset by disease demons. They were in my head, in my throat, in my blood, and I longed as I had never longed before to be held in loving arms and to hear a forgotten voice murmuring words of comfort and reassurance.

Several times during the night I half woke, my mind confused, feeling as if I were another person and my true self was somewhere else. Once I came awake to hear voices. The stranger and Sembur were talking, not urgently but in a slow, almost idle fashion.

". . . and you don't consider ten years a long time?" the stranger was saying.

"Not by Army standards, sir." Sembur's voice was steadier now, for his breathing had eased, but he still spoke very slowly. "They got a lot of things to think about. But I knew my case would still be on file, to be dealt with when things settled down."

"Well . . . I confess it amazed *me*, Sar-major. Ten years." A brief laugh. "I was in the Third Form when it happened."

"Beg pardon, sir, but I got longer experience of the service than you. Thirty-five years. The Army works slow, but it never forgets."

There was a long silence. I had followed the conversation only vaguely, for I hung between sleep and wakefulness. At last the stranger said quietly, "I think it unlikely that I shall succeed in taking you back, Sar-major."

"Quite so, sir. I've done me time. I fancy I won't be any 'indrance to your departure tomorrow."

"For my report, would you care to tell me if it's true that you killed the Maharani and her husband?"

The question seemed to hang in the air for a moment, then Sembur said, "Yes, sir. That's quite correct, in a manner of speaking."

"You stabbed them both to death with your bayonet?"

"I did, sir."

"And took the jewels from her body? The jewels of which some still remain in this box I've found in your pack?"

"Yes, sir. I took 'em."

"And ran away?"

"Quite so, sir."

CHAPTER FOUR

I lay feeling a remote astonishment. What Sembur said he had done was quite impossible. I heard the stranger give a little sigh, as if puzzled, then he said, "And that's the truth?"

"True as you're sitting there, sir."

"The whole truth?"

"Ah . . . now that's a hard question, sir, because nobody knows the 'ole truth about anything, I reckon."

"I should have thought you of all people would know the whole truth about that night. *Why* did you do such a terrible thing?"

"Private reasons, sir."

The stranger gave a grunt of impatience. "I'm damned if I can make you out, Sar-major."

"I wouldn't bother, sir. Not important really. Can I 'ave a word with you about the child, sir? About Jani?"

"Yes, I think you'd better. To start with, who is she?"

"Mine, sir. I lived with an Indian woman in Jahanapur, when I was serving with the Maharaja's forces there. Jani was born about two years before . . . before I left. I took 'er with me that night."

"We know you lived with a woman called Parvati, but there was no record of her bearing you a child."

"There's no record of *any* child being born in Jahanapur, outside the palace, begging your pardon, sir. It's an Indian state, not like at 'ome."

I did not hear what was said next, for my muddled mind was struggling with a new puzzle. Sembur my father? True, he had been a father to me, and I loved him as one, but I had never truly felt I was his child. If my feeling was right, then Sembur was lying to the stranger. I had never known

61

him lie to anyone before, and could see no reason why he should do so now. When my mind drifted back to the conversation again, Sembur was saying, "I brought 'er up as Hinglish as I could, sir, an' she's a good little girl. Old for 'er age, but that's only natural, growing up in Namkhara with no mother."

"What do you want me to do about her?" The stranger's voice was cool and wary.

"Take 'er back to Gorakhpur with you, sir." There was an urgent pleading in Sembur's voice now. "Try and get the Widows an' Orphans Association to take care of 'er."

"She should be taken back to her mother, surely?"

"Parvati's dead, sir. I got word three years ago, last time I went down over the border to get some ammunition and one or two things."

"Well . . . I don't know much about these matters. I mean about orphans, and what one does with them."

"Sir, will you try?" Sembur's voice was hoarse and shaking. "You're an officer, a gentleman. Try to get 'em to send 'er 'ome to England for some schooling. They'll listen to you, an' she'll be safe there."

"Safe?"

"Well . . . I mean, there's proper arrangements for looking after children back 'ome. But think of the kids you've seen in Calcutta, sir, living in the gutters. For pity's sake don't let that 'appen to Jani, sir. If you could just—"

"All right, man, all right," the stranger broke in sharply. "I'll do what I can."

"Thank you, sir. Greatly obliged . . ." Sembur's voice trailed away as if he had used up the last of his strength. I heard the stranger stir, finding a more comfortable position. Job or Flint blew through his nostrils and shuffled his hooves. I felt nothing. Sembur was dying, and had put me under the care of this Hinglishman, this foreign demon, this strange soldier who made it clear with his every look that he disliked me very much. Yet I felt nothing. I should have been torn with grief and afraid of what was to come, but I was empty.

I slept and woke again, slept and woke. A fever demon possessed me. Now my shoulders ached, and my head was full of pain. I could only breathe with my mouth open. At last there came a time when I sank into a deep sleep, to be woken by a hand gripping my shoulder, shaking me.

I opened my eyes and looked up into the face of the stranger. It was a face hard as stone, and I almost flinched from the anger of his stare. Then, as my burning head seemed to float up towards him, I had a sudden insight which astonished me. The foreign demon was not angry with me. His fierce glare hid some kind of dismay and uncertainty.

He said stiffly, "Jani, I'm sorry but I have to tell you . . . well, I'm afraid your father died during the night."

"My father?" I was sitting up now, and looked toward the place where Sembur had lain, but he was no longer there. The stranger said, "It happened a couple of hours ago. I took him out at first light, while you were still asleep."

Slowly I dragged myself out of the sleeping bag, and rested on my hands and knees before making the effort to stand up. Nothing seemed real. When I looked toward the cave entrance I could tell by the light that it was past dawn. I swallowed to clear my aching throat and said, "Where is 'e, Mister?"

"Outside." He looked past me, scowling at nothing. "There's not much snow beneath the overhang. I was able to find enough rocks to make a cairn."

I nodded slowly. That was the way Sembur would have wished. In Namkhara his body would have been taken out to the hills and cut up for the vultures, so that it would return to the four elements of fire and water, earth and air, of which our bodies are composed. But Sembur always said this was shocking and showed no respect.

Outside the cave I stood looking at the long, low pile of stones, knowing there was something I should do but unable to think of it because my mind kept slipping away. Then I remembered, and I went back to fetch the Holy Bible from Sembur's pack. I wished I could cry, but although everything inside me seemed to be burning and melting, no tears would come. When I knelt down by the cairn, the stranger took off his cap. The Bible fell open at Ecclesiastes, Chapter Three, and I began to read. I had to read very slowly, and keep stopping for breath, because my throat felt so small that it was hard to get any air into my lungs. *"To every thing there is a season, and a time to every purpose under the heaven. A time to be born, and a time to die: a time to plant, and a time to pluck up that which is planted . . ."*

I had to pause, and lift my head to swallow. A winter sun glittered on the blanket of snow, and I saw a great elongated shadow skim the white slope. An eagle flashed over the pass and dipped out of sight.

"*. . . a time to weep, and a time to laugh; a time to mourn, and a time to dance . . .*"

I fell over sideways, fighting for breath. Everything about me became black for a while, and when the blackness went away I found that the stranger had picked me up and carried me out from beneath the overhang so that we were no longer in shadow. He kicked some snow away with his feet, then went down on one knee as he lowered me, supporting me with one arm round my shoulders, and tilting my head back with the other hand.

"Open your mouth, Jani," he said harshly. "Wide, so I can see your throat."

He turned my head toward the light, his forehead almost touching my nose as he peered down my throat. I heard him catch his breath, and mutter a strange long word, then he scooped me up and went striding back into the cave.

Moving from the light into the darkness seemed to make an end and a beginning, for from this moment I began to live in a faraway world where time sometimes went very fast and sometimes very slowly. There were many bad dreams which seemed to come while I was awake, and many times when a wood demon sat on my chest and kept holding my throat so tightly I could not breathe.

There was night and day, night and day, and I had never been so afraid before. Whenever the dreams were very bad, or I thought the wood demon was going to kill me, I would cry out for the stranger. I had heard his name only once, when he first spoke to Sembur, and had long forgotten it, so when I needed him I always called for Mister.

Once, and I thought it was at the beginning of this time, I heard the sound of a shot outside the cave, and wondered vaguely at the cause. Later, in one of those short periods when my mind was clear, I realized that I was in bed close to the entrance of the cave, with a well-banked fire against the wall. Somehow Mister must have known that I needed fresh air to breathe, but did not want me to be cold. Within the blankets and sleeping bag I was undressed, except for Sembur's spare shirt.

Such moments of clarity were rare. Often in my nightmare world Mister seemed to be coaxing me to swallow a warm drink he had made. Sometimes, when I whispered my need, he would wrap me in a blanket and carry me to a corner right at the back of the cave where a mound of dirt had gathered over countless seasons.

And sometimes, when I fought for breath, he would bend above me, with something like a thin stick in his mouth, probing to the back of my throat and sucking away the webs the demon had spun there to choke me. In all that time of confusion and terror I remember saying only three things to him: the choking cry of *"'Elp me, Mister!,"* the whispered *"Could you lift me please, Mister?,"* and the grateful *"Thanks ever so, Mister."*

There came a time at last when the heat in my body, the pounding in my head, even the sense of being choked, all faded slowly between one day and the next, leaving me almost too weak to lift my head, but with a feeling of having been freed from the demons. By the light from the cave entrance I judged that it was almost dawn. Beyond the fire, Mister was bending over a bucket of steaming water, stripped to the waist, washing his body.

I said in a feeble voice, "Mister . . ."

He came to me quickly, drying his chest with a towel, and knelt beside me, looking at me searchingly, as if not quite daring to hope. "Jani?"

"I feel . . . much better. You been ever so good, looking after me."

"I hadn't much choice," he said in a dry voice.

"I'm sorry."

"I'll get something for you to eat now. You've lost a lot of weight, and we have to build up your strength a little before we can move."

There was a fine chain round his neck, with a thick silvery disk on it, and something golden set in the face of the disk. I remembered now that this medallion, or whatever it might be, meant a great deal to me, for I had several times seen it fall from beneath the collar of his shirt when he bent over me with the stick-like thing in his mouth, to clear my throat so I could breathe.

He pulled on his vest, shirt, and a fine jacket of thin leather, then turned to a pan which stood over a low flame on the spirit stove. In a moment or two he came to sit beside me with a little stew in a bowl, and a spoon.

"Come along now." He helped me to sit up, put his white fur coat round me for warmth, and held me with one arm while he fed me. As he laid me down and drew the blankets up round me again, I said in a voice that was still stupidly weak, "Thanks, Mister, that was lovely. I'll soon be all right, honest."

"I hope so. We've a long way to go."

"Is it long since I was took ill?"

"It's five days since you passed out."

"Five! Did we get a lot of snow?"

"There's been none at all, so far." He gazed toward the cave entrance. "You were ill when you left Namkhara. You must have picked up the germs there."

"Kachke's little boy wasn't very well, and I gave 'im a carry the day we got 'ome."

"Yes. Well, you've had a very bad thing called diphtheria. It attacks children, and I'd have thought you were almost too old for it, but evidently not."

"It nearly choked me." I shivered at the memory.

"That's what it does, blocks the throat."

I remembered him bending over me, and said, "You kept doing something to get the muck out, didn't you, Mister?"

He picked up an almost empty sack of oats and moved to where Flint and Job stood. "I used a big quill cut short, and sucked it out. Very crude, but it worked."

Few people could have brought themselves to do such a horrible and dangerous thing, and I felt so grateful I would have given anything to have him like me a little, but there was no reason why he should. A thought floated into my mind and I said, "Where did you get a quill from?"

"I managed to shoot an eagle." He spoke curtly, as if this was something he did not want to remember, and now I recalled hearing the shot outside. "Stop talking and rest, Jani."

"All right, Mister. And thanks ever so much. *Ever* so."

When I woke again it was night, and I was sobbing. Perhaps it was because Sembur's death had at last become a reality for me, or perhaps it was simply from weakness. Mister was bending over me, a hand on my brow, his face anxious in the glow of the fire. I saw the glint of the medallion hanging from the chain about his neck. "Jani? Are you all right?"

I groped for his hand and clung to it, trying to find my voice. At last I whispered, "I'm all right. Just ever so frightened . . . I dunno why."

"Try to sleep." His voice was stiff.

I touched the silver disk and said, "Can I 'ave this to 'old, please?" At once I felt ashamed for having said such a thing.

"This? All right." He unclasped the chain, wrapped it round my wrist, and pressed the medallion into my hand. "Like that?"

I nodded, staring up at him, the fear draining away from

66

me, no longer feeling that dreadful sense of being completely alone. He said, "Can you sleep now?"

I nodded again. "Yes. Thank you, Mister."

"Good." He moved away, and I was listening to the sounds as he settled down again when sleep suddenly engulfed me.

I was still clutching the silver disk when I woke in the morning. Mister was holding a bucket of water for Job to drink from. The light from the cave entrance told me that the weather was good, and for the first time since the sickness struck I began to think clearly. I lay for a few moments going over everything in my mind, then said, "Excuse me, Mister."

He looked over his shoulder. "Ah, you're awake. How do you feel?"

"Much better, thanks. I'm sorry I made a fuss in the night." I fumbled at my wrist and unwrapped the chain, holding it up with the silver medallion as he came across the cave to me. "You'd better 'ave this back now."

He took the chain, fastened it round his neck, then gazed down his long thin nose at me. "Are you ready for breakfast?"

"Well, yes please, but we'd better 'ave a talk about what we're going to do, Mister, because there's not much time."

His eyebrows went up, and for the first time I saw the stern, foreign-demon face break into a grin. He looked young then.

I said, "When it snows again, it'll keep snowing an' we'll be cut off 'ere for the winter. There'll be nothing for the 'orses to eat. We'll 'ave to slaughter them an' freeze the meat to last us about three months till spring. So it's best if we can get back down the pass before it snows again."

He had stopped smiling as I spoke, and was looking at me curiously. After a few moments he said as if to himself, "How you'd shock them in Sussex. Such grim realism so young. But I suppose you've never been sheltered from reality, being brought up in a Godforsaken country like this." He gave me a little nod, as if he did not totally dislike me now, and went on, "I've been very much aware of the situation, Jani. Certainly I've no wish to spend the next few months in this cave, and it would break my heart to slaughter the horses. But we can't move till you're strong enough."

"I've only got to sit on Job. You could tie me on 'is back if need be. He's a good pony, and it'll only be 'ard for the first few miles, till we're below the snow line."

"Do you think it's going to snow soon?"

I glanced toward the cave entrance. "Not today. I could tell for two or three days, if I go outside."

He knelt, slipped an arm under my shoulders, wriggled the other under my knees, and lifted me as I was, swathed in blankets and sleeping bag.

It was a joy to be outside the cave and in the tingling cold air. The whiteness was dazzling, and at first I could scarcely see. Mister stood holding me in his arms near the edge of the overhang as I blinked about me, my eyes slowly adjusting to the light. A bright sun shone from a milky-blue sky. There had been no fresh snow and no thaw. When I turned my head I saw the cairn which was Sembur's grave, and for a few seconds I pressed my face against Mister's shoulder to stop the tears coming.

At last I looked carefully at the sky, especially at the texture of the haze to the north and east. Sembur had sometimes been irritated with me because I could never explain to him exactly what I was looking for, or how I could tell what weather was building up for us, but the truth was that it simply would not go into words, especially when I stopped using my eyes and began to sniff the air. I did this now, eyes closed, and found a strong tang with none of the heavy yellow smell that heralded snow. But beneath the tang there was a taste of blandness, like unsalted food, which for me was a distant warning.

I said, "We've got two days for sure, Mister. P'raps three. I'll know better about that tomorrow. But no more than three."

When he took me back into the cave and laid me down, I felt exhausted, too weak even to lift my head. He said quietly, "Now listen, Jani. You're sensible enough to be treated as an adult, thank God, so I'm going to tell you exactly how you stand. You're over the diphtheria, but in another three weeks, or perhaps longer, you're likely to be quite ill again in a different way, as a result of having had the disease. I'm not a doctor, so I can't explain why, but I had experience of diphtheria in the family some years ago, and I remember it only too well."

He looked down at me, frowning. "Now, assuming we get back down the pass to Galdong, we'll press on south, into Nepal. From Pokhara we can go on down through Tansing to Gorakhpur. There's a hospital there run by a nursing order of nuns, so you'll have proper attention. And they can make arrangements for the Army Widows and Orphans Association to take charge of you when you're better." He paused, thinking. "If we make steady progress on our journey we ought to reach Gorakhpur in less than three weeks, so you'll be in good hands before you're ill again."

I hated the thought of almost everything Mister had just said. Of falling ill, of the long journey south, and above all of what would happen to me when I was placed in the charge of strange Hinglish people in a world completely unlike the world I knew.

I said, "If we've got a long journey, Mister, I think I'd better rest an' get me strength back a bit for a couple of days."

He nodded. "Three, if you decide the snow will hold off. I've been rationing the horses, and I've brought in the other sacks of grain you abandoned. There's still enough for a small feed each today. After that they'll have to go hungry till we get down to Galdong. Still, that won't do them any harm."

He began to make a pot of stew, frowning, and I felt his mind was far away, probably on the problems of the journey ahead. Having rested a little I felt stronger now, and said, "Would you do me a favor, Mister? Would you warm up some water to fill the bucket, so I can 'ave a bath?"

He looked at me in surprise. "A bath?"

"Well, not a real bath. A wash all over. I can do meself a bit at a time. I must smell all sweaty and 'orrible, an' I can't bear being like that."

"Ah. You've been brought up by a Regimental Sergeant Major, of course."

"Eh?"

"Your father was an Ahressem. He'd naturally be smart, clean, disciplined." I realized he was speaking of Sembur, but at this moment I did not want to ask what an Ahressem was, or to say that I did not believe Sembur was my father.

When he had filled the bucket with warm water, Mister set up a blanket screen by the fire for me, but I was so weak I fell over when bending to wash my legs, and he had to come and help me, which he did in silence, scowling all the time. When it was over, when I had combed the tangles from my hair and was snug in bed again, I felt like a new person. Mister brought me big bowl of stew and I ate it hungrily, feeding myself for the first time. It was only when I finished that I noticed he had eaten no stew himself but was chewing a strip

69

of dried yak meat. I was dismayed, and said, "When you going to 'ave yours, Mister?"

"I've only three tins left, and you need building up. But I won't go hungry, there's plenty of dried meat." He stared at me in exasperation. "Oh, don't start grizzling, girl. What's the matter now?"

I rubbed some tears from my cheek, feeling angry at my own weakness, and said, "I'm not grizzling. Well, not really. I just felt wobbly because of you being nice to me."

"Oh, for God's sake." He got up and went to attend to the horses. I looked about the cave. The pile of wood and great layer of dry dung we used for fuel were almost exhausted. Soon we would have no fire. I made up my mind then that I would be strong enough to travel in two days, and fixed this thought firmly in my head as I went to sleep.

All that day I slept, only waking to eat when Mister roused me. By the following morning I was much stronger. After breakfast I got up, washed and dressed, then tried my legs for ten minutes before lying down again. When an hour had passed I took a little walk outside the cave, going round in a small circle beneath the overhang. So it went on throughout the day. I would rest, then exercise; rest, then exercise a little more.

Mister and I hardly exchanged a word. I was too busy concentrating on what I was doing, and I suppose he had nothing to say to me, though once or twice I became aware that he was watching me with a half-puzzled, half-annoyed look on his face, as if there was something he could not quite fathom.

At dusk I went out to look at the sky and sniff the air. When I returned to the cave I said, "We'll 'ave to start at first light tomorrow."

"Will you be strong enough?"

"Yes, Mister. You might 'ave to tie me on Job's back, but I'll manage."

He stared at me hard, then nodded slowly. "All right, Jani. Tomorrow."

When we led the horses out next morning I knew we had left no time to spare. The sky to the north was heavy with the threat of more snow, and the temperature had dropped sharply. I stood by the cairn for a few moments, silently saying goodbye to Sembur and thanking him for looking after me. As I did so I remembered the moments when I had lain half stupefied by fever, hearing Mister and Sembur talk, hear-

70

ing Sembur calmly admit that he had killed—who was it? A Maharani and her husband . . . ?

I had the vague notion that a Maharani was some kind of Indian princess, and the idea that Sembur would kill any woman was unbelievable to me. But then, he had told Mister I was his daughter, and I could not believe that either. I looked at the pile of rocks under which Sembur lay, and thought that whatever the truth might be, it no longer mattered to anybody now.

The day was to come when I would learn that the strange and terrible truth mattered to many people, not least to myself and to the man who in these last days had saved me from dying.

CHAPTER FIVE

Mister helped me mount, and we set off down the slope to where the pass ran north and south. He was leading on foot, breaking trail to make it easier for the horses, who were very hungry now. Flint followed, laden with our tent and baggage, and I came last on Job.

Just to sit in the saddle was hard work, for we were constantly lurching, swaying, and slithering. Beneath the walls of the pass the snow was up to three feet deep, and I marveled at the way Mister thrust on against it, forcing a narrow path for us to follow. We covered half a mile in the first hour, a full mile in the next, for the snow was less deep, and another mile in the third hour.

Then my strength ran out, and I had to call to Mister. He trudged back, placed a folded blanket in front of me so that I could lean forward on it, fixed a rope round my waist, and knotted the ends under Job's chest. He said no word, but rested his hand against my cheek for a moment and gave me a sudden grin, the kind that wiped away all his sternness and arrogance. It was like a tonic, and gave me new heart.

After five hours of cruel struggle which seemed unending, we were below the snow line at last. Without the rope I would have fallen a dozen times, but it did not save me from the effort of riding, and my whole body ached with a weariness I had never known before. When Mister trudged back to me, his boots making a welcome sound on rock now, instead of being muffled by snow, I saw that his eyes were sunken with strain, and his grin had become a fixed snarl, as if in defiance of the mountain, the pass, the wind and snow, and all that was trying to destroy us.

He paused to get his breath, then panted, "Jani . . . can we camp in the upper valley?"

I shook my head, and forced my cold lips to frame words. "No good, Mister. There's a ton of snow coming. It'll be right down to the foot 'ills tonight."

"I thought as much. This is what I've been saving Flint for." He unfastened the rope, lifted me down and sat me on the folded blanket, then spent several minutes moving all our baggage from Flint to Job, and strapping it securely. I marveled that he should do so much for me when he had no liking for me. The Lo-bas would have considered that it was my fate to die on the mountain, and would have left me in the cave days ago.

Mister picked me up and set me astride Flint, then swung into the saddle behind me, with Job's rein looped about his wrist. A great easement crept through my bones and muscles as I sagged back. With his body behind me, his arms supporting me on each side, all strain was taken from me, and I could almost have slept in the saddle.

I knew the worst was over now, and Mister had won. The horses, eager for grazing, would move on down the winding pass at a good steady pace, and we would come to Galdong before dusk.

During the next few hours I dozed many times, lolling drowsily in Mister's arms, feeling safe and secure. At some time after the sun had passed its zenith I roused and said, "Mister . . .?"

"Yes?"

"Thanks ever so much."

"You must have said that ten times already."

"Did I? I'm sorry, but I dunno what else to say."

"Try shutting up for a change."

The mountain demons had closed in on Mister at last. When you were very tired, and had been very high up for a long time, they danced invisibly round your head and made you bad-tempered, but I knew the demons would not stay with Mister once we reached the plain, and I dozed again.

Much later there came a time when I opened my eyes to see the great golden spires of the Galdong monastery only two miles away across the fields. I felt suddenly refreshed, renewed, and hungry. It was warmer now, the air was richer, and I saw that Flint was stepping along briskly with head high. As he was not trying to stop and graze, I realized we must have halted earlier for the horses to feed, and I had slept through it.

That night we stayed in a house in the small village of Galdong, which lay west of the monastery. Mister would have paid a gold piece for the two rooms we rented, but I was so shocked at his stupidity that I forgot myself and spoke quite rudely to him.

"A piece of *gold*? You gone barmy or something?"

"It's only a half sovereign."

"Don't let 'er see it!" I snatched it from his hand before the woman I was bargaining with returned with her husband in support. "Let's 'ave a silver rupee, quick!"

When the woman and her husband appeared I began politely to point out the poverty of their home, the lack of all things necessary to persons of quality, and the extraordinary goodness of our hearts in condescending even to consider spending a night or two under their roof. They in turn pointed out the splendors of the little mud-brick house, and the dangers they were risking by taking a foreign demon within its walls. In the end we agreed on a price of one silver piece for two nights, with three meals each day, one to include meat, and a tub of hot water.

Mister watched in silence, seeming to follow the discussion even though he did not know the language. When the bargain was closed and we were alone, I told him the terms. It was then I saw him laugh for the first time. "You're a card, Jani. You're really quite a card."

I did not entirely understand what he meant, but felt rather proud of myself for having made him laugh.

We saw that the horses were comfortable, took turns to bathe in the tub, ate a big meal, then slept the night through. In the morning I felt much stronger, and was glad to see that Mister looked his usual cool and arrogant self. As I expected, the High Lama had heard of our arrival at once, and sent for me. Mister frowned when I told him, and said, "I'd better come along."

"No, you can't if you 'aven't been invited. Anyway, Rild's just going to ask about Sembur. Then he'll say I can stay on 'ere and become a nun if I like."

"And do you like?"

I shook my head. "No. And anyway I can't become a nun 'ere because Sembur says they're a lot of 'eathens 'oo don't

74

believe in the 'Oly Bible. An' I wouldn't do anything to upset Sembur."

Mister gave me one of his long frowning looks, as if trying to puzzle something out. I looked back at him, because Sembur had taught me so. *"Never look away, Jani. Always look a person straight in the eye. Superior or subordinate. Straight in the eye."*

Mister said at last, "Well, whatever Sembur did, you're fortunate to have had a father who inspired such loyalty."

"Sembur wasn't my pa. And what you and 'im were saying when I was 'alf asleep, that wasn't true either. Sembur never killed those people an' stole their jewels."

"He had the jewels in his possession."

"Then 'e got 'em honest."

"You're saying Sembur lied to me when he confessed to the murders? He was a liar?"

I felt trapped, and a sudden rage against Mister swept me, making me tremble. "No 'e wasn't a liar!" I stormed. "Sembur just told you all wrong that night for some special reason. And if I was big enough, I'd *'it* you, except Sembur said I was to be polite to you."

With that I turned and stalked away, making for the monastery. My audience with Rild went just as I had expected. I told him how Sembur's heart had failed going over the pass, and how I had been taken ill. He agreed that a very bad disease-bearing demon had killed several children in Namkhara, and said I was fortunate to have overcome one so powerful.

His eyes closed, and after a silence he went on, "Your way is dark to me, the veil hard to penetrate . . . but I see the women in red who will be your friend, and through her will come the one to fear, who will be your enemy, the Silver Man—" He broke off with a hiss of indrawn breath, eyes opening suddenly very wide with shock. I had thought it impossible for the High Lama's calm to be disturbed, but now it was as if he recoiled from the sting of a scorpion.

"Ahhh . . ." he breathed. "Within the bounds of earth and incarnation I had never thought to feel such power." Again he closed his eyes, and I saw his lips moving as he murmured mantras to bring quietness to his mind. I was beginning to fidget impatiently, anxious to be gone, when he spoke. "With the turning of the stars you will come to us again, child. Till then, go with my blessing."

I made the proper response, "May it aid my release from

the wheel of rebirth, Highborn." Then Mudok came to conduct me through the many passages, chambers, and winding flights of stairs which brought us at last to the great doors of the monastery.

I had taken scarcely any notice of Rild's words, for I was busy thinking about preparations for our journey south. Not until the Year of the Iron Mouse came, when I had been living for years in another world, would I remember the words spoken by the High Lama of Galdong on this wintry day in the land of Smon T'ang.

When I returned to our lodging I found Mister rubbing down the horses. I began to help in silence, then swallowed my pride and said, "I'm sorry I was rude to you, Mister."

He gave me an amused look. "That's all right. What happened at the monastery?"

"Nothing much. Only what I said."

"I'd like to start south tomorrow, so we can get you under medical care as soon as possible."

"I don't *feel* as if I'm going to be ill again in three weeks."

"If I'm wrong, there's no harm done. Do you advise buying a yak for the journey?"

I thought about it, then said, "It'll be all right us taking a yak as long as I'm there, and it's certainly a big 'elp with the baggage."

"What do you mean, it'll be all right with you there?"

"Because if I wasn't, you'd take twice as long on the journey. But I can talk to yaks, and they do what I ask 'em."

"Talk to yaks?" He paused in his work to stare at me.

"Well, any animal, really. Not lower ones, like snakes, but four-legged ones like goats or 'orses or bears."

"Bears?"

"They're nice. I once talked to a snow leopard. She was suspicious at first, but after a while we made friends. I don't mind if you laugh, Mister."

"I'm not laughing." Instead, his face was thoughtful. "I saw you make friends with Flint that first day I met you, and I'd say he's more difficult than a snow leopard. All right, we'll buy a yak and supplies for the journey today, and start tomorrow."

By the sixth day I felt completely myself again in health, with all weakness gone. There was still an aching emptiness within me for Sembur, but during the long days of travel through the quiet hills I had had much time to think, and I

76

was sure that Sembur would have chosen to die in the high mountains rather than be taken back into India to face whatever awaited him there. I had stopped wondering about my own future, and pretended that Mister and I would simply go on and on, through mountains and foothills, across tumbling rivers and over wide plains, our journey never ending.

As the days passed, we had fallen into a simple pattern. Each morning I would make a good hot breakfast while Mister folded our two tents and attended to Flint and Job, who had become good friends now. Neither of them liked the yak, whose name was Neb, and he disliked them just as heartily. I had called him Neb after Nebuchadnezzar, who ate the grass in the fields.

As we busied ourselves with our tasks, or rode on our way, we would sometimes talk a little but not very much. Our silence was not unfriendly, though. It was more that we had little to say to each other, as we came from different worlds and had almost nothing in common. Well before sunset we would stop, make camp, and wash the dust and sweat of the day's travel from us before making our second and last meal of the day. This was the time I liked best, when we sat by our fire in the dusk, and all the world was quiet but for the shuffle of a hoof, or a little snort from one of the animals.

Often on the trail I had to coax Neb to move faster, or to move at all. This always fascinated Mister. He would watch with a half smile, then give a baffled shake of his head. Once he asked, "What are you saying to him, Jani?"

"Oh, just what comes into me 'ead. Sometimes I flatter 'im, sometimes I scold 'im."

"And you have to do it in the language of Smon T'ang?"

"It doesn't matter what language. It's not really what you say, it's what you're thinking. No, more what you're *feeling*."

Mister pointed toward Neb, who had stopped just beyond a little river we had forded, and now stood with his head turned sulkily away from us. "Talk to him in English this time, Jani."

I got down from Job and went to Neb, rubbing his jaw roughly with a bare hand and blowing gently on his nose. It came to me that he felt sad and needed encouragement, and I said, "Poor old Neb, you've been such a good little boy, 'aven't you? I'm ever so pleased, the way you've been carrying all that load. An' just look at the way those funny 'orses with no decent 'air on 'em go showing off, acting as if you can't keep up with 'em . . ." Neb stirred and turned his head

77

to look at me. When I had chattered on a little more he started to move, stamping past the horses with a lofty and determined air.

Mister took off his felt cap, ran fingers through his black curly hair, and gave a little chuckle of delight. "I'll be damned. I wish the grooms who look after our polo ponies had your gift."

From Smon T'ang we crossed the border into Nepal and moved steadily south down the great valley between the white peaks of Annapurna and Dhaulagiri, descending from the high country where fir and birch and the huge-bloomed rhododendrons grew, to the slopes where the wind blew more gently among pines, oaks, and walnuts. We swung east to Pokhara, where Mister refilled our panniers with fresh stores, then moved south again for Bethari and the Indian border.

On the tenth day, when it was Mister's turn to wash first in the bucket of water we had heated, I looked for the silver medallion hanging against his chest, as I always did now, for since that night in the cave it had been a kind of talisman for me.

Summoning up my courage, and making myself look at him instead of down at the strips of meat I was frying, I said, "Can I ask you something, Mister?"

He looked up from the razor he was putting away with its twin in a leather case and said absently, "Why not?"

"I'm not sure if it's polite."

"Try asking, and I'll let you know."

"I was wondering what that medallion was."

He came towards me, unclasping the chain, his teeth chattering a little in the early-morning wind, then put the whole thing in my hand and turned away to pull on his fine woolen undershirt. Now I saw that the thick disk of silver, about twice the size of my thumbnail, was inset with a star which had five points. I turned the medallion over. On the back was a spiral of tiny little squiggles and curlicues, and I realized that this must be some kind of writing.

I said, "Is it a foreign language, Mister?"

"Yes. A language of India, called Hindi."

"What's it say?"

"Oh, it's a poem of some sort. Nothing important."

"Did someone give it to you?"

"A lady. Now stop asking questions."

"I'm sorry. I just wondered." I gave the medallion back to him, then returned to watching the strips of meat in the pan.

Almost from one day to the next the air became warm and moist, and we found ourselves moving through country quite unfamiliar to me. For a whole day we traveled along a trail through a forest, passing small villages where dark-skinned people stared at us as we went by. Early that day we sold Neb to a party of merchants going north, for he was unused to this climate and showed signs of distress. I was in the same case as Neb, for the air seemed far too thick and heavy, but I hid my discomfort. We rode lightly dressed now, I wore one of my tunics, Mister wore a shirt, but we still needed our warmer clothing after sunset, for the nights were cold.

As long as I was able to shut out of my mind the fact that our journey would come to an end, I was strangely happy during all this time. I could not have said why. Perhaps, with Sembur lost to me, it was because I was so glad to be in Mister's care for a little while.

I often wished I knew more about him, but he would never talk about himself. Sometimes, when we made camp and were waiting for our meal to be cooked, he would ask me quite a lot of questions, not about myself but about the land of Bod. He called it Tibet, as Sembur had called it, and evidently it was a great mystery to the outside world. Mister asked me how the people were governed, whether there were many soldiers, how many passes there were through the mountains from Smon T'ang, whether the old forts on the plains beyond were strongly manned, and many other such questions. I answered as well as I could, but felt surprised, because from some of the things he asked I felt sure he knew more about Bod than a complete stranger would.

When I asked if he had been into Tibet before, he said, "Yes, but not the way you go. I was further to the east, between Lhasa and the border, for six months last year."

"Why d'you go there, Mister?"

"Don't ask so many questions."

"Me?" I stared at him indignantly. "You're the one keeps asking questions, 'undreds of 'em?"

He gave me one of his heavy scowls. "Little girls should be seen and not heard."

I liked his scowl and did my best to imitate it as I looked back at him across our little cooking fire. "You've got a long nose," I said, "an' hooky eyebrows, an' you look like a foreign demon."

His face shifted in a funny way, and he said, "I thought you were supposed to be polite to me."

"Oh. Yes, I am, but sometimes I forget. Beg pardon."

"Don't mention it," Mister said.

On the fifteenth day I woke in the night feeling ill, my heart palpitating and an awful weakness creeping through me. When morning came I barely had strength to stand. Mister felt my pulse and forehead, and bit his lip.

"It's come sooner than I thought, Jani," he said shortly. "We've done well, but we still have another three days to go." He laid me down on my bedding and drew a blanket over me. "You rest while I get breakfast and strike camp."

That morning I rode tied to Job's back, lolling and lurching in the saddle. At some time during the afternoon I realized that I was on Flint, with Mister seated behind me, holding me as he had held me on the way down from the pass. Or perhaps it was a different day, for often I seemed to drift right away to a place of nothingness where time itself stood still.

For a while I came back briefly from that faraway place to a new day, with the sun no more than two hours risen. The air was warmer, the smell of the land different. I was no longer astride Flint, but sat across the saddle on something soft, a folded blanket perhaps, with Mister's arm cradling my shoulders, my head resting on his chest.

I whispered, "Where's Job?"

He looked down, and I saw that his face was drawn with weariness. "Behind, on a leading rein, carrying the baggage. How are you, Jani?"

"Sort of . . . funny. You're ever so tired, Mister, carrying me like this."

"Go to sleep, Jani. That's the only medicine I can offer."

There came a time when I roused to the chatter of a tongue unknown to me. I was in a small cart, a thing unheard-of in Smon T'ang but which I had seen in a picture in my *Tales of Jessica* book. I seemed to be lying on a mattress of straw, and I could hear Mister's voice speaking sharply, warningly, as if telling the driver to go carefully. Vaguely I realized that we must have reached a village where he had hired a cart and driver. After another time of blankness I heard a whole medley of sounds, the rattle of wheels, the clatter of hooves, the chatter and murmur of many voices. I could smell fruit, vegetables, smoke, animals, humans, and knew we were in a town.

Then the noise was left behind. The cart stopped. Mister lifted me out and carried me through a big doorway into a cool place. Somebody spoke to him. I heard his voice, sharp and demanding: "I don't give a damn about the proper channels. Get this child into nursing care at once, then give my respects to the senior sister, or whatever you call her, and say I'd be obliged if she would have a word with me as soon as she can spare a moment."

I was lying on a narrow bed that moved along a corridor. A lady in a white cap was speaking to somebody and starting to take my clothes off. Her hair was the color of corn, and I stared dazedly. I had never seen fair hair before. Then everything faded, and I went far away again to the distant place where nothing happened and time did not move.

I came back to the world unwillingly, and knew I had been away for a long time. I lay in a bed with white sheets and was wearing a faded flannel nightdress. The room was small, and a dark-skinned girl wearing a white apron over her dress was washing the floor. When I made a sound she smiled, said something in a strange tongue, then went out. A few moments later she returned with a lady all in black except for a white peak to her hood. I was to learn that she was an English holy woman, a nun, and this was a nursing order of nuns who ran the small hospital attached to the Catholic Mission in Gorakhpur. They were helped by a few nurses who were not holy women, like the lady with fair hair I had seen that first day.

The nun stood beside my bed, smiled, and said, "Well, young lady, you gave us all quite a fright. It's been five days now, you know. How do you feel this morning?"

"A bit . . . a bit weak. But all right, thank you, miss."

"You call me Sister. Sister Ruth."

"Yes, Sister."

"You've been something of a puzzle to us all, Jane."

"I'm Jani, miss. Sister."

The nun picked up a board with a paper fastened to it at the foot of my bed. "We have you entered as Jane. Jane Burr."

I wondered vaguely why someone had chosen that name for me. No doubt Jane was the Hinglish way of saying my first name, but in Smon T'ang I had never had a second name, and could not think why they should call me Jane Burr. The nun was saying, "Major Crossland, from the military hospital, came on his usual weekly visit yesterday. He's

81

the best of doctors, and he gave you a thorough examination. Do you remember?"

"Well . . . not really, Sister."

"Never mind. He was concerned about your heart, because there is sometimes damage to the heart in these cases, but it seems you're very strong and healthy." She beamed at me. "We expect to have you up in a few days now, and off home to England within a month."

I said, "Please . . . where's Mister? Will 'e come an' see me?"

"Who, dear?"

"Mister. I . . . I forget 'is name. The gentleman 'oo brought me 'ere."

"Oh, the young captain. No, he left three days ago, Jane. He had orders to report to Calcutta, and he went off by train, with that lovely horse in a horse box."

I had known he would be gone, back to his own world, and that I would not see him again. Yet to be told so was like the shock of being struck an unexpected blow. I flinched, panic-stricken by the thought that I was now truly alone. My mouth twisted under the need to cry, and I turned on my side, sliding my hand up to hold my throat where a great lump had suddenly risen. My fingers touched something beneath the nightdress, something small and round. Scarcely daring to believe my hope could be true, I fumbled at my neck, found the slender chain, and drew it out. Next moment I was staring at the medallion with the inset gold star.

I turned the medallion over and peered with tear-blurred eyes at the spiral of tiny writing on the back. A thought came to me, and I whispered, "Sister . . . excuse me, but . . . do you 'appen to read . . . Hindi?"

"I don't myself, dear," I heard her say brightly, "but Sister Maria does. She used a magnifying glass to read the inscription on that medallion the young captain left you, if that's what you're wondering about."

"D'you know what it says, miss—I mean, Sister?"

"Yes, Sister Maria wrote it down." She turned over the little board she held, and looked at a piece of paper clipped to the back. "Apparently it's more poetic in Hindi, but it means something like this:

'Here is a token to remind you of a friend
It may not bring you good fortune
Or protect you from fate

> *Or from your enemy*
> *It is for remembrance only*
> *Keep it until a friend has need of it*
> *Then give it gladly and go your way.' "*

I turned my face into the pillow and let the tears come. There was heartbreak in me, but gladness too, for I held the medallion gripped tightly in my hand, this token which said I was his friend. He had given it to me . . . to *me*, in remembrance.

And while I remembered, I would never ever be quite alone.

CHAPTER SIX

I first set eyes on England three months later when I saw the Isle of Wight. In another hour our ship was sailing up a wide stretch of water called the Solent, and we landed at Southampton in a steady drizzle of rain.

I no longer called this country Hingland, because I had noticed that other people did not use an extra aitch for emphasis, as Sembur had done. In fact, I no longer spoke at all, and had been mute for almost eight weeks. Everybody thought it was from wickedness, and that my ingratitude was disgraceful, but they were wrong. When I was alone I could speak to myself, but if I tried to say anything to another person my throat and tongue seemed to become locked.

I was afraid all the time. In *Tales of Jessica* I had read at least a little about the world outside Smon T'ang, and over the years Sembur had told me many amazing facts. But it is one thing to be told about a great iron locomotive, or a huge ship, about a town teeming with people like ants, or a sea reaching to the horizon; to experience such unbelievable sights is very different. I was as frightened as an English child would have been to find herself with a caravan of yaks and ponies traveling through the land of Bod.

Throughout the journey I was in the care of Miss Foot, who had been a governess in India and was now going home. She was being paid a small sum by an Army charity to escort me to London, where a place had been found for me in an orphanage called the Adelaide Crocker Home for Orphan Girls, which had been founded more than fifty years ago by a lady called Miss Adelaide Crocker.

Miss Foot was a thin lady with gray hair and a nose like a beak. We hated each other. I was afraid to move a finger because I knew it would be wrong. In Miss Foot's opinion I walked badly, stood badly, sat badly, and was bad-mannered, bad-tempered, and badly bred. I hated her because I remembered all the trouble Sembur had taken to bring me up properly, and I felt that everything she said was a slur on him. Miss Foot hated me for all my many faults but in particular because I was a half-caste. I gathered this meant that I was half English and half Indian, and was deeply puzzled as to why she considered this to be such a sin.

Because I was mute, she seemed to think I was without hearing or feeling, and she would talk about me, while I was sitting beside her, as if I were not there.

". . . we all have our cross to bear, Mrs. Stoddart, and Jane is a great burden to me. I had hoped for peace and quiet on this voyage, but—*don't* cross your feet, Jane!—I have very little peace, I assure you. The child is a half-caste, of course. Her father was a common soldier who married an Indian woman in Jahanapur, then perpetrated some dreadful crime and ran off with the child to Tibet—*don't* hang your head like that, Jane!—I beg your pardon, Mrs. Stoddart? Oh yes, she *can* talk. She was talking quite freely the day I first saw her in Gorakhpur, but like a *costermonger*, Mrs. Stoddart, so dreadfully common. I was *amazed* that the Army authorities should send a half-Indian child to England, but it seems *somebody* exerted a great deal of influence and also paid her fare—keep your *knees* together, Jane!"

I put my knees together, rested my folded hands upon them, and sat up very straight, hoping to avoid any more complaint. If somebody had paid my fare to make sure I was taken to England it could only have been Mister. He had honored the promise he had made when Sembur lay dying in the cave that night, the promise that he would do all he could to ensure I was sent to England.

On a gray day in January I saw the last of Miss Foot and entered the Adelaide Crocker Home for Orphan Girls, in a part of London called Bermondsey, where I was to spend the next two and a half years. For me, once I had grown used to the life, they were not unhappy years.

On the day of my arrival, as soon as Miss Foot had handed me over and left, I found myself able to speak freely. This was an enormous relief, and helped me through my first awkward week, when the other girls eyed me warily and seemed hostile. I was to find that they were always like this

85

with a new girl until they came to know her, and indeed I later behaved in the same way myself.

The number of girls varied from sixty to seventy, and their ages from five to fourteen. The Principal was Miss Callender, who looked rather like Miss Foot but was very different. She had two assistants, one who was liked and one who was feared.

Of the grant made each year to the orphanage under Adelaide Crocker's will, Miss Callender spent every possible penny on food, so though we ate simply we ate well enough. Our clothes were dreadful because Miss Callender hated to spend money on them. We wore a strange assortment of dresses, skirts, and underclothes, remade by the older girls from bundles of old clothes collected for us by what we called Rectory people. These were patched, dyed, turned, handed down, and remade yet again for as long as the threads would hang together. Old woolen garments sent to us by the Rectory people were washed, unpicked, then knitted or crocheted to make mittens and shawls for the winter.

Our boots came to us secondhand from a School for Young Ladies, and were repaired again and again by Douch, the gloomy caretaker and handyman who detested every one of us. All boots had the toes cut away so that they would fit a wide range of feet. Most of Miss Callender's grudging expenditure on clothes went on stockings and undergarments. Our stockings were of heavy worsted, our shifts of thick flannel, our drawers of horribly stiff unbleached calico.

Some of the girls in the orphanage were timid creatures, some were bold. Three, when I first arrived, had been on the street. They were just under fourteen. I did not know what the phrase meant then, to be "on the street," but by the time I had spent six months with the mixture of girls in the orphanage there was little I did not know about the horrors of life among the poor in London.

We had lessons every day, and were taught reading, writing, sums, sewing, knitting, and crochet. The older girls were expected to look after the small ones, which meant that we were always busy, getting them washed and dressed in the morning, helping make their beds, teaching them how to do things for themselves, and looking after them at meals.

I had only one patch of real trouble while settling in, and then I was glad that even as a small child in Namkhara I had played many rough games with boys bigger than I was, and had learned a useful lesson . . . that the way to deal with a bully was to surprise him, and hurt him, and to do it right at the start. One of the orphanage girls who had been taken from the streets was a vicious creature and a bully. The other girls were afraid of her, and she would make them do things for her as if they were her servants.

At the end of my first week she turned her attentions to me, and ordered me to hand over the boots of plaited yak hair I had brought with me and still wore. With a fluttering in my stomach I looked at her and said, "You're miles too big for 'em. And anyway, as long as they fit me, they're mine, Daisy. When they get too small, I'll give 'em to 'oo I like."

Daisy advanced slowly upon me, fists on her hips. "Coo, 'ark at 'er!" she jeered. "You fancy a good 'iding, Little Miss Cocky?"

I decided that this would not end with mere words, and I would have to settle it quickly. I said gently, "I don't want any trouble with you, Daisy, honest I don't . . ." and hitching up my skirt I kicked her very hard on the knee. She gave a great howl of shock and pain, and went hobbling away to her bed, wailing that I had crippled her.

I won a lot of friends that day, and became a kind of protector for many who had been bullied by Daisy. For the six months that she remained at the orphanage she caused me no more trouble.

The seasons came and went, and the orphanage became my small world. I enjoyed the lessons, enjoyed contriving to remake old garments when it seemed scarcely possible, and gained pleasure from looking after the little girls and having them rely on me and trust me. But the best part of every day was when we went out, moving in pairs in a long crocodile, for our walk to the park a mile away.

I had spent more daytime hours of my life out of doors than indoors, and sometimes I felt the walls of the orphanage were suffocating me. To go for an hour's walk round the park was a small enough outing after the journeys I had made, but to me it was a daily joy, no matter what the weather.

When a girl became fourteen, a position was found for her, usually in service, but sometimes with a dressmaker or in one of the East End factories, or very occasionally on a farm. I stayed until I was fifteen, a year longer than I should have done, because Miss Callender found me a great help with the smaller children. I might even have remained to become a kind of unpaid assistant, if I had not fallen out with an unpleasant girl called Big Alice, who was in charge of another dormitory. She was always sneering, and one day I lost my temper and hit her. It was the first time I had done such a thing since kicking Daisy at the end of my first week, but a great fuss was made about it, and Miss Callender decided it was time for me to go.

Although I had always tried hard with my sewing, I had no gift with a needle; neither did I want to go into a factory, for I had heard grim tales from some of the other girls about conditions in such places. I imagined that I would go into service, but to my great joy Miss Callender sent for me one day, about two weeks after the incident with Big Alice, and said she had found me a place on a farm in Hampshire.

"A farm, miss!"

"Well, perhaps not quite a farm, Jane. A small holding, rather. It's run by the owner and his wife, Mr. and Mrs. Gammidge. They have a cottage and a few acres. It seems they have not been blessed with children, and now they are in middle age they need a pair of hands to help in the house and on the land."

"Will I 'ave some animals to look after, miss?"

"They keep a few chickens and pigs, I'm told."

"Oh."

"And they're sure to have a horse, or an animal of some kind to pull a cart."

"Ooh, that's nice. Thanks ever so, Miss Callender."

"Mr. Gammidge has sent the money for your rail fare, and you will leave on Saturday. He will meet you at Tenbrook Green, which is the nearest station." She sat back, her hands folded on the desk. "I'm sorry to lose you, Jane. Do control your temper in future."

"Yes, I'll try, miss. It was just . . . well, I was telling the girls a story about someone I knew 'oo was ever so special to me, an' that Alice said something 'orrible about 'im."

"That was wrong of her, but you should not have struck her, Jane. It was most un-Christian behavior. *'Vengeance is mine,'* saith the Lord."

"Yes, miss. I suppose I was thinking more about that bit where it says, *'Whatsoever thy 'and findeth to do, do it with thy might.'* "

She gave me a long stern look. "We will not use scriptural quotations for argument, Jane."

"No, miss."

Her face relaxed and she almost smiled. "You're a sound girl. I wish we could have done better for you, but it's always a struggle here. I hope all goes well for you in your new life, Jane."

"Thank you, miss."

My new life at Crabtree Cottage, with Mr. and Mrs. Gammidge, lasted exactly two weeks and three days. She was a quiet, stolid woman who worked hard but whose mind always seemed to be somewhere else. Her husband was cheerful but lazy, a lanky man with a long face and a jumble of big white teeth.

On the second day, when we were getting grain for the chickens from the shed where it was stored, Mr. Gammidge put an arm round me and pressed his hand on my bosom. I pulled away, startled, realizing that I had an awkward problem to cope with, and one that was new to me.

From then on, almost all my thoughts were devoted to avoiding being left alone with Mr. Gammidge. If that was impossible, as it so often was, I would try to keep something between us and at the same time pretend not to be doing so. I found it very difficult to appear natural as the pair of us circled the big table in the kitchen, or the small cart in the barn. He did not speak at such times, but just kept grinning and trying to put his hands on me. Once, when he cornered me in the barn, I had to stamp on his foot hard to get away, and pretend it was an accident, apologizing as I scuttled out.

It ended when I came down at half past five one morning to light the fire in the big range, and found Mrs. Gammidge there before me. The range was lit, and on the long scrubbed table was a package with an outer wrapping of butter muslin. Mrs. Gammidge turned from the sink, where she was washing up a plate and one or two knives, and said quietly, "Goo an' pack yer things, girl, I'm wanting 'ee gone 'fore Muster Gammidge come down."

I made no pretense of being puzzled, and said, "I'm sorry, Mrs. Gammidge, honest I am. I 'aven't done anything to . . . you know, make 'im think—"

"I know. Tes no blame to you, girl." She gave a weary shrug. "He was allus like that. I thowt he'd a growed out of it by now, maybe, but he've been after you like an ol' rooster ever since you been wi' us. It's a lad we need, and it's a lad

89

we'd 've had, if it weren't for Vicar sayin' we should tek an orphanage girl."

I went up to my tiny room and packed my belongings in the small canvas sack I had brought with me from the orphanage. The task did not take long. I had one set of spare undergarments consisting of shift, drawers, and stockings; a shawl, and a threadbare blue velvet dress which had surely belonged to a lady at one time, for it was of good quality; a comb, a long apron, two handkerchiefs, a piece of toweling, *The Holy Bible* and *Tales of Jessica*.

I had already washed in the bowl in my room, had done my hair, and was wearing my working clothes, a skirt and a flannel blouse which had once been a man's shirt. My silver medallion hung round my neck next to my skin, as always. I never left it off, and never displayed it, for fear that somebody might try to steal it from me. Now I put on my well-scrubbed but rather frayed straw hat with a ribbon round it, a special treasure Miss Callender had provided, and went down to the kitchen.

Mrs. Gammidge sat in a wooden rocking chair, gazing at the fire in the range. As I entered she spoke without looking round. "That on the table, tes for 'ee, girl. A packet o' bacon san'wiches an' a sixpence. Best I can do."

"Thanks ever so, Mrs. Gammidge. I'm sorry about . . . everything."

She shrugged, still gazing into the fire, but said nothing, and after a moment or two I went to the door and let myself out, the canvas sack on my back, its neck tied by a piece of rope with a loop for me to hold.

I walked the three miles to Tenbrook Green station, and waited there for Bert Taylor, who worked on the big dairy farm, to arrive with his churns of milk. Bert was a friendly man with eight children, and I had talked with him three or four times when he had called at Crabtree Cottage for eggs. I only knew him slightly, but there was nobody else I knew a all.

When he arrived with his heavy cart, drawn by the two great shire horses, I told him what had happened and asked if he could suggest where I might seek work. He showed no surprise that Mrs. Gammidge had got rid of me, but rubbed his chin doubtfully when I spoke about finding a position.

"Well now, that's askin' summat, Jane. Best thing is for you to get down to Bournemouth, I reckon. Lots of gentry in big 'ouses there, and lots of big 'otels, too. Might find a job as chambermaid wi' a bit o' luck."

"Where's Bournemouth, Mr. Taylor?"

"That way, me dear." He pointed along one of the three roads leading from the green near the station. "You go along wi' the river to Romsey, then keep west of Southampton an' take the road down through the New Forest, but it's thirty mile or more. You best go by train if you got the money."

"I got a sixpence, but I'm not spending that on a train. Anyway, it's a nice 'ot summer, Mr. Taylor, so it won't 'urt if I 'ave to sleep under an 'edge tonight."

"Well, take care now, an' good luck."

I walked seven miles that morning, not hurrying and keeping to the greensward between the road and the river as much as possible, so that there would be less wear on my boots. As usual, the toes had been cut open, but Douch the handyman had repaired the heels and soles just before I left the orphanage, so they were now quite good boots. For all that, I did not know how long they would have to last me, and so I was very careful.

At noon I ate one of the three thick bacon sandwiches Mrs. Gammidge had made for me, and two hours later, after crossing two roads which led from the west into Southampton according to the signposts, I was making good progress on a track which led through a quiet and beautiful forest. I kept an eye on the sun to make sure I was moving south all the time, and soon began to see some of the wild ponies who lived in the forest.

I sat under a tree for an hour or more until a pair of them came grazing close enough for me to talk to them, and then began to say one or two things, very idly at first, giving the ponies plenty of time to make up their minds that I would do them no harm. After a while they came close and I was able to rub their noses and chatter to them, but when I spoke about being allowed to sit on their backs they became nervous and uneasy, not truly understanding. I did not persist, but gave them greeting from my old friends Pulki and Job before going on my way.

That night I slept well enough under an old yew whose branches spread low to the ground and formed a shelter to keep the dew from soaking me. I had begun to feel very lonely now, not because I was alone at this moment but because once again I had nobody to care for, or to care for me.

I would have been glad to be back at the Adelaide Crocker Home, looking after the little girls again.

Next morning I woke very early with the birds, and very hungry. I walked to the brook I had noted the evening before, washed as well as I could, combed my hair, which I still wore as short as I had worn it in Smon T'ang, and then thankfully but very slowly ate my second bacon sandwich. I was keeping the last one, and my precious sixpence, in reserve, for I had no idea how long might pass before I could earn myself a meal.

Throughout the morning I went on at a good pace, and judged that by noon I had walked ten or twelve miles. I felt sure that I had not far to go now before reaching the coast, for I could smell a difference in the air, and was sure it came from the sea. I was not only very hungry again, but also tired and in a bad temper with myself, though I did not quite know why.

I rested for an hour as the sun moved overhead, then set off once more. I hoped to find, when I reached Bournemouth, at least some casual work there for a day or two while I sought a permanent position. If I failed, I would sleep out again tonight, spend a penny of my sixpence on food, and eat my last bacon sandwich. Then tomorrow I would try to find the Salvation Army people, for I had learned from the girls at the orphanage that they would never turn anybody away.

I had the feeling that if I now moved a little more westerly I would find the main road, and might save myself time and extra distance at the end of the journey. I hoped to reach the town before three o'clock, for then I would have six hours of daylight in which to look for work.

I was so absorbed in my thoughts that I was startled when a voice quite close to me called, "Stop!" The word was spoken not very loudly and rather shakily. I was passing through a narrow glade, and when I stopped and looked to my left I saw that a man stood in a patch of grass to one side of the glade. He wore a tall black hat, check trousers, a frock coat, and gold-rimmed spectacles. In his hand he held something which looked like a large note pad. He was standing in a strangely awkward way, one foot advanced and with his weight on it, as if he had stopped suddenly in mid-stride. It looked a very tiring way to stand.

As I stared, the man lifted a hand to raise his tall hat, and I saw that his hair was gray and rather thin. I also saw, with a touch of shock, that his face was a bad color. The last time

I had seen anyone look like this was the day when I had helped Sembur down the pass at the end of our last caravan.

The man said rather breathlessly, "Pray forgive me, young lady, for calling to you in such peremptory manner, but I should be greatly obliged if you could assist me."

He spoke in the nice posh voice I had heard the gentry using on the ship that brought me to England. At first I thought he was mocking me with his politeness, for I must have looked a poor creature in my working clothes, toeless boots, ancient straw hat, and with my sack over my shoulder. But there was sweat on his face, and with his color so bad I knew he was in no case to be making fun of anybody.

I began to move toward him, lowering my sack, and said, "You been taken bad, sir? You ought to lie down and 'ave a little rest."

"Oh, stop, please stop!" he croaked anxiously, waving his hat. "Don't come any nearer, miss—ah . . . ?" I stopped short, completely bewildered, and he gave a sigh of relief. "The—er—the fact is," he went on feebly, "I am standing on a snake, of the genus *Pelias berus, Vipera communis,* or common viper."

My stomach felt cold. I put down my sack and said, "You mean it's poisonous?"

"Indeed, yes. If . . . if you approach with caution, you will observe that the creature is trapped under the instep of my . . . let me see, yes, my right boot. At first, and most fortunately, it was trapped very close to the head. But we have been in this position some time now, and I believe he, or possibly she, has been slowly gaining more freedom . . ."

I put down my sack, went quickly forward, and dropped to my hands and knees. The snake was about thirty inches long, with a thick body and a flat arrow-shaped head. It coiled and thrashed under the man's foot, tongue darting. The head and perhaps three inches of the body protruded from beneath the instep on the inner side of the boot, and the reptile was constantly writhing, trying to thrust forward. If the man ceased to press down hard, it was clear the snake would quickly gain enough of its own length to strike into the leg. Even now it was gaining slowly.

I would have been happier to face a wolf than a snake, for I knew that nothing could pass between this creature and myself. My small gift for coaxing the best out of animals did not extend to the serpent, with its tiny cold brain. With a forked stick I could have pinned the viper's head while the man

93

moved away, but even if I had possessed a sharp knife it would have taken me several minutes to find and cut a forked stick strong enough for the task.

The hestitant voice said, "I . . . I think you had best move away, young lady . . . my head is swimming and I . . . I fear I may fall . . ."

I glared up at him, and my face must have been as pallid as his own, for I had decided what I must do, and it terrified me. "Don't you dare fall down!" I said furiously. "Don't you *dare!*"

I got up, moved round to his right, and crouched down by his backward-reaching leg, where the main body of the snake emerged from under the instep of his boot. Nerving myself to do it, I gripped the dry scaly body with both hands near the tail and slowly drew it straight. On the other side of the boot I could see the head weaving madly, the tongue flickering.

The man said, "No, really . . . you mustn't, my dear child . . ."

"For Gawd's sake shut up!" I snapped quaveringly, the sweat running into my eyes. Then I added "sir" to make amends for my rudeness. "Listen," I said, "we got to be quick. When I say '*Go,*' you lift this foot an' take a big step forward, see?"

"But . . . but the creature will turn on you and—"

"Don't *argue!* You're worse than the kids, you are! I'll count three. Are you ready? One, two, three . . . *go!*"

The man lunged clumsily forward, and I was vaguely aware of him sprawling headlong in the thick grass, his hat dropping from his hand and rolling away. But I had little attention to spare for him. I was watching his right boot, and the instant it began to lift I straightened from my crouch like a spring, swinging to my right and hurling the viper away from me with all my might. At the instant of release it had already curved in a half hoop as it sought to reach my hands, but then it was gone, soaring through the air to fall amid bushes twenty paces away.

I dropped to my knees, shaking in every muscle, wiping my palms again and again on my skirt. When I looked up I saw that the man was crawling toward me, his leaden face full of anxiety. "Child . . . are you unhurt?"

"It's all right, 'e didn't get me."

The man gave a great sigh, then rested on all fours, his head hanging low. I got up, picked up his hat and the large note pad, which I vaguely noticed had a drawing of a butterfly on the open page, then moved toward him and said, "I'm sorry I 'ollered at you, sir. It's just I was scared. We'd better get out of this long grass, 'adn't we? There might be more of 'em."

"They . . . are not hostile"—he lifted his head and gave me a painful smile—"except when one is so foolish as to step upon the creature." Slowly he got to his feet, then stood gazing at me as if I were a curiosity he had never come across before. I judged him to be about sixty, a tall and quite heavily built man with a wide mouth and a very small nose, which was turned up in a way which gave him an almost comical appearance. His eyes were brown, kind, and friendly.

After a moment or two he seemed to come to himself and said, "Oh, pray forgive me. I am Graham Lambert of Merlin's Keep, Larkfield."

I dropped him a curtsy, as we had been taught in the orphanage. I had decided to go back to my proper first name now, and to go on using the surname which had apparently been Sembur's real name. I said, "I'm Jani Burr." I could not help a slight giggle. "Of nowhere special."

Mr. Lambert gave a little bow. "Your servant, Miss Burr. I am . . . profoundly grateful, and full of admiration." He swayed and I caught his arm to steady him. "I'm sorry, my dear. I have a heart which is . . . inclined to sulk if called upon to do more than it deems necessary."

"Are you far from 'ome, sir?"

"About . . . two miles. Just this side of Larkfield. I have a gig close by." He pointed vaguely. I put my arm round him and made him lean on me as we moved slowly in the direction he had indicated. The road was much nearer than I had thought, only a long stone's throw away. There, on a grassy patch where the forest lay back a little, a beautifully groomed horse of about fifteen hands stood grazing in the shafts of a two-wheeled carriage. A nearby signpost pointed to Larkfield.

Mr. Lambert had fallen silent now and his eyes kept wandering. I knew he could not drive himself home. With much pushing and heaving I managed to get him into the gig, and put my canvas sack in beside him. I hesitated, then said, "Would it 'elp if you 'ad something to eat, sir? I got a sandwich you can 'ave." I raked in the sack, took out the package, unwrapped the butter muslin, and showed him the last of Mrs. Gammidge's bacon sandwiches, which was becoming stale now.

He whispered, "Thank you . . . no, thank you, my dear.

95

Most kind . . ." Greatly relieved, I put it away. In the same croaky whisper he said, "Can you . . . drive the gig?"

"I don't think I'll 'ave any trouble once I've 'ad a word with your mare, Mr. Lambert. What's 'er name?"

"Oh . . . ah . . . Sally."

I moved up to stand where she could see me, and scratched her ear, talking to her first in English but then in the tongue of Smon T'ang, which was better for animals because it was more polite and dignified. She was a little aloof at first, but then warmed to me and became friendly. I asked her to take us home, rubbed cheeks with her, then climbed up beside Mr. Lambert and took the reins. I had never driven a cart before, but once I had stopped foolishly nudging at nothing with my knees to control Sally, and concentrated on letting her feel me through the reins alone, it was very easy.

Our route led away from the forest and along a lane that twisted and turned between thick hedgerows of hawthorn. After ten minutes we climbed a long hill, then began to drop down again. Mr. Lambert was leaning heavily against me now. I saw a village below, a pleasantly rambling pattern of little houses with slate or thatched roofs, and a church with a square tower. We had only just started down the hill when I saw a gravelly lane forking to the right.

Sally swung into the lane and went trotting briskly along between shrubbery and tall silvery trees. These gave way to a low stone wall with green fields beyond. Ahead, on our left, I saw two huge gate pillars. Sally turned in between them. We were moving along a gravel drive which curved to the right, away from a line of very big old trees which I was later to learn were elms.

Then I saw Merlin's Keep, and in the same moment a blue-gray bird with a white-banded tail flashed across the drive in front of us. A merlin, though I did not know it then. The house was of gray stone and mellow brick, its front made up of a center span and two short wings which slanted forward from it. Strangely, it seemed the center span was curved, as if it formed part of a circle. This much I saw at a glance, for I could spare little attention to the house.

Sally wanted to take a spur leading off the drive, which perhaps led to stables at the back, but I coaxed her on toward the portico and drew her to a halt on stone flags at the foot of some broad curved steps. We must have been seen from a window as we approached, for even as we stopped the big front door opened and a woman came flying down the steps. The skirt of the wine-colored satin dress she wore swirled and rustled. Her hair, piled high on her head, was rich auburn, almost red. She was in her late twenties, or perhaps a little older, with a strong handsome face and gray-green eyes which were wide and full of anxiety as she strode toward the gig. Behind her came a thin, older woman wearing a dark dress.

A little beyond where we had stopped, a gardener was working on a flower bed, a strapping young man who now paused and stared at us. The lady in the red dress turned her head briefly toward him and said in a penetrating voice, "Haddon! Here, quickly!" She looked up at me. "What happened?"

I had not descended, for I was still supporting Mr. Lambert. "I found 'im in the forest, miss," I said. "Trod on a viper, 'e did, and couldn't move. He never got bitten, but I think 'is 'eart's gone a bit wonky."

"Father? Father, do you feel very bad?" She had taken his hand and was holding it, her voice warm and gentle as if she were speaking to a child.

Mr. Lambert sighed and opened his eyes. "Ah . . . there you are, Eleanor dear. Such a stupid thing . . . I stepped upon a snake. And then this child . . . so brave, my dear. She saved my life, I'm sure . . ."

The lady looked hard at me for a moment, then said, "Wait here, please." She turned to the young gardener. "Give me a hand to help Mr. Lambert down, Haddon. Steady now. All right, Father, we've got you." She turned to the thin lady. "Burkey, run on ahead and call Mayes, then have young William take the gig and fetch Dr. Vine at once."

A minute later I was alone. I got down from the gig, lifted out my canvas sack, and looked about me. All was quiet again. I made a little fuss of Sally, thanking her for being a good girl, then went and sat on the steps. Suddenly I felt very tired and close to tears.

A young man came running from somewhere at the side of the house. He looked surprised to see me, said with a cheerful grin and a broad country accent, "Well, there's a noice 'at!" then climbed quickly into the gig and went clattering away at a great pace.

I looked first to one side, then the other, studying the house. As I had thought, the front was indeed curved. I got up and walked toward the end of one wing, intrigued despite my tiredness. I had seen bigger houses on my train journey from London to Tenbrook Green, but I had never been as close as this to a gentleman's house. There seemed something a little odd about the wing. The wall at the end turned back more sharply than I felt it should have done. I walked back to the steps, looking up, and again had the impression that the center span was part of a circle.

Soon I was to learn that Merlin's Keep had been built sixty years before by a rich man with a passion for falconry, his favorite bird for this sport being the merlin. He must have been a crank, for the house had been designed as a squat tower three stories high, like a castle keep, with two long triangular wings, so that if anybody could have seen the building from above it would have looked something like a bird in flight. When the man died, a new owner had converted the triangular wings into rectangles, to make the appearance quite pleasing, though there remained some odd effects within, such as curving walls, and rooms which narrowed somewhat from one end to the other. There were still merlins in the pinewood which bordered the grounds on the western side. I saw another, soaring high over the tower, as I walked back to sit on the steps again.

Five minutes passed. I looked at the sun. Now that I had lost so much time, and had turned back two miles to Larkfield, the sooner I started walking again, the better. With any luck I would have an hour or two at least to get my bearings in Bournemouth before the light failed. I picked up my sack and set off, but had gone no more than a hundred paces round the curving drive when I heard a cry behind me. Looking back, I saw the lady in the red dress, waving an arm as she marched vigorously across the lawn between the flower beds. I stopped and put down my sack. As she came near she said rather fiercely, "What on earth are you doing, girl? Didn't you hear me ask you to wait?"

"Yes, miss. But I got to get into Bournemouth soon as I can."

"Where are you going in Bournemouth?"

"I dunno yet, miss."

"I see." She gave me a searching look. "When did you last eat?"

"This morning, miss. I 'ad a bacon sandwhich."

"Ah. And did you offer my father one? He keeps saying something about a sandwich."

"Yes, I thought it might 'elp, but 'e didn't want it."

"And you are Jane Burr? Janey Burr?"

"Jani, with an 'i,' miss."

Her gray-green eyes studied me. I felt she was very strong inside, and very spirited, the way Flint had been. She said, "Jani, I want you to come into the house. My housekeeper will give you something to eat. Then I want you to tell me exactly what happened in the forest, and to tell me something about yourself. Afterward, if you wish, I'll have you driven into Bournemouth, so you'll lose no time and be much fresher when you get there. What do you say?"

"Thank you very much, miss."

I walked beside her across the lawn, up the steps into the house, through a paneled hall twice as big as my whole home in Namkhara, then down some stairs and into a huge kitchen. Here, the thin lady she called Burkey was giving orders to a maid, while another maid sat at a long scrubbed table cleaning silver cutlery.

"Now," said the lady in red briskly. "This is Mrs. Burke, our cook-housekeeper, this is Annie and this is Meg. They will look after you, and I'll see you in my study in an hour." A bell rang, one of a row of bells fixed high on the wall, each with the name of a room below it. Mrs. Burke glanced up and said, "Front door, Miss Eleanor. That'll be Doctor, I expect." The lady hurried out, and I heard the clatter of her feet as she almost ran up the stairs.

During the next hour I discovered quite a lot about Merlin's Keep and the Lambert family, for Mrs. Burke chatted slowly but almost unceasingly, and whenever she paused for more than a second or two either Annie or Meg would seize the chance to put in a few words. While they talked I washed my hands and face at the kitchen sink, tidied my clothes and hair as well as I could, then sat down to a plate Mrs. Burke set in front of me with cold meats, tomatoes, lettuce, and small new potatoes served cold, with some kind of white sauce on them.

I learned that Miss Eleanor Lambert was Mr. Graham Lambert's daughter, and these two were the whole family, since Miss Eleanor's mother had died giving birth to her, and Mr. Lambert had never remarried. Mr. Lambert was a retired solicitor, and also a naturalist. "Writing a book on butterflies, so 'e is," Meg put in impressively. "A book wi' pictures painted by 'is own self."

Miss Eleanor was no less clever, for she knew all about wildflowers. "Very high up in wildflowers she is," said Mrs. Burke, who had put on an apron and was mixing something

99

in a big basin. "What they call an authority on them, see? And not just here in England, mind. She goes off abroad, does Miss Eleanor, abroad to foreign countries."

"Lookin' for special flowers," chimed in Meg, polishing a spoon.

"Painting 'em, like 'er father does wi' butterflies," added Annie, shaking flour into a bowl.

"Ooooh, they're clever, mark my words," said Mrs. Burke. "I've known Miss Eleanor since she was a baby, and I always said she'd be a clever one, like her father. But she's handy with it too, mind. Now the master, bless him, he's so wrapped up with this and that, he sometimes doesn't know what day it is. But Miss Eleanor, she's got her wits about her all right."

Meg sighed. "Tes a pity she's an old maid."

Mrs. Burke gave a sniff of contempt. "Old maid? Don't you go talking nonsense, my girl."

"But it was Miss Eleanor's birthday last May, an' she were twenty-eight, Mrs. Burke. I mean, twenty-*eight!*"

"Miss Eleanor could have married anyone she liked," Mrs. Burke declared firmly. "*If* she'd wanted. But just because she didn't want, that doesn't make her an old maid. She's a single lady, that's what she is."

They talked more between themselves than directly to me, and it soon became clear that this was a happy household. The servants were proud of their master and mistress, regarding them as much superior to other gentry in the parish, even to the squire. "Squire he may be, Annie, but where's his manners, I say? Coming into church straight from the hunt, with mud all over him, and breathing out brandy fumes. And does he know the name of a single butterfly, eh?"

Some time after I had finished eating, a man called Mayes came downstairs. He was about fifty, a quiet man with a soft voice, and I learned that he was Mr. Lambert's manservant. There was no butler. These four were the only indoor servants, though two women came daily to do cleaning. I was to discover that this was considered a very small living-in staff for such a house.

Mayes said that the doctor had been, had left some pills for Mr. Lambert, and had prescribed complete rest for a week. Mr. Lambert himself looked much better and was making little jokes about his adventure. And Miss Eleanor was ready to see me now.

I felt very nervous, for as I sat there in the servants' hall I had begun to hope, though scarcely daring to, that Miss

100

Eleanor might offer me a position in service, as a kitchen maid, perhaps. This would be wonderful beyond all words. I had seen that Mr. Lambert was a kind and gentle person. Miss Eleanor might not always be kind and gentle, I thought, she was too fiery for that, but I felt she was just, and without malice. I had already taken to Mrs. Burke and the maids, for here I was, a stranger in their kitchen, speaking in a strange way, very different from their soft country accents, and looking like a tramp in my working clothes, with my toes poking through the cutaway caps of my boots. Yet the girls had not giggled at me, and Mrs. Burke had not looked down her nose.

Miss Eleanor's study was in one of the angles of this strangely designed house, and was shaped like a triangle with one corner cut off. The walls were paneled in dark wood up to one third of their height, with a nice light wallpaper above, a cheerful yellow with a simple silvery pattern. Miss Eleanor sat behind a large desk on which folders and papers were laid out. There was an easel in one corner by the big window, a very large glass-fronted bookcase, and a long narrow table with paints, cartridge paper, and half-finished sketches and paintings lying about.

As Mrs. Burke ushered me in she said, "A nice snack she's had, Miss Eleanor. And asked if she could wash herself an' tidy up before she sat down to it." She gave a nod of approval.

"Thank you, Burkey. Off you go." When the door had closed, Miss Eleanor gave me a brief, rather thoughtful smile, and pointed to a chair near the desk. "Sit down, Jani. What have you got in that little sack?"

"Just my belongings, miss."

"May I see?"

I felt ashamed as I set them out on the desk. My spare undergarments and dress were clean but very rumpled, and the butter muslin wrapped round my last sandwich was becoming greasy. Miss Eleanor pointed. "Is this the famous bacon sandwich?"

"Yes, miss. Well, I dunno about famous."

"And what are these?"

"*The 'Oly Bible* and *Tales of Jessica*. They're my books, miss. I covered 'em in brown paper."

She looked taken aback. "Where do you come from, Jani?"

"Well, first of all from Smon T'ang, miss."

"Where?"

"Smon T'ang. It's a country in the 'Imalayas, north of Nepal and south of Tibet."

Her eyes narrowed. "Are you joking?"

"No, miss. Honest."

"You speak the language?"

"Yes, miss."

"What is it called?"

"I don't think it's got a name in English, but it's almost the same as Tibetan, with bits of some Indian langauges mixed in."

"Say something in it, please."

"Which kind, miss? There's a posh kind for talking to 'igh-up people, like lamas or nobility, and there's an ordinary kind."

Her lips twitched. "Let me hear the posh kind."

When I had spoken a dozen or so words she asked, "What have you just said?"

"Well, it sounds sort of funny in English, miss. I said, *'Gracious lady, I thank you with 'umble gratitude for the 'os-pitality shown me by your 'ouse. May your kindness gain you much merit to aid your release from the wheel of rebirth.'* "

She gasped and sat back in her chair. "Good heavens above! I apologize for doubting you, Jani. How did you come to England?"

"It's ever such a long story, miss. The man 'oo looked after me an' brought me up was called Sembur. He died, an' then I was taken down into India, and they sent me to an orphanage in England because I'm 'alf English."

"You have a gift for précis, Jani. What happened to you between going to the orphanage and walking through the New Forest to Bournemouth?"

"I was at the Adelaide Crocker Home for nearly three years, miss. Then something 'appened and I 'ad to leave. Miss Callender got me a job on a small 'olding at Tenbrook Green, but I was only there a couple of weeks."

"Why?"

"The man kept trying to get 'is 'ands on me. It was ever so difficult. Then the woman said I'd better go, an' I was glad to."

Miss Eleanor glared down at her linked hands on the desk, her lips tight. "Why did you have to leave the orphanage? You said something happened, I believe."

My heart sank. I had been trying very hard to make a good impression, sitting properly and struggling to avoid everything the horrid Miss Foot had long ago admonished me for doing. But now I had been asked the question I dreaded, and my answer would surely destroy all hope of gaining a position here at Merlin's Keep.

"Well, miss, there was this girl called Big Alice," I said rather tiredly. "One day I was telling some of the little girls I looked after a story. It was about someone 'oo saved me from dying in a cave on the Chak Pass, someone ever so special to me. An' this girl Big Alice, she sniggered and said something 'orrible about 'im."

Miss Eleanor looked at me curiously, head tilted a little. "Go on, Jani."

"So I clouted 'er on the nose with my fist, as 'ard as I could, miss." I wanted to look down at my hands in my lap, but remembered Sembur's teaching and kept my eyes fixed steadily on Miss Eleanor's face. She rested her chin on cupped hands and said, "What happened then?"

"She didn't 'alf bleed, miss." I could hear the shameless satisfaction in my voice, but no longer cared. It was all over now anyway.

Miss Eleanor pressed her hands over her mouth and made a funny snorting sound, then got up quickly and moved to stand gazing out of the window. I began to put my belongings back in my sack, hoping she would still keep her promise to have me driven into Bournemouth. At last she said very quietly, as if to herself, "And that was three years later . . . how does one earn a loyalty so fierce and enduring? It must lie within the child herself, of course . . . but what joy to win such staunch devotion. It is something no riches can buy."

She turned and looked at me hard with what I had so far thought of as her stern expression, but was now dimly beginning to realize was the way she looked when moved by excitement or emotion. "Jani. Would you like to stay here at Merlin's Keep?"

Suddenly my eyes felt wet and there was a funny pain at the back of my nose. I said fervently, "I'd like that more than anything in the world, miss."

"I'm not taking you into service." Miss Eleanor began to pace up and down the room, hands clasped behind her back. It seemed a mannish sort of habit, but she moved very gracefully, and in womanly fashion. "Oh, you'll start off below-stairs, of course. You'll be more at home there to begin with, and I don't want to go too fast . . . make Burkey and the

103

girls jealous." She spun round and raised a finger at me warningly. "But you have a brain, Jani, and character. I'll not see you wasted. And it will please my father, too. *'Keep that girl, Eleanor, keep that girl,'* he said. And he was right."

She moved back to her desk, sat down, and slapped her hands emphatically on the top. "I'm going to make something of you, Jani. I'll give you lessons in everything you've missed, I'll teach you to talk properly, I'll make a young lady of you in time. Oh, what a splendid notion! I work for half a dozen charities, but it's so impersonal, there's no giving of the self. Can you write, Jani?" I nodded dazedly. "Good! That will save time. You shall become my secretary in the long run, heavens knows I need one. And my father will help. I suspect he's often lonely——"

"Miss . . . please, Miss Eleanor." I felt confused and frightened. "I'll never do all those things you said."

"Oh yes, you will, Jani."

"But . . . even then, you'll only make trouble for yourself, miss, I mean, if you teach me 'ow to be a young lady an' mix with the gentry. They don't like someone that's 'alf Indian, I found that out on the ship. They'll think badly of you."

Miss Eleanor's gray-green eyes opened very wide, and though she spoke quietly I could hear a whiplash in her voice. "I have never allowed myself to be troubled by what others may think, Jani. It's true that in this country, as in most, there is a totally unscientific attitude of superiority towards those of mixed blood. *I* think you have the character to overcome this, and you can be quite sure that you will have total support from both my father and myself."

I felt a strange peace come upon me, as if suddenly all my burdens had been shifted to other shoulders, to shoulders far stronger than mine. I could have fallen asleep as I sat in the chair, and from the past a long-forgotten memory came drifting into my mind. I was standing in the sunlit chamber of the High Lama, Rild. His eyes were closed and his voice quiet as he said, ". . . *Your way is dark to me . . . but I see the woman in red who will be your friend . . .*"

I had never doubted that Rild could catch glimpses of the future. Now I sat looking sleepily at the woman in red, Miss Eleanor Lambert, who would be my friend. There had been something more Rild had said . . . what was it? I had been paying scant attention at the time. Something about . . .

Miss Eleanor was saying, "Meg and Annie share a room, but I think we'll put you in a small room of your own, Jani, then it won't be too difficult to make changes later. Mind you, we shall have to see how we get along together, so you'll be on trial for a while, but I'm sure I've judged you rightly."

"I'll try very 'ard, miss." I meant it. I would give my whole being to the task that lay before me. Rild's voice faded from my mind. Three long and wonderful years were to pass before I remembered those words of his I could not now recapture.

It was then that the Silver Man would come into my life, and his coming was to be like a great shadow cast over the sun.

CHAPTER SEVEN

On a fine day in July, three months after my eighteenth birthday, I saddled Nimrod and rode out from Merlin's Keep,
down through the village and then up Goose Hill to give
Nimrod a gallop along the grassy ridge.

When we had exercised I dismounted and let him wander
to find the juiciest grazing while I sat gazing down at the village below, and at Merlin's Keep on the hill beyond. I was
remembering, taking stock, my mind roving over all that had
happened since my coming to Larkfield on this very day
three years before.

There were few in Larkfield I did not know by name
now. I had exchanged constant greetings as I rode through
on Nimrod. The farm laborers would touch their hats or give
a tug at a forelock. "Ar'ternoon, miss." Shopkeepers and
tradesmen would call me Miss Jani, because that was how
Eleanor had first introduced me to them. The gentry of the
district, usually in their carriages, would greet me as Jani, or
as Miss Burr if they came from a neighboring village and
only knew me slightly.

Anybody not born and bred in Larkfield would always be
considered a foreigner, but the villagers were warm, friendly
people and had long since accepted me as a permanent visitor
among them. I had been the subject of much discussion, of
course, particularly during my first year at Merlin's Keep.
My move from Belowstairs to Abovestairs had been a nine-
day wonder, but on the whole the village folk seemed to feel
rather pleased with me on this point, as if in some way I reflected credit on them. Also, I was under the wing of Miss
Eleanor Lambert, and this had put me in good standing from
the beginning.

The village was very proud of Eleanor. She sometimes bullied them unmercifully, but always in their own interests, and she did not in the least mind quarreling with the doctor, the vet, the vicar, or the squire himself on their behalf. Her unladylike behavior sometimes startled them, but they did not hold this against her. Miss Eleanor was a character, and Larkfield was glad to have her. "She's a rare 'un, that Miss Eleanor," they told one another.

During my first six months at Merlin's Keep I had done housework and kitchen work with Meg and Annie every morning from six o'clock till noon. After we had served a light luncheon, and taken our own in the servants' hall, there followed three hours of lessons for me, with either Miss Eleanor, Mr. Lambert, or a retired schoolteacher brought in from Bournemouth. At least one hour out of that time was devoted to elocution lessons, so that I might learn to speak properly.

In the evenings I would take turns with Meg and Annie, two of us serving dinner, the other helping Mrs. Burke in the kitchen. After dinner I was free to spend whatever time I wished in studying for myself in the library, a room with shelves bearing almost two thousand books. I had never dreamt that so many existed.

Amazingly, Annie and Meg were not in the least jealous of my privileges, in fact they pitied me and were always warning me of the danger of getting brain fever. Both were courting, and they each had one simple ambition, to get married and live in one of the little cottages belonging to Mr. Sangford, who farmed his own land and was the best-liked employer in the district. Progress toward this had been achieved before my coming to Larkfield, and the ambition was fulfilled when both girls married within a few weeks of each other, six months after my arrival. This was the time, with new servants to be engaged, that Miss Eleanor chose to move me from Belowstairs to Abovestairs.

Mrs. Burke sniffed a little, and made dark remarks about the Good Lord having appointed us to our station in life, but within a week she was calling me Miss Jani and behaving as if she had never in her life seen me scrub out a pot. Mr. Lambert's manservant, Mayes, had no interest in anything except looking after his master. If I had suddenly disappeared I doubt if he would have noticed, and the fact that I did disappear from Belowstairs, and reappeared Abovestairs as Miss Jani, made no impression on him at all.

For the first few days it was a great ordeal for me to sit at table with Mr. Lambert and Miss Eleanor, to retire to the drawing room afterward, and there to chat about village news, general events from the newspapers, or whatever work Mr. Lambert and Miss Eleanor happened to be doing. It was an even greater ordeal for me to start calling her simply Eleanor. At first I tried to avoid using her name at all, but this seemed rude, and in the end I forced myself to do as she had asked. Within a few days the awkwardness vanished. "Good girl, Jani," she said at breakfast one morning when I used her name quite naturally without even thinking about it. "That's another big step you've made."

My lessons continued, but for longer hours now that I had no other work to do. Even so, the hours were not long enough for me. There was so much to be learned, and I was so greedy for knowledge, that I soaked everything up like a sponge. The library was my constant joy. I would sit with a book, sometimes a book of travel, sometimes a novel, sometimes a history book, and work slowly through it, page by page, a dictionary at my elbow so that I could look up unknown words and write them down to fix them in my memory.

Despite my studies, we spent a great deal of time out of the house, much to my pleasure. Eleanor liked riding. She had no knack for cooperating with a horse, but simply dominated it, being filled with such powerful certainty it would obey her that the creature almost always did. She wore breeches for riding, and had a pair made for me. On our first outing she said, "Mrs. Wheeler will disapprove. She's long since given me up as hopeless, but she'll have a few words to say about me putting you in breeches, too. Don't let it worry you, Jani."

Mrs. Wheeler was the vicar's wife, a plump lady with a loud voice and a sense of mission, but always very amiable to me. Sure enough, we met her next day as we returned by the country road from Goose Hill. She was in a gig with her rather pale and dumpy elder daughter beside her.

"Eleanor, really! What can you be thinking of, bringing little Jani out dressed like that? It simply isn't proper, dear. I know you flout the conventions, but you really shouldn't embarrass a young girl like Jani."

Eleanor smiled. "She's not embarrassed, Mrs. Wheeler."

"But she *must* be, dear, sitting . . . . well, sitting *astride* in that fashion. Besides, it's the wrong way for her to begin."

"Begin? Mrs. Wheeler, this girl could ride before she could walk. I had my first view of her in the saddle yesterday, and in my opinion she could ride anyone in Hampshire into the ground, man or woman. Also, she never wore anything but trousers until she was nearly thirteen, so she's no stranger to them."

Mrs. Wheeler sighed and gathered the reins. "You're impossible, Eleanor, quite impossible. But God bless you anyway. Be sure to come to the fete next Saturday."

The golden months passed. We rode, played tennis, joined in the village activities, read, worked, played chess and card games; walked or bicycled for hours with sketchbooks and paints, looking for wildflowers; were sometimes silent, sometimes talkative. I loved to help Eleanor in whatever she was doing, whether it was cataloguing her flower paintings, checking the names in Latin, visiting a sick or bereaved villager, helping with her charities, or simply being with her when she set out to do battle with a farmer, landowner, or anybody who had offended her sense of justice.

Soon it became hard to remember she was not my elder sister, for that is exactly how she behaved with me, and I adored her. If Eleanor treated me as a younger sister, Mr. Lambert treated me as a younger daughter. When we met at breakfast each morning he would kiss me on the cheek, as he did Eleanor, and wish me a happy day. At bedtime he would do the same, and say, "God bless and keep you, child."

Although he was often absentminded, and had a long-winded way of saying things, almost in legal fashion, which sometimes irritated Eleanor, he was a cheerful man with a good sense of humor. When we were at table he always made pleasant conversation, recalling times past, and telling amusing stories of his days as a young solicitor in London.

Many a time during the summer I would take the gig and drive him out into the country, searching for some creature or plant he wished to study and sketch. I never saw him pluck a wildflower or try to catch any wild creature. He had a belief about the wrongness of killing anything except for food, even an insect, and this was very like the beliefs of the Lo-bas in Smon T'ang, except that they avoided it partly because they might be killing a reincarnation of a relative.

Whenever we returned to the gig after walking in the New Forest he made the same little joke about the pretty girl in the straw hat, with no toes to her boots, who had offered him her last bacon sandwich. This kind of thing, telling the same story or making the same joke, sometimes annoyed Eleanor, but I never minded with Mr. Lambert. During our expeditions we talked of many things, and I grew ever more fond of him as time went by.

It was the custom of the gentry, the ladies in particular, to pay morning calls on each other, though in fact these calls were always made in the afternoon. They were very formal, with a set procedure to be followed. At Merlin's Keep we neither paid morning calls nor received them officially, for Eleanor thought they were a great waste of time. Visitors were not unwelcome, but they could come as they pleased. If we were truly not at home, Mayes, who answered the door, would say so. If we were at home but the visit was inconvenient, he would politely say as much to the visitor, instead of telling them we were "not at home" as etiquette demanded. It was very rare that a visit was inconvenient, for both Eleanor and her father enjoyed company, and would cheerfully put aside whatever work they were doing.

There was one activity of Mr. Lamber's which at first surprised me. Regularly every Thursday evening he spent four or five hours at the Manor playing a card game called whist with Squire Tarleton, Major Elliot, and a retired engineer called Matley, who was very rich and lived in Cranwood. They played for money, and Mr. Lambert always won. This was because whist was a very mathematical game and he had a remarkable brain for it, being able to remember every card that fell, and able to work out what cards the other players held.

Among some of the gentry there was much whispered disapproval of this playing for money, though not among the men of the village, who had their own local betting games. Two or three times a year the vicar would preach a sermon on the evils of gambling. On these occasions the squire would glare sulkily and put nothing in the plate. Major Elliot always slept through every sermon, so he did not mind. Mr. Matley attended church in his own village of Cranwood. And Mr. Lambert would sit nodding grave approval but with a great twinkle in his eye, and then congratulate the vicar afterwards on a splendid sermon.

At breakfast one morning after the weekly card-playing evening, Eleanor said, "I really can't think why you do it, father. You're not a gambling person at all. I know the squire

110

is, he's always making wagers about something or other, and I imagine Mr. Matley is, too, though I scarcely know him. No doubt Major Elliot plays to please squire, whether he enjoys it himself or not. But for you it's quite out of character, Father."

Mr. Lambert put down his coffee cup, leaned back in his chair, and said amiably, "Eleanor dear, every man needs to display some small spark of rebellion, to indulge in some small vice, and this is mine. I love the mental battle, and playing for money adds salt to the game, which, if you will forgive my immodesty, I play very much better than my fellows." He chuckled. "This is why I am able to run our stables mainly at their expense, and I have no intention of giving up a practice from which I derive both pleasure and profit."

"I didn't say you should give it up, Father, I simply said I couldn't think why you did it."

Mr. Lambert beamed at us both. "Well, now I have explained, my dear. I also do it because I dread perfection, and wish to have one small blot upon my otherwise unblemished virtue. Furthermore and moreover, it is an act of charity towards the Reverend Hubert Wheeler, who would otherwise be sermonless for three Sundays every year."

I gave a splutter of laughter, and Eleanor said, "Jani, you encourage him." But she was smiling herself now.

In the summer Eleanor gave a small garden party at least once a month. During the colder weather she held what Mr. Lambert, with some amusement, called Eleanor's soirées, but which she called musical evenings, when guests would come from Larkfield and from neighboring villages to gather with us in the big circular ballroom at Merlin's Keep.

Eleanor was a very good pianist, and Mr. Lambert played the cello beautifully, but they were not the only ones to entertain the guests. Dorothy Wheeler, the vicar's dumpy daughter, had a soprano voice that was a joy to hear, and there were several others in the district, both men and women, of good voice or sufficient musical skill to help in providing most enjoyable entertainment.

Once again, these occasions were very informal. First there would be a little music. Then our new maids, helped by girls hired from the village for the occasion, would bring in simple refreshments. After some more music or singing, people would mingle and chat together for a while before settling down to listen to the next piece of entertainment.

During my second year, Eleanor had a young man come to

give me violin lessons, but although I tried hard I had no gift at all for music, and after a few months Eleanor told him to come no more. That evening, at dinner, she said, "Jani, I cannot for the life of me understand how a bright girl like you, who *likes* music, can be so thoroughly obtuse when it comes to reading a simple score."

"Eleanor dear, I'm so sorry. The notes just won't seem to come off the paper for me."

"Now that was remarkably well put," said Mr. Lambert, looking up from his roast lamb. "A most apt description of a mental process, or perhaps one should say a mental *non-*process. What a pity. You know, I do so wish we had a harpist in the district. Do you feel you might do better with a harp, Jani?"

"Heaven forbid!" Eleanor exclaimed. "After listening to what she does with four strings can you imagine letting her loose on forty?"

We all laughed. We laughed often, and very easily, in those good years at Merlin's Keep, especially once I had put behind me the early difficulties and awkwardness of being brought Abovestairs to become one of the family.

If I had to decide on a moment when the change was made within me, when I first felt certain that Eleanor and Mr. Lambert would succeed in the strange task they had set themselves, it was the moment a few weeks after my sixteenth birthday when I was officially presented to the gentry of the parish at the first of Eleanor's garden parties that summer. The new "Indian" girl the Lamberts had taken up had been much discussed, of course, but this was the day when I was to take my place in the community officially, if they accepted me. And I knew very well that not everyone was well disposed towards me.

On the day of the garden party I was so frightened I kept fearing I would faint, something I had never done in my life. I wore a dress of very pale apple-green ninon over a silk foundation, with a bertha collar from which a chemisette of creamy lace rose about my throat. Eleanor was surprised that I knew what the different pieces of the dress were called, but of course I had worked on many good dresses collected by the Rectory people for the Adelaide Crocker Home.

On Eleanor's advice I had kept my hair shorter than most girls wore it. She had cut it for me herself. "Plenty of time for you to let it grow and put it up, Jani." Standing behind me as I sat before the big looking glass, she lifted the hair from my neck. "Yes, you'll look very elegant with that lovely neck, but this suits you well." I had a short thick fringe across my brow, and on either side the black hair fell straight and square to the level of my jaw, framing my face.

Eleanor studied me in the looking glass. "If you didn't look like a frightened doe, you'd be very beautiful. Nobody's going to eat you, Jani."

I tried to swallow but my mouth was dry. "Oh, Eleanor, you should have *told* them you were going to present me officially today, then people who didn't want to come could have stayed away."

"Which is exactly why I didn't tell them," Eleanor murmured, still studying my reflection. "Yes . . . I'm glad we've done your hair this way. It emphasizes the Indian part of you which isn't very noticeable, but that's what's going to worry the squire and his cronies, so let's hit them in the eye with it and make no pretense."

"Oh, Eleanor . . . I'm so afraid of letting you down."

"That's impossible, dear. You have all the qualities of a young lady. You're dressed well, you carry yourself well, your manners are excellent, and you have an admirable speaking voice, thanks to your very quick ear. You don't in the least sound like a Cockney putting on an accent, you sound as if you'd been speaking this way all your life."

It was not until all the guests had arrived, and were strolling and chatting on the lawn, or sitting in deck chairs, that Eleanor came into the house to fetch me. Standing beside me at a window from which we could watch unseen, Mrs. Burke had been pointing out some of the guests, though I knew most of them by sight from attending church. There was Squire Tarleton, Major Elliot and his wife, the Wheeler family, Judge Boscombe, now retired from the bench, and a score of others, with the maids moving among them serving tea and dainty sandwiches.

Eleanor linked her arm in mine and began to take me round the lawn, introducing me. My face felt frozen, and my legs were trembling, but I tried to smile and look each person in the eye as I touched hands in the rather feeble way that was correct.

"How do you do, Mrs. Markham? Good afternoon, Mr. Sangford." Here was the vicar's daughter. "How nice of you to come, Dorothy, I hope we shall be friends." I tried to keep my voice from becoming mechanical as face after face passed before me. I was vaguely aware that Mr. Lambert, seemingly strolling in one of his absentminded fits, was never more than a few paces away and a little ahead of us as we moved. His hands were clasped under his coattails, his head bent, but every now and again I saw him dart a surprisingly keen glance at us.

There came a moment when I felt Eleanor tense slightly, then she turned so that we moved directly to where Major Elliot and the squire stood chatting, with one or two other ladies and gentlemen grouped about them.

"Squire Tarleton, Major Elliot, I should like you to meet a young friend who is very dear to my father and to me, Miss Jani Burr."

The squire screwed up his heavy red face doubtfully as I dropped a small curtsy to him and said, "How do you do, sir?"

"H'mm! Hallo, young lady." He looked down into his teacup as if seeking inspiration there.

Major Elliot was a tall, thin, dried-up man, very erect and brisk. I knew from Eleanor that he had spent several years in India with the British Army. He looked at her and said, "The child is part Indian?"

Eleanor was beckoning to a maid with a tray of tea, and spoke absently as if the matter were completely unimportant. "Oh, half Indian, half English, I believe, Major."

His lips tightened. "I'm bound to say that in our society a person of mixed blood—"

"Quite right, too, Major." It was Mr. Lambert who had interrupted. He strolled through our little group, still talking. "They are indeed to be envied, but we cannot all expect to be so privileged."

"I beg your pardon?" the Major began blankly, but Mr. Lambert went on speaking without pause. He had stopped and turned, almost a dozen paces away, and his usually quiet voice had become remarkably penetrating, so that people all around fell silent in surprise.

"How chastening it is to think, Major," Mr. Lambert went on, beaming amiably, "that she carries the blood of a people who had achieved a high state of civilization when your ancestors and mine, and the squire's, God bless him, were still wearing half a goatskin and a few daubs of woad. And as I am sure you were about to say, Major, where would we in England be today, nay, in the whole Western world, I hear you add, if it were not for Brahmagupta?"

The Major said, "Eh?" But nobody heard him, for Eleanor
114

now came in with a voice she could have used for hailing a ship. "Did you mention Brahmagupta, Major? Surely he was the great Hindu mathematician and astronomer who made such a huge contribution to civilization while our poor ignorant ancestors in England were wallowing in the Dark Ages? Did he not devise the symbol for zero, which gave us our system of numerals, when we would otherwise have found ourselves trying to multiply and divide with the absurd Roman numerals?"

Major Elliot gasped at her and said, "I'm—ah—not quite sure I—er . . ."

"Precisely, Major," cried Mr. Lambert from twenty paces away now. "As you were about to point out to Eleanor, it was not in fact the great Brahmagupta, but a quite unknown Indian scientist who gave us that particular benefit. Oh, I can well understand your high admiration for the Indian race. No doubt it stems from your personal experience. You have had the pleasure of seeing the Taj Mahal, have you not? What amazing architects and masons, to produce such a marvel of beauty. Let me see . . . about 1640? We would be busy burning witches here at that time, would we not? But of course the Taj Mahal is modern for India, who evolved an agricultural system some two thousand years before we managed it ourselves. As you say, if we are to speak of architecture, what of the Classical Age?"

"I take it you refer to the period of the Gupta Empire, Major Elliot?" It was Eleanor again now, standing tall beside me, her rich hair glinting red in the sun. She proceeded to enumerate several instances of India's historic attainments in art, philosophy, and literature, then handed over, rather out of breath, to her father, who added some further loud reflections of his own.

I kept my face straight and solemn, but inwardly I was giggling, and all my fears were draining away. I realized now that Eleanor and her father had planned this shattering onslaught, ready to be launched at the first hint that I might not be acceptable.

". . . and of course," Mr. Lambert was saying now, gazing up at a wood pigeon floating lazily across the garden, "it is not only for her inheritance of intelligence that we should envy Jani, as I am sure you would be the first to observe, my dear Tarleton . . ."

"Me?" The squire grunted in surprise.

". . . for you are the first to admire a physical skill, squire,

115

providing it is seemly in a young lady, and as the most honest of men you would never fail to recognize superiority wherever you might find it." The absent air suddenly vanished, and for a moment it seemed that Eleanor was looking out of her father's eyes as he said with an aggressive stare, "You have seen her ride, my dear fellow. You were watching her last week, Eleanor tells me. As a sporting man will you make a wager with me? Will you back *any man you care to name* in a race against the child, let us say from the Plough at Langley to Goose Hill? Loser to pay a hundred pounds—perhaps to the Church Restoration Fund, if the vicar will accept?"

The sudden challenge came like a thunderbolt, and I heard gasps and whispers all around me. It was a challenge never to be taken up, and indeed I think Mr. Lambert did not expect it to be, but it served its purpose, and his final words left the vicar floundering, gulping back whatever protest he may have been about to make. It was only later I realized just how cleverly Eleanor and her father had done their work that afternoon. They had known that the two men who would lead opinion on the matter of Jani Burr were the squire and Major Elliot, and they had defeated each on his own ground.

At the time, as Mr. Lambert's challenging words hung on the air, I wondered what on earth the outcome would be. It seemed the squire might well be furious at the notion that a young girl was better on horseback than anyone he could name, but Mr. Lambert had judged his man well. The squire's florid face turned from me to Eleanor, to her father, and back again to me. First there was astonishment, then the beginnings of a scowl, but quite suddenly he flung back his head and gave a great laugh.

"D'ye take me for a fool, Lambert? She'd need a half-hundred-weight handicap for a man to have a chance! Confound it, you've a look more innocent and benign than the vicar himself, but you're crafty as Old Nick." He turned to Eleanor. "And you're as bad, my lass. You're forever brewing up some sort o' mischief." He nodded at me and said regretfully, "I suppose you'll not allow her to ride to hounds, hey?"

Eleanor had a smile she used seldom, a warm, radiant smile that made her handsome face beautiful. She gave it to Squire Tarleton now, and said gently, "Indeed I don't wish Jani to ride to hounds. Let us not have our old hunting argument again, squire."

"Pity. She'd be a picture to watch, up there with the leaders. But as you say, we'll not quarrel today, m'dear."

Major Elliot stood gazing blank-faced, rubbing his chin with the ivory knob of his cane. I had the feeling that he was trying to catch up with events which had moved much too fast for him. "Yes," he said at last with a judicial manner, looking at Mr. Lambert. "There is a great deal in what you say."

Squire Tarleton crooked his arm at me and said with an air of cheerful acceptance, "All right, young Jani, let's take a walk to the stables and look at the horses, hey? And you can tell me where you learnt to ride."

It would be untrue to say that from this moment on I was completely accepted in Larkfield as a member of the Lambert family, but this was the critical point. Most people followed the squire's lead, and the village folk were content to accept me because of the affection they had for Eleanor and Mr. Lambert. The people who took longest to forget that I was half Indian *and* had moved from Belowstairs to Abovestairs were the gentry of lower rank in the community, but very soon they were swayed, as were many others, by an extraordinary rumor which swept the village and rippled far beyond.

It was whispered that Jani Burr was really an Indian princess, her parents being a Raja who ruled one of the princely states of India and a beautiful Englishwoman, daughter of a nobleman. It appeared that Jani had been kidnapped as a child by agents of a wicked relative of the Raja who wished to seize power from him. Her mother had died of grief, the Raja had given up everything and gone away to become a holy man, and the villainous relative now ruled the princely state. But Jani had been discovered in Tibet by an agent of the British Government and brought to England, her true identity concealed until she came of age, when the Army in India would throw out the usurper and she would come into her inheritance as the Rani, ruler of a state half as big as England.

This was the basic rumor, though there were many astonishing variations of detail, depending upon who was telling it. But regardless of variations and additions, the effect on those who still doubted whether it was proper to mix with a half-Indian girl was very positive. I found I could expect to be accepted anywhere in the country, in the homes of the very highest, as an Anglo-Indian, provided I was a princess as well.

On the day Eleanor first found the village buzzing with this new rumor she came straight back to Merlin's Keep, where Mr. Lambert and I were playing croquet on the lawn, went up to her father and hugged him, her green eyes sparkling with mischief and joy.

"Father, you clever old thing!"

He blinked. "Of course, my dear. But in what respect are you complimenting me at this moment?"

"You've started a rumor about Jani, and it's sweeping the village like wildfire."

"Rumor? Come now, Eleanor, I am a respectable retired solicitor. How can you suggest that I might spread a rumor?"

"You didn't spread it, Father, you started it. I know your style too well to be taken in. But oh, it's a lovely rumor! Our Jani, an Indian princess, incognito!"

I said blankly, "A what?"

Eleanor took my arm, still bubbling with merriment and delight. "I'll tell you in a moment, dear. Father, how did you manage it? Ah, wait now. Your old clerk, Penfold, he'd do it beautifully. Foxy Penfold. You always did make a fine pair, you two. Then he'd just have to breathe a word to Mrs. Gravett, that widow who's always trying to marry him. She has the longest and quickest tongue in Hampshire."

Mr. Lambert sighed, laid down his mallet, gazed up at the sky, and began to polish his spectacles. "Really, Eleanor, you do run on," he said gently. "I suggest we all sit down quietly in the shade while you tell us about this extraordinary rumor."

He would never confess to having started it, but as I came to know him ever more closely with the passing of time, I was quite sure Eleanor had made no mistake. Mr. Lambert knew the power of snobbery in the world we lived in, and he had made good use of it. In time the rumor faded, or became taken for granted, it was hard to know which. But the effect of it remained, to give me good standing in Larkfield at all levels, and smooth what might have been a difficult path for me.

Eleanor was gradually accumulating material for a book on European wildflowers and took me abroad with her twice during my first two years Abovestairs, once to Austria and once to Italy. My childhood had made me a hardy traveler, and I greatly enjoyed our long walks in search of rare flowers. I had also worked hard to make myself a capable secre-

118

tary, and was able to take notes at Eleanor's dictation while she made color sketches.

By the beginning of my third year at Merlin's Keep I sometimes felt that Larkfield was rather proud to have me, in the same way that it was proud to have Eleanor, because we were different. I had long since told my whole story to Eleanor and Mr. Lambert, including the mysteries it contained, and had shown the precious medallion I always wore. They were fascinated to hear of my life in Namkhara, of the monasteries, the lamas, the beliefs and religious practices, and of my journeys with the caravans into Tibet.

Because I owed them everything, I had hidden nothing from them. They knew that an Army officer, known to me only as Mister, had come north from India to arrest Sembur for a terrible crime of murder and theft. They knew I had heard Sembur admit his guilt and claim to be my father, but that I was sure he had lied deliberately for some unknown purpose, perhaps for my sake, because he felt some danger threatened me.

Now that I was grown up, and no longer saw through the eyes of a twelve-year-old child, I was much better able to realize just how much Sembur had done for me. A poorly educated man, he had come to the strange land of Smon T'ang with a girl-child of two, ignorant of the language and customs. He had settled there, contrived to house and feed us, and brought me up according to his simple beliefs and soldierly habits.

He must surely have been desperately homesick for his own kind, for men to talk with, for a woman to care for him, for everything he had given up. Yet through all the years he had never faltered, and I had never heard him complain. Sometimes, when I had special cause to remember him, on his birthday perhaps, or when snow fell to remind me of the mountains, I would go to my comfortable bedroom, think of Sembur, and weep quietly, wishing so much that I could put my arms round his neck, my cheek against his, and thank him from a full heart.

We did not speculate much on the mysteries my past held, for as Mr. Lambert said, "One cannot make valid deductions from insufficient data." But one small puzzle we did solve was the question of Sembur's name. Since I had been registered at the hospital in Gorakhpur as Jane Burr, presumably by Mister, we took it that Burr was the correct surname. And

I had heard Mister speak of him more than once as Ahressembur . . . as I had thought.

"I fancy," said Mr. Lambert, "that this is the phonetic sound of R.S.M. Burr, or to put it in full, Regimental Sergeant Major Burr, for your friend—ah—Mister would surely address him by rank in the first instance. Now this is interesting, because Sembur is evidently a baby-talk corruption of R.S.M. Burr, would you not agree?"

I said eagerly, "Yes, I'm sure you're right Mr. Lambert. And I'm sure Sembur *was* a Regimental Sergeant Major because Mister called him 'Sar-major.' I'd forgotten that." A thought was trying to take shape in my mind, something significant, but I could not quite grasp it. Next moment Mr. Lambert was speaking it for me.

"It would be very odd for a child to address her father by a corruption of his military rank and surname. How does a child come to know a name? By hearing it spoken, of course. 'Come to Mama.' 'Here is your papa.' 'Give your sister Elsie a kiss.' So I think we can make the strong assumption that during your babyhood R.S.M. Burr was present in some capacity, from time to time, and some person or persons *referred* to him as R.S.M. Burr. A name which you, Jani, lisped as 'Sembur.' I believe we can therefore be certain that he did not speak the truth in claiming to be your father, which gives excellent reason to believe that his confession to murder and theft was also false, though we can never hope to guess why."

We were having tea on the lawn when this conversation took place, and I was so full of delight at the logical way in which Mr. Lambert had argued for Sembur's innocence that I got up from my seat to put my arms round him and kiss him on the cheek. Often during those golden years at Merlin's Keep I would make some such impulsive gesture with Mr. Lambert or with Eleanor, for I was always bursting with happiness and a sense of wonderful good fortune. Also, I had never even begun to show Sembur the gratitude I owed him, and now it was years too late. I did not intend to make the same mistake again.

From where I sat on Goose Hill I could see the long shadow of the church moving slowly across the gray headstones of the churchyard, and I thought of the great shadow which had been cast over Eleanor's life and mine only a week or two before my third Christmas at Merlin's Keep.

It was then, without warning, that Mr. Lambert died peacefully one night in his sleep. To say I was heartbroken tells little of the grief I felt, for with his passing I lost not only a man who had treated me as a daughter but also one who had been a wonderful companion and friend. In my sorrow I did not forget that he was Eleanor's true father, and I fought hard to keep my feelings under tight control, for Eleanor needed comfort, and it was to me that she turned while showing a stoic face to the rest of the world.

I had never thought to see my strong, brisk, fearless Eleanor so dazed and shaken. This was foolish of me, for I had known her long enough to recognize that though she did not display her affection freely, her feelings ran strong and deep. I was thankful to lift from her shoulders all the sad tasks which had to be dealt with on such occasions, and I think in the end it was this which enabled me to pass through my time of grieving more quickly than Eleanor.

When the will was read, I was alarmed to discover that Mr. Lambert had left me a legacy of two thousand pounds. I felt guilty and almost panic-stricken at the idea of such a fortune, and at once begged Eleanor to take it.

"Don't be silly, dear," she said gently. "Father spoke to me about it before making the codicil to his will a year ago, and I fully agreed." Her voice began to shake. "He was a man who lived a happy life, Jani. And you gave him almost another three years to live it."

In March, three months after the funeral, Eleanor decided to go away on one of her trips abroad, to seek and paint wildflowers in Greece. I was torn between the wish to go with her and a feeling that it would be best for her to go on her own and look after herself, as she had always done before my coming to Merlin's Keep. When we talked about it, I found she had the same feeling.

"I've been leaning on you, Jani," she said as we walked a frosty footpath to the village for exercise after breakfast, our hands muffed, our fur-edged hoods keeping the keen wind from our ears. "I've been leaning on you for too long, and it simply won't do."

"I don't mind your leaning on me, Eleanor dear. It's just that . . ." I hesitated.

"It's not like me?"

"Well. Yes."

"Exactly. So I shall go away, and work very hard for a few

weeks, then come back home and be my old self again. Are you sure you can manage while I'm gone?"

"Don't worry, I shall enjoy having lots to do. There'll be Mrs. Burke and Mayes in the house if I need domestic advice, and for anything else I'll go to David Hayward." David Hayward had come to Larkfield eighteen months ago, taking over old Mr. Kingley's veterinary practice, and had quickly become a welcome visitor at Merlin's Keep.

"Yes. Yes, do that, Jani," said Eleanor. "David is very reliable."

I sighed. "I do wish you hadn't refused him when he wanted to marry you last year."

I saw her flush, and she said, "Oh, stop nagging me, Jani. David Hayward can't be more than a year older than I am. It's quite unsuitable. I became an old maid five years ago, and I'm perfectly happy about it."

"Well . . ." I took a hand from my muff and slipped it through her arm as we walked. "I hope he asks you again, anyway."

Eleanor laughed. It was the first time I had heard her laugh for many weeks, and the sound made me glad. I hoped that soon she would be herself again, that she would come back to Merlin's Keep strong and happy once more, her sorrow transformed to loving memory. Then perhaps she would marry David Hayward after all . . . and perhaps some handsome and exciting man would fall in love with me and want to marry me, and perhaps we would share Merlin's Keep, and everything would be quite wonderful . . .

Such foolish dreams. By the calendars of Smon T'ang, we had now entered the Year of the Water Hare. Next would come the Year of the Wood Dragon, the year named by the Oracle of Galdong. But I had lived in England for more than five years now, where oracles and prophecy had no place outside the Bible and fairy tales. I had long dismissed from my memory the blank-faced girl who had stood before Rild, the High Lama, staring down into the black pool of ink as she spoke strange and ominous riddles.

weeks, then come back home and be my old self again. Are you sure you can manage while I'm gone?"

Oh, don't worry. I shall enjoy having her to ...

She stopped and listened to the noise of ...

CHAPTER EIGHT

A voice behind me on Goose Hill said, "Miss Burr, I should like to make a proposal."

I came to myself, startled for a moment, then smiled and managed to stop myself looking round, "A proposal? Oh, sir, this is so sudden."

For almost as long as I had known David Hayward he had been teasing me with pretended proposals of marriage. He came into my view now leading his big gray, Smoky, gave it a slap to go and join Nimrod, then dropped down beside me on the dry grass. "Hello, young Jani. Mrs. Burke said I'd find you up here."

"I'm getting less young all the time, Mr. Hayward. You'd better start being careful, in case I say yes when you propose."

He laughed, then looked at me thoughtfully, his head on one side. "Well . . . if I do it again, you'll know I'm serious."

I knelt up and glared at him. "Don't talk like that! You know very well you want to marry Eleanor."

He spread a hand. "She won't have me."

"Well, you must just try again."

He grinned, got to his feet, and reached a hand down to me. "Come on, Jani."

"Come on where?"

"Oh, I forgot to tell you my proposal. What I'm proposing is that you come along with me to Stafford's Farm and talk to one of his cows while I get her womb back in."

"Oh, so that's it. But you'd better not make proposals of that sort to any other young lady, Mr. Hayward."

"No. They'd run screaming. Will you come? She'll cooperate if you tell her to, and it makes all the difference."

"Is it Mabel again?"

"The same one as before. I'm not on first-name terms with her."

"All right."

He took my hand, drew me to my feet, then stood waiting as I called Nimrod and Smoky to come to us. "It's not fair, Jani," he said wryly. "I give Smoky food and shelter, but he wouldn't come to me like that unless he felt inclined to."

"Ah, but I talk to him in the honorific form of Tibetan, and it flatters him."

"Nonsense." He linked his hands to give me a leg-up into the saddle. "But I have to confess it works."

I liked David Hayward. The youngest son of a titled landowner in Lincolnshire, he was of independent means, and had left university to take the long training of a veterinary surgeon simply because his great ambition in life was to heal animals.

A quiet, serene man, he showed politeness to all, deference to none. Within a few weeks of setting up in practice in Larkfield, he had discovered through Eleanor that I had a way with animals. At first, by his own admission, he had been skeptical, but he had lost no time in putting me to a practical test at the earliest opportunity. I had pacified Mr. Sangford's big Airedale when it was mad with the pain of a poisoned foot and would let nobody come near. Afterwards, when the foot had been opened, cleansed, and bandaged while I held the dog's head, David Hayward had looked at Eleanor and smiled. "You were right, Miss Lambert. This girl is amazing."

"You surprise me, Mr. Hayward. Pleasantly, let me add," she said.

"I'm flattered. May I ask how I surprise you?"

"You deal in the science of medicine. Most people who deal in any form of science refuse to believe anything which cannot be explained by science."

"I lean in that skeptical direction myself, Miss Lambert." He looked at me, and gave a sudden warm smile. "But when I see an ability demonstrated which science cannot explain, then I conclude that science has not yet advanced far enough to explain it."

Since that day it was rare for more than three or four weeks to go by without David Hayward asking me to help with one of his patients. He was a slender, wiry man of surprising strength, as I had seen when he was delivering a diffi-

124

cult calf. His hair was thick and brown, his face quiet and rather nondescript except when he smiled, but then the warmth that lit it made him almost handsome.

Sometimes, when I was helping him in his surgery or out on one of the farms, we would work together for an hour or more with scarcely a word exchanged between us. Eleanor had spoken of this once to Mr. Lambert. "It's so funny to watch the pair of them, Father. There's David busy with his knives and syringes, and Jani whispering her jabber-jabber in the horse's ear, and they scarcely seem to notice each other. You'd almost think they had quarreled, and sometimes they do. I mean, they tend to snap at each other when they do speak."

It was true, though I had not thought about it before, but I remembered it now as we cantered down the grassy slope of Goose Hill, falling into an easy trot when we reached the footpath at the bottom which would take us west of the village to Stafford's Farm.

David Hayward said, "Is everything all right at the house, Jani?"

"Yes, thank you. Mrs. Burke and Mayes keep everything running smoothly."

"And you're not lonely?"

"Well, I miss Eleanor, of course, and I still miss Mr. Lambert, but I'm not lonely. I see quite a few people during the day, and in the evening I usually have a light dinner in the garden, then work on household accounts, or Eleanor's book, or just read for a while before I go to bed. I have a typewriting machine to copy out all the indexing for Eleanor's book, and I'm becoming quite good with it."

"Well . . . if you haven't any household problems, what's wrong, Jani?"

I looked at him, a little startled. "Why do you think there's something wrong?"

He shrugged. "I've come to know you quite well, and I think I can tell when you're worried, even when you try to hide it. Besides, you once told me that you like to go up on Goose Hill and sit there alone when you want to think things out. I saw you sitting up there when I started riding down from Stafford's Farm, and I don't think you had moved when I crossed the valley and reached the top ten minutes later."

"Oh . . . I was just looking back over the years, and dreaming." I hesitated. "And perhaps worrying about Eleanor a little."

"Ah." He looked at me quickly. "Why, Jani?"

"I expect I'm just being silly. She was going to be away for six or eight weeks, and for the first month she wrote me two letters each week. But then her letters became . . . I don't know. Strange. They weren't like Eleanor."

"In what way?"

We had slowed to a walk now. I said, "Well, they weren't regular for one thing, and they were rather scrappy. She'd start to write something, then she'd jump to a fresh thought so suddenly you could scarcely follow her. Oh, I know that seems nothing, but I really am worried, Mr. Hayward. Before her letters changed, she wrote saying she had met an Englishman who was staying at the same hotel, and she was always trying to avoid him, but wherever she went he always seemed to appear on the scene, and it was like being haunted by a ghost. She was quite amusing about him, just like the old Eleanor."

I paused for breath, a little embarrassed. Now that I had begun to voice my fears, I was almost gabbling them out to David Hayward. I thought he might smile at them, for I had so far given no solid reasons for my anxiety and in fact had none to give, but he said soberly, "Go on, Jani."

"Not long after that, her letters became even more strange, as if she wasn't herself at all. They were very short and she spoke of this man two or three times in a vague sort of way, but not laughing about him now, more as if they had become friends. Then, when she moved from Trikkala down to Corinth, she made some brief reference to him again, as if he was still with her."

"She's not a child," David Hayward said quietly. "If she's made friends with the man, it's because she wished to."

"But Eleanor wouldn't travel about with a man. I know everyone says she's outrageous and unconventional, and it's true in some ways, but in other ways she's very correct about standards of behavior. Oh, it's so difficult to explain. She mentions receiving my letters, but she never really answers them any more, as if she hasn't taken in what I've said. And . . . she's been gone more than three *months* now."

We turned at the corner of the copse and began the gentle climb to Stafford's Farm. David Hayward said, "Perhaps she's in love. That could account for everything, I suppose."

I felt in the pocket of my breeches for the two rather crumpled pieces of writing paper covered in Eleanor's bold hand, and after a moment of hesitation passed them to him.

126

"That's the last letter I had from Eleanor. It came about a week ago. I took it up to Goose Hill to read again."

I had done so in hope of wringing some previously unnoticed shreds of comfort from the letter, but my hopes had been vain. It read:

Dearest Jani,
Your letter came on Thursday, I think. I hope you are well. I have no notes for you to type on your typewriting machine as yet. Why have I done no work this past week, or is it longer?

So deep, the Corinth Canal. So far below. I was seized by vertigo, and could have cast myself down from the bridge, but he was holding my arm. What shall I do?

It has been very hot, and Mr. Quayle advised me to rest, as I had been doing too much and felt exhausted. It was a very tiring climb to the headland at Cape Sounion, especially in the early hours.

Keep well and strong, and always be yourself, Jani, always be yourself. Greece is so beautiful. I think I have been away for quite a long time now, and hope to return soon. Perhaps that will help.

This evening we had a most pleasant dinner on the rooftop of this small hotel, with a gentle evening breeze to keep us cool, and some Greek musicians playing. It was quite enchanting. I'm sure you would so enjoy it.

I am writing this letter before going to bed. Please pray for me, Jani.

With fondest love,

Eleanor

We had halted a stone's throw from the farm while David Hayward read the letter. I saw his frown deepen as he read it through twice, then he looked up and slowly handed it back to me, dismay in his eyes. "I don't understand, Jani."

"Neither do I. But I just wanted you to see that she isn't behaving oddly because she's in love. It's not that sort of letter, is it?"

"No. Far from it. There's an underlying note of . . . desperation."

"That's how it seemed to me. But what *can* be wrong? And if there is something, why doesn't she say?"

He shook his head, troubled. "Lord knows. It's a mystery."

127

"I've looked up in the encyclopedia about Cape Sounion. It's a headland south of Athens where the Temple of Poseidon was built, and a lot of the temple still stands. But it's not near Trikkala or Corinth, and why on earth would she be going up to an ancient Greek temple in the early hours?"

He nudged his horse into a walk, and I fell in beside him again. "I've no idea, Jani," he said grimly. "None at all. Is this fellow Quayle the Englishman she met earlier?"

"Yes."

"If it was anybody but Eleanor I'd be inclined to think Mr. Quayle was one of these parasites who ingratiate themselves with lonely women. But she'd spot that kind in a flash."

"Yes, and anyway she's not lonely, Mr. Hayward. She just wanted to be alone for a while, that's all." We were nearing the cowshed now, and Mr. Stafford was coming towards us, calling a greeting to me. David Hayward's little trap stood in the courtyard. He had taken Smoky from the shafts to ride up to Merlin's Keep, then on to Goose Hill to fetch me.

Veterinary work was usually a messy affair, and Larkfield had taken some time to get over the shock of knowing that young Jani Burr was often involved in such unseemly matters, and was sometimes present to assist Mr. Hayward when he was actually stripped to the waist and struggling to deliver a difficult foal or calf. The Reverend Hubert Wheeler and several ladies had remonstrated with Mr. Lambert and Eleanor for permitting it. Mr. Lambert had genially advised them that if they objected to my exercise of a God-given talent, then they should complain to the Almighty in their prayers. What Eleanor said, I never knew, but my activities as an animal nurse soon became just one more eccentricity of the many displayed by the folk at Merlin's Keep.

I had great admiration for David Hayward's skill as a vet. In Smon T'ang a cow yak would sometimes push out her calf bed, and it usually took three men a lot of hard work to get it back. David Hayward used a trestle to keep the hindquarters raised when he made the cow kneel, and this prevented her straining against him, but he always insisted that the task was twice as hard without me there to soothe the creature, and that I was more use than two strong men. I was very proud of this, because I knew he would not flatter me.

I stood talking to Mabel while David Hayward made his preparations, then coaxed her to kneel and be still while we helped her. She almost went to sleep, so he and Mr. Stafford had little trouble in pushing the great uterus back into her, and she continued dozing with closed eyes even when I went back to help him stitch her so that she would not push the calf bed out again.

When we had finished, David Hayward took off his long calico apron, washed his arms and shoulders in a bucket of soapy water, then put on his shirt and jacket. I washed my hands with him, and then Mr. Stafford invited us into the cool kitchen for some lemonade before we left.

"Always a favorite wi' Miss Eleanor when she calls," his wife said as she set down two of her best glasses on the big scrubbed table. "Says I make the best lemonade anywhere, she does."

"I'm sure she's right, Mrs. Stafford," I agreed. "It's lovely."

The farmer said, "When's she comin' back from foreign parts then, miss? Been gone longer this time, surely?"

"Yes, but I expect she'll be home again soon."

"Ah." Mr. Stafford nodded his head. "Well, anything you want, Miss Jani, I mean from the farm like, you just say. Don't you go to the shops now. Robbers they are, all of 'em. You tell your Mrs. Burke to come an' see Tom Stafford, and she needn't bring her purse, neither."

David Hayward insisted on escorting me home, and I rode back to Merlin's Keep in his trap, with Nimrod hitched behind. We spoke very little on the way, and not at all about Eleanor until we drew up outside the stables, then he said quietly, "I think you're right to be worried. It's very disturbing. But there's nothing you can do, except wait for Eleanor to come back."

I shook my head slowly. "No. I've been thinking about it all the way back from the farm, and I know what I must do. I've made up my mind now. I'll wait just ten days, till the end of the month. If by then I haven't had a letter from Eleanor to say she's returning, I must go out to her."

"Go out? To Greece?"

"I have my own money, and Mrs. Burke can look after the house. But I must *see* Eleanor, and *talk* with her." My voice began to tremble. "I don't know what's wrong, and I can't even begin to guess, but I know there's something, and I'm sure she needs help, so I must go to her, and whatever's wrong I must put it right, and if somebody is . . . is harming her in some way, then I must stop them."

I had climbed down from the trap as I spoke, and by the time I had finished I found my whole body was shaking with a mixture of fear, anxiety, and a kind of unfocused rage.

"Eleanor's father is dead," I ended more quietly, "and I'm all she has left, so it's up to me now."

He stared down at me in silence with a wondering look, then got down from the trap, paced back and forth for a few moments, and said abruptly, "It's no good, Jani, you're too young to travel on your own."

"Too *young?*" I glared at him. "Oh, don't be stupid, Mr. Hayward! You know enough about me to know better! Too young to travel on my own? I was riding across the roof of the world with a salt caravan when I was *ten,* Mr. Hayward, with Khamba tribesmen and bears and snow leopards to worry about. Do you really think I can't find my way to a hotel in Corinth? There's even a railway station there!"

That was the first time I saw David Hayward's calm broken. Chin jutting, my own anger reflected in his eyes, he wagged a finger in my face. "Don't shout at me like that, please! You're a very rude little girl—"

"I am *not* a little girl!" I said through my teeth. "I'm eighteen, and I'm worried to death about the person who took me from the gutter and gave me a wonderful home, and education, and love. You may think you know what Eleanor has meant to me, but you can't even begin to know. Nobody can, so—"

"All right, Jani, all right." He made a placating gesture, and the anger faded, leaving him troubled but calm again. "Please let us not quarrel."

I turned, put my arms on the side of the trap and rested my brow on them, trying not to cry. When I could speak I said, "I was very rude to you, and sarcastic. I'm sorry, Mr. Hayward, please forgive me."

I felt his hand on my shoulder. "I know you're worried about Eleanor. So am I. Then, when you spoke of going off to Greece, I started worrying about you as well."

I turned to look at him in surprise. "Me?"

"Yes, of course." He regarded me soberly. "You said you were going to wait ten days for another letter, and that strikes me as being very sensible. It allows time for you to make travel arrangements and decide what's best to be done. But will you at least agree to discuss this with me again a week from today?"

"Yes. Yes, I'll do that, Mr. Hayward."

"Thank you." He unhitched Nimrod, climbed into the trap, and sat looking down at me for a moment or two. "Few people remain grateful for long, Jani. You're certainly one of the few."

I scarcely paid attention to his words, for I was busy with a thought of my own, and said, "Mr. Hayward, when Eleanor comes back will you ask her to marry you?"

He laughed, and gathered the reins. "Well, I'll ask one or other of you, Jani. I haven't quite made up my mind which."

He was teasing me again, and I was able to laugh with him, for I felt relieved, almost happy, now that I had come to a decision and made up my mind to act. During the next few days I obtained railway timetables which listed cross-Channel ferries and train connections on the Continent, and spent quite a lot of time between my other duties in studying these together with brochures from shipping companies, trying to work out how best to travel from Bournemouth to Athens.

I found the quickest way was to take the train ferry to Paris and catch the Orient Express from the Gare de l'Est. This would bring me to Istanbul in only sixty hours, and from there I could reach Athens by ship in less than two days. On the afternoon that I made up my mind to take this route, I wrote out my itinerary carefully, with a list of the reservations to be arranged and preparations to be made, then had some tea and went out into the garden.

There I spent an hour or two doing some light pruning of the many fine rose bushes, dead-heading the petunias, staking some border carnations, and stopping the early-flowering chrysanthemums. I had known nothing about gardening before coming to Larkfield, and still knew very little, but I was fascinated by it and had long ago persuaded old Dawson, the head gardener, to teach me one or two simple tasks and allow me to do them.

By the time I had finished I was hot and sticky, and ready for my bath before dinner. I think this was the moment I enjoyed most each day. Merlin's Keep had a boiler in the cellar which gave us taps with hot water, and I had never ceased to revel in the joy of lying in a warm bath, comparing it with the baths of my childhood, standing up in a bowl of water.

When Mr. Lambert died, Eleanor and I had made ourselves continue to dine in the dining room, even though our grief was sharpened by Mr. Lambert's empty chair. Now, for me at least, that sadness had passed. With Eleanor away, I still dined there on my own, and instead of feeling heartache I felt glad and thankful to remember all the laughter and happiness I had known at that table.

I had cold meats and salad for dinner, and afterwards Mrs. Burke came to me in the drawing room to discuss housekeeping matters. We went over the week's accounts, talked about shopping for the week to come, and then, at her firm request, and feeling quite inadequate for the task, I had to send for a new maid we had recently engaged and reprimand her for skimping her work. I tried to feel very grown-up, and to do it in the way I thought Eleanor would have done, but from the way Mrs. Burke sighed and rolled her eyes up when the maid had gone I think I was not very successful.

When I went to bed I read Eleanor's letter again, and as had happened every night since I received it, one line in particular held my eye.

Please pray for me, Jani.

Strange words, for Eleanor. Her father had always declared, in his amiable way, that she was an automatic Christian rather than a thinking one. They were strange words in any event, for they seemed to arise from nothing in the letter, and to have no sequel. I had little doubt it was these words which had made David Hayward speak of an underlying note of desperation.

I sat on the side of my bed, frowning over the letter, and fingering the silver medallion which hung about my neck. Having heard the vicar preach against the evils of superstition, I sometimes had a little sense of guilt about my feeling that it was this talisman, given to me by Mister, which had brought me all the miraculous good fortune I had known. The Hindi poem itself denied any such notion, yet it was one I could never make myself reject. Apart from the medallion, all that remained from my past lay in the bottom of my chest of drawers, the ribbon from the straw hat I had been wearing when I found Mr. Lambert, and my two books, the Bible and *Tales of Jessica.*

Carefully I took out the worn Bible, knelt beside the bed, and began to turn the pages. I knew I was not very good at praying, and in fact I had no very clear idea of my own beliefs. Under Sembur, I had begun reading the Bible when I was six or seven, but with almost no understanding of it. Such ideas as I had even now were vague, and had mainly been shaped by passing my childhood in a world of monasteries, lamas, prayer wheels, karma, and reincarnation.

Please pray for me, Jani.

I knew that Eleanor had been christened and confirmed in

the Church of England. She had asked me to pray for her, and I would do so every day until we were together again. When I had finished, I read through the Twenty-third Psalm aloud, but in a quiet voice, then, feeling very inadequate for the second time that evening, I got to my feet. In doing so I must have leaned on the bed in such a way that the Bible began to slide from the counterpane. I made to put out a hand quickly, but half caught my thumb in a ribbon of my nightdress, and instead of holding the Bible I knocked it sideways so that it slid right off the end of the bed and fell to the floor. Finally, in my haste to pick it up, I stubbed my toe on the leg of the bed.

I sat on the floor with one foot in my lap, nursing my toe and feeling furious with myself for being so clumsy. When the pain eased I got up, limped round the bed, picked up the Bible, and sat on the bed to examine it, fearful lest it was damaged. To my relief I found that the binding had held, and that none of the sections had broken away from the spine. I laid the Bible down again to look at what Mr. Lambert had taught me were the endpapers, the sheets at the back and at the front which were glued down to the inside of the leather-bound covers.

The back endpaper, brown with age, had split down the inner side, but it was a curiously straight slit, more like a cut than a natural tear. I decided it would not be difficult to stick the paper back in place, but felt an urge to do it at once rather than leave the Bible damaged until tomorrow. I put on my dressing gown, lit a candle, put the Bible under my arm, and made my way down through the dark house to the small pleasant room I called my office. This was the room Mr. Lambert and Eleanor had furnished for me when I first became competent enough to take over the household management and secretarial work for them. There I lit the gas, snuffed the candle, settled myself at the desk, took the jar of paste from its pigeonhole, and picked up a paper knife. Sliding the blade under the slit, I lifted the endpaper gently to find out how far I would have to spread the paste beneath it. And then I sat very still, staring at something which lay beneath the endpaper.

It seemed to be a sheet, or several sheets, of very thin paper, folded once and resting between the endpaper and the board of the cover. Through the thin paper I could see a line of small dark marks . . . writing of some kind. It dawned on me that this was something which had been deliberately hid-

133

den in the Bible, either by Sembur of by whoever had owned it before him.

It seemed an exciting discovery, and for a moment I felt a pang of sorrow that Mr. Lambert could not share it with me, for it was just the sort of unusual event he would have enjoyed. Carefully I edged the folded papers out with a pair of tweezers, then made myself attend to sticking the endpaper down securely before I allowed myself to turn to what had been hidden within. There were nine sheets of flimsy rice paper. It was the kind of paper I had sometimes seen in Namkhara, made by the yellow men to the north of Bod. One side of every sheet was crammed with writing, tiny letters laboriously set down with a fine nib, almost like the printing in a book.

My first feeling was one of disappointment, for already I had jumped to the conclusion that this was something Sembur had hidden, and that I would find his large rounded handwriting on the paper. Then, peering, I saw that the first words were: *Dear Jani.*

I turned quickly but carefully to the last page. There the small print-like writing ended halfway down, and was followed by Sembur's signature in the rather ornate hand I knew. My heart jerked as I realized that the papers I held were indeed from Sembur, and were meant for me. He had used tiny writing, and crammed line close to line, to use as few sheets as possible, knowing that what he wrote was to be hidden, and where.

My mouth was dry, and I was trembling a little as I moved to the wall, turned up the gas so that the mantle burned brightly, then went back to the desk and picked up the first page. As I did so the past suddenly burst from the caverns of memory, sweeping over me so that it seemed only yesterday I had ridden into the mountains with Sembur. For a long time now those past years had been scarcely real to me, but the writing before my eyes brought everything back so sharply that for a moment I wondered if all about me was no more than a dream from which I was now awakening.

I shook my head impatiently, drew a deep breath, and began to read.

Dear Jani,

Today you were eight years old and I have decided to spend my evenings these next few weeks writing down your story. Perhaps you will never read this. I don't know. But I will write it down and leave it to Chance.

Your father was Captain Francis Saxon, of the First Battalion, 2nd Queen Victoria's Own Gurkha Rifles. He was seconded to the State of Jahanapur, with the rank of Colonel, to command the Maharaja's armed forces, three companies of infantry and one battery of artillery. It was to do with politics, because some of the Indian Princes are friendly to us and some are not, but I won't go into all that.

I was the only British R.S.M. in any Gurkha regiment, which was something special, and I was nearly due to retire, so when your Father asked if I would sign on for seven years as R.S.M. of the Jahanapur Army I was very pleased as I have no family in England to go back to. Also he was the best man I ever knew.

The ink took on a slightly different shade at this point, as if Sembur had stopped writing for a while and then begun again with a thicker mixture. I was to find there were many such changes during the time it took Sembur to compose and write down his strange and terrible story. I read on:

The Maharaja was a good ruler, and very educated. He had been to Cambridge University, I think it was. His daughter was Sarojini. She had been to school in England and Switzerland. They were both popular with the people. We had some trouble with Ghose, who was the half-brother of His Highness. Ghose wanted the throne of Jahanapur, and tried to start a rebellion, but your Father soon put a stop to that. I wish His Highness had ordered Ghose to be shot, because he was a traitor all right, but he pardoned him.

Well Jani I must try to keep this short. Colonel Saxon and Princess Sarojini fell in love. It was really something to see, made in Heaven as the saying goes, I only wish I had the words to tell you. Old Mohan, I mean her father, the Maharaja, he was very pleased, and so was some high-up man from the Viceroy's Office who came to see the Colonel, but your Father blistered this man's ears because he wasn't marrying your Mother for politics.

I looked up from the cramped writing. Colonel Saxon, my father? Princess Sarojini, my mother? I recalled the story Mr.

135

Lambert had so mischievously put about in Larkfield, to make people think I was an Indian princess. Now it seemed his story was partly true, except that he had reversed the nationalities of my parents.

I had stopped trembling now, but I think even a pencil dropping would have made me jump out of my skin. I was hovering between laughter and tears, and bit my lip hard to steady myself. I could have laughed at the absurdity of Jani Burr being an Indian princess, or I could have cried at the thought of Sembur, sitting up at night in the hovel we called home, slowly penning word after word of his story, so that the truth should be set down, even if it might never come to light.

I put aside the page I had finished, and read on.

Some people in Jahanapur were against the marriage because of religious reasons, but your Mother had become a Christian while she was in Switzerland, and your Father didn't bother much about such things anyway. He said it would please the people if they had a wedding in Indian style as well as Christian, so they did that, and then you were born nearly a year later Jani. You were fifteen months old when the Maharaja, your grandfather, died and your Mother became the Maharani, which meant she was the ruler of Jahanapur.

Chandra Ghose, her uncle and the one who made trouble before, he acted like he was very pleased for her to be Maharani and went round saying how good she was. We didn't trust him, but as long as he behaved like that the Maharani couldn't very well banish him. Anyway, your Father controlled the Army, so there was nothing Ghose could do we thought, but we were wrong.

I've got to come to a terrible bit now Jani. I still have nightmares about it and always will. You and your parents lived in the palace of course, and I lived in a nice bungalow between the palace and the barracks, with a woman called Parvati to do housekeeping for me.

Parvati . . . that was the name Sembur had sometimes spoken in his nightmares, and I recalled that in the cave at the top of the Chak Pass I had heard him tell Mister that Parvati was his wife. Perhaps it was true he had married an Indian woman, or had simply lived with her, but he would

136

not say that when writing for a child who was then no more than eight.

I focused on the laborious writing again.

The Maharani's personal maid came for me one night, bringing you with her. She said her mistress and the Colonel were both dying. The Colonel had said I was to come at once and tell nobody. We left you with Parvati, and the maid-servant took me into the palace by some sort of secret tunnel that ran from a dry moat. Her name was Pawala.

As soon as we reached the big bedroom I saw they were done for, your Mother and your father. It was poison, I don't know what sort or how it was given them. The girl said it was two things, something from the gland of a frog, but from another country, and very finely chopped whiskers from a tiger. She said they act like steel splinters, I don't know, but I never saw such agony. Their muscles kept going into spasms so bad I thought their bones would break. I'm sorry but I have to tell you how they were suffering Jani or you will think badly of me for what comes next.

The Colonel was on the floor, with blood running down his chin. He was biting on his swagger-stick and it was near chewed through. The Maharani was near him, poor girl, and he was holding her wrists because she had gone over the edge and kept trying to tear her own stomach out with her nails. I won't describe any more Jani but I just pray that Ghose burns in Hell for ever for what he did that night.

Sitting at the desk, I cringed and felt the blood draining from my cheeks. Sembur had no gift for words, but his simple telling called up a scene so dreadful I felt I could bear no more. I do not know how long I sat with palms pressed to my eyes, screwing up my courage to go on, I only know that there came a time when I found myself reading again.

Your Father spits out the stick and gasps at the maid-servant to go. Then he says between spasms, We're finished Sar'major. For the love of God give my darling rest.

At first I did not understand, and then I did, and I wanted to run away. Sir, I can't, I says to him, I love

137

her like a daughter. Then help her God damn you he says in a kind of screaming whisper.

When I came from the bungalow I had put on my belt with the bayonet in the frog, so now I took it out and knelt down, and slid it in quick under the second rib, and she went limp and quiet right away.

The Colonel let go her wrists and fell over sideways, both hands holding his stomach now and he said, Thank God, you have never served me better Sar'major. Then came a spasm and I prayed it would finish him but it did not. I said, Sir, I will turn out the whole Army and have that dog Ghose hanging in the Palace Square at sunrise.

Don't be a fool he wheezes. This is India. Winner takes all.

I knew it was true. The Army would not follow me against Ghose, not with your Mother dead. They would know Jahanapur needed a new ruler quickly before one of the border states laid claim to it. Both the Army and the people would accept Ghose rather than be swallowed up. They might be almost certain that he had done away with the Maharani, whatever tale was put out, but that kind of thing was nothing new, not in India. Underneath they would admire his cleverness a bit.

Then I remembered the new ruler was you, Jani, but you were only two, so Ghose would act for you and you would not live long enough to grow up. Your Father had worked that out all right even with all the pain. He said, Viceroy's Office want stability here so they will back Ghose. Matter of policy. You have to get Jani away. I promised Her Highness before she . . . Then he stopped, but he meant before she went out of her mind with pain.

I said, Yes sir. What orders?

Get her away now, he said. Go north. Have Parvati bring you news of what happens here, then use your discretion. You will need money. Take the jewellery Her Highness is wearing. Then he closed his eyes and another spasm started tearing at him. I took the jewels from her body, and after what I had done I think I would have gone and put a bullet through my own brain rather than remember, but there was you to think of Jani.

Then your Father says to help him because he could

138

not hold the bayonet himself, and so I did, same as I had done for your Mother. God forgive me for what I did that night but I still don't know what else I could have done.

My poor Sembur. I sat weeping silently, for my mother, for my father, for Sembur himself, leaning back with my arm pressing the sleeve of my dressing gown across my eyes so that no tears should fall upon the flimsy paper. As soon as I could see again I went on reading, for I knew now that there could be nothing worse to come.

I went north with you as ordered, and a week later Parvati came into the hills where I was hiding. She said Ghose and his boot-licking friends had put out the story that I had gone to rob the Maharani of some jewels because I wanted to run away with Pawala, her maid-servant, but I had been caught in the act and had brutally killed both the Maharani and her husband. They said Pawala had confessed to all this before hanging herself in her prison cell in shame for what she had done.

Parvati said the Army did not believe it but they pretended to because with Her Highness dead they would be relying on her successor for their pay, and Ghose was promising to be generous. She said the British Army and the civil authorities had been informed and a reward had been posted for me. All the palace staff had been dismissed and Ghose had moved in with his own people.

I was not surprised at any of this Jani, because I had time to think and had guessed the sort of thing Ghose would do. What did surprise me was that he did not give out that I had taken you with me. I suppose he thought it would not fit in with the story he had told about me murdering your Mother and Father. So instead he gave out that you were quite safe and being looked after in the nursery by an ayah he had engaged. Parvati said they might soon get hold of a girlchild from somewhere and pretend she was you for a time, then she would die of a fever or something. But she said Ghose would never stop looking for you to destroy you because you were the rightful ruler of Jahanapur.

I brought you here to Mustang so nobody would ever find us and I went down to meet Parvati two years later in Bethari near the border. She kept her promise and

139

was waiting there for me. She said the child had died six months later and that Ghose was ruling Jahanapur and everything had settled down again, but the British were still after me because only a month ago a Civilian had come to question her about that night and she had said she did not know anything otherwise Ghose would have her killed.

We met again after another two years and nothing had changed, but she never kept the next appointment. I waited two weeks in Bethari for her but she did not come or send any message so I think she must have died.

Well now I have put it all down Jani. Sometimes I think I should take you down into India and go to Army H.Q. and say what really happened. But I am afraid. The last thing Parvati said to me was that if ever Ghose discovered you were alive you would surely die. Parvati was Indian and I believe her.

Perhaps I will tell you all this when you are a big girl, then we can decide together, but I just wanted to put this down in case anything happened to me.

I can't think of any more to say so will close now.

With love.

Sembur (R.S.M. George Burr)

My head was throbbing, my throat parched. I turned to the first page and read the whole story through again, very slowly. A dozen questions pricked my mind. I wished desperately that Sembur had described my mother and father, for then I could have pictured them and felt a sense of belonging. As it was, the two who had died so terribly were as strangers to me.

I made myself visualize the whole story, forcing my imagination to fill in the gaps left by Sembur's terse and unvarnished telling, letting the full horror of it sweep through me so I could face and accept that horror now, in this present hour, rather than struggle constantly to ward it from my thoughts in the days to come.

Now I knew why I had sometimes awakened from a fading dream of high cool rooms with white pillars, of a flower garden and a fountain, of hard hands lifting me and a deep voice laughing, of soft arms holding me and a sweet voice

140

singing. The memory began to make my parents more real for me, and I felt tears burning my eyes again.

Poor Sembur. It was little wonder that the boundless horror of that scene had lived on for him in nightmares. Poor brave, troubled, faithful Sembur. Even at the last he had struggled to protect me from the smallest chance of discovery by Ghose. He had told Mister I was his own child, and that Parvati was my mother. He had begged Mister to see that I was sent home to England, where I would be "safe." Now I understood what he had meant, and as I recalled that conversation in the cave as he lay dying I understood, too, why he had appeared to confess to robbery and murder under Mister's questioning.

"Is it true that you killed the Maharani and her husband?"

"Yes, sir. That's quite correct, in a manner of speaking."

"And took the jewels from her body?"

"Yes, sir, I took 'em."

"And ran away?"

"Quite so, sir."

It had not even been necessary for Sembur to lie. He had simply held back some of the truth, to make sure my identity was not suspected. And in doing so he had knowingly died with the stain of brutal murder upon him.

After a long time I sat up, rubbed my eyes, and looked about me, empty as a husk. Even this room I knew so well seemed strange and unfamiliar, for Sembur's story had carried me away into another world, a world of passion, savagery, and greed for power, where life was cheap and where corruption and treachery sprang from the very soil. I was half Indian and had lived in the East for most of my childhood, but even so the world of Sembur's story was completely alien to me. It was strange to think that both he and my father, both English, had understood the nature of India better than I ever would.

Winner takes all. My father's bloody lips had uttered those cold harsh words in his last agony. Yet he had denied Ghose something by contriving to save me. That evil man had put another poor child in my place, then killed her so that he would become Maharaja of Jahanapur. But even now there must surely be times when he would wonder what had become of the vanished baby princess, and whether she was alive today, and where.

CHAPTER NINE

Later I had only a vague recollection of tidying the desk, putting the thin sheets of rice paper between the pages of the Bible, and returning to my bedroom.

For a long time I lay staring into the darkness, trying feebly to find myself in a world which had suddenly turned upside down. The little baby in the palace at Jahanapur, whose father was Colonel Francis Saxon and whose mother was the Maharani, Princess Sarojini . . . that baby had been myself. But this was something which would not become real for me, no matter how hard I tried to make it so.

For me, the baby princess remained another person, quite separate from Jani of Namkhara, or Jane Burr of the Adelaide Crocker Home for Orphan Girls, or Jani Burr of Merlin's Keep, Larkfield, in the county of Hampshire.

I felt astonished and somewhat awed at the thought of my parents' rank and position, but above all my heart ached with sorrow and pity for them in the hideous end they had suffered. Yet my blood did not reach out across the years to them, and I had no deep sense of belonging.

After a while I began to wonder what I should do about my discovery. Presumably I was the true ruler of a princely state in India, a thought which made me want to giggle, for so much emotion combined with weariness had left me lightheaded. If Chandra Ghose still ruled there, sixteen years later, he had nothing to fear from me. I did not want to be a princess and own an Indian state. I wanted to remain as I was, living in England, occasionally traveling abroad, working with Eleanor, perhaps in time falling in love and marrying.

My ideas for the future were vague and very flexible. I had

known three different lives, for I had come from Smon T'ang to Bermondsey and then to Mr. Lambert and Eleanor. They had opened the door for me to the kind of life in which I was as happy as any human could ever hope to be. I wanted no more new lives. It would be easy to do nothing, to put the papers and the Bible away and pretend to myself that I had never made this strange discovery . . . but surely I had a duty to my tragically murdered parents? If Chandra Ghose still lived, surely somebody in authority ought to be told what he had done?

When at last I fell asleep I dreamt I was riding my pony, Job, through a strange pass in a blizzard, following Mister, who was mounted on his great black horse, Flint. We were looking for Sembur, who was lost. I kept calling to Mister that we were going the wrong way, but he seemed not to hear me. At last, when I spurred Job closer, Mister turned in the saddle to face me . . . and it was not Mister, for there was no head at all in the hood that rose from his shoulders. I could see the lining in the back of it.

I screamed, and turned Job, and went galloping back through the pass, calling for Sembur. Then we were out of the blizzard, in sunshine, and beside the track ahead of me I saw a gallows, with soldiers standing round it. Sembur was there, mounted on Bugler, wearing only shirt and trousers, his arms bound to his sides by a great chain wrapped round him many times.

A huge fury possessed me. I rode at the gallows, whispering to Job, turning him so that when he kicked out, his hooves smashed the wooden struts and planking. The soldiers kept shouting, but I called to their horses, making them buck and rear wildly. Then I rode at Sembur, snatched at the end of the chain and jerked it free. The coils fell away, and next moment we were riding knee to knee down a slope of sunburnt grass. I was crying with relief. When I looked at Sembur I saw that he was younger than the Sembur I remembered, perhaps as he had been in my first memories of him. The points of his waxed mustache, stiff as needles, glinted like copper. His head was thrown back and he was laughing joyously, free from every care, in a way I had never in his lifetime known him laugh.

At six o'clock the next morning I came from sleep to wakefulness with a start of dismay, suddenly aware of how thoughtless and selfish I had been in my reflections the night before. Not for one moment had the most important point of all crossed my mind. Pulling on my dressing gown, I ran downstairs to the kitchen, calling to Bridget, who was lighting the big range. I told her to draw a bath for me now, and to prepare no more than some bread, butter, and ham for my breakfast, with a pot of tea, as I would be going out early.

"Yes, miss." Bridget looked a little put out as she got to her feet, which puzzled me. I could very easily have drawn my own bath, and would gladly have made myself a quick breakfast in the kitchen, but Eleanor had cured me of such behavior. "You must never encroach upon a servant's work, Jani. It upsets them. It might sometimes be easier to do something yourself, but in a way it's a threat to their livelihood, and it also disturbs their own belowstairs hierarchy."

I had not made this mistake now, and as Bridget clumped up the stairs behind me I said, "Is something wrong?"

"No, miss."

"Oh, come now, Bridget. I know you."

"Well, you didn't ring, miss. That Polly over at Major Elliot's, she'd just enjoy laughing at me if she knew my young lady came running down to the kitchen instead of ringing."

I sighed, was about to apologize, thought better of it, and simply said, "All right, I won't do it again."

It seemed Eleanor had not quite cured me of upsetting the servants.

David Hayward lived in a cottage set in an acre and a half of very informal garden, bordered on two sides by the little stream which crossed beneath the Cranwood Road just outside Larkfield. It was a large, rambling cottage, and he had brought in builders to make three of the rooms into a surgery and miniature hospital for small animals. Each day the blacksmith's sister, Rosie, a rather silent and brawny spinster of forty, came in at seven to keep house for him. She worked steadily throughout the day, keeping the whole cottage spotless, providing meals at all odd times, and guarding her employer jealously against thoughtless farmers and any others she suspected of "a-puttin' on my young gennelman" or failing to show proper consideration.

David Hayward was an early riser. In this fine weather he took breakfast under a vine-covered trellis at the side of his cottage. Often when I had been out riding early we had waved to each other as he sat at the small table set on flags beneath the vine, in his shirt sleeves, with the morning paper propped against the milk jug.

At half past eight on the morning after my discovery of Sembur's letter I was sitting at David Hayward's table, my throat dry from having talked almost without stopping for the best part of half an hour. In that time I had spoken briefly of my childhood in Smon T'ang, which in a general way he knew about, and then gone on to tell of Sembur, and Mister, of Sembur's death in the Chak Pass, and of my near-death; how I had come to England, to the orphanage, and at last to Merlin's Keep.

He had interrupted me only twice as I told my story, to have something made clear. Now he was reading the last page of Sembur's letter. I sat fidgeting with my crop, waiting. He lifted his head, gave me a long curious look, then called, "Rosie."

She came from the kitchen, eyeing me suspiciously, and David Hayward said, "Some fresh tea please, Rosie. Miss Burr must be very dry." Rosie nodded grudgingly, her bare forearm rippling with muscle as she picked up the teapot. David Hayward turned back to the first page of Sembur's letter and began to read it again.

Five minutes later, as I poured fresh tea, he passed his cup to me and said quietly, "Why did you come to me, Jani?"

"Well, you can see I need somebody to talk to, Mr. Hayward, somebody to help and advise me."

"Of course. I meant, why me in particular?"

I felt a little baffled as I handed him his tea, and repeated the question silently to myself. Then I said, "Well . . . because there's nobody else."

"I'm genuinely flattered, but by no means confident that I'm qualified to advise you." He waved a hand and smiled ruefully. "Your story seems to raise a daunting number of issues. What in particular is worrying you?"

"Oh, only one thing." I sat forward on my chair, and words began to tumble from me. "It's Sembur. You see, to save me he let himself be blamed for a terrible murder, and even confessed to it just before he died, to make sure I'd be safe from this man Chandra Ghose. And it was especially dreadful for Sembur, because he was a soldier, and very proud of it, yet when he died, he was under military arrest on a charge of murder." I rested my hands on the table, fingers clenched round my crop. "So I have to clear his name. I have to make sure the Army knows the truth and that they do the

145

right things, I don't know what things, but like holding an inquiry and saying Sembur was innocent and brave and loyal, and putting it on his record."

I sucked in a long, loud, and unladylike breath, for I had gone through the whole of the final sentence without drawing one. David Hayward leaned back, hands linked behind his head, and continued to stare at me with a kind of profound but absentminded wonder.

"Yes," he said at last.

"Yes *what?*"

"Sorry. I mean, yes, I'm not surprised that of all the issues raised by this letter the most important thing to you is clearing Sembur's name."

"Mr. Hayward—" I began impatiently.

"I think you're quite grown-up enough to call me David." He was still looking at me, his face serious.

"Well ... David, then. How should I go about it?"

"Two points occur to me. First, if you set out to do this, then you can't keep it secret. All Larkfield will buzz with gossip about Princess Jani of Jahanapur, probably the whole county."

"Oh, it won't amount to anything. They've been saying for ages that I'm an Indian princess, ever since Mr. Lambert set the rumor going."

"Very well. Now the second point." He hesitated. "Yesterday you were worried about Eleanor, I think rightly. She's alive, and Sembur is dead. Clearing his name isn't urgent. Shouldn't Eleanor come first?"

I stared. "Of course she must! I'm still going to Greece if I don't hear from her by Thursday, but I do so want to make a start in setting things right for Sembur, and I thought perhaps something could be going on while I'm away. If I go."

"Oh, Jani." He laughed and stood up. "You do like to get to grips with a problem. Come on my rounds while I look at my in-patients." I knew he wanted to think about all I had said, and when I had put Sembur's letter carefully away in the stiff envelope I had found for it, I went with him through the cottage to the room beyond the surgery.

There was little in the way of small-animal work for a vet in the Larkfield area, but at present in the tiny hospital he had a cat which had been badly mauled by a fox, a small black-and-white sheep dog, a child's pet guinea pig, and a parrot belonging to the landlord of the Plough. We spoke a little about the animals as he examined them, and I was able

146

to help with changing the cat's bandages. I had thought I might at first feel awkward about calling him David, but it came quite naturally to me. Twenty minutes later he strolled down the garden with me to where I had left Nimrod, and said quietly, "I think we should go to Major Elliot with your story first."

"The Major?" I was a little surprised.

"Yes, I know he's pompous, Jani, but he's very knowledgeable about the Army and about India. I think he's probably a man who's at his best when he has an object in view, a campaign to carry out. If he decided to take up your cause, the cause of clearing Sembur's name, I think he might well go at it like a lancer in a cavalry charge. And he's a snob, like most of us, so I think your standing as daughter of a Maharani and a Colonel will have a splendid effect on him."

"Well . . . if he believes it."

David touched the envelope I held. "I've never yet read anything with a greater ring of truth," he said. "I'll have Rosie's young nephew take a note to the Major this morning. You'll hear from me later, Jani."

We saw Major Elliot that same afternoon, in a study where the walls were hung with spears, guns, and the stuffed heads of several wild animals. He greeted us rather awkwardly, and was clearly dubious about the propriety of an unrelated young man and young woman calling upon him together.

"I gather from your note, Hayward, that Jani is seeking my advice in a matter of some importance. May I ask your connection with the matter?"

"None, Major." David leaned back comfortably in a deep armchair and crossed his feet on a tiger-skin rug. "It's simply that I'm privileged to be a friend of Jani's, and when I heard what she needed advice about, I said that you were the man best fitted to help her."

"I see." Major Elliot pondered. Perhaps he was wondering whether to pronounce some slight criticism of my behavior. If so, he must have reflected that Eleanor's behavior and mine had always been considered too bold and unladylike anyway. It might be somewhat shocking that I had been left alone in charge of Merlin's Keep, and that occasionally I helped a veterinary surgeon, albeit a gentleman vet, in his sordid and sometimes revolting work, but all this was nothing new and had long been accepted as a matter of eccentricity rather

147

than a cause for scandal, so there was little point in admonishing me.

At last Major Elliot moved to a large ornate desk in a wood that was almost black, sat down, placed some writing paper in front of him, and picked up a pen. "Very well," he said, "you had better tell me all about it, Jani."

Once again I told my story and showed the sheets of rice paper covered with Sembur's cramped printing, but it took very much longer than when I had told David, for Major Elliot kept interrupting with questions, and would then make me pause while he wrote notes.

It was a full hour before the thing was done, and during that time the Major displayed no surprise, interest, or any other emotion, not even when reading Sembur's letter. But when I had spoken my last word, and he had made his last note, he took up Sembur's letter, read it again, then moved from his desk to stand looking at me with his thin face full of wonder, the faded blue eyes sparkling with zest.

"No doubt at all," he said, his creaky voice a little higher than usual. "I recall the case, of course. Thousands miles away at the time, in Bombay, but it made a big stir. Senior British Warrant Officer murdering his own C.O. and royal memsahib. Couldn't understand it. And old Baggy Ryman, he'd known this chap Burr as a sergeant years before, in Lahore. Or was it Bahawalpur? Baggy said he wasn't the type at all. Fishy. All very fishy. But he bolted, d'you see, so what else was there to think? However, at last we've got to the bottom of it, hey? Splendid, splendid!"

He fell silent, still gazing at me, and now there was a hint of embarrassment in this look, a slight flush to his cheeks. Suddenly he moved towards me purposefully. I had perhaps two seconds to wonder what he was about before he reached out, picked up my gloved hand, and was making a small bow over it, saying, "I am truly honored that you should have come to me for advice, Your Highness."

"Oh no, please, Major!" I rose to my feet, not without difficulty since he was looming over me, then moved aside and drew my hand away. My cheeks were hot, and I felt a complete fool as I shot a frantic glance at David, who had risen as soon as I stood up. "Please call me Jani," I said, floundering. "I don't want to be . . . I mean, it was all so long ago, Major . . . and really—oh, don't sit there grinning like that, David!"

"Eh? No, indeed." Major Elliot gave David a very frosty

glare. "Now, look here, young Hayward, you don't seem to understand that as Maharani of Jahanapur, this young lady is ruler of some two million souls in a state half as big as England! And under the suzerainty of the British Crown she is entitled to a fifteen-gun salute, and to be addressed as Your Highness. That is no cause for amusement. Are you a confounded Radical or something, hey?"

"I was laughing at myself, Major," David said soothingly. "It's not every vet who can claim to have had a princess help him deliver a calf."

The Major snorted. "Well, all that nonsense will have to stop, of course." He looked at me. "If you wish to remain incognito, as it were, and not to assume your proper style and title, I shall of course respect your wishes—ah—Jani. Perhaps that would be best for the moment in any event, until the Foreign Office has looked into all this and confirmed your right to Jahanapur. H'mm! There's a pretty pickle, too. Wonder if what's-his-name, this swine Chandra Ghose, is still on the throne, hey? We're into politics now, d'you see, so honesty goes out of the door. If they want to unseat Ghose, you'll suit them very well. If not, we might have a bit of a tussle on our hands."

I said, "Major Elliot, all I really want is to clear the name of R.S.M. Burr. I suppose if Ghose is still alive he ought to be punished, but I'm not interested in being a Maharani or living in India or anything like that."

The Major pinched his nose. "H'mm. Well, we'll have to see. But I agree with you about clearing Burr's name, poor devil. Terrible blot on the regiment, d'you see. Ha! Now that's where we should start, if I may advise you."

"Start where, Major?"

"With the regiment, of course, child. Oh, I beg your pardon. Ah, Jani. Now look, I'll go up to town this week, and talk to some old friends in the War House and the Foreign Office. Find out the situation in Jahanapur at this moment—"

"But I don't care about that part, Major."

"Hold on now, hold on." He lifted a triumphant finger and beamed at me. "I shall also go to see Lord Kearsey! How about that?"

"Lord Kearsey?"

Major Elliot blinked at me. "Lieutenant General Lord Kearsey. He's Colonel of the Regiment, and as such he has the right of direct access to the sovereign. Good heavens, I thought everybody knew that! Kearsey's all right, I served under him for three years before he retired, and if we give him a chance to wipe out this nasty stain in the regiment's history, he'll go at it like a rogue elephant. Declare war on the Foreign Office itself if they get in his way, I shouldn't wonder."

He turned to pace across the room, rubbing his hands together, and I realized that David Hayward had judged him correctly. Major Elliot still relished a campaign. "By George," he said slowly, "this is going to spread through every cantonment in India. Court of Inquiry set up to re-examine the case. They'll find Burr innocent, of course. No sane man can look at the facts together with that letter and decide otherwise. Lord, I'd like to be in the battalion mess the night that news reaches them!"

He turned towards me, a gleam in his eyes. "I know what they'll do, Jani, with or without permission from any confounded political johnnies. They'll send a party of Gurkhas up through what-d'you-call-it? Mustang, it says in the letter. Right up through the Chak Pass, to bring that old soldier home from where you laid him to rest, and they'll bury him in their own military cemetery in Gorakhpur where he belongs. That's what they'll do, by George!"

It was then, quite unexpectedly and with scarcely a sound, that I began to weep as I stood there, the tears rolling down my cheeks. Major Elliot stared aghast, and looked frantically at David. "What happened, Hayward? Did I say something wrong?"

David gave him a glance of rather surprised respect, put a clean handkerchief in my hand, and tucked my other arm under his as he spoke. "I think you said something exactly right, Major. Thank you for your help, and we'll leave you to carry on as you think best."

That night I slept poorly, and the following day I was listless, unable to settle to anything, but then came a sound night's sleep, and I was myself again next morning, having absorbed the shock and emotion of my bewildering discovery. It was a relief to feel that for the moment I had done all I could for Sembur, and his cause was in good hands. Now I could concentrate on Eleanor.

There were only five days left of the time I had allowed, and still no new letter had come from her. That day I sent off a telegram to reserve a passage for myself on the cross-Channel ferry, and a place on the Orient Express. Eleanor was now more than six weeks overdue to return, yet she had not said why, had not answered my anxious inquiries, and indeed had not even referred to the fact.

I sometimes tried to imagine what might have happened to make her behave so strangely and write such odd, disturbing letters, but my imagination failed. I only knew that something was badly amiss, and I was quite sure that Jani Burr was going to put it right.

Looking back later, I saw what a fool I was and how conceited. Eleanor was strong and independent, and had infected me with her spirit. Because she had taught me how to run a household, and how to do her secretarial work, arranging journeys, writing business letters, helping with her books, I now believed that nothing was too much for me. So I would go off to Corinth, all on my own, find out what was wrong, and bring Eleanor safely home, thereby repaying some small part of the measureless debt I would forever owe to her.

Wonderful Jani Burr.

My vain and silly dream was shattered two days later, when a letter came from Eleanor, on the writing paper of a hotel in Athens, a cool gray letter which left me dazed, and afraid of I knew not what.

> Dear Jani,
>
> Mr. Vernon Quayle and I were married in the Anglican Church here yesterday, and we shall leave for England in two days' time.
>
> We expect to reach Bournemouth on Monday 29th, by the train arriving at three o'clock.
>
> Please have us met, and make suitable arrangements for our taking up residence at Merlin's Keep.
>
> Yours sincerely,
>
> Eleanor

It might have been a letter from a stranger.

I rode up to Goose Hill, read it a dozen times in the hour I spent there trying to collect my wits, then rode home and made a feeble attempt to busy myself while waiting for David Hayward to call, for this was the day I had agreed to talk with him about my journey. But there would be no journey now.

I was in the stables, grooming Nimrod with a body brush and pouring out my anxieties to him, when David arrived. I

151

showed him the letter and he stood reading it through several times, his face startled at first, then becoming impassive. At last he looked up, handed me back the letter, and said, "Do you understand it?"

I shook my head. He rested a hand on Nimrod's withers and stared down. "Well . . . that's it, then."

I touched his hand. "I'm sorry, David."

"Thank you, Jani dear. And you're worried, too, I fancy."

"Yes. I'm almost frightened. Frightened for Eleanor, I mean."

He shrugged and gave a wry smile. "Don't let your imagination run away with you. Mr. Vernon Quayle is probably a very nice man. I'm sure Eleanor wouldn't have married him otherwise."

"But she's different, David. Her letters are different."

"Being in love can make people behave in strange ways, I suppose. It must all have been very exciting for her, and everything else has been swept from her thoughts for a while. Even you, Jani. But I'm sure this won't affect your situation here."

"I hadn't thought about that. I don't mind anything as long as Eleanor's happy. There are all sorts of things about myself I'm not very proud of, but honestly and truly I've never never taken my position here for granted."

He nodded, still absently running a hand over Nimrod's freshly groomed coat. "No, I didn't imagine you had. But I'm quite sure you'll be staying on here with Eleanor. I've heard her say she couldn't do without you, and she meant it. New husband or not, she needs you, Jani."

I hoped then that David was right, and that Eleanor would need me, but if I had known how horrifyingly true my hope was to be, I would have wished otherwise for Eleanor's sake.

For the next two days I was very busy, for there was much to be done. Mrs. Burke, Mayes, and the maids were all startled to be told the news, and received it with more unease than enthusiasm. I decided that Eleanor would prefer to retain her own bedroom, which was very large, for herself and her husband, so I arranged to have the big bed and some of the furniture moved in from Mr. Lambert's old room.

My room adjoined Eleanor's, and I thought it best to move along the passage to a spare bedroom, partly to give them more privacy and also because I thought my old room might be used as a dressing room for Eleanor. The maids cleaned the house from top to bottom, though we had completed spring cleaning only three months ago, and I set old Dawson and his assistant to tidying the flower beds, trimming the lawn edges, and making the gardens look as fresh and smart as possible.

After a long discussion with Mrs. Burke I decided that Eleanor and Mr. Quayle would be glad of a change from foreign food, so we would have a roast beef dinner on the evening of their arrival. I also found time, on the Saturday morning, to drive into Bournemouth, draw some money from my account in the bank there, and buy a lovely four-piece silver tea and coffee service made almost eighty years ago by Benjamin Smith of London. This was to be my wedding present to Eleanor and her husband.

By noon on the Monday I had done all that I could in the time available, and after luncheon I put on my best dress and bonnet, ready for the drive into Bournemouth. At first I had thought to drive the landau myself, for truth to tell I handled the pair of horses better than Mayes or the young gardener who sometimes acted as coachman. But then I felt Mr. Quayle might think it unladylike for me to drive a landau, so in the end we went with Mayes up on the box in front of me and young William following us with the gig.

We reached the station twenty minutes before the train was due. I brought a platform ticket, then tried to sit composedly on a bench with my parasol instead of giving way to a fretful longing to pace up and down. The last time Eleanor had returned from a journey abroad, I had been with her. We had spent three weeks in the Savoie region, and Mr. Lambert had been here at the station to meet us. It was so different today.

The train came in at last, no more than a minute late, puffing self-importantly, great pistons gleaming, and I remembered how afraid I had been when first I saw one of these huge steel monsters. Then I thought of nothing but Eleanor, and I was standing on tiptoe, craning my neck, stupidly worried that I might miss her amid the bustle of alighting passengers.

My heart leapt as I saw her, rich auburn hair glowing beneath the green straw hat I had helped her choose before she went away, and I almost ran as I hurried through the dwindling crowd on the platform. I was vaguely conscious of somebody beside her, but I had eyes only for Eleanor, and called her name as I drew near.

"Jani?" She was staring at me from a rather drawn face, fingers of one hand touching her temple as if trying to recall

153

something. Then suddenly her eyes lit up and she threw out her arms. "Oh, Jani! Jani!" We hugged each other, and my hat was pushed all askew, for she was taller than I, then she stepped back, clutching both my hands.

"Oh, Jani, how good to see you. I kept trying . . . trying to remember, but I couldn't see your face, dear. Everything seemed so far away . . . I mean, Larkfield, and Merlin's Keep, and everybody, really. I couldn't make any pictures in my mind—oh!" I felt her jump, and saw the animation suddenly vanish from her face. She loosed my hands almost guiltily, and said in a flustered fashion, half turning to the figure beside her. "Oh, forgive me, Vernon. This is Jani Burr, I'm sure I've told you all about her." without looking at me she continued, "Jani, this is my husband, Vernon Quayle."

For a moment I saw an old man, then a much younger man, then I was lost and confused. His hair was silver gray, and spread thinly over a skull that seemed too large. The long face was strangely unlined, the eyes remote, gray as cobbles. Vernon Quayle's ears were large and jutting, his mouth large and loose, so that he seemed always to have the beginnings of a foolish grin. He carried a hat in his hand, and wore a rather ill-fitting suit of silver gray.

Time seemed to have stopped. I began to feel as if a spring were being slowly wound up inside me. We were standing on the platform of a railway station in an English town on the Hampshire coast, yet I felt suddenly as if I were standing poised on the edge of a precipice. At first glance there was nothing unusual about Vernon Quayle, nothing to cause unease. An unkind person might even have found his appearance slightly clownish. But I had a powerful conviction that nobody, nobody in the world, could have looked carefully at this man and laughed.

I felt a sense of nausea, a sense of danger, and I shuddered. Abruptly the spring that coiled within me seemed to break joltingly free, ripping aside the veils of my memory and opening the gates of a cold and paralyzing fear. Years ago in Galdong, the girl who was the Oracle had looked into the pool of ink and spoken of the Silver Man . . . the bloodless one . . . Eater of Souls. And later, the last time I had seen the High Lama, Rild, he had foretold my meeting with the woman in red . . . *"who will be your friend, and through her will come the one to fear, who will be your enemy, the Silver Man . . ."*

154

I knew he stood before me now. Bloodless he was, for while Eleanor had a slight tan from the sun, Vernon Quayle's face was unnaturally white, as if from lack of pigment rather than ill health.

One part of my mind kept telling me that I was being stupid and over-imaginative, that because Eleanor's husband was silver-haired there was no reason to believe he fulfilled some strange prediction made by a dull-witted girl and an old monk, six years ago and half a world away. But somewhere deep in my being I felt that I was looking at the one the Oracle had called the Eater of Souls. And as I stared, with horror creeping through me, I could almost begin to understand what she had meant. I remembered how Rild, normally so quiet and serene, had given a little gasp of shock, and whispered, ". . . *within the bounds of earth and incarnation I had never thought to feel such power.*"

Vernon Quayle said, "Good afternoon." In contrast to his appearance he had a beautiful voice, quiet and mellow, but I heard no trace of warmth in it. I dropped a little curtsy and said, "Good afternoon, and welcome to Larkfield, Mr. Quayle. You have my warmest good wishes and congratulations." When I put out my hand he merely touched it with cold fingers, yet I had to repress a shiver, and make a positive effort to withdraw my hand naturally rather than snatch it away.

Eleanor stood quietly watching her husband. My heart sank as I looked at her, for it seemed to me that all the old energy and vitality had gone from within her. Vernon Quayle said, "I have three trunks of important chattels in the luggage van."

"William will see to it, Mr. Quayle. If he can't get it all on the gig, he can make another trip." I caught at Eleanor's arm and made a frantic attempt to be cheerful. "Oh, it's so lovely to see you again! I'm longing to hear all your news, and to look at your paintings and notes. Did you find any rare wild-flowers?"

Eleanor frowned a little, as if trying to remember. "Flowers? Well, not really, dear. I wasn't able to do a great deal of work."

When we took our places in the landau I sat facing Eleanor. Vernon Quayle sat beside her and took her hand. I hoped this was a gesture of affection, but as we drove through Bournemouth and out onto the Larkfield road he

155

said no word to her but simply looked about him, silver head turning slowly this way and that, the empty gray eyes gazing without seeming interest. I waited for Eleanor to speak, but she sat stiffly, with an embarrassed air, giving a timid smile when she caught my eye.

I had never dreamt that it was in the bounds of possibility for Eleanor Lambert, my Eleanor of the fearless eye, ready tongue, and fiery spirit, to be timid or embarrassed, and as I looked at her now I felt utter misery. Somehow I managed to keep chattering away about nothing in particular during the drive home, but it was a heavy ordeal.

We came to Merlin's Keep, where Mrs. Burke and the other servants appeared on the steps to welcome their mistress and new master. This should have been a happy and exciting moment, but everybody seemed ill at ease, except for Vernon Quayle himself. He eyed the staff absently as they were introduced in turn, but seemed much more interested in studying the house itself. I had planned to have a refreshing cup of tea brought out to us in the garden, and thought Eleanor would then be glad to take a bath and rest for a few hours before dinner, but as we entered the big hall Vernon Quayle said, "I should like to see the house, my dear."

"Of course, Vernon."

I set my teeth and said as cheerfully as I could, "Won't you rest first, Eleanor? You must be so tired."

Vernon Quayle gave me a long, slow stare, and Eleanor said quickly, "No, dear, no, I'm not at all tired, thank you."

During the next twenty minutes we made a brief tour of Merlin's Keep. In some parts of it Vernon Quayle showed no interest, in others he lingered. It seemed to me that to the extent he showed any concern at all it was in the matter of aspect and direction, whether a room faced north or south, and how wide a view the windows gave. When we were upstairs, and I explained the arrangements I had made, he said in his fine mellow voice, "We shall require separate rooms." He glanced round the big bedroom I had made ready for him and Eleanor. "No doubt this will suit you well enough, my dear. I will take the east-facing bedroom across the passage." He looked at me. "Perhaps you will see to it."

"Certainly, Mr. Quayle."

Eleanor said, "I do hope you will find a room suitable for your study, Vernon. There is mine, of course, or the room that was my father's study, or Jani's office, all on the ground

156

floor, as you have seen." She sounded nervous, and I could have wept.

Her husband said, "None is suitable, Eleanor." He gazed at a flight of stairs leading up from the passage where we stood. "Does that go up to the servants' quarters?"

"Not exactly, Vernon, though it leads to the same floor. Their quarters are in the two wings, each with a separate staircase. This leads to what we call the Round Room."

The Round Room had no connection with either wing, and the stairs we now mounted provided the only access to it. The room was part of the original folly that Merlin's Keep had been, and its purpose was a mystery. It rose slightly above the level of the rest of the roof, and had four windows. One was wide and deep, looking out from the back of the house over the grounds. The other three, equally spaced round the circular room, were of necessity high up near the ceiling and slot-like in shape, looking out only upon the roof. Mr. Lambert had always suspected some architectural error, for in fact the room was not really round, or even symmetrical, but bulged on the southern quadrant.

Vernon Quayle stood in the middle of the newly cleaned but unfurnished room, gazing slowly round him. He began to nod, and the loose mouth tautened for a moment into something approaching a smile.

"This will do admirably," he said, and looked at me. "Perhaps you will be so good as to have a furniture maker call at the earliest opportunity."

"Very well, Mr. Quayle." I felt suddenly that I must get away if only for a few minutes, for I could scarcely bear to see Vernon Quayle and Eleanor together. "Please excuse me while I attend to one or two matters," I said, and went to my room. I took off my hat, rang for Bridget, told her to ask Mrs. Burke to come and see me, cried for a few moments, sponged my face in the washhand basin, and was ready for Mrs. Burke when she arrived.

"Is Miss Eleanor all right?" she said anxiously. "She doesn't seem herself at all, Miss Jani. We all said so. I mean . . . you know, not a bit like herself."

We looked at each other. Mrs. Burke nodded meaningly. I said a little wearily, "Let's hope she'll be herself again soon. In the meantime, we have to make a spare bedroom ready for Mr. Quayle." I told her what needed to be done, and when she had scurried off I practiced some cheerful smiles in

157

the looking glass before returning along the passage to tap on the door of Eleanor's room.

Entering at her call, I found her sitting at the dressing table, hands in her lap. Despite the warmth of the day, she still had not taken off her hat or the jacket of her costume. I looked about me, and said, "Where is Mr. Quayle?"

She looked down at her hands. "He's up in the Round Room."

I moved toward her. "Take your hat and jacket off, dear, it's so warm. Come along, let me help you." She sat listlessly as I drew out the pin and lifted the hat from her beautiful hair, then suddenly she caught at my hand and gasped, "Don't leave me, Jani! Don't ever leave me, please promise!"

My nerves jumped with shock, then I put my arms round her and held her tightly to me. "Of course I won't leave you," I whispered fiercely. "Never, never, never while you need me. Oh, Eleanor, what is it? What's wrong, dear? Is it—?" I broke off. I could not ask a bride of a few days if it was her husband who had changed her from a mettlesome, self-reliant woman to a meek and timorous wife.

For a moment she clung to me, then twisted suddenly away and stood up, her head cocked as if listening, a puzzled frown between her eyebrows. "What did you say, Jani?" She asked after a moment or two.

"I asked what was wrong."

"Wrong?"

"Yes. You begged me not to leave you, and you seemed so distressed."

"Did I?" She stared at me in what seemed genuine bewilderment. "Oh dear, I seem to do such funny things these days. I'm sorry, Jani."

I stood undecided, with the feeling that I was trying to cope with something I could not begin to grasp. At last I said, "I'll make some tea, and fetch it up here, shall I? Mrs. Burke will have enough on her hands for the moment."

"Yes, dear. That would be very nice," Eleanor said absently.

I went out of the room, glancing at the stairs leading to the Round Room as I passed. I knew that something quite dreadful had happened to Eleanor. It seemed she was almost unaware of it herself, except in occasional flashes of realization, as when she had suddenly begged me not to leave her. That had been the true Eleanor, in deep distress and crying to me for help, and there had been similar tiny flashes of herself in those strangely disjointed letters. But for the most part she had ceased to be Eleanor Lambert, and had become . . . I flinched from the truth, then made myself face it. My beloved Eleanor had become horribly like a submissive puppet.

CHAPTER TEN

I had promised Eleanor I would never leave her. Within seven weeks I had broken that promise, not of my own failing but because she herself made it impossible to keep.

In only a few days the easy and pleasant atmosphere I had always known at Merlin's Keep was changed to one of somber unease. At the end of the month, Mayes left to live with a widowed sister in the Midlands. In his place Vernon Quayle engaged a sour, burly man from Southampton. His name was Thorpe, he spoke scarcely at all, and appeared to have a grudge against the whole world. Mrs. Burke stayed on only because I begged her to.

Less than a week after Vernon Quayle entered Merlin's Keep, workmen were busy in the Round Room redecorating and doing whatever else he required there, under his constant supervision. Later the furniture he had ordered to his own design was delivered and installed. Neither I nor any of the servants climbed the stairs to the Round Room during this time, for Eleanor had said nervously that this was her husband's private domain. I was so distracted by worrying about her that it was some time before I wondered who kept the Round Room cleaned and dusted, for it was always locked now, and I was shaken to my bones when I discovered that it was Eleanor herself who did this duty.

Vernon Quayle spent much of each day in the Round Room, and often summoned Eleanor to be with him, sometimes for a few minutes, sometimes for several hours. I could not imagine why, for at other times they seemed to have little to say to each other. He always spoke civilly to her, and sometimes addressed her as "my dear," but I never heard them converse on any general subject. At table he could sit completely unembarrassed throughout a whole meal without uttering a word, the dull gray eyes withdrawn, absent, while Eleanor and I talked.

I say that we talked, but it was not as before. In the old days we had talked of everything under the sun, sometimes arguing, sometimes agreeing, but never lacking in subjects. In those days, when all three of us were constantly busy at our various pursuits, there was always news and gossip and discoveries to be exchanged. But now Eleanor did nothing. Her notes, manuscripts, and paintings gathered dust in her study. She no longer served on committees or worked for charities. She gave no soirées or garden parties. Once her energy had seemed boundless. Now she rose late, went to bed early, and seemed to spend most of her waking hours in an uneasy dream.

Sometimes, fleetingly, I would catch a glimpse of the old Eleanor, trapped in the husk of the new. Twice when we were alone, she unexpectedly caught my hand in a desperate grip and said, "Help me, Jani!" Yet almost before I could cry, "Tell me what to *do!*" the moment was gone, and she would look at me blankly as if she had not spoken.

On another occasion, as she sat watching me layer some border carnations, she suddenly echoed the words in her letter and said in a strange, shaking voice, "Pray for me, Jani." Even as I dropped the knife and the peg I carried, and hurried toward her, the flash of fearful animation faded from her eyes, and she said, "I'm a little tired. I think I shall go in and rest for a while."

I watched her walking slowly across the lawn, and felt my heart would break.

When Vernon Quayle was not in the house he was out walking or riding alone. I never saw him abuse a horse, but they all feared him. The first time he came into the stables when I was there, I felt a tremor of fear run through all six horses. Eyes rolled, ears twitched, hooves shuffled uneasily. I was thankful when he picked Hector for his mount, and not Nimrod.

On these country journeys he carried a haversack containing a number of small, thick glass bottles. Eleanor had said vaguely that he was interested in botany, but it was from the village folk I discovered he was solely interested in collecting herbs and particular small insects. In Larkfield there was much whispering and shaking of heads over Vernon Quayle, and over "poor Miss Eleanor." Once, when I was in the

161

smithy and he rode past, I saw Rosie furtively point crossed fingers at his back in the ancient gesture to ward off the Evil Eye. I shivered, wondering what instinct made her regard Vernon Quayle in such a light. She was not alone, as I found when I talked with David Hayward one afternoon.

"They all think Quayle's some sort of wicked wizard," he said. "Old Mrs. Spicer vows that he just looked at her goat and it died in the night."

We were dealing with Old Wilfred, the cantankerous bull on the Colbrook Farm, who had an infected hoof. David had sent a note asking if I could spare an hour to help him, and I had jumped at the chance. It was the first time I had seen him since Eleanor's return, and I suddenly realized how I longed for somebody I could talk to, somebody I could trust.

I said, "If I still lived in Namkhara, I'd be making signs like Rosie, spinning a prayer wheel, and putting out demon traps. Vernon Quayle is like Rild, that High Lama I told you about, except that Rild was a good man and I think Vernon Quayle is bad."

David had the hoof clamped between his knees and was working on it with a hoof knife. He said. "Bad? What has he done?"

"He's changed Eleanor. You wouldn't know her now, David."

"I suppose people can change on marriage."

"Oh, don't be stupid and reasonable!" I said angrily. Then, to Old Wilfred, in Tibetan, as he snorted and stirred, "Be at ease, my little one. Gently now, gently. Be patient a while and we will wipe away the pain. Then you can tread the soft cool grass again . . ."

David and I talked no more until we left the farm. I was sitting beside him in his trap, with Nimrod tied behind. Then I told him how changed everything was at Merlin's Keep, or tried to, for much of it was hard to put into words. He listened in silence, keeping Smoky to a slow walk, and when I floundered to a halt at last he said somberly, "I don't know what to make of it, neither does anyone else, Jani. My work brings me in touch with everybody, from the squire to the knacker man. Quayle makes no overtures. If spoken to, he's civil. For the rest, he goes his own way, whatever that may be, ignoring everybody, gentry and village folk alike. That's his own business, I suppose, but he seems to have cut Eleanor off from the rest of the world. Is he going to make her into a recluse?"

162

"I don't know, David." My throat ached and tears were very close. "I don't know what he's going to do, and I feel so helpless."

After a silence he said tiredly, "Eleanor has married Vernon Quayle, for better or for worse. There's nothing anybody can do about it." As we turned from the road onto the woodland track which led down to his cottage he glanced at me and said, "Have you told her about your discovery? I mean, Sembur's letter, and all about your mother and father?"

"Yes. I read her the copy I made of the letter. I thought she'd be so excited, and that we'd laugh together about my being a Maharani, and then she'd want to see Major Elliot and find out what was happening, and . . . oh, there would be so much to talk about. But it didn't happen like that, David. She just nodded and smiled a little and said, 'How interesting, Jani dear.' That was all."

David bit his lip, and I realized that what I had just told him must have given him a clearer picture of how Eleanor had changed than anything else. When we had driven on a little way he said, "Does Quayle know all about you?"

"He knows the last part, because he was there when I told Eleanor and read out the letter, at dinner one evening. He never seems to listen to anything we say, but he must have heard. I don't know whether Eleanor has told him all that happened to me before I came to Merlin's Keep."

David turned his head to look at me incredulously. "You told the whole story of Sembur's letter, and Quayle took no notice? Didn't ask a single question?"

"That's right."

"Good God, the man can't be human."

I shivered at those words. We spoke no more until we reached David's cottage, and there he invited me to have tea with him in the garden. "Have you heard anything from Major Elliot yet?" he asked as we sat waiting for Rosie to bring the tea.

"Oh, I'm sorry, I should have told you," I said contritely, "but somehow I've been so taken up with Eleanor since she came home."

"That's all right. What should you have told me?"

"Only that Major Elliot wrote to me. He stayed in London at his club for two days while he was seeing what he calls 'the right people.' It seems the Army was interested, but the Colonial Office people were rather cool, so then he took the story to a friend of a friend at the Foreign Office, and they

163

got quite excited. They said the Marquis of Lansdowne, the Foreign Minister, was away on holiday, but he would look into the whole matter when he returned. In the meantime, it was to be regarded as highly confidential."

David gave a short laugh. "Confounded cheek. They've no right to tell you whether you can speak of it or not."

I shrugged. "What does it matter? Major Elliot said it might take weeks before I heard anything further, because London would want to discuss the political significance with Delhi, and—oh, I don't know. I'm just glad he saw Lord Kearsey, the gentleman he told us about who's Colonel of the Regiment. Apparently he's *very* eager to have Sembur's name cleared, and that's all I care about."

Three days later Vernon Quayle astonished me by appearing in the drawing room after dinner. I had never known him to do so before. Eleanor and I were seated by the open french window enjoying the cooler evening air. I had a small table set in front of me, and was busy pasting into my scrapbook some pictures and small items of interest from *Country Life* and *Vanity Fair*. Eleanor held a tambour frame on her lap, her skeins of silk in a box at her elbow, and was embroidering a flower design on a silk shawl.

I always tried to ensure that both Eleanor and I had something to occupy us when we sat together after dinner. When she first came home I had exhausted myself with the effort of keeping a conversation going in the face of so small a response. Now we could exchange a few words about nothing of importance, then work in silence until I could think of something fresh to say.

We were both startled when the door opened and Vernon Quayle walked in. Eleanor said, "Oh . . . Vernon." I made myself smile at him but offered no greeting, for we had parted in the dining room less than half an hour before. He pulled an armchair forward a little to sit facing the window, ignored Eleanor, rested his chin on clasped hands, and gazed at me curiously for several seconds before saying in that mellifluous voice: "I understand that when you lived in Smon T'ang you visited Tibet on several occasions."

I stared in astonishment, then slowly put the brush back into the paste pot and wiped my fingers. "Why, yes, Mr. Quayle. We called it Bod."

"I take it your route was through the Chak Pass rather than the Sharba or the Kore?"

I was even more bewildered. "Yes, the Chak isn't quite so

164

high as the other two. But however do you know about them, Mr. Quayle?"

"I have visited Tibet," he said absently, in the same way that he might have mentioned visiting Winchester.

"*You* have?" My words and tone must have sounded impolite, though I had not meant them to be. I simply could not imagine this thin, white-faced Englishman of indeterminate age traveling into the land of Bod.

Eleanor said with a flustered air, "Oh, Vernon is very widely traveled, Jani, have I not told you? He has been to India, China, Egypt, the West Indies, so many places."

"I'm sorry if I sounded rude." I addressed Eleanor and her husband together. "It was just surprise, because very few people have been to Tibet. After all, there are no roads or carriages, so it's a very harsh country for traveling, especially in the high altitudes."

Vernon Quayle's loose mouth twitched in what might have been a grimace of scorn. "Where the body is obedient to the mind, there is no problem," he said distantly. "I entered Tibet by the main route, north from Darjeeling. I do not know the area in which you traveled."

"I never knew it very well myself, Mr. Quayle. We just followed the old trade route to Magyari, and came back the same way."

"Then you must have passed within a few miles of Choma La, and the great monastery there."

"Yes, I've seen it from the ridge where the trail runs. It's on the far side of a broad valley, and it seems to be partly built into the mountain."

"You have never been inside it?"

I half smiled. "Oh no, Mr. Quayle. I would never be allowed inside, except by command of the High Lama."

He gazed out across the garden. "What do you know of Choma La?"

"I hardly know anything about it, except that it's important. It must be, because the Dalai Lama visits it once a year for a special festival."

He half closed his eyes. "But surely when you were on the trail to Magyari with your companions, and you saw the great monastery across the valley, they must have spoken about it, made comments, told what they knew of it?"

I sat thinking, trying to remember, but shook my head at last. "I suppose they did, but I can't recall anything now. I expect I was too busy coaxing the yaks along to pay much attention to anything else."

Without another word Vernon Quayle rose to his feet and walked from the room. There was silence for perhaps half a minute after the door had closed, than Eleanor said vaguely, "Perhaps I should use a paler green for the leaves of this design."

I had always been very careful never even to hint at my feelings toward Vernon Quayle, or to question anything he did, but now I could not resist saying, "Eleanor, how strange that was. Why do you think Mr. Quayle asked me about Choma La?"

She got up, chafing her fingers as if they were numb. "Oh, he has so many interests," she said, her eyes screwed up as if in an effort of memory. "He studies the natural sciences, astronomy, mathematics, metaphysics . . . so many subjects, really, but it's all quite above my head, Jani."

"Oh, you can't say that. You're a scientist yourself."

"Yes. I suppose I used to dabble a little. But Vernon's knowledge is quite remarkable. He understands so much that even clever men cannot comprehend. There are reaches of the mind . . . reaches of the mind, Jani, which . . ." Her voice trailed away, I saw her eyes suddenly fill with tears, and she went on agitatedly, "He collects beautiful things. Did you know? They contain beauty, you see, an intangible quality but with genuine potency. All intangibles are potent. Light and dark, order and chaos, good and bad. It is a matter of understanding how to . . . how to absorb and direct the force—"

She stopped abruptly in mid-sentence, sat down in her chair, and gazed fixedly at her hands, clenched together in her lap. I ran to her and put an arm round her shoulder, pressing my cheek to hers. She felt cold. I had not understood her strange, disjointed outburst, but there was something about it which filled me with horror.

"Eleanor, Eleanor dear," I whispered, "I know you're unhappy, I know it. Please talk to me, tell me how I can help. Is it—?" I hesitated, then plunged on recklessly. "Is it your husband? Are you afraid of him? I'll take you away, dear, I'll take you right away if you want me to. But you must tell me, you must *speak*."

I felt her stir. She turned her head, and when I looked into the gray-green eyes which had once been so serene, it seemed that far away in their depths I could see the old Eleanor looking at me with desperate appeal. Then slowly she shook her head. "No," she said softly, "not you, Jani. I'll not bring you down."

Her eyes closed. After a few moments she sighed, opened her eyes, and picked up the tambour frame. "What do you think?" she said, wrinkling her brow. "Would it be better to use a paler green for the leaves?"

Ten days later, at a few minutes before noon, I was in my little office when Vernon Quayle entered. My office was a very special place for me, and I hated his intrusion.

I was also surprised, for he had never set foot here before, and had merely glanced inside that first day when we had shown him round Merlin's Keep. I put down my pen, stood up, gave the polite smile I always gave Eleanor's husband, and said, "Please come in, Mr. Quayle. Can I help you?"

He did not answer at first, but simply looked at me. At other times his gaze had been absent, or he had looked through me or past me, but it was not so now. The eyes, like gray raindrops, looked steadily into mine, and I was suddenly aware how huge the pupils were. The gaze was so troubling that for a moment I felt dizzy, but somehow I continued to meet it, and kept the forced smile on my lips.

At last he said, "I should be obliged it you would assist me for half an hour, Jani."

I hid my surprise and said automatically, "Of course, Mr. Quayle. Do you mean now?"

"Yes." He turned away. "In the Round Room, if you please."

I blinked at the empty doorway and listened for the sound of his footfalls, but heard nothing. I had never known man or woman move so soundlessly as Vernon Quayle. I closed my account books, put them away in a drawer, tidied my desk, picked up my note pad and pencil, then made my way upstairs, a flicker of uneasiness stirring within me.

I knew that Eleanor was in her room, resting before lunch, something she had never dreamt of in the time before Vernon Quayle, when her energy had been boundless. My disquiet did not arise from any fear that he planned to make advances to me, for I was quite sure he had no feeling for me whatsoever, and doubted that women held any attraction for him. I was almost sure, though I did not like to think about it, that he had never visited Eleanor in her bedroom since their coming to Merlin's Keep. I could have put no name to the cause of my unease, but it was very real, and grew stronger as I mounted the stairs to the Round Room, tapped on the door, and entered at Vernon Quayle's call.

I would never have believed that a room I knew could have been so transformed. My first impression was one of lightness, for the four windows allowed sunlight to bathe the curving walls. The floor was of white tiles, the furniture stark and strange, in a glossy black wood, with nothing upholstered. There were two armchairs, a broad settle, a stool with an octagonal seat, and a semicircular desk with an inlaid surface of black leather.

Two quadrants of the room had been fitted with shelves to hold hundreds of books, many of them quite old, to judge by their bindings. Another quadrant held a curving bench with a sink and a long tap which swiveled above it. On the bench were several retorts, some racks of test tubes, and a Bunsen burner. Above, on shelves, were dozens of glass bottles holding powders and substances of various colors. The fourth quadrant of the Round Room had been fitted with a rack which held a number of scrolls, and beside it an ancient-looking star map hung on the wall. The center of the tiled floor was clear, but round the edges of the room were long rugs, strangely patterned but with the flavor of the East, and glowing with rich colors.

There was more, much more, for the Round Room was very large, but I could not take it all in, for something was disturbing me. I looked slowly about me, seeking the cause, a sense of agitation growing within me. And then it came to me, even as I remembered the way Vernon Quayle had smiled when he first saw the Round Room. As I have said, the room itself was not symmetrical but a somewhat mis-shapen circle. Now I saw that this theme was echoed everywhere. In the furnishing, in all the decoration, there was a slight but positive distortion.

Between the shelves, the walls were white with an apparently simple recurring design in black lines. But the shape formed by these lines troubled the eye, for it would conform neither to two dimensions nor to three, but produced a disturbing optical illusion. The chairs stood steadily enough, but were in some peculiar way lopsided in every direction. The desk top was not truly a half-circle, yet not sufficiently different to be something else. I felt almost sure the surface was not entirely level, and that the same could be said of the

168

shelves, but I could not tell to what extent my eyes were being tricked. When I looked down at one of the rugs I saw it tapered slightly, but not evenly, and that it had not been cut but was woven in this way.

No single thing in the Round Room seemed quite round, or square, or straight, or of any symmetrical shape. There was nothing pleasing or artistic about this lack of symmetry pervading Vernon Quayle's room. The whole effect was one of leering ugliness which nudged at the senses as if relishing the affront it offered them.

Vernon Quayle said, "Sit down, please." As I obeyed he pulled on a cord which drew curtains across two of the shallow windows. The curtains were dark blue with a triangular pattern in gold, but again the pattern tricked the eye and troubled the senses. I remembered Eleanor's artistry, her taste which I had so envied, and wondered how she could bear to be in such a room, or how any man could choose to live among such monstrosities of shape and pattern. As if reading my thoughts, Vernon Quayle said, "If the mind is to be free from emotion, and to become truly objective, it must be trained to disregard external trivialities." He moved to open a small cabinet.

I had little understanding of what he meant, and would have had none at all if I had not heard so much talk about monks and lamas during my years in Smon T'ang. I knew they performed all sorts of rites and practices to free their minds from concern with the material world, but this was in order to enlarge and uplift the spiritual element of their being, and I was quite sure the same could not be said for Vernon Quayle.

He turned from the cabinet, and as I saw what he carried I froze, my scalp creeping as if the hair were trying to stand up. In his hands he held a round tray with a black-and-white mosaic design. On the tray stood a small bowl of flint glass, and beside it a tall flask of inky black liquid. He set the tray on the desk, seated himself, poured the black liquid from the flask into the bowl, and reached across to set the bowl down on the far side of the desk, in front of me.

"Take the bowl in both hands, if you please," he said abstractedly, "and look at the surface of the liquid. Make no mental effort. Simply look."

I sat upright, every muscle stiff, gripping the arms of my chair, and when I could find my voice I said hoarsely, "No!"

"I beg your pardon?" His faded gray eyes were as cool as

ever, his beautiful voice as mellow, but I saw that the loose mouth had tightened momentarily.

"No, Mr. Quayle," I repeated doggedly. "That's what they use in Galdong to make the Oracle go into a trance. I'm not going to be mesmerized, or whatever you call it."

"Mesmerized?" He ran a hand over his thin silver hair, and I saw contempt in the bloodless face. "Franz Mesmer was an ignorant charlatan, a novice who . . ." He stopped, shrugged, and made a languid gesture toward the bowl. "But let us proceed. This is merely a device for enhancing the memory. I am interested to learn more of Choma La, and I believe you may know more about it than you can now recall. The black liquid offers a focus for the mind, which in turn allows the doors of memory to be opened by correct questioning. It is a simple scientific operation, and entirely harmless."

I stared at him. "Scientific?"

"Oh yes," he said softly. "Oh yes, Jani. Scientific. Whatever the narrow-minded fools who write the textbooks may say."

I stood up, my heart pounding. "Does Eleanor do it? Have you made her look into the ink?"

Every scrap of life vanished from his eyes, and I could almost feel myself shrivel under his gaze, but I kept meeting it even though I could feel perspiration break out on my brow. "You are impertinent," he said at last. "What my wife does is no concern of yours. Take up the bowl, if you please."

I shook my head. "I don't wish to offend you, but I'm not going to do it. I hate anything of that sort. I don't like people being put into trances, or making prophecies, or doing things that seem like magic. I lived with all that in Smon T'ang and I think it's bad and unhealthy."

Vernon Quayle's shoulders moved in a tiny shrug. "I had thought you too intelligent to use meaningless words like 'bad.' Very well. I shall not press you."

I moved to the door, and hesitated there, trying to find something suitable to say, but there was nothing. I did not intend to apologize for my refusal.

In the days that followed I wondered if Vernon Quayle would be hostile toward me, but his manner did not change. For most of the time he ignored me, just as he ignored everybody else, not with deliberate rudeness but as if unaware of those about him.

I now hated this man. I knew it was very wrong of me, but I simply could not help myself. I was quite certain that in some way he had acquired almost complete power over

Eleanor, shackling her mind in bonds she could not break. I had heard of mesmerism and hypnosis, but I knew little about them except that they were ways of inducing a trance. Perhaps Eleanor had been gradually brought to submission during those long weeks in Greece before she married. One thing was quite certain, that Vernon Quayle was responsible for the heartbreaking change in her. When I remembered Eleanor as she had been when I first came to Merlin's Keep, strong and vital, ever ready to laugh, ever ready to do battle, impulsive, warm, affectionate, I could not hold back the hatred I felt toward the man who had made her an empty shell.

I do not know if Vernon Quayle decided to be rid of me because I refused to obey him in the Round Room or because he sensed my hatred. The blow fell one evening when I had persuaded Eleanor to play a game of croquet with me on the lawn after dinner. It was a day in late August, and the sun was touching the treetops to the west when Vernon Quayle came from the house, walking slowly as he usually did, hands behind him, moving across the lawn to where I stood watching Eleanor as she prepared to make a stroke. She was unaware of his approach, and I did not want her to be startled, so I said softly, "Eleanor." She looked up, gave a little start, then began to bite her lower lip anxiously.

Vernon Quayle halted a few paces away, looked at me, and said as if making some casual remark about the weather, "I have decided that it is inconvenient for us to retain you here at Merlin's Keep any longer, Jani. Perhaps you will be so good as to leave within the next two or three days."

Eleanor looked suddenly like a ghost, and I felt my own face must have mirrored hers, for I was cold with shock. Struggling against it, I gathered my wits and tried to speak calmly. "I don't understand, Mr. Quayle. Why do you want me to go?"

"You are not in a position to demand reasons," he said, without any hint of anger or malice, "but I will extend you the courtesy of replying, quite simply, that you have no satisfactory position in this household."

Eleanor stood with her head bowed, her eyes closed. I could see that she was gripping the croquet mallet with such force that her knuckles were white. I looked at her husband again, and could not quite manage to prevent my voice shaking as I said, "Eleanor and her father took me into their home three years ago, Mr. Quayle. I'm content to be what-

171

ever Eleanor wishes me to be, whether it is servant, companion, or friend. If you feel that the work I do here is not sufficient for my keep, then I have a small income from which I can pay——"

"No!" Eleanor cried in a low and terrible voice that made my heart turn over. "No, no, no!"

Her husband looked at her and said, "Eleanor." Her eyes were open now, and slowly her head came round to meet his gaze. I saw the fire go out of her, saw her body go slack, the mallet fall from her hands. There was a silence. Vernon Quayle looked at me again and said, "You are no longer required here in any capacity, Jani. Now that Eleanor is married, she has no need of a companion or female friend. She has outgrown the botanical work in which she once dabbled, and has no need for your secretarial services. As regards household servants, we shall employ them as required."

Apart from the incident in the Round Room I had always avoided the slightest disagreement with Vernon Quayle, for he was Eleanor's husband, but now I was forced to outface him if I was to keep my promise never to leave her. I pressed my heels hard into the soft grass, stood erect, and said very slowly and politely, "Excuse me, Mr. Quayle, but it was Eleanor who invited me into this house, her own house. I won't be told to go by anyone but Eleanor."

The bleak gray eyes with their huge pupils bored into me. "Eleanor?" he said softly.

I looked, and saw her pale face working as if she were under some dreadful stress. Then she said in a harsh, frantic voice, "Go, Jani, it's no use. You can't stay here." Her splendid eyes fixed on me suddenly with a wild glare. "Go!" she cried again. "I don't want you here! Go, Jani! For pity's sake, *go* when I tell you!"

She turned, caught up her skirt, and began to move toward the house at a stumbling run, a hand to her face.

"I suggest to you," Vernon Quayle said quietly, "that the longer you remain, and the more you protest, the more my poor wife will suffer, since your presence here is obviously a cause of distress to her."

I knew then that I was defeated, for this man held Eleanor in his hand, helpless as a puppet, and it was she who would pay for any defiance I showed. I made no attempt to hide my hatred and loathing as I said, "If I am gone by noon tomorrow, will that be satisfactory?"

"That will do very well." He turned to stroll away in the

direction of the rose garden. I put the croquet mallets and balls away, then went into the house and down to the servants' hall to tell Mrs. Burke I would be leaving.

She shook her head miserably. "I knew it, Miss Jani. I could see it coming. He's a devil, that one. A devil, that's what he is. If I was young enough to start again in a new position I'd be off before you could whistle."

"Oh, I hope you'll never do that," I said unhappily. "I can't bear to think of Miss Eleanor being all alone, without any of us who were here before."

I spent the rest of that evening, and two hours before breakfast next day, sorting out my belongings and packing them in the two trunks Mr. Lambert had bought for me when I made my first trip abroad with Eleanor. It was surprising to find how much I had accumulated over my time in Larkfield, all the clothes and books and personal items I had bought out of the allowance Mr. Lambert and Eleanor had always made me for the work I did for them.

I thought of the day I had come to Merlin's Keep, in my tattered skirt and straw hat, toes poking through my boots. Here I had been given great and wonderful gifts, of trust, affection, education, and work to do, and none of this could be taken away from me. But here, where I had found happiness, I had now lost it, and I felt I could never be truly happy again, for how could I ever rid myself of the memory of Eleanor and what she had become?

Following a plan I had worked out during the night, I drove out to Stafford's Farm and was back in my room before breakfast time. Mrs. Burke sent Bridget up with breakfast on a tray, but I could only pick at it, for I had no appetite. I asked Bridget to let me know when Mr. Quayle had gone to the Round Room, and as soon as she tapped to tell me so I went downstairs to spend an hour tidying my office and Mr. Lambert's old study.

I took everything I had of Eleanor's in the way of manuscripts and drawings, and also Mr. Lambert's unfinished work. I knew very well that I had no right to do this, but I had a sick feeling that if these things were left in the care of Vernon Quayle they would be destroyed, and I simply could not allow that to happen.

When I had packed everything in a suitcase, I sent for young William and had him carry this and the rest of my luggage down to the hall. I said goodbye to the servants, including old Dawson and his assistants, but not Thorpe, the new man engaged by Vernon Quayle, then went to the stables and spent ten minutes talking to Nimrod and the other horses, saying goodbye to them. Young William came to harness Sally to the gig, and we walked back together to the front of the house. I went inside, up to my room, put on my hat and gloves, then walked along the passage to Eleanor's room and tapped on the door. All this time I was being very brisk, businesslike, and strict with myself, for otherwise I would have cried my heart out.

I went in when Eleanor called, and found her sitting in a chair near the window, a glass of milk on a table at her elbow. She wore a dark blue dressing gown buttoned to her neck, her long auburn hair was loose, her face wan. Again I was swept by a blend of rage, pity, and utter helplessness. It was all I could do to prevent myself bursting into tears, but somehow I managed to smile as I moved toward her.

"Jani," she said. "I'm so glad you've come to say goodbye. I was afraid you . . . might not want to."

I took off my gloves, held her cold hand, and bent to kiss her cheek. "Never think such things. You'll be in my thoughts every day. And I didn't come just to say goodbye, Eleanor dear, I wanted to say thank you again. I grew up without a mother or sister, but you've been both to me, and the dearest of friends as well."

Her mouth began to tremble, and she looked away. After a moment or two she said, "Will you be able to manage, Jani? Will you have enough to live on?"

"I shall manage wonderfully well, silly. Just think what I had when I came here. Now I have an income of a hundred pounds a year from what your father left me, and I've learned to do all kinds of work, so I haven't anything to worry about."

"Where will you go?"

"Oh, that's all settled. You know the little cottage just before you reach the farmhouse at Stafford's Farm?"

"Where Tom Stafford's father lived?"

"Yes. It's been empty since he died last year. There are just the two rooms, one up, one down, and a kitchen, but that's quite enough for me. I went to see Mr. Stafford this morning, and I can have it for two shillings a week." I gripped her hand hard. "And if you ever need me, just send for me, Eleanor dear. Nothing and nobody will stop me coming."

She pressed my hand to her cheek and gave a strange little laugh. "My fiery Jani, who hit Big Alice on the nose when

174

she spoke ill of her friend Mister. Do you remember telling me, that first day?"

I nodded. "I thought you'd send me away because of it."

"I'd sooner throw away gold, Jani. Such friendship can't be bought. I could only win it from you, as Mister did."

I released her hand and groped for the clasp of the chain at the back of my neck, beneath the collar of my dress. "Do you remember the gift he left me, Eleanor? The silver medallion with the gold star on it, and the poem in Hindi?"

For a few brief moments Eleanor had shown a glimpse of her old self, but now her animation faded as if her energy had drained away. "Why yes, I recall something of the sort, dear," she said vaguely, rubbing her temple. "What was the poem about? I don't seem to remember things very well these days."

I held the medallion in my hand now, looking at it, and spoke the translation I had never forgotten.

> *"Here is a token to remind you of a friend*
> *It may not bring you good fortune*
> *Or protect you from fate*
> *Or from your enemy*
> *It is for remembrance only*
> *Keep it until a friend has need of it*
> *Then give it gladly and go your way."*

I took Eleanor's hand, and dropped the medallion and chain into her palm. "Please wear it for me sometimes," I whispered.

"Oh, Jani . . ."

The door opened and Vernon Quayle entered. He said, "Good morning, my dear. Good morning, Jani. I see you are about to depart."

I said, "Good morning, Mr. Quayle," and left it at that, hoping he would go, for I did not want to make my farewell to Eleanor in his presence. To my disappointment he closed the door and walked across the room. Eleanor had not moved. Her hand was still held out, with the medallion in it, the chain hanging down a little. Vernon Quayle stopped, and his silver eyebrows lifted slightly as he said, "What is this, eleanor?"

I answered for her. "It's just a little present from me, Mr. Quayle."

"May I see?" He reached out, and as he picked up the me-

175

dallion from Eleanor's palm I saw a tremor pass over his putty-white face and heard a tiny hiss of indrawn breath. He raised the medallion almost defiantly, as if he wished to drop it but would not. Then he placed it on the table and stood gazing down at it, slowly rubbing his hands together in a kind of washing movement.

His face showed more emotion than I had ever seen in him before, though of what nature I found it hard to tell. His mouth was tight, his eyes slitted. When he stopped rubbing his fingers and lowered his hands to his sides, an extraordinary stillness came upon him. For a moment I was reminded of the stillness of Rild, when I had stood before him in the monastery at Galdong for the last time, and he had spoken of things to come.

Suddenly Vernon Quayle made a sound in his throat, an unpleasant, regular catching of the breath, and it was several seconds before I realized, with a shudder, that he was laughing. After a few moments he stopped. The intensity faded from his face, and his body relaxed. Without taking his eyes from the medallion he said, "Where did this come from?"

I said, "It was given to me by a friend."

"And before that?"

"I only know that it was given to him by a friend."

"Ye-e-es," Vernon Quayle said slowly, his head on one side. "Yes, indeed. A potent talisman. When you wish to find one who is lost, you may come to me with it."

Those strange words were spoken so casually that I thought I must have misheard him, and said, "I beg your pardon?"

He gave a half shake of his head. "I am sure you will recall what I said when the time comes."

"But . . . I don't understand what you meant."

"That is something we both have yet to discover." He nodded toward the medallion. "You will take it with you, please. Eleanor is very touched by your kindness, but the gift is . . . unsuitable."

Every instinct in me urged me to argue, to insist that Eleanor should decide for herself. But she sat with head bowed, the lovely hair falling forward so that her face was partly hidden, and she did not look up. I remembered what had happened the day before, when I had made a small attempt to defy Vernon Quayle, and I did not want to see Eleanor so distressed again.

I picked up the medallion and chain and put them in my handbag. I was not going to fasten the clasp and slip the me-

176

dallion down inside my dress with Eleanor's husband watching me. I said, "Goodbye, Mr. Quayle," then moved to kiss Eleanor on the cheek again. "Goodbye, Eleanor."

She whispered something I could not catch, but she did not lift her head. Then I turned and walked from the room without looking back, for I could not bear to.

CHAPTER ELEVEN

Within a week I had made Withy Cottage into a very pleasant home. Some might have thought it tiny, but it was larger than the home I had lived in for more than half my life. Tom Stafford had sold off the furniture when his father died: "Lot of owd rubbish anyway," he told me. But I spent very little money in getting together all I needed.

Many people knocked on my door to wish me well, and when they were ladies I was able to invite them in. When David Hayward called, we had the freedom of Mrs. Stafford's parlor in the farmhouse. The vicar and one or two others were a little disturbed at the idea of my living on my own, but according to David and Rosie there was no gossip about me.

I had no enemies in Larkfield, a blessing bequeathed to me by Mr. Lambert and Eleanor, and in any event Larkfield had never forgotten that I was an Indian princess, a story which had gained new life of recent weeks, and so I had never quite been judged as a native-born girl would have been.

There was a small kitchen in the cottage where I made breakfast and luncheon for myself, but in the evenings I took dinner with the Staffords in their big kitchen. Time did not hang heavily on my hands. I began to help David Hayward more frequently, and would have been glad to help on the farm except that Mr. Stafford would not hear of me doing any heavy or dirty work. He regarded me as an animal expert, and seemed delighted to have me spend an hour or so going round the farm with him and telling him if I felt the animals were in good fettle or if any of them needed attention.

With so little expenditure, I was able to live comfortably

on the income from the money Mr. Lambert had left me, but at the same time I felt I ought to provide for the future by setting myself to regular work of some kind.

One afternoon I talked of it with David Hayward. We were sitting on bales of hay in the Gratton Dene stables, after spending five hours struggling to deliver a foal from a great shire mare, Molly, and bickering with each other, as we so often did when working together. Now it was done. The hairy little creature was already standing on wobbly legs, suckling from its massive mother, who weighed little less than a full ton, and our anxious squabbling had ceased.

David, stripped to the waist, was massaging his bruised, aching arms. Mr. Rooke, the owner, had gone to tell his wife to put a cold meal together for us, as we had neither of us eaten since breakfast time. My blouse and breeches clung to me, for my body was damp. I had not undergone the same physical exertion as David, but I had shared Molly's nervousness and fear for long hours, and from time to time she had leaned some of her weight against me, as if to test me, to reassure herself that I would not leave her.

Buttoning his shirt, David gave me a tired but satisfied smile and said, "That's a mare and a foal Rooke owes you. I'd never have managed without you to make her relax. She's so confoundedly strong."

"You were very good with her," I said, and meant it. "David, could I learn to be a vet?"

"You'd have a lot of prejudice to overcome," he said slowly. "But you'd make a marvelous vet, Jani. The only thing is, you'd have to go away to college and be properly trained, which takes seven years."

"Oh. I don't want to go away."

He said soberly, "Would you be interested in a partnership?"

"With you? But I don't really do anything, David. Oh, I know it helps if I'm there to talk to the animals when things are difficult, but I'm not qualified, and I couldn't . . . well, I couldn't take money for it."

"I was thinking of a more permanent partnership." He wiped his brow with a forearm. "Would you marry me, Jani?"

He had said it often before, but this time I knew he was not joking. Strangely, I was neither startled nor embarrassed by his words, only a little proud and a little sad. I answered at once, "Oh, David . . . you know you don't love me."

"Love? Well, that's hard to pin down, Jani. I enjoy being with you, I feel completely at ease with you, and there's nobody for whom I have a higher regard."

"But you love Eleanor," I said gently.

"No." His voice was a little sharp. "You mustn't say that. Eleanor is married now."

"I'm sorry, I didn't mean to offend you."

"You haven't offended me, Jani dear." He was fumbling with one of his shirt cuffs, trying to button it, but his fingers were still clumsy with numbness. His pleasant, nondescript face was thoughtful as he said, "I hope and believe you are as content in my company as I am in yours. Do we really need more? Is love something else, do you think?"

I got to my feet and went across to button the cuff for him. As I bent by the bale of hay where he sat, Mister's silver medallion slipped from the neck of my blouse and hung suspended on its chain. I said, "Yes, I think love must be something more, David, and I think in your heart you know it."

He studied me curiously, then took my hand. We were very close, and I could smell the carbolic lingering on his body from when he had washed his arms and shoulders after the delivery. "Perhaps you're right, Jani," he said, "but I wonder how *you* know that love is something more." He gave a slow smile, and lifted his other hand to touch the medallion with a finger. "You know, I've sometimes had the odd feeling that Jani Burr is in love with that mysterious Mister of hers."

I gave a gasp of surprise and was about to laugh, but without warning I felt the color suddenly flooding up my neck and making my cheeks burn. Pulling my hand away, I snapped, "Oh, don't be ridiculous, David!" Heart thumping, I turned away, and was aware that for the first time in my life I had actually flounced.

Even as I had the thought, David said accusingly. "That was a flounce."

"Nonsense!" I whirled round and glared at him, slipping the medallion down beneath my blouse again. "I *never* flounce, and anyway I was only twelve when I knew Mister, and he called me a liar, and I kicked him, and he didn't like me, and I didn't even bother to ask his *name*, so—"

David lifted both hands, palms out. "Peace, Jani, peace. I didn't mean to upset you."

"I'm not in the least upset," I began angrily, then my annoyance suddenly faded and I stared at him with growing
180

alarm. "Yes, I am. I'm all hot and embarrassed! Oh, David, I couldn't be so silly, could I?"

"As to be in love with Mister?" He laughed and shook his head. "Heavens knows, Jani. I suppose a little girl might hero-worship a man like that."

"No, I'm sure I didn't think of him in that way."

David shrugged and stood up. "Not much point in dwelling on it, Jani. I should imagine there's very little chance you'll ever meet again."

"I suppose not. I'm sure I'd be very nervous, but . . . I would like to see him, David. I'd even be glad just to discover his name."

I did not know then how soon I was to hear that name, the name of the demon on the black horse, who had saved me from death in a cave at the summit of the Chak Pass.

In the third week of September I was in my little garden soon after breakfast one morning, pruning a loganberry bush which had finished fruiting, when one of Major Elliot's stable hands arrived on horseback. I went to the gate as he dismounted, and greeted Bruno, a red roan with a white sock on the nearside foreleg. The boy touched his cap and handed me an envelope.

"Letter from the Major, and I 'ave to wait for a reply please, miss."

The letter read:

> Dear Jani,
>
> Sir Charles and Lady Gascoyne are in Bournemouth and would be grateful if you would consent to receive them. I propose to conduct them to you at three o'clock this afternoon, if that is convenient to you, or at such other time as you may suggest.
>
> J. R. Elliot (Major)

I read the letter again. The Major did not waste words. I assumed that this must be something to do with his activities concerning Sembur, but had no idea who Sir Charles and Lady Gascoyne might be, or why they should wish to see me. Not for the first time, I warmed to Major Elliot. He had not asked me to go to his house for the meeting, but was bringing the titled lady and gentleman to my tiny cottage.

I hurried indoors, wrote a brief note to say I would be happy to receive the Major and his companions at three, and sent the boy off with it. I decided firmly that I would not speculate about Sir Charles and Lady Gascoyne, then spent most of the following hours doing so.

At two o'clock everything was as clean and polished in Withy Cottage as I could make it, and I had a throbbing head. I carried hot water up to my bedroom, took a bath standing in the bowl behind a curtain I had hung across one corner, then put on a fresh dress and composed myself to wait.

At one minute past three, Major Elliot came riding up the lane on Hero, followed by his best carriage. I did not wait for him to knock, but opened the front door and greeted him as he dismounted. He bowed over my hand and said, "After-noon—ah—Jani. Shan't be staying myself. This isn't quite to do with R.S.M. Burr, do you see. More of a side issue that's come up. Private matter between you and the Gascoynes. they'll explain all about it. Ah, there you are, Sir Charles."

The footman had assisted a lady and gentleman to alight from the carriage. The Major bowed to me again and said, "Your Highness, may I present Sir Charles and Lady Gascoyne." He turned to my visitors. "Sir Charles, my lady, may I present Her Highness the Maharani of Jahanapur."

I was startled and embarrassed, for he had presented them to me first, indicating that I was of higher rank. I had already begun to drop a curtsy when the lady did the same thing. quickly I reached out to take her hand, and feeling very flus-tered, said, "Please come in."

There was perhaps a minute of vague confusion during which I shook hands with both my visitors, ushered them in, thanked Major Elliot and said goodbye to him, then invited Sir Charles and his wife to be seated on the small but com-fortable couch I had bought secondhand in Cranwood.

Now I saw that Sir Charles was a man nearing sixty, or perhaps a little more, heavily built without being fat. His hair was thick and dark with gray streaks. His face was square and stern, the big jaw having little bumps at the hinge of the jawbone where the muscles knotted. There was something in him which made me think of a gray-muzzled snow leopard I had called a greeting to on the Magyari trail one day. Per-haps it was the hint of cool, stubborn pride in the deep blue eyes. His wife was a good ten years younger. She had dark eyes, black hair untinged by gray, and a thin high-bridged nose which gave her the look of an eagle. Yet in her eyes there lay some deep and long-enduring sorrow which had brought gentleness to her face.

I said nervously, "May I fetch you some tea, Lady Gascoyne? I'm afraid I shall have to leave you for a few minutes while I prepare it."

She did not answer at once. They were both staring at me intently. Then she gave a little start and said, "Oh. Thank you, but I would prefer not to take tea just at this moment, Your Highness."

"Oh, please. I'd much rather you didn't call me that. I was so embarrassed when Major Elliot introduced us."

Sir Charles took a large envelope from a pocket inside his morning coat, opened it, and stood up to hand me a photograph about the size of a postcard. "My wife addressed you by your proper title," he said. His voice was deep, rather throaty, and very decisive, the voice of a man accustomed to obedience.

I took the photograph wonderingly and looked at it. Two people stood against the background of a pool with a fountain, and a white clematis-hung wall beyond. The man was of medium height with a strong humorous face, wearing a uniform but hatless. Beside him, her arm linked through his, and wearing a sari, was . . . myself.

The room seemed to spin about me, and I braced myself, staring down, waiting for the dizziness to pass. When my vision cleared I studied the photograph for a full minute, then lifted my head. My face felt pinched and drawn. I said, "This is my father and my mother?"

"It is Colonel Francis Saxon and his wife, the Maharani of Jahanapur," said Sir Charles, "taken shortly after their wedding. This photograph appeared in *The Tatler* in May 1884. I think that if any vestige of doubt existed as to the veracity of R.S.M. Burr's letter, the likeness between you and your mother is the final proof. Forgive me, but you have become very pale, Your Highness, won't you please sit down?"

"Thank you, sir." The photograph still in my hand, I moved to the small armchair. "But . . . please do not address me by my title."

"As you wish," Sir Charles said gruffly. "How do you prefer to be addressed?"

"Almost everybody calls me Jani." With an effort I lifted my gaze from the photograph. "Are you from the Government, sir? Major Elliot said I would be hearing from one of the Ministries sooner or later."

Sir Charles sat down again. "This is an entirely private visit, though in fact I have been a diplomat all my life and retired from the service only a year ago. At this moment the advisers of the Secretary of State for Foreign Affairs are trying to decide what counsel they should give him regarding this remarkable matter which Major Elliot has sprung upon them. Since the War Office is involved, on behalf of the Army in India, and the India Office is involved on its own behalf, and since all Ministries are invariably at loggerheads, I suggest some time may pass before you are approached officially."

I shook my head. "I don't want to be approached at all about my being . . . who I am. I just want R.S.M. Burr's name to be cleared."

"That is in hand. Kearsey's got his teeth into it, and he's not the sort to let go. I talked with him myself the other day, and he gave me a piece of information which must be of interest to you. Chandra Ghose, the man responsible for the murder of your parents, was killed two years ago while hunting, clawed to death by a tiger which managed to reach his howdah."

I felt no satisfaction, only a vague sense of relief that I no longer needed to feel I must try to have the man brought to justice.

Sir Charles went on, "There was an immediate outbreak of civil strife in Jahanapur, but the British Army sent in a battalion to restore order. They also put into power there a man highly approved by the India Office. His name is Mohan Sudraka, a distant relative on your mother's side, who had to flee for his life during the reign of Chandra Ghose because he had fought against the many oppressive measures Ghose adopted. Sudraka is the present *de facto* ruler."

When I realized Sir Charles had finished what he had to tell me I said, "Thank you very much." I was not greatly interested in what had happened in Jahanapur. After a rather long and awkward silence, I said, "Forgive me, Sir Charles, but is there a particular reason why you have come to see me?"

He gazed round the little room, then looked at me from beneath black eyebrows. "A friend who is still in the Foreign Service passed on Elliot's story to me because he well knew that my wife and I would be deeply interested." He hesitated.

"Does our name, the name Gascoyne, mean anything to you?"

I shook my head slowly, perplexed. "I can't recall that it has any special meaning for me, sir."

His wife leaned forward. "Jani . . . do you possess a little pendant, a silver medallion inset with a gold star?"

I stared. "However did you—? But of course, Major Elliot will have told you." I slipped a finger under the collar of my dress and drew out the chain until the medallion came free. "This is what you mean—oh!"

The last word was a gasping cry of astonishment, for even as I held the medallion suspended from my finger a vivid flash of memory darted across my mind. "Gascoyne? Of course, *that* was his name! He only said it once, to Sembur, and I was very ill at the time. I never called him anything but Mister, but I remember now. Captain Gascoyne, I think he said, of . . . of a Gurkha Rifle Regiment?" As I spoke I felt the first true joy I had known since Eleanor's homecoming, a joy I could not have explained, and in the next instant it was wiped away, for Sir Charles said in a low voice, "Adam Gascoyne is our son . . . or was our son. We do not know what has become of him."

I stared stupidly, my hand to my lips. "Do you fear he is . . . that he may be dead?"

Sir Charles nodded. His wife closed her eyes, then braced herself and opened them again. "We are hoping," she said, "that you may be able to tell us something of him."

I held the medallion tightly in my hand, as I had held it when I was near death in the cave. "I? But Lady Gascoyne, it was six years ago!"

She said quietly, "It is more than eleven since I last saw my son, Jani."

I shook my head, shocked and perplexed. "How dreadful for you. But . . . why haven't you seen him?"

"We quarreled," Sir Charles said harshly. "Adam and I quarreled."

I stared in horror. "Do you mean you quarreled so bitterly that he went away and never came back? Oh, but that can't be so. Surely anyone who has the good fortune to be part of a family would never . . ." My voice trailed away as I realized that I was making a criticism of my visitor. "I beg your pardon."

Sir Charles gave a short laugh. "Families?" he said. "I fear

185

you are being a little ingenuous, child. Half the upper-class families in the country are in a state of civil war."

"Nonsense, Charles," his wife said calmly. "A few, perhaps, and more shame to them."

Sir Charles shrugged. "We are a belligerent race, my dear. It has made us rich and powerful, but it does not make for happy families. However"—he looked at me—"I wanted Adam to go into the Foreign Service, and he wouldn't have it. Ran away from school, went to sea for a few years, then got himself a commission in the Army and did very well, by all accounts. But he gave it up in . . . when was it, Mary? In June ninety-nine, that's right, four years ago. Bought himself out and went to South America, breeding horses there, I believe. Then he moved up to the Caribbean in oh-one, and that's the last we heard of him."

I felt dazed, and had taken in very little of what Sir Charles had just said. I unfastened the medallion, held it in my palm, and said, "But surely Mister—I mean your son—must have come home to England to see you during all those years!"

"Adam wrote to his mother from time to time," Sir Charles said gruffly. He looked suddenly tired. "But if and when he came to England, we saw nothing of him. I was able to keep track of him as long as he was in the Army, of course."

Lady Gascoyne put a hand over her husband's. "Charles," she said gently, "please do me a great service. Please go and walk in the garden or in the lane while I talk to Jani."

He nodded somberly and got to his feet. As I rose to open the door for him he paused and looked at me with a weary sadness. "You'll think badly of me, my dear," he said, "and you'll be right to do so. I'll say only one thing in extenuation of myself, which is that my foolish and stiff-necked pride has been equaled only by that of my son."

When I had closed the door behind him, Lady Gascoyne patted the couch beside her. "Come and sit with me, Jani."

I went to her and put the medallion in her hand. "You must have this. Do you know what the poem says?"

"Oh, yes." She gave a pale smile. "It was given to me when I was not much older than you, by the man I loved. We could not marry because he was not considered a suitable match for me. He went away, and I never saw him again. Fifteen years later he was killed in a skirmish on the North-West Frontier."

186

She fell silent, gazing distantly down at the medallion on her palm. I did not know what to say, and after a few seconds she went on. "I married Charles. As a diplomat's wife I have lived with him in several different countries. He has been a successful man, and I have learned to respect him, admire him . . . yes, and to love him, despite his faults." She raised her eyes and gave me a rather timid, wondering look. "I am telling you secrets I have never told anyone, Jani, I can't think why."

I said quickly, "I shall never repeat them, Lady Gascoyne, please trust me for that."

She made a little gesture. "There's no need to reassure me, my dear. We have some kind of rapport, you and I. I feel as if I have known you for a long time." She gave a smiling sigh. "I always longed for a daughter. Now I wish she could have been you. But Adam was an only child, for after he was born I was unable to have more."

"Your son is a very fine brave man," I said. "Has Major Elliot told you how he saved my life, and brought me back safely to India?"

"After a fashion, Jani. But another day I would like you to tell me everything, all the small unimportant details which matter little to the story, but which matter to me because Adam is my son."

"Yes, I'll gladly do that."

Again she fell silent, wrapped in her thoughts, then said abruptly, "They are not alike, Charles and Adam, but they have one thing in common, and that is pride. Foolish, unyielding pride. Charles demanded unquestioning obedience from Adam, who would not give it, and so the anger grew and the stubbornness grew . . . and between them they broke my heart, for when I tried to heal the quarrel, each thought I was taking the side of the other."

Her eyes swam, and my heart went out to her. I remembered the pride and arrogance I had seen in Mister. It had been there in the very way he sat his great black horse, Flint, and in the cold haughty eyes which had reminded me of a snow leopard. Now I knew that these were his father's eyes, and I remembered the thin nose and that fierce eagle-look in Mister which must have come from his mother, though her face had now been softened and made gentle by years of sorrow.

What had the Oracle said? *"He is born of the eagle and the snow leopard, yet is he feared by both . . ."*

187

As if to echo my thought, Lady Gascoyne said, "I sometimes wonder if we were not both a little . . . afraid of Adam. I mean, afraid of the fire in him, of that hard will to go his own way, never yielding, never bending." She closed her eyes for a moment. "Or perhaps I was afraid *for* him. Those who do not bend, life will surely break." She lifted her cupped hand and looked at the medallion. "I gave this to him the day he came to me and told me he was going away. I am sure you have discovered what the poem says, Jani. *'Here is a token to remind you of a friend . . .'* I prayed that he would always feel I was his friend, but I fear it was not to be. He said he realized that he and his father made me constantly unhappy, and so he was going away."

Her mouth twisted and she brushed away a tear with the back of her hand. "Oh, Jani, these men hurt us so. It isn't that they don't care, it's because they simply don't know."

I took her hand and held it, trying to think what to say and feeling very inadequate. "But he wore your keepsake," I said at last. "And there is great kindness in him. He was truly gentle with me when I was very ill, Lady Gascoyne."

"Then you must have exerted a good influence on him," she said with a shaky laugh. "No doubt I'm a foolish woman to have expected my son to realize how desperately I would worry about him. Sons are not made that way, I fancy." She drew in a deep breath and made an effort to compose herself. "I'm sorry, my dear, I must be causing you great embarrassment."

"No, please don't feel that. I do sympathize, and I wish I could help, but I don't know how."

"I'm clutching at straws, Jani. Let me explain. When Adam went away, Charles declared that he would never permit him to return to us, and until a few months ago my husband remained as adamant as ever. This is a situation I have known and accepted for ten years. I also knew, from Adam's very occasional letters, that he would never attempt to return unless invited to do so by his father. It was hard for me to bear, but supportable as long as I heard from Adam, or of him, from time to time, just to know that he was alive. But it is three years since I heard, Jani. Three years."

I said, "Lady Gascoyne, I'm so sorry. I feel very anxious and troubled myself, to think something may have happened to him, but I know it must be a hundred times worse for you.

Is it because of the long silence that your husband has . . . well, become more concerned?"

She put a hand to her throat and swallowed with an effort. "No, dear. It is because a few weeks ago he was informed by his doctor, a Harley Street specialist, that he has a diabetic condition which will prove fatal within the next two years."

I felt myself jump with shock. "Oh. Oh dear, I don't know what to say, Lady Gascoyne. I'm sorry, so very sorry."

"Thank you, Jani. I think, with death so close, Charles realized how much had been wasted in his life, and in mine, because of a needless quarrel and foolish pride. Adam is not only my son, remember, he is Charles's son, too. My husband has always hidden his feelings well, but I am sure he must often have felt the emptiness I have felt, with our son gone."

I said, "And now he wants to find Adam? To ask him to come home?"

"Yes. So that I shall not be . . . quite alone when the time comes. But for his own sake, too. He wants to make his peace with Adam. When we heard of you, Jani, when we heard your story, Charles felt that during those long days of travel, through lonely mountains and passes, Adam might have talked to you as he would not have talked to another adult. He might have voiced his thoughts and plans for the future, feeling that what he said would mean nothing to you anyway."

I shook my head slowly. "No. "I'm afraid he didn't tell me anything about himself. I once asked him about the medallion, and he said it had been given to him by a lady. I didn't know he meant you, his mother. But that was all."

"I'm glad he wore it," she said softly. "It must have meant something to him. We have had inquiry agents at work both in the Caribbean and in America, trying to find somebody who knew him there, or did business with him there, who might be able to say what he planned to do next, where he planned to go, but there has been no result. He just seemed to . . . disappear."

She took a small handkerchief from her pocket and dabbed her eyes. "As told you, I'm clutching at straws, Jani. Will you do something for me?"

"Anything I can, Lady Gascoyne."

"Please spend a little time today thinking back, remembering your journey with Adam, then allow me to come to see you again tomorrow. Perhaps we could walk in the woods together, while you tell me every tiny thing you can remember. And perhaps"—her voice faltered—"perhaps there will be something to help our search. I have the strangest feeling, Jani, a feeling that in some way you are still linked with my Adam. It's just foolish hope, I expect, but I shall cling to it."

She stood up, and I rose with her. "Poor Charles," she said, and sighed. "But he is so different now, so patient. I suppose we are all the same, we human beings. We always learn too late."

Sir Charles stood by the low hedge at the side of my garden, hat in hand, idly watching the bees moving busily around the pyramid-shaped hive of straw which stood just on the other side of the hedge. He half turned as we approached, gave a rather sleepy smile and said, "You know, I remember my grandmother used to follow the old custom of telling the bees. Have you ever heard of it, Mary? Or you, Jani?"

When we both said we had not, he went on: "It's simply that you're supposed to get a fine yield of honey from them if you keep them fully informed of all your household affairs. Oh yes, and you must carry a key, I forget why. I remember my grandmother standing with the key, muttering away over the hive, telling them all the family news." He rubbed his eyes with a finger and thumb. "Well, I imagine my wife has been telling you, Jani, instead of telling the bees." He gave me one of those hard looks which reminded me of Mister. "Everything?"

I met his gaze, and said, "Everything, sir." I did not add another word, for suddenly I understood something of his nature, and I knew he did not want me to utter words of sympathy or of worthless hope.

He eyed me in silence for several seconds, then gave a quick warm smile and said, "Good girl. Well, what's the outcome?"

"Just that Lady Gascoyne is calling to see me tomorrow, and I shall tell her everything I can remember."

"I see. H'mm. Yes, I'd be somewhat in the way, I fancy. More of a female occasion. But I'd be more than pleased to see you again and have a chat, young lady. We go home by the evening train tomorrow. Will you come and visit us in London? Stay for a few days?"

I looked at Lady Gascoyne, who said, "Please, Jani."

Sir Charles smiled ruefully. "When I retired from the service we discovered that as a diplomat I had made hundreds of acquaintances but few friends, and we are sometimes rather lonely now."

I said, "Thank you, I should like to see something of London. The only part I know is the road between the Adelaide Crocker Home for Orphan Girls and Southwark Park."

He laughed. "I'm sure we can find more pleasant vistas to show you."

"May I write to you in two or three weeks, when I'm more settled?" I asked.

"Of course. Mary will give you our address when she calls tomorrow."

I felt sudden pleasure, and in it there was a sense of relief. I had taken to Sir Charles and Lady Gascoyne, and was at ease with them now, but beyond that I felt I would be glad to get away from Larkfield for a little while, away from the shadow of Merlin's Keep. I had not heard from Eleanor since leaving, but this did not surprise me. Mrs. Burke, who had called to see me once or twice, could only tell me sorrowfully that nothing had changed at Merlin's Keep, except that it had become ever quieter and more tomb-like than ever.

If I went to London, I would certainly come back. I was forewarned against Vernon Quayle now, since he had tried to put me into a trance with the crystal bowl of ink, and I was able to contain my fear of him, perhaps because the pursuits he practiced were less strange to me than they would be to anyone who had not been brought up in a country where lamas and demons, magic and prophecy, were part of everyday life. Yes, I would come back, and perhaps I would try to see Eleanor, try to bring her back to life, try to fight the Silver Man for her soul. But it would be good to go right away for a little while first, to clear my mind.

Lady Gascoyne took my arm. We walked to the gate and out into the lane where the carriage was waiting just off the road. Sir Charles followed. As the coachman held the door open, Lady Gascoyne said, "Turn round for a moment, Jani." Wonderingly I turned my back. Her hands came over my head holding the medallion suspended on its chain, and then she was fastening the clasp at the back of my neck.

I said, "Oh please, no! You must keep it, Lady Gascoyne."

She turned me towards her, put her hands on my shoulders, and smiled. "I have already given it, for remembrance, as it was given to you by Adam, and as you will give it to a friend when the moment comes. Goodbye till tomorrow, my dear."

I watched the carriage go, holding the medallion, glad to be still wearing it, my mind whirling with a dozen different thoughts and feelings at the same time. Adam Gascoyne. So that was Mister's true name. Knowing it seemed to bring him nearer to me, and I was glad. But he had vanished. All trace of him had been lost for three years. He might well be—I made myself think the word—he might well be dead. But I could not imagine it and would not believe it.

For the rest of that day, as I went about my work, I thought about Mister, from the moment I first met him on the road to Yamun, through the pursuit up the Chak Pass, the blizzard, Sembur's death, my sickness, and the journey back to Galdong and then on down to Gorakhpur, to my last recollection of Mister, when he had lifted me barely conscious from the cart and carried me into the hospital. I wanted to remember as much as I could for Lady Gascoyne next day, and found it no effort, for the memories came flooding in, clear and vivid, bringing with them a blend of emotions which moved me deeply.

Before going to dinner in the farmhouse I put on my breeches and rode down to see David Hayward. I had Mr. Stafford's permission to borrow his dogcart at any time, or either of the two horses he used to draw it in tandem. David listened to my story without comment, then gave a nod of satisfaction. "It will do you good to get away for a while, Jani. I'll miss you, of course, but I'm sure you'll come back refreshed."

"I feel . . . well, a little guilty about leaving Eleanor. I mean, not being here if she suddenly needed me."

"Vernon Quayle rules in Merlin's Keep," David said grimly. "Eleanor won't suddenly need anybody." He looked away. "I've sometimes thought about wringing that swine's neck."

I was in full sympathy with such a notion. Sometimes I had thought about Vernon Quayle being thrown from his horse and breaking his neck, though I had managed not quite to wish it. But now I said angrily, "David, don't you dare even to think of such a thing! You can't go about wringing people's necks!"

He gave a half laugh. "Just Quayle's. It would be worth it to see Eleanor herself again."

"Stop it, David, please. They'd take you away and hang you."

"Don't worry. I'm not a violent man, Jani." He gave a bitter shrug. "I sometimes wish I were. What do you think a fellow like your Mister would do about Quayle?"

I said hastily, "If you keep talking nonsense, I shall go straight home."

"All right, I'm sorry. Come and chat to a terrier with a poisoned paw. He's mending, but he's very miserable, and I'm sure you can cheer him up."

I was restless that night, my head full of too many thoughts. In the morning I put on some old clothes and a smock and worked in the stables till I was tired, grooming the horses, cleaning out their feet, sniffing for any hint of thrush, and keeping an eye open for scurf. Mr. Stafford kept looking in, tut-tutting anxiously and saying that it "warn't proper work for a young lady."

Major Elliot's carriage brought Lady Gascoyne soon after three o'clock, and this time I made tea for us both. Then, for the next hour or more, I talked my way through all the memories I had so recently refreshed of those weeks with Mister. Even as I talked, more and more came back to me, and I found that often I could remember a whole conversation, almost word for word. To make a clearer picture, I sometimes reached back across the years for the Cockney accent and way of speech I had used in those days.

Lady Gascoyne listened like a child hearing a fairy story, lips parted, eyes aglow, drinking in every word. Sometimes she gave a laugh of delight, sometimes her eyes filled with tears, sometimes her face grew taut with anxiety. I did not soften any part of the picture for her. I told of the times when Mister had been arrogant, or brusque, or angry, and I told of the times when he had been kind, or friendly, or sympathetic.

When at last it was finished and I could say no more, she sat for a long time simply looking at me with a kind of joyous wonder. "Oh, thank you, Jani, thank you," she breathed. "You've made Adam come alive for me after all these years. I've read his letters a hundred times . . . but I have only a dozen, and they say so little. Today you helped me to see him."

I said, "It's hard to understand how he could have been so cruel, writing so seldom, for he can be wonderfully thoughtful."

She sighed. "It's a rare son who realizes just how much he means to the woman who bore him, Jani. Sons go off happily to war, or to climb mountains, or seek adventure in any number of ways, and never realize the unending pain of the woman who waits for news of them."

At half past four, when the carriage returned to take her back to Bournemouth, I said, "Please, Lady Gascoyne, do let me know if you have news of Adam. I pray it will be good news."

"Thank you, Jani. Somehow you have given me fresh hope. I so much look forward to your coming to stay with us in London."

During the week that followed I was unlike my usual self. Although impulsive, I had never been given to quick changes of mood but had always been something of an optimist, putting worries behind me and forgetting them. Now I found myself sometimes full of excitement, though I could not have said why, and sometimes low-spirited for reasons equally unknown to me. Above all I had a tremendously strong feeling that I should be doing something, that I was wasting time when there was something very urgent to be done, though I knew not what.

On the night of the tenth day after Sir Charles and Lady Gascoyne had gone back to London I dreamt I was riding slowly across a broad plain under a sky without moon or stars. I could see nothing but a silver ribbon on the horizon, a ribbon extended in jagged peaks across my view, for it marked the division between earth and sky by outlining the mountain range towards which I rode.

I could not see the ground beneath me, and I rode with eyes half closed, for I was listening. I was searching for Mister, and I was listening for his voice. As I rode on, I began to hear a sound, a whisper at first but growing gradually louder. It was a voice which droned the same meaningless syllables over and over again, but to my sorrow it was not Mister's voice. Yet it was a voice I knew, and struggled to recognize.

Then I began to hear the mantra-like chant in a slowly changing way: . . . *smanap-oten-tali* . . . *manap-oten-talis* . . . *napoten-talisma* . . . *apoten-talisman* . . . *a-potent-talisman* . . . *a potent talisman* . . .

Vernon Quayle's voice, mellow and beautiful.

I woke with a huge start and lay propped on an elbow, my heart thundering. What had he said? What had he said that day as I was leaving Merlin's Keep?

194

The medallion. He had actually flinched as he picked it up, then he had behaved very strangely, his manner reminding me of Rild, the High Lama. He had asked me questions, and then he had said, "A potent talisman." And something else. But what? When I begged his pardon he had replied, "I'm sure you will recall what I said when the times comes."

What, then? What?

I was sitting up in bed now, fists clenched and pressed to temples, a furious urgency rising within me. Then it came. *"A potent talisman. When you wish to find one who is lost, you may come to me with it."*

CHAPTER TWELVE

At dawn I was still awake, my mind in confusion. How could Vernon Quayle possibly find "one who is lost" for me, if that one was Mister? Only a credulous fool would believe such nonsense. Yet only a credulous fool would believe that the Oracle in Galdong could foresee the coming of the foreign demon in search of Sembur, or that Rild could tell me of the woman in red who would be my friend, and of the Silver Man who would be my enemy.

I had witnessed all these things, and more, during my life with the Lo-bas of Smon T'ang. They regarded such gifts or powers as entirely natural, as natural as we in England regarded a talent for painting or singing, or any similar art.

I had long ago decided that England was my country, and had long ago embraced her ways, customs, and attitudes, as imparted to me by Mr. Lambert and Eleanor. I looked on my earlier way of life in Smon T'ang as primitive, despite Sembur's unceasing efforts to keep us Hinglish. But I still knew, beyond all doubt, that among the Lo-bas and the people of Bod to the north, there were many who possessed abilities which had perhaps been lost or smothered in our more civilized world. It was only since the coming of Vernon Quayle that I had sometimes felt there might be a few, a very few, in our Western world who knew the old secrets, understood the old mysteries, and could wield powers we no longer believed in.

At four o'clock that afternoon, wearing my second-best dress and driving Mr. Stafford's borrowed dogcart, I returned to Merlin's Keep, handed one of my recently printed cards to Thorpe, the surly man who had replaced Mayes, and asked if Mr. and Mrs. Quayle were at home. The man returned

196

after less than a minute and showed me into the familiar drawing room. Vernon Quayle, white-faced, silver-haired, gray-eyed, loose-mouthed, rose to his feet and greeted me with a slight inclination of the head. "So you remembered," he said.

I had been determined to remain cool and possessed, but those first words startled me. "Were you expecting me, Mr. Quayle?"

He made a movement of his lips which I had learned to recognize as a smile. "In a general sense, yes. You have had a visit from the Gascoynes, and they seek a lost son, the man who brought you out of Smon T'ang. It was logical to suppose that this was the moment for you to remember what I had said."

I could feel my eyes growing bigger. "How did you know about Sir Charles and Lady Gascoyne?"

"There is no mystery. Major Elliot talks to Mrs. Elliot as they dine together. The servants at table gossip with servants of other households, and Thorpe conveys that gossip to me."

"Oh."

"You have come to ask me to find Adam Gascoyne?"

"Yes." My tone was as brusque as the single word was terse. Between Vernon Quayle and myself there was no call for formal politeness. I had not come to beg. He would do as he pleased, to suit himself, and my greatest doubt in coming here had been exactly that. *Why* might it suit Vernon Quayle to find Mister?

He said, "Very well, let us make the attempt. I have not yet looked into this matter deeply. It is always possible that Adam Gascoyne is dead, which can be quickly ascertained. If he lives, the problem becomes more complex, for the world is wide. However, perhaps we shall be fortunate. I am very much inclined to believe he is alive, since I have knowledge of matters to come which I am almost certain will involve his participation. We will go to the Round Room now, if you please."

I preceded him from the room and up to the floor above, my nerves taut, half my mind wondering where Eleanor was and if I should see her, the other half trying to decipher what Vernon Quayle had just said. When we reached the flight of stairs which led up to the Round Room he said, "Allow me," and went up before me to unlock the door.

The room was full of sunlight, so that the immediate impression was pleasant. It was only as the eye picked up the small disproportions in everything that the ugliness broke through and the room seemed to become cold. Vernon Quayle waved me to the chair where I had sat before, and moved to a long curving bench against one wall. On a shelf behind the bench were many small stoppered bottles in clear glass, drop-shaped, but each one slightly awry. Each was labeled in black paint with some kind of hieroglyph or character in a script unknown to me.

Vernon Quayle took down several bottles and unstoppered each in turn, taking out a tiny portion of the powdery contents with a pair of broad tweezers and dropping it in a mortar of black marble. When he had accumulated a pinch from each of ten bottles there could have been no more than enough to cover a shilling in the mortar. He began to grind the mixture to a still finer powder with a pestle, and the sound grated so horribly on my taut nerves that I had to speak to break the tension, and said the first thing to come into my mind.

"I am wondering what you have in those bottles, Mr. Quayle."

He said absently, "Preparations of essential elements from herbs, plants, insects, animals. Beautiful things. Valuable things. Things which have intrinsic potency or have acquired it in one way or another."

"Oh. They just look like powder."

"Powder. Ashes. The items of inanimate potency have been crushed or burned, destroyed in suitable fashion."

"Destroyed? But why?"

He stopped using the pestle and tipped the little pinch of grayish powder onto a small flat piece of glass. "There is no point in my answering your question," he said, "since you lack the knowledge you would need in order to understand."

"Pray excuse my ignorance. May I ask what you are going to do?"

He was washing his hands carefully in the small laboratory basin at the end of the bench, and now he glanced at me from those ashen eyes with heavy-lidded contempt. "I suggest you contain both your fears and your curiosity. Do you imagine I shall echo the claim which Shakespeare put in the mouth of Glendower, that I can 'summon spirits from the vasty deep'? Rubbish."

"I . . . I hadn't imagined anything, Mr. Quayle. But in your study of the natural sciences you explore unusual areas of knowledge, I believe."

"A discreet phrase, carefully rehearsed, perhaps?" He was holding his hands high over a small spirit stove to dry them, not using a towel. "Because you have a slender hope that I can assist you in a certain matter, you have no wish to call me crank, occultist, devil-worshipper, or whatever dramatic epithet happens to come to your mind."

He gazed musingly down at the almost invisible blue flame. "There will be no summoning of spirits, I assure you. Let me tell you something very simple. There are no spirits, no demons, no angels, no elementals, nothing in the whole universe which is supernatural. There are only energies and forces, neither good nor bad, which may be employed by those with the knowledge and craftsmanship to harness them. So-called supernatural powers are merely those which scientists cannot explain because they have no understanding of causation on any but the material level."

I had only the vaguest grasp of his meaning, yet I felt a chill run through me, for at this moment he seemed even more inhuman than some wicked man truly attempting to conjure up demons. He picked up the small plate of glass, sat down at his desk, put the glass down, and touched a finger to the little pinch of gray dust. As I watched, he dabbed the finger on his tongue, touched the dust again, sniffed some of it first at one nostril, then at the other, repeated the whole process several times, then tipped the few remaining grains into his palm and began to rub his hands slowly together.

I felt nausea touch my stomach, and the room seemed to grow darker, even though sunlight still streamed through the high windows. He put the glass plate aside, folded his hands on the desk, and said, "Eleanor will assist me now."

My nerves twitched and I repeated, "Eleanor?" Vernon Quayle did not answer, but sat gazing before him with blank eyes. There was a remoteness about him which made me think once again of Rild, when I had stood before him in the great monastery of Galdong, waiting . . .

I felt little surprise when the door of the Round Room opened and Eleanor came in. "Why, Jani, it's you," she said in a faraway voice, and a little hint of pleasure came into her eyes, to be followed almost at once by a look of troubled alarm. "Oh. Whey have you come?"

I rose, smiling, and started to move toward her to kiss her. She wore a dress of white linen with a pouched bodice, trimmed with strips of pale brown velvet. Above the collar her face was pallid, and her hair lackluster. Vernon Quayle's voice halted me. "No contact, if you please," he said sharply. "This matter will be hindered by any emotional disturbance. Take your seat, Jani. And, Eleanor, kindly occupy your usual chair."

I obeyed resentfully. Eleanor did not even show resignation as she took the largest of the three black-lacquered armchairs, her back to the western quadrant of the Round Room. For the first time I noticed that this chair was set upon a not quite circular platform, two inches above the floor, raised on casters so that the chair could be swiveled round.

Vernon Quayle moved to one of the cabinets, took out the tray, bowl, and flask of inky liquid. I twisted my fingers together to prevent my hands shaking, and watched as he poured the fluid into the crystal bowl and carried it to Eleanor. Without a word spoken, she took it between her hands and stared down at the inky surface. Vernon Quayle stood before her, hands in front of him, fingers interlocked, palms pressed together. Her breathing became slower, slower, and her eyelids fell, half closing. A few seconds later she gave a long sigh, and her eyes closed completely.

Vernon Quayle removed the bowl from her hands, which fell very slowly to her lap. "She will require the medallion now," he said, and I jumped to hear him speak in so normal a voice. I unfastened the clasp at the back of my neck, and hesitated. "Is it all right for me to move?" I whispered.

"Certainly." He did not take his eyes from Eleanor, but his voice was waspish. "You may move or speak unless I tell you otherwise. Eleanor is far beyond being disturbed."

I went to him and held out the medallion. He nodded downward and said, "Give it directly to her." I held it close to her limp hands, and he said, "Eleanor, you will take this medallion." Her hands lifted, she took both the silver disk and the chain in her cupped palms without groping, and her fingers closed. Vernon Quayle said, "This object was for a long time in the possession of, and in close contact with, a person I wish to find. Do you understand?"

"Yes." Her voice was flat, lifeless.

"You will need to go back six years or more to know this person."

There was a seemingly endless silence, then Eleanor said, "A man. Young. Dark. He wears uniform, and——"

Vernon Quayle interrupted her quite brusquely. "You have the man. This is he. Now give yourself to knowing him."

For a full five minutes no word was spoken. I saw

Eleanor's hands clutching, squeezing the medallion, saw perspiration gather on her brow and along her upper lip. At last Vernon Quayle said, "Now you must move forward to this day."

After another few minutes she said, "Yes."

"He lives?"

"Yes." She answered in the same dull voice but without hesitation.

In spite of the awed horror which lay upon me, I felt my heart lift at that single word. Vernon Quayle said, "Do you see him?"

A long pause, then, "No."

"Do you see his surroundings?"

"No."

"Why not?"

"There is a barrier."

"Material?"

"No. Dark. Potent."

"Rest."

Eleanor's taut body relaxed. Her husband turned and very carefully picked up a pair of white gloves, which he began to put on. "Most interesting," he said. "We have encountered an unexpected energy which resists Eleanor's penetration." He moved to a chart on the wall which seemed to show a night sky with various constellations of stars, then consulted a worn leather-bound book. "Be so good as to draw all four blinds, please," he said, "we must gather more strength, it seems."

I rose and moved round the room, pulling on the four cords which controlled the blinds of the high windows. When I had finished there was still some light in the room, a little from the spirit lamp which Vernon Quayle had moved onto a pedestal, and the rest from some luminous lines now showing on the tiled floor, forming a large circle with spokes radiating from the center to the circumference. The chair on which Eleanor sat moved easily as Vernon Quayle drew it to the center of the circle and then began to turn it an inch at a time, watching the luminous lines. There was a similar circle on the star chart, and I realized that this design on the floor was no more than a huge compass which he was using to position Eleanor precisely.

"Sit down," he said to me, "and kindly do not speak or move until I say you may."

As I obeyed he drew off the white gloves, seeming to take

care that his bare fingers did not touch the outside of them. He threw the gloves onto the desk, moved behind Eleanor, and placed the palms of his hands against her temples. In the eerie glow of the spirit lamp and the luminosity, I saw his eyes open wide, and those eyes were no longer dull but suddenly like two huge glowing embers.

His mellow voice said, "Now, Eleanor. We seek the man."

For what seemed an age there was no sound in the room. I could not even hear their breathing above my own. Then Eleanor said, "I have his surroundings."

Vernon Quayle said, "How close? How far?"

"I think . . . close."

"Does any sea lie between us?"

A long pause, then, "No. No sea."

"Describe."

"A river. A wide river. Much smoke. Much traffic. Cranes."

"A port." It was a statement rather than a question.

"Ye-e-es . . ." The word came slowly, doubtfully. "But I cannot find the sea. Not close."

"A river port, then."

"Yes."

"The man. Can you see him now?"

"No. There is darkness." her voice slowed. "But he is there . . . above the place underground . . . with the great casks . . . and in his hand is the tusk from which the warriors spring . . ." The last words were slurred, as if her strength had drained away and she were close to exhaustion.

Vernon Quayle said, "Go on."

"I have no more." It was a whisper.

"Go on."

Something gathered in the room, pulsing, demanding, intangible, and after a long silence she said quaveringly, in a voice filled with pain, "The river flows past . . . flows between the two towers . . . where the bridge is . . . and is not . . . the river flows down to the place . . . the place where the dead man lay . . . heavy with chains . . . for three tides . . ."

Her words ended in a sob of exhaustion, and she swayed in the chair. Vernon Quayle snatched his hands from her temples and caught her by the shoulders. His head turned toward me and he snapped, "The blinds." In the spectral blue-green glow I saw something gleam in his eyes, but whether it was triumph or frustration I could not tell.

By the time I had raised the blinds he was seated at his half-moon desk again. Eleanor sat slumped in the chair, but her eyes were open now. I ran to kneel beside her and began chafing her icy hands. She gave a weak smile and whispered, "I'm all right, Jani, don't worry."

"You're *not* all right!" I turned my head to glare at Vernon Quayle. "I didn't know you were going to use Eleanor as a . . . a medium."

He raised one silvery eyebrow. "If by that word you mean somebody who is a medium for communication between this world and another, you are talking nonsense. I have simply traced the etheric lines which connect that talisman with its erstwhile owner by making use of Eleanor's very substantial mental energies." He glanced down at his hands. "And of my own, which are somewhat more substantial."

Distressed and unnerved, I drew breath to say something angry, I scarcely knew what, when he continued. "I imagine that with a little diligence on your part you will find the results of the experiment adequate."

I stared, then said, "I beg your pardon?"

"We set out to discover the whereabouts of your friend, if you recall."

Eleanor pressed my hand and stood up. As I rose with her she closed my fingers about the medallion and chain, and said, "I shall go and rest for a little while now. Goodbye, Jani."

"Oh, please let me help you to your room, please, Eleanor dear."

She shook her head. "No. No, Jani. Goodbye." She turned and went slowly from the Round Room, closing the door behind her. Vernon Quayle said, "I am sure you will find you have sufficient material for your task."

With a great effort I dragged my thoughts from Eleanor and tried to remember what had been said during those eerie minutes when Vernon Quayle had sent some part of her being out into a world of shadows in search of a man she had never known. At last I said, "I'm afraid I don't remember her exact words, Mr. Quayle. She spoke of a river port, and some underground place with barrels. No, casks." I reached back in my mind, trying to recapture that lifeless voice. "There was something about the river flowing between two towers. That sounds like a suspension bridge. But then I thought she spoke of a bridge which is, and is not. It didn't seem to make sense."

He gazed through me with remote disdain. "Your friend is to be found in London. Probably the East End of London."

"*What?*" I was too startled to speak politely.

"It was established that no sea lay between your friend and us, therefore he is in this country. We require a bridge adjacent to a busy river port. Very well. A bridge which is sometimes there, and sometimes not there, can only be a swing bridge or a drawbridge. She spoke of a wide river. This eliminates the swing bridge, and at first seems to eliminate the drawbridge, until we remember the two towers. Indeed we have a drawbridge, or rather a pair of drawbridges, spanning the River Thames between two great towers. It is Tower Bridge, which must be close to wherever your friend is at this moment, or Eleanor would never have perceived it."

"Oh!" I felt my heart beat faster, as much with anxiety as with excitement. It almost frightened me to think that Mister could be so near. I had always thought of him in faraway places. And how could he be living in the same city as his parents yet be lost to them? I said, "What do you think she meant by the underground place with casks? And that he was holding the tusk from which the warriors spring?"

"I do not know what she meant, and neither does Eleanor. She is an instrument of perception, not of interpretation. She spoke of a place where the dead men lay, heavy with chains, for three tides. Note the past tense. You would be wise to remember this reference, together with the rest. It is probable that their significance will be come clear as you pursue your search, and they will act as signposts for you."

I stood feeling confused and inadequate. Vernon Quayle seemed confident that I would solve the riddles posed by Eleanor's words, but I did not share his confidence. For all I knew, the riddles might be quite meaningless, and have no answer.

At last I said, "Very well, Mr. Quayle. I will go to London, and seek Adam Gascoyne. You say that he is probably to be found in the East End, but surely that is where the very poorest people live?"

"Perhaps he has taken up missionary work," Vernon Quayle said dryly. "However, I do not propose to waste time in idle speculation." He rose to his feet, moved to the door and held it open for me. "I trust you have found this visit interesting. Allow me to show you out."

An hour later I was sitting in Mrs. Stafford's parlor with David Hayward. He had been awaiting my return there, for I had told him earlier that afternoon what I intended to do. When I finished my story he let out a long breath of perplexity.

"Lord, Jani, it sounds so . . . weird."

"Well, it would to you, but what it sounds like doesn't much matter. What I have to do now is discover if Mister really is there, in this place near Tower Bridge."

"But what place? It's all so vague."

"I suppose, a place with big casks underground, and . . . and all the rest."

"M'mmm. Sounds rather like the cellar of a tavern to me."

I started, and caught his hand. "David, how clever of you! Of course, a tavern would make sense."

He smiled. "It's only a guess, Jani, and I can't make much sense of the rest of it. Will you write to his parents?"

"No. That was my first thought, but I don't want to raise their hopes in case it all turns out to be mumbo-jumbo nonsense."

"But you don't think it is?"

"Well . . . no, I don't. I believe Vernon Quayle has powers that very few people would believe in, and I also think there's . . . some kind of pattern to be worked out. I wish I could remember things the Oracle said in Galdong, and things Rild said, but they only come back to me after they've happened."

David said quietly, "Be careful, Jani. You need a long spoon to sup with Quayle. Is Eleanor just the same as before?"

"I'm afraid so." I pressed my palms to my eyes. "That's why I hate him so. I think he's using her for his horrid practices, and draining the life from her. David, if I go away for a while to find Mister, please don't think I'm deserting her." I lowered my hands and looked at him. "I have such a strong feeling that all these happenings are part of the same thing. I think I *have* to find Mister if I'm to help Eleanor, but don't ask me to explain, because I can't."

He looked away from me and I saw his jaw tighten. "How can anyone help Eleanor?"

"I don't know, I just have to follow my instinct."

His head turned and he studied me again. "Yes," he said. "All right, I'll trust your instinct, Jani."

Two days later I arrived at Waterloo Station with a suitcase, and took a hansom cab to an address in Grays Inn

205

Road. This was a shop which sold tobacco and sweets, run by an ex-soldier and his wife, Mr. and Mrs. Bailey. Until the retirement of her ex-sergeant husband five years before, Mrs. Bailey had been a cook for thirty years at Laydon Hall, the Lincolnshire home of David's parents. He had known her from his childhood, was very fond of her, and wrote to her two or three times a year. She still sent him a homemade birthday cake and a Christmas pudding each year.

David had sent her a telegram followed by a letter, and she and her husband were expecting me when I arrived in the late afternoon. They lived over the shop, and a small spare room had been prepared for me, with the furniture polished till it shone, the linen crisp and snowy, and flowers in what was clearly a highly prized vase of red-and-green glass.

Mrs. Bailey was plump and motherly, and fussed over me as if I were a child of ten. Mr. Bailey, ex-Sergeant Bailey, had a forbidding air, but after the first five minutes in his company I could have hugged him, for his way of speaking and his mannerisms were so like Sembur's.

"Right then, Miss Jani. Got all your kit put away an'. everything shipshape, eh? Good. Then we'll 'ave a nice cup of tea I 'ope you left Master David in the best of 'ealth. My good lady's always certain he never gets enough to eat. Now you just sit yourself down nice an' comfy." With a courtly gesture he drew out a chair from the well-scrubbed kitchen table, held it for me to be seated, and lifted his voice. "Harriet! Come along, my dear. Miss Jani's down now. I'll see to closing the shop while you get the tea."

They were both kind, warm people, and as we sat round the fire in the parlor after supper that evening I told them something of my quest. David had suggested that as they were both London born and bred they might be of help to me. I could not tell them the whole truth about Vernon Quayle and Eleanor, and I did not want to lie, so with David's help I had prepared a simple version of the story.

I told Mr. Bailey and his wife that I was trying to find a friend from my childhood, and that a woman I knew well and trusted completely had had a strange dream about the man I sought. Then I simply recounted what Eleanor had said, but as if it were a dream. To my relief they both listened very seriously, Mr. Bailey in judicial silence, his wife giving an occasional gasp of "Oooh!" or "Well I never!"

"David and I think it must have been Tower Bridge she

saw in the dream," I ended, "and the underground place with great casks might be the cellar of a tavern."

Mrs. Bailey shook her head doubtfully. "The trouble is, they say as how dreams go by opposites, don't they?"

"Now don't talk silly, Harriet, my dear," Mr. Bailey said briskly. "You can't 'ave a hopposite of all Miss Jani's just been saying, can you? There's no such thing."

"That's all very well, Albert, but why did this lady see all these dead men and chains and tusks, eh? P'raps we ought to ask Mrs. Skinner to look in the tea leaves."

"We don't need Mrs. Skinner *or* 'er ten leaves, thank you, Harriet." Mr. Bailey rose with dignity, his thumbs in the pockets of his waistcoat. "If you will be so kind as to hexcuse me for a few minutes, Miss Jani?"

"Oh, of course, Mr. Bailey."

He marched from the room, and I heard his slippered feet flapping on the stairs. Mrs. Bailey leaned toward me and whispered, "Books. A terrible bookworm, he is, Miss Jani. Gets 'em second 'and from the stalls in Farringdon Street. Ever so educated is Albert."

Two minutes later Mr. Bailey reappeared carrying a large book bound in red cloth. As he joined us by the fire he proudly displayed the title. *"Illustrated London* it's called, see? I put my 'and on it right away." He sat down in his chair and opened the book. "Now, let's see if I remembered right. Ah, yes, 'ere we are."

He sat reading to himself, lips moving slightly, for two or three minutes while Mrs. Bailey and I sat waiting ever more impatiently for what he had to say. At last he looked up, a finger on the page. "Right, then. You can read it all for yourself, Miss Jani, but this is the interesting bit, about Judge Jeffreys, him they called the Hanging Judge." Mr. Bailey pointed vaguely across the room. "There was Execution Dock on the north bank, by Wapping Wall, see? That's where they used to 'ang pirates and suchlike. Well, this Judge Jeffreys, after he sentenced 'em, he'd go and sit in a tavern by the river, 'aving a bottle of wine while he watched the 'angings." Mr. Bailey referred to the book again. "And it says 'ere that after the bodies were cut down, they were weighed with 'eavy chains—*chains,* mind you!—and then left on the foreshore till they'd been covered by the tide three times. *Three,* Miss Jani!"

My heart was thumping, and for a moment I could not speak. Mr. Bailey ran his finger down the column, paused, then read slowly aloud: "There are several taverns on the riverside here, but tradition has it that the tavern where Judge Jeffreys took his . . . his deplorable pleasure was the Red Cow." He looked up, his face aglow with triumph, then passed the open book to me.

I felt hot and my face was tingling with excitement as I said, "Thank you with all my heart, Mr. Bailey. I didn't know where to begin, and now you've made it easy for me." I rested my hand on the book. "I want to read the whole article. Perhaps I'll find something to explain the tusks and warriors, but anyway I shall certainly visit the Red Cow, in Wapping, tomorrow morning."

Mrs. Bailey drew in a shocked breath. Her husband, tamping his pipe with a dark brown finger, nodded agreement and said, "Right. She can't go alone, Harriet. I mean, Wapping. Very low class, full of rogues."

I said quickly, "Oh, please don't worry, I'll take a cab right to the door, and anyway I'm not frightened. I was in an orphanage in Bermondsey, so I'm used to . . . to people like that."

"You'll go with her, Albert Bailey," Mrs. Bailey said firmly. "I could never face Master David if anything happened."

"Right, my dear. That's settled." Mr. Bailey glowered at me in the way Sembur had so often done when he anticipated an argument and was trying to prevent it by pretending to be very stern. I did not intend to argue, for I was a stranger in London and would be glad to have a Londoner with me, but I guessed Mr. Bailey would be pleased with a small victory just as Sembur had always been, so I said meekly, "Very well, Mr. Bailey." I did not let him win next morning, however, when I vowed that I would walk all the way to Wapping unless he allowed me to give him sufficient money for the cab fares before we started.

If I had not been so keyed up, I would have been fascinated by the cab journey, for all the way along Mr. Bailey kept pointing out whatever he felt might interest me. We clattered along Holborn and across the viaduct into Newgate, past the great dome of St. Paul's, and on through Cheapside and Poultry. Now the traffic was heavy, the pavements crowded with bustling people. Near the Bank of England we were held up for a while in a great cluster of cabs, carts, drays, and carriages, then our cabbie turned down toward the Monument. Less than ten minutes later I saw Tower Bridge, and the Tower of London itself, but I had little time to stare, for almost at once we plunged into another world, a place of narrow, grimy streets, smoke-blackened warehouses, and mean dwellings.

Stray dogs with rib cages showing through their skin foraged for scraps. Groups of children played in the rubbish-littered streets, games I had played at the orphanage, Fox and Chickens, Hopscotch, Eggy Peggy. In their tattered clothes, cut-down, remade, outgrown, they looked very much as I must have looked when I lived at the Adelaide Crocker Home, except that we had always kept ourselves clean. Men in leather aprons, in overalls, in worn corduroy trousers with braces, drove carts, pushed trolleys, carried sacks, came and went, or stood gossiping on corners. Women called to each other from doorways or windows across the street.

The cab drew many stares, and soon the cabbie was cursing and using his whip to keep the children from trying to hang on behind. At last he came to a halt and refused to go farther.

"Eh?" cried Mr. Bailey, outraged. "What? Stoppin' 'ere, you say?"

"I'm not just stopping, guv, I'm goin' back, that's what," the cabbie said firmly. "These little beggars'll 'ave my wheels orf, given 'alf a chance. They'll 'ave the legs orf me 'orse, I wouldn't wonder!"

Mr. Bailey was calling him a miserable little earwig and threatening to pull him off his box and teach him a lesson when I intervened. "Please, Mr. Bailey, let's just walk the rest of the way. Look, this street is called Wapping Wall, so we can't be far away."

Watched by a dozen curious children of both sexes, we alighted from the cab. Mr. Bailey paid the cabbie, told him to whistle for a tip, then offered me his arm with a flourish. In his other hand he was carrying a Malacca cane, which soon proved very useful, for we had an escort of children dancing along with us and around us, chanting and taunting, some of the girls mincing along in exaggerated fashion.

"Coo, look at Lady Sadie!"

"Where did you get that 'at, duckie?"

"La-di-dah-di-dah . . ."

Mr. Bailey caught one or two of the jeering, face-pulling boys across the legs with his cane, but could not bring himself to do the same to the girls, who promptly moved closer, skipping along beside us and growing bolder all the time. On any other occasion I would have enjoyed the incident and found it hard not to laugh, but today I could not bear the noise and distraction. The biggest girl must have been fourteen or fifteen, and was almost my own height. I waited till she pranced close to me, chanting some silly rhyme, then reached out suddenly and caught her by her ear with my finger and thumb.

She gave a yelp of pain, and we all stopped. There was a complete and astonished silence as I drew her toward me, thrust my head forward, glared at her threateningly, and reached back across the years for the voice of Jane Burr when she had been in the Adelaide Crocker Home. "Listen, duckie," I said shrilly, "if you want a thundering good clout round the ear'ole, you can 'ave one!"

I thrust her away from me, and with my arm still in Mr. Bailey's walked steadily on. Behind us the astonished silence continued. When I glanced sideways I saw that Mr. Bailey's eyebrows had almost vanished under his hat brim, and his mouth was open. "Oh, my word," he said. "Oh, my *word!* You're a card, you are, Miss Jani. A deep 'un." He began to chuckle. "Couldn't 'ave stopped 'em quicker with a Maxim gun! Oh, my word."

Two minutes later we came to a corner where a public house called the Red Cow stood. A fat man wearing a grubby apron was outside, using a hook to lift a stout wooden trap set in the cobbles against the wall. A thin youth with bare feet black as mud stood watching, holding a coil of heavy rope.

Mr. Bailey said briskly, " 'Scuse me," and continued as the fat man straightened up, "I'm acting on be'alf of this young lady. She's inquiring after a missing person, as you might say, and we 'ave reason to think this said person might be staying at this establishment or 'ereabouts."

The fat man said suspiciously. "You a rozzer?"

"No. Just lookin' for this bloke, that's all. On be'alf of the young lady."

"What's 'is name, then?"

Mr. Bailey looked at me. I said, "Adam Gascoyne. He's dark, with blue—"

"Never 'eard of 'im." The fat man grinned. "What's 'e done, then? Put you in the family way an' run orf?"

Mr. Bailey said softly, "Come round the corner, you dirty-mouthed skunk, and we'll see 'ow you look with no teeth."

I said sharply, "Stop it!" And at that moment the scrawny

210

youth went into a fit of coughing which ended with him leaning against the wall, gasping. For some reason we all stood waiting while he coughed, then, as I took Mr. Bailey's arm to draw him away, the youth said, "P'raps she means Molly's feller."

The fat man said, "P'raps," and bent to open the other flap of the trap.

The youth wiped his lips with the back of a hand and said to me, "Is 'e a toff, this bloke?"

I nodded. "About thirty, with dark hair."

"Ah, that's 'im. Took the back room at the Grapes, 'bout two years ago. On'y five minutes down the road." He pointed "Everyone calls 'im Buff."

"Buff?"

The fat man said irritably, "Come on, 'Arold," and the youth turned away.

"D'you reckon it's the one you want, Miss Jani?" Mr. Bailey said as we began to move on.

"I just don't know," I said helplessly. "Why would he call himself Buff? Or live in a place like this? And who can Molly be?"

"Sounded like what you might call a lady friend, Miss Jani, begging your pardon. Molly's feller, that young bloke said."

"Well, at least that's not strange, like all the rest."

"Ahem!" Mr. Bailey cleared his throat. "No, I suppose not, really, looking at it in a matter-of-fact sort of way, which is 'ighly unusual in young ladies. But then you're an 'ighly unusual young lady, if I may say so, Miss Jani."

The dingy tavern stood beside a slipway where a decrepit rowing boat lay on its side near a rusting iron ring set in a moss-green beam. A skin of litter and scum had gathered on the edge of the water where it lapped against the slipway. Mr. Bailey said, "You 'ang on a tick, Miss Jani." he pushed open the door, and I saw two or three men standing at an L-shaped counter. The floor was covered with sawdust.

I realized that Mr. Bailey did not want me to go in but was equally reluctant to leave me alone outside. He stood on the threshold, holding the door open, and called to a man in a dirty apron behind the counter. "You got a toff lodging 'ere, friend? Name of Buff, some kid said."

The man said without interest, "Might be, 'oo wants to know?"

"'Oo wants to know?" Mr. Bailey echoed indignantly. "It's 'is sister of course." He pointed a thumb toward me.

"That's different then, innit?" The man jerked his head sideways. "Along the path, round the back, up the stairs, first door on the right."

"Ta." Mr. Bailey stepped back and the door swung to. "I 'ope I didn't do wrong, saying you was 'is sister," he whispered, "but the sort of people you get round 'ere, they're suspicious of strangers, see? But they can understand if you're 'is sister."

"I think it was very clever of you, Mr. Bailey."

There was only just room for the two of us to walk along the narrow path between the side of the tavern and the railing. Halfway along, Mr. Bailey stopped suddenly, frowning, "'Scuse me asking, but d'you want me to come up with you, Miss Jani?"

"Oh, no, thank you." The answer was automatic. If I had found Mister, which I still could not believe, then I wanted to be alone when we came face to face. He would almost certainly not know me, and I had no idea what to expect from him when I told him who I was. Above all, I had a task to perform for his parents, and I was afraid he might be furious with me for my intervention.

Mr. Bailey rubbed the back of his neck with a harassed gesture. "It's not proper, miss, going to a gentleman's room alone."

"I can't help that, Mr. Bailey. Anyway, I'll be quite safe. this gentleman sick-nursed me through diphtheria, and we traveled hundreds of miles alone together, in the wilds, so you could scarcely call us strangers."

"Gawd 'elp!" said Mr. Bailey, and shook his head resignedly.

We moved on to the end of the path and turned left onto a broad terrace from which weed-covered stone steps ran down to the slipway. When we turned our backs to the river we faced a half-open door in the rear wall of the tavern, a door from which every scrap of paint had been peeled by weather. To our right, beyond the low crumbling wall where the terrace stopped, a large bay window of the tavern looked out upon the river. Above the window was a narrow balcony, and there a man in shirt sleeves sat at a small table, his back toward me, his hands busy with something on the table I could not see.

My heart gave a huge leaping thump of fearful delight,

and for long seconds my mind stood completely still. It did not matter that I could not see his face. I knew the way that black hair curled, knew the shape of the head and the set of it on the wide shoulders. When I lay sick in the cave, and later during our long journey south, I had watched him for hours, for days and weeks. And now, six years later, I could have picked Mister out in a crowd of a hundred, even going away from me.

CHAPTER THIRTEEN

I turned to Mr. Bailey and nodded wordlessly. He cocked an eye at the balcony, then looked at me with a smile and lifted one hand with fingers curled and his thumb sticking up. He glanced about him, moved to sit down on a small cask in one corner of the grimy terrace, and took out his pipe and tobacco pouch.

I drew in a deep breath, moved to the half-open door, pushed it wide, and began to climb the dingy staircase. It consisted of two short flights, the second turning to the right and rising to a narrow passage of bare floorboards and smoke-filmed walls. At the first door on the right I stopped, felt my hat to make sure it was on straight, clutched my handbag in a shaking hand, and tapped on the door.

His voice called; "Hello? Come in, come in whoever you are." He continued to speak as I opened the door and entered, but my mind was too full to hear what he said. The room was small, but in contrast to all else I had seen it was very clean. A faint smell of carbolic hung in the air. An iron bedstead stood in one corner. It sagged a little in the middle, and on it was spread a very faded pink counterpane.

There were two wooden chairs, a table, a washstand with a big china basin and jug, and a curtain across an alcove beside the chimney breast. The curtain was partly drawn, and I saw that the alcove was used as a wardrobe. One or two shirts, a jacket, topcoat, and trousers hung there, all of which had seen far better days. There was also a hanger with a well-patched blue cotton frock on it. That would be Molly's, I thought vaguely.

He sat framed in the window, the gray river beyond him, his left side toward me, his hands busy. On the table were

214

several small white objects. I moved forward, and saw that they were chessmen, rooks, knights, and bishops, but roughly shaped, as if in the process of being carved. Ivory. I remembered Eleanor's words . . . *"the tusk from which the warriors spring."* Mister was carving warriors of the chessboard. He held a king or queen in one hand, a steel tool in the other. He was turning the piece deftly, paring away tiny scraps of ivory, constantly running the ball of his thumb over the area he was carving. Then I began to hear what he was saying.

He spoke with a lilt of cheerful humor I had not heard in his voice before, never taking his eyes from the chess piece in his hand. " '. . . It is the voice of my beloved that knocketh, saying, Open to me, my sister, my love, my dove, my undefiled.' " The words were vaguely familiar, and then I placed them. They were from the Song of Solomon, a book in the Bible which Sembur had reluctantly allowed me to read only after I had pointed out that there surely could not be anything wrong in the Bible.

" '. . . Who is she that looketh forth as the morning, fair as the moon, clear as the sun, and terrible as an army with banners?' " Mister grinned down at his hands. "And are you over your bad temper yet, Molly? If so, then feel in the pocket of my jacket, and you'll find enough coppers to buy us a jug of ale and some pease pudding each."

I moved another pace forward, trying to speak, and as I did so his head turned and he looked at me, still smiling, his hands not ceasing to work. "Well, say something, girl, even if it's only 'To hell with you, Buff.' " His head tilted, and now his hands were still as he stared at me. "Molly? Is that you?" He put down the chess piece and tool, and stood up. "Molly?"

They came to me together, the understanding and the pain, and it was as if a spear had been driven through me. The deep blue eyes were looking not at me but past me, a little to one side, and there was no sight in them. Shock, grief, and horror welled up within me, bringing a huge burning ache to my chest and throat. I heard my handbag fall from my hand, felt my face twist, and clutched my hands together painfully hard, shaking my head as if to deny what I saw.

"Molly?" he said again.

At last words broke from my throat in a protesting cry. *"Oh, no! Not you, Mister, not you!"*

Slowly he pushed back his chair and moved a pace to stand in the window, facing me, head tilted back a little now, eyes half closed as if in puzzlement. I saw his lips shape the word "Mister . . . ?" slowly, thoughtfully. Then he said, "Nobody ever called me that except . . ." His blank eyes opened wide, and his face, paler than I remembered it, was suddenly alight with pleasure. He gave an incredulous laugh. "Jani! By all that's wonderful, little Jani Burr!"

He reached out both hands, and I ran to him without a moment's hesitation, throwing my arms round his neck, pressing my cheek against his chest. In the last days of our journey, when I was very weak, he had often held me in this way. His hands touched my waist, then I heard him laugh again, as if taken aback, and his arms moved up to embrace me. I was crying, struggling not to, my whole body shaking. I heard him say, "Lord, what a fool I am, Jani. I was expecting to scoop up the skinny little creature you were . . . how long ago? Six years now, surely. But you've grown up since then!"

I said in a muffled wail, "I'm making your shirt all wet."

"It's just an old shirt. That's the only kind I have." He laughed yet again. In these few moments I had heard him laugh more than in all the weeks I had spent with him before. One of his hands moved, lightly touching my arm and shoulder, my dress, my cheek, my hat, which was knocked askew now, and my hair. "Yes," he said, "you've grown up, Jani."

Reluctantly I stepped back, turned to pick up my handbag, found a handkerchief, and began to dry my eyes. He stood very quietly, listening as if following my movements. When I could speak without my voice shaking too much I said, "Oh, I'm so glad I've found you, Mister. I mean, Mr. Gascoyne. I'm sorry, I'm all confused, and I'm so dreadfully upset about . . . about your being blind."

"Sit down, Jani. No, don't move the chair, I have to know where everything is. There, that's fine. Whatever made you seek me out? And what's been happening to you all these years? What happened to that funny Cockney voice? And how on earth did you manage to find me?"

I put my hand to my head. "Oh, dear. There's so much to tell, and so much I want to hear. It's hard to know where to begin."

"I have any amount of time, Jani. Oh lord, what about your reputation? I keep forgetting you're no longer a child."

"I have a friend with me, down on the terrace, but it doesn't matter anyway?"

"Do you want him or her to come up?"

"No. We can talk more easily on our own."

He smiled. "You're different, but you still don't mince words."

"You're different, too. Not so . . ." I hesitated.

"Arrogant? Haughty? Conceited?" He grinned. "Yes, I think I've mellowed a little, maybe even improved."

"You were a very young man. I didn't realize at the time."

"I was frightened out of my wits, having a little girl on my hands." He chuckled. "I saw myself as a dashing soldier, not a nurse."

"You were so kind to me."

"I didn't dare be otherwise, in case you kicked me on the shin again."

"Oh, dear. I did apologize."

"So you did." He paused, then: "You called me by my name just now."

"Yes. You're Mr. Gascoyne. Mr. Adam Gascoyne, or do you use your military rank?"

"No I don't. Do you think you could call me Adam?"

"I'll try." I found myself smiling. "It might be a little difficult at first. I've been thinking of you as Mister for six years now."

His sightless eyes gazed past me for long seconds, then he said quietly, "I'm very flattered that you should have thought of me at all, Jani Burr." He stood up, picking up his chair. "Whatever you say, I don't intend to endanger your reputation, so we'll go out onto the balcony. Then I can carry on working while you tell me all about yourself, and we'll be chaperoned by the river traffic and your friend below. Come along."

I took off my hat and followed him onto the balcony. He moved with great certainty, placing the chair opposite his own so that we would face each other across the table. Before I sat down I said, "Until you knew who it was, you were saying something about pease pudding and ale. Are you hungry?"

"Well, there has been a slight hitch in the commissariat arrangements this morning."

"Molly went off in a temper?"

"Ah." He looked rueful. "Well, yes. I'd go out and get something for us, Jani, but I couldn't offer you a decent meal."

"Are you short of money?"

"Just until I've completed this chess set." He waved at the

217

ivory pieces. "Next week I shall be rich again. Two whole sovereigns old Cheng Wu down in Limehouse pays me."

"Well, I happen to be rich today, Mister. I mean, Adam." I leaned over the rusty balustrade and called softly, "Mr. Bailey."

Mr. Bailey snatched his pipe from his mouth and jumped to his feet. "Miss Jani?"

"Would you be very kind and try to find some food for us?" I asked him. "A cold chicken, perhaps, and some ham, cheese, bread. I leave it to you. Oh, and a jug of ale, please, and lemonade or ginger beer for me."

"Right, miss."

"And fetch enough for yourself, Mr. Bailey. I shall be here with Mr. Gascoyne for quite a long time. You have some money?"

"I've got 'eaps left out of what you gave me. Just leave it to me, Miss Jani." He marched off briskly.

Adam Gascoyne said, "That's an old soldier. Like Sembur."

I stared. "How did you know?"

He shrugged. "The voice. The manner. I've developed a quick ear, I suppose. Well . . . thank you kindly for your hospitality, Jani." He waited, listening while I sat down, then seated himself and picked up the chess piece and carving tool. "Lord, there's so much to talk about." His hands became busy. "You first, Jani. Right from the beginning."

Because he could not see me I was able to study him closely. His patched shirt, open at the neck, was freshly laundered, his worn boots were polished. His face was a little thinner, his hair a little longer. He looked older, though perhaps not six years older. I said, watching him, "Well . . . when I woke up in that hospital in Gorakhpur I found you'd left me your medallion." I put a hand on his forearm to stop him working, drew the medallion from under my dress, and pressed it against his fingers. "I've worn it ever since, and I can never thank you enough. It's been my talisman . . ."

Without haste, I began to tell my story. He went on working, stopping me with a question from time to time, listening intently, his face showing surprise, anger, concern, laughter, and a whole range of emotions as I unfolded my tale. I remembered how impassive he had been, and was glad.

After half an hour Mr. Bailey returned, bringing us a basket of cold foot, together with some cheap plates and cutlery. "Borrowed 'em," he explained. "Nice little shop up near the

Tower. Couple o' beer mugs 'ere." There was also a quart jug with a lid, a stone bottle of ginger beer, some fresh warm bread, a slab of butter, pepper and salt, and a jar of pickles.

I said, "Mr. Bailey, you're wonderful."

"My pleasure, miss." He stared fiercely at the ceiling to make it quite plain that he was not being inquisitive, and did not lower his eyes until I introduced him to Captain Gascoyne, when he sprang to attention, held his hat over his heart, gave a slight bow, and barked, "Sir! Sarn't Bailey, Third Tower Hamlets."

Adam said, "Have you secured your own rations, Sergeant? Miss Jani has been well-trained, and she won't sit down to eat until all men and horses under her command have been properly catered for."

"I 'ave the honor to report, sir, as 'ow I've secured me own rations and 'ope to partake of same on the terrace below."

"Very good, Sergeant."

"Sir!" Mr. Bailey took one pace back, made a smart about-turn, stamped his feet together, and strode out.

We took our food and drink onto the balcony, and as I set the cold meats out on plates, buttered slices of bread, and poured some ale for Adam, I continued my story. Below us the river lapped at the wall of the tavern. Beyond the far bank, amid a haze of smoke, rose the cranes of Surrey Docks, familiar to me because I had seen them so often from the Adelaide Crocker Home. Small craft and barges passed up and down, ruffling the gray water. From far and near, the river sounds carried to our ears as the sun moved slowly across the upthrust jibs of the distant cranes.

When I told of Sembur's letter, and read out my copy which I had brought with me, Adam Gascoyne put aside his work and made me read it all through for a second time.

"So that was the truth of it," he said quietly. "What a truly hideous business. But I'm very glad for Sembur, I always found it hard to believe his confession. I hope the story doesn't haunt you, Jani."

"No. I was terribly distressed at first, but I don't dwell on it now. It's all in the past."

"Good." He pondered for a few moments, then grinned suddenly. "Good Lord, to think I've bathed a Maharani and tucked her up in bed, without knowing it!"

We had long finished eating when I came to tell of my leaving Merlin's Keep for the cottage on Stafford's Farm, and there I left a gap in my story, saying nothing of Sir Charles and Lady Gascoyne, but going on to tell how I had followed up Vernon Quayle's claim that he could find "one who was lost" through the medallion I wore. I described the half-eerie, half-prosaic proceedings in the Round Room, and Vernon Quayle's deductions from the impressions Eleanor had received. I went on to tell how David Hayward had sent me to lodge with Mr. and Mrs. Bailey for a few days, as a base for my search, which had succeeded far more quickly than I had dared to hope.

"I've left out one piece of my story," I ended, "because I haven't explained what happened to make me go to a man like Vernon Quayle and ask to try to find you. But please let me keep that until you've told me your story, Adam. It's . . . something separate, really."

"All right, but first you have to make me a promise, Jani." His face was hard and serious. He had begun to carve a new chess piece, but now he put it down and reached across to find my hand. "You must have nothing more to do with this man Quayle. Ever. I don't have to tell you he's dangerous, more dangerous than that viper you dealt with in the New Forest. What did you say Rild call him . . . Eater of Souls? Rather dramatic, but not far wrong, I fancy. Quayle is a destroyed, Jani."

"Do you mean you know him?"

"No." He gave an impatient shake of his head. "But I've come across some strange things in my travels. So have you. Thank God you refused to look in that bowl of ink. He might have begun to get hold of you as he did your friend Eleanor. You simply mustn't go near him."

"I can't promise that. You see, there's Eleanor, and I have to go to her if ever she needs me."

"But you can't *do* anything for her, Jani." He was squeezing my hand hard now, as if by doing so he might in some way perceive the essence of me with his inward eye. "I'm afraid Eleanor is lost. Unless Quayle decides to let her go."

I shook my head stubbornly. "Anyone might have said there was nothing you could do for *me*, when I kept nearly choking to death in the cave. But you saved me, you didn't give up hope, and I won't give up hope for Eleanor. I owe her so much, Adam, so much."

He rubbed my knuckles gently with the ball of his thumb, in the same way that he felt the ivory as he was carving it. "All right, Jani," he said at last, very quietly. "I suppose you can't be other than the way you were made."

With relief that the argument was over, I said, "Well, that's settled, and now it's your turn."

"My story?" He laughed and picked up the ivory and the scraper. "It's very dull compared with yours. I hoped to stay in Gorakhpur till you'd recovered a little, but I was summoned to Calcutta, then sent back into Tibet, but to the east, up through Darjeeling. I had two engineers with me, and we were supposed to be carrying out a survey, but in fact we pushed up into Tibet for reconnaissance."

He turned the chess piece, feeling it carefully. "I should think there'll be an armed expedition moving north soon. The Government has been fidgeting with the idea for years now, afraid of Russian influence there." He began to scrape at the ivory again. "I spent a few months spying out the land, then came back to Calcutta, fell out with a Brigadier, was posted to Egypt, found myself in the invasion of the Sudan, got slightly wounded at Omdurman, was posted to Cairo, fell out with a Major General there, and decided to let the Army get on without me."

He frowned and held out a bishop. "Can you see a flaw there, Jani? A little blemish? I can feel something here, on the cope."

I looked closely. "Yes, but it's only a speck."

"Ah, they can use it for one of the black pieces, then. As a matter of no interest, this is ivory from a cow elephant, the best sort for carving, especially if it's from the east coast of Africa. Most people use a hand vise, but I seem to manage well enough without. Where was I, Jani?"

"You'd just left the Army."

"Well, let me see . . . then I went to Santa Fe, in Argentina, to breed horses. Bought a share in a stud farm, and after a year we were in a very promising position, my two South American partners and I. But then Ramón's sister conceived a passion for me, and when I didn't return it she accused me of dishonoring her." Adam threw back his head, laughing without restraint, and it was several seconds before he could continue. "It being Argentina, her brothers had to take it up, of course, whether they believed her or not, but I jumped a train for Buenos Aires and managed to out with a whole skin."

Chuckling, he put down the scraper and picked out a three-cornered file from a box at his elbow. "Then I wandered up through the Caribbean for a while, looking for something to do. In the end I settled in Haiti and started exporting mahogany and rosewood. There were all sorts of problems, but Haiti's a fascinating place and I was rather enjoying myself there." He shrugged. "Then I went blind."

He was leaning back a little now, as if glancing idly at the sky while he worked. I felt a heavy echo of the grief and shock I had known when I first realized he had no sight, and my voice was unsteady as I said, "How did it happen?"

"Lord know, Jani. There wasn't an accident. I picked up a fever and it laid me low for three or four days. When I came out of it, I was blind. I saw a French doctor in Cap Haitien and an American doctor in Port-au-Prince, then I came back to England and saw a specialist here. The American said he was baffled, because he couldn't find anything wrong. The Frenchman said positively it was due to pressure on the optic nerve from causes unknown. The Englishman said that was rubbish, and I had contracted a disease of the optic nerve from some foreign germ which had got into me. I saw three or four more doctors, but the only thing they agreed on was that they couldn't cure me."

He laughed again, and there was no hint of bitterness in it. "I must say, I liked the American best."

"How long have you been in England, Adam?"

"Oh, about eighteen months. After four or five I was running out of money, so I went to old Cheng Wu. He sells antiques and oriental objects of all kinds, the old villain. I'd often bought from him, and sometimes traded with him when I was a young seaman—that was long before we met, Jani. Anyway, he found lodgings for me here and said I could learn to carve ivory. It seems his grandfather had been blind, and he'd become a master at it. Well, I'm afraid I'll never be that, I can't do the fine filigree work yet, but I can make very reasonable chess sets which Cheng Wu sells to people who think they were carved in China."

Again he threw back his head and gave that wholehearted laugh which stirred a strange blend of happiness and sorrow in me.

He said, "I've been very lucky. After about a month here, Molly took me under her wing. She's an Irish girl who goes totting for old lumber with her own donkey and cart. She keeps this place clean, sees to my clothes, quarrels with me, and won't take a penny for her pains, even when I have any to spare."

"Does she live here with you?" I asked, remembering the

blue cotton frock that hung with his own clothes. "Will she be cross if she finds me here?"

"Truth to tell, I never quite know what Molly will be cross about." He began to use a slim round file very delicately. "She has a junk shop up near the Mint, with a room above it, but she stays here off and on. Two or three days in a week, usually. She's very generous, very good to me." He paused, and lifted an eyebrow. "You don't seem to have grown up into a young lady who's easily shocked, Jani."

"No, I suppose not. I grew up partly in Smon T'ang, where getting married was very casual, and partly in the Adelaide Crocker Home, with girls like Big Alice and Soppy Kate, who'd been on the streets." I hesitated, then took the plunge. "Adam, your mother and father want you to come home."

His hands became still, his face a mask, and after a moment he said slowly. "What do you know of my parents, Jani?"

"Somebody in the Foreign Office told your father about Sembur's letter, and he already knew through Army reports that you were the one sent to arrest Sembur. They came to see me at my cottage. Oh, Adam, I know you quarreled with your father all those years ago, but did you never think of all the pain and anxiety you've caused your mother?"

He put down the file and picked up the scraper. "This isn't your business, Jani."

I caught his hand and said hotly, "Oh, yes, it is! Stop scraping at that thing and listen to me, Adam Goscoyne! You saved my life and you gave me your medallion, your mother's gift to you, *for remembrance, as a friend*. So if you meant it, if we're really friends, then what you do *is* my business. You've been thoughtless and heartless, but what's past is past. You said you would never come home unless your father asked you to. Well, he's asking you to come home now." I still held his hand tightly. "Adam, he's dying. I don't mean he's on his deathbed, but he hasn't long to live. Please go home, if not for his sake, then for your mother's."

There was a long silence. His sightless eyes turned toward the river, his face without expression. At last his free hand moved to cover mine and he said thoughtfully, "I do wish I could see you."

My eyes filled suddenly. "Please, Adam. Will you do it?"

"I didn't mean to be cruel, Jani. I thought it best for my mother just to forget me. And when I lost my sight I felt it

223

was better for her to think me dead than to discover I was blind and useless."

"Oh, Adam, you're such a fool," I whispered, and bent to put my cheek on the hand that covered mine. "Don't you understand anything about a woman's heart? Did you really imagine she could forget her son? Or that she'd rather you were dead than blind?"

He did not speak for a while, then gave a long sigh. "First you soak my shirt front, now my cuff. I don't know what's happened to you, Jani Burr. Or Jani Saxon. Or Your Highness. In all the weeks we were together, and with all that you went through, I only ever heard you weep once."

I lifted my head, wiped my eyes again, gave a quavery laugh, and spoke a few halting words of apology. Adam Gascoyne did not know what had happened to me, but suddenly I knew very well. I was in love, and was beginning to suspect that I had been in love with Mister since long before David Hayward had jokingly suggested it. If I wept, it might be for happiness, sorrow, yearning, despair, jealousy, or all of these together.

We sat in silence for a time, and at least he said, "Very well, Jani. I'll come home if you'll come with me. I shall need you there, especially at first."

"Adam, I—I can't thrust myself on your parents like that."

"You won't be. I'm the one who's insisting, and if they really want me it's a very easy condition to meet. Lord knows, the house is big enough, and so is the staff. Besides, if they've met you I'm sure they'll be delighted to have you. I mean it, Jani, I shall really need you. They're both going to be strangers to me, and I won't know how to talk to them, but I feel comfortable and at ease with you, so you'll be a . . . a kind of catalyst. Do you feel at ease with me?"

"Yes. Yes, I do, Adam. But I must go to see your mother and father first, to warn them. I'll go this afternoon and tell them I've found you. I shall have to break it to them that you've lost your sight, but I'll do it as gently as I can, and I'll say you're coming home to them."

"Providing you come with me."

"Yes. I'll tell them. I hope that part is going to be all right. When will you come, Adam?"

He gave a wry grimace and seemed to brace himself. "Let's get it over with. Tomorrow morning? Will you call for me?"

"Yes."

I felt suddenly as if every ounce of strength had drained out of me, and knew I could have put my head on my arms and fallen asleep at the table. Adam said, "Are you tired, Jani?"

"M'mm." A great yawn seized me without warning. "I'm sorry."

He laughed and stood up. "I'm not surprised. Come along, I'll walk with you and Mr. Bailey to the Tower."

"Oh, but who'll see you back?"

"I don't need a guide, I walk miles on my own."

I moved into the room, carrying the baskets which had held our food. "I must wash up the crockery for Mr. Bailey to give back as we go."

"All right, there's some soda on the dresser."

It was quickly done, for the plates were barely greasy. I packed everything in the two small baskets, and moved to a cracked looking glass which hung near the bed, about to pin my hat on. Molly's looking glass, I realized with a pang; Adam had no use for it.

Even as the thought came, the door opened and a girl stepped into the room. I would have guessed her age to be twenty-two or twenty-three. She was a little taller than I, with a small waist swelling to a large bosom and broad shoulders. Her face was plain and red, her eyes beautiful. Her mousy hair was gathered in a bun at the back of her head, beneath a tilted-forward hat with some rather battered imitation grapes and cheeries on the brim. The dress she wore was a patchy maroon and had clearly been dyed. The white lace on the bodice collar, and sleeves was freshly laundered and ironed.

Adam, leaning against the wall by the window, said, "Ah, you've forgiven me, Molly. When I can smell the lavender water on you I know I'm forgiven. Jani, I present Molly. Molly . . . Jani."

She pushed the door to behind her and stood looking at me, hands on hips, thumbs to the front, her wide-spaced eyes sharp and suspicious at first, then gradually softening to a kind of rueful regret.

"Sister, is it?" she said with a toss of her head. "If it's his sister y'are, then I'm the Pope hisself." She tilted her head back, studying me. "So you're the one, then."

Adam said, "None of your Irish riddles, Molly me dear. She's what one?"

Molly gave him a glance of pitying contempt. "It's as well you have the education, Buff, for you're stupid as any man."

225

She moved to stand in front of me. "Have you come to take him away, then?"

I said, "He's going home to his family. His father is dying."

She shrugged. "Well, there's an end of it, an' who cares?"

I said, "Somebody does, Molly. Somebody has given him a great deal of care."

Tears shone in her eyes and she rubbed them angrily away. "I've had him a year an' more, an' there's none to take that from me. But I'm glad for him to go back to his own now. When will you be taking him?"

"I'll come tomorrow morning, about ten o'clock."

"Then I'll have him ready an' neat, with his bits and pieces all darned an' clean."

"Thank you, Molly."

Adam said stiffly, "I'd be glad if you'd both stop talking of me as if I weren't here."

Molly laughed, and moved toward him till she stood very close, looking up at him. "You know what, Buff? Wait'll I tell you now. I'll marry Sid, like he's always askin' and like you're always tellin' me." She put up her arms and clasped her hands at the back of his neck. "But you'll be the one, Buff, you'll be the one, damn you."

She stretched up, pulled his head down, kissed him hard on the lips, then swung round and went out of the room with her head in the air. Adam ran long fingers through his thick black hair. I turned back to the looking glass and put my hat on, thinking about Molly, thinking that I might have been living much the same life, totting with a donkey and cart, if I had not had the good fortune, some six years ago in the New Forest, to meet Mr. Graham Lambert of Merlin's Keep.

Adam was putting on a threadbare jacket. He buttoned it, moved to the door, and held it open for me. A question I had thought of several times, but had not yet asked, came again to my mind, and I said, "Adam, why do they call you Buff?"

He thought for a moment, then gave a little laugh. "Do you know, I'd almost forgotten. But it was the children, of course. They dubbed me after that game they play, Blind Man's Buff."

Three hours later, in the lovely drawing room of a house which looked out over Regent's Park, a white-faced Lady

Gascoyne said. "But may I not go to him, Jani? May I not go to him now, and bring him home?"

Emotion had emptied me, and in my weariness I had to grope for words as I said, "Please don't, Lady Gascoyne. It isn't going to be easy for him, and I'm sure it's best for him to come here in his own way."

Standing by a window, staring out over the park, Sir Charles said, "Pay heed to the child, Mary. She found him, she has talked with him. She knows best."

"But, Charles . . . *blind!* And living in such an awful place."

"An hour ago you would have thanked God that Jani found him alive, in whatever condition. Pull yourself together, my dear."

"Yes. I'm sorry, Jani. I must seem so ungrateful."

"No, no, Lady Gascoyne. I know what a shock it all is, both the good and the bad." I looked across at Sir Charles for support, and went on, "Please don't think me impertinent, but if you wish Adam to settle here happily, I think you should make as little fuss of him as possible. He won't want . . . well, he won't want a lot of sympathy or . . . emotion."

Sir Charles moved away from the window and came to where I sat beside his wife on a deep-buttoned sofa. "Understood," he said gruffly. "Mary's a diplomat's wife, and she'll school herself to the necessary restraint, I promise you." He looked at me anxiously. "And we can count on you coming to stay here indefinitely?"

I put my fingertips to my brow, trying to rub a nagging headache away. "Well, for a little while, Sir Charles, if you'll have me. I can't really say for how long."

"Of course, of course, we must not exact promises from you. But for the moment, may I suggest that I send you and the very patient Mr. Bailey back to Grays Inn Road in my carriage? Will you return tonight with your luggage? We shall have a room ready for you within the next hour. Or shall I send the carriage for you tomorrow morning?"

I said, "Tomorrow, please. I only have a suitcase at Mr. Bailey's. Then in a day or two I must go down to Larkfield on the train and pack some more of my clothes to be brought up here."

His wife said anxiously, "Jani must be our full responsibility, Charles. I shall open accounts for her with Harrods and my dressmaker, so that she can set herself up with a wardrobe here in London."

"Of course, Mary."

I did not want to be under such an obligation, but decided to postpone any argument. I was too tired for it at this moment. I said, "Will you send the carriage in good time, please, Sir Charles? About nine o'clock? I have promised to be Wapping by ten, and could not bear to be late."

CHAPTER FOURTEEN

It was on an unseasonably gray day in September that I brought Adam Gascoyne home to the family house in Chester Gardens, and took up residence there myself.

The first week was a nightmare for everybody. We all struggled to be completely natural, and only succeeded in being stilted, awkward, and forced. It was nobody's fault. A gulf of many years lay between Adam and his parents. He had gone away from them as a boy and returned as a man nearing thirty, who had no interest in relating his adventures, or in anything of the past.

When first greeting his father he had offered his hand and said quietly, "Shall we agree to forget the past, Father?"

Sir Charles had said, "I should be truly grateful if you would do so, Adam."

When his mother was fighting back tears that came partly from joy and partly from the shock of seeing the neat but pitiful clothes, the unresponsive eyes, he said, "Jani has told me I've been very cruel, Mother. I am sorry."

It was as good a beginning as I could have wished for, but then it suddenly seemed there was nothing more to say, perhaps because there was too much to say. After the first two days I feared the ordeal might be too heavy for Adam, and made him promise me that he would not quietly leave one night and vanish into London's sprawling populace. The reluctance with which he promised showed that the notion had already entered his mind.

The fourth day, to Adam's evident relief, he and I spent alone together, for we took the train to Bournemouth and then a cab to Larkfield, so that I could fetch a trunk of clothes and personal belongings from Withy Cottage. His new suit was ready-made, for those he had been measured for were not yet finished, but I was able to tell him truthfully that he looked most elegant and handsome, which made him laugh.

I was enormously thankful that what might have been the most dangerous problem had already disappeared. I had dreaded that Adam's pride would not permit him to live on his parents' bounty for very long, but this did not arise. On the morning after his arrival at Chester Gardens I was summoned by Sir Charles to read out and confirm to Adam a portion of the will of Adam's maternal grandfather, who had died fifteen years before. A rich man, he had left a third of his fortune to Adam, in trust until he attained his twenty-fifth birthday, which was now already past, so in fact Adam was of independent means.

On the day of our visit to Larkfield I had hoped to see David Hayward and introduce him to Adam, but as luck would have it David had set off for Southampton early that morning to supervise the unloading and transport of a racehorse which had been brought over from France by a breeder in Bishops Tenby. Mr. and Mrs. Stafford gave us a splendid luncheon in the farmhouse, during which they brought me up to date with Larkfield gossip and overpraised me embarrassingly to Adam.

"You oughter see Miss Jani wi' animals, sir," Mr. Stafford said, wagging his head as if mystified. Then, with a look of horror as he realized he had told a blind man what he ought to see, "Oh, my goo'ness, I didn't mean—I 'ope you'll pardon me, sir . . ."

Adam laughter, completely unruffled. "That's all right, Mr. Stafford. As a matter of fact. I've seen and heard Jani quite a lot with animals. We had a yak she used to hold long conversations with."

"A yak? Now what might that be, I wonder?"

"It's a sort of Indian ox, covered with long hair."

"Ah! Now, did she talk to it in foreign?"

"Indeed she did. And I'll swear the yak understood every word."

"Then what would you say, sir, if I told you as 'ow Miss Jani talks to our own proper English animals in foreign, an' *they* understand? Now, 'ow d'you rackon that, sir?"

Adam shook his head solemnly. "It's beyond me, Mr. Stafford. I suppose she must just be a very clever young lady."
230

"Ooooh, she's that all right, sir. I mind the time when she come along to 'elp Mr. 'Ayward wi' owd Mabel . . ."

Before we left to catch the London train I asked after Eleanor, but there was no fresh news of her. "Not at 'ome to anyone nowadays, Miss Eleanor isn't," said Mrs. Stafford, "not even when the vicar's wife called to see 'er."

Next day I wrote to Eleanor, saying I had found Mister and that he was reunited with his family. I should have written to Vernon Quayle, since it was he who had really enabled me to find my friend from the past, but I could not bring myself to do so, and in any event I was bitterly sure that he would see any letter Eleanor received. I also wrote to Major Elliot, telling him that I had been able to help Sir Charles and Lady Gascoyne to find their lost son, and that I was now staying with them at their London home for a time.

My letter to David Hayward was longer and more detailed. I ended it by saying I felt guilty at being so far from Eleanor, but that Adam needed my help to settle down with his mother and father. This was not the whole truth, for I did not say I had fallen in love with Adam and never wanted to be away from him; or that when his hand rested on my arm for guidance as we walked together, I felt my heart swell with a great longing to have him take me in his arms, and hold me close, and kiss me till I was breathless. It was a beautiful feeling, like suddenly becoming molten inside.

David replied promptly, saying that there was nothing I could do for Eleanor and I must stop feeling guilty. He was sorry to have missed our short visit to Larkfield, but hoped we would come down again soon.

At the end of the first ten days at Chester Gardens everything was a little better and we were all more natural in our behavior. I realized that time was the only answer to our problem. If Adam was to settle down happily here, then we all needed to build up a background of day-to-day experience, trivial though it might be, which was common to us all and would provide a source of conversation as well as giving us a sense of belonging to one another.

When Adam and I were alone together he was always at ease and seemed happy to talk about the past, to remember the weeks we had shared, to have me tell him about my life in Smon T'ang, and to argue with me on any subject under the sun. I sometimes felt he was arguing against his true feeling on a subject, simply to make me think hard and bring forward an opinion of my own.

231

It was embarrassing to realize that he was more at home with me than with his parents, but they showed no resentment, and in fact anxiously sought my advice as to how they should act in this matter or that, in order to please Adam. Like a fool, I was greatly flattered by this until it dawned upon me that I was not really helping the situation by playing Little Miss Know-all, and that I ought to be pushing Adam and his parents closer together instead of acting as a go-between.

Soon I had arranged for Sir Charles to accompany us when we went riding in the park for an hour every morning. During that time I contrived to let him be responsible for guiding Adam, and I was tremendously glad when I say that not only were they beginning to chat more easily together as they rode side by side, but also they were content to jog along in silence from time to time, without feeling bound to make idle conversation.

I was not very good at thinking of ideas, and I lay awake for half one night seeking something interesting in which Lady Gascoyne could join us. At last, with many qualms, I suggested to Adam that he should take up his ivory carving again, simply for the pleasure of using his hands to make something beautiful. He seized upon the notion with delight, but was startled when he discovered that I had invited his mother to come down to Limehouse with us, to see the oriental shop of Cheng Wu and perhaps one of the beautiful chess sets her son had made.

Adam spent the whole coach journey there in trying to prepare his mother for the sights and smells of Limehouse, for the mockery and mimicry we might suffer, and for the squalor of Cheng Wu's shop, though not its contents. In his concern, Adam took her hand and held it as we rattled along Commercial Road and past Regent's Canal Dock. Lady Gascoyne responded by looking as happy and excited as I had ever seen her.

Cheng Wu was an old man with a wispy beard who showed not the slightest hint of surprise when Adam escorted two very well-dressed ladies into his cluttered shop and introduced them. To Lady Gascoyne this was another world, and she stood gazing about her, stupefied, giving a little shake of her head and an unbelieving laugh every now and then, as if she felt she might be dreaming.

I knew that the Chinaman came from Chungking, for Adam had told me so, and when he bowed to me I spoke a few of the words I had learned when bargaining with the yellow men in Magyari, guessing that this would be the form of Chinese he spoke. Even he could not restrain a glance of surprise at this, and he answered politely in the same tongue, asking me how I came to know it.

I explained that I had traveled in the land of Bod, but then went on in English, saying that I must not delay his business with Mr. Gascoyne. When Adam began to talk I drew his mother aside and pointed out two or three ivory chess sets of the kind I had seen Adam carving. There was much to catch the eye in Cheng Wu's shop, colored lanterns, paper dragons, joss sticks, brass idols, ivory carved in filigree, big colored stones in rings and bangles, kites, hand-painted china, nests of colored boxes, carved jade, and brightly colored fireworks.

Suddenly I heard Cheng Wu say in his singsong voice, "So you will buy the ivory, Mr. Buff?"

Adam said, "Yes, all right. But if I make a chess set for you, you ought to cough up something for it, you miserable old devil, whether I need the money or not."

"Ah, Mr. Buff, Mr. Buff, how can you speak so, after all my kindness to you when the goddess of fortune turned her head from you? Come. I will pay you a whole sovereign."

Adam had drawn breath to agree when I said sharply, "Wait, Adam!"

I moved to face Cheng Wu, and it was as if I had moved back seven years in time, and was facing one of the yellow men across a stall in Magyari. I smiled into his eyes and said apologetically, "Let us talk a little first, honored sir."

For a moment I glimpsed wariness combined with a kind of pleasurable anticipation in his eyes, then he smiled back, and said in Chinese, "Let us speak in my tongue, most charming lady, for it is the best tongue for bargaining."

"Would you put a poor and inexperienced female child at such disadvantage?" I asked in English, shaking my head. "But if you wish, we may talk in the tongue of Bod."

"Forgive this unworthy person for being unfamiliar with that most excellent tongue."

"Then it must be English, honored sir, and I have small hope that my poor eloquence can secure a fair price for our friend, Mr. Buff, since you are a man of great business talent, and infinite persuasion. Therefore I must trust to your kindness and generosity."

"My heart grows heavy with fear, dear young lady, for I

233

recognize one who will outwit this dull and untutored person at every turn."

It took us five minutes to come to the subject of Adam's payment, and another ten minutes of polite bargaining before we both knew that we had arrived at the final meeting point, when we both dolefully acknowledged defeat at the hands of the other. For me, it was just like the old days of trading in Magyari, and I enjoyed it immensely. Though we spoke in English, we used the forms and structure of the tongues in which each of us had learned the art of the marketplace, so that our words and phrases were most flowery and ornate. Throughout the whole time Adam and his mother uttered not a single word, but stood with arms linked listening to us.

At the end Cheng Wu said, "So we have agreement, dear young lady, and I must take a heavy loss. Mr. Buff to be supplied with the ivory at my expense, as before, and the fee for each complete set to be four pounds and eight shillings, the rough ivory to be collected by Mr. Buff or his representative from this shop, and all offcuts to be returned."

"Each party to pay the cab fare one way," I amended.

He rolled his eyes up to the ceiling, shrugged, nodded, bowed and turned away, saying, "I will fetch ivory for two sets now."

As he vanished into a back room I looked at Lady Gascoyne. "I'm sorry," I whispered, "I ought to have done much better, but he knew from the start that Adam would settle for almost nothing."

She nodded, lips compressed, but said nothing. Adam, too, had a strained look on his face, and my heart sank as I realized that in trying to be clever I had made an exhibition of myself. We collected a parcel of ivory pieces from Cheng Wu, wished him good day, and went out to the waiting carriage. As it moved off I started to apologize, but almost before I had framed the first words Adam collapsed in the corner of the seat with an explosion of pent-up laughter. I saw that Lady Gascoyne's shoulders were shaking, and she was dabbing at her eyes as spasms of mirth caught her.

"Ah, Jani," gasped Adam, "that was splendid! Even without your Cockney accent you're as funny as ever. Isn't she priceless, Mother? I'll wager old Cheng Wu hasn't been squeezed so hard in donkey's years."

At first I felt indignant at being thought funny, but then I found myself laughing with them. That evening, at dinner, conversation flowed more freely and happily than at any time since we had come to Chester Gardens. Most of it was taken up by Adam and his mother vying with each other to tell Sir Charles of our journey that day, and particularly of my encounter with Cheng Wu.

Later, when we were alone for a few minutes, Sir Charles thanked me for all I was doing to help Adam's reunion with his family, and I went to bed that night with a feeling of hope, and without my usual dread of ordeals to come next day.

For some time I lay awake, daydreaming about how wonderful it would be if Adam were to fall in love with me and ask me to marry him. I knew it would not happen, for I was not convinced that to him I would always be the funny little half-Indian Cockney girl he had known in Smon T'ang. In a way I was glad it would not happen, for if it did, I knew I might be tempted beyond endurance, tempted to turn my back on Eleanor and try to forget what had befallen her. And if I abandoned Eleanor I would never forgive myself.

I knew that eventually I would go back to Larkfield and wait . . . wait for however long it might be for the time to come when Eleanor needed me. It might never come, but I knew that I must always be ready. One day Eleanor might be free. Vernon Quayle might die, or might discard her, and then I could go to her and fight to restore her to health. So it would not be good if Adam fell in love with me. I could not let him, or any man, be bound by a debt that was mine alone, the unpayable debt I owed to Eleanor and her father.

As week succeeded week, a true family atomosphere slowly burgeoned in the Gascoyne household. We began to receive and pay calls, and if Adam found this boring he concealed it splendidly. We would often go to the theater, to an opera or musical concert, sometimes all four of us, sometimes just Adam and myself. They were days which would have been wonderfully happy for me if the shadow of Eleanor's pitiful entrapment had not always lurked in the back of my mind. Even so, there were days when my heart lifted as I saw Adam's hollow cheeks filling out, the color coming back to them, and the growing contentment in him.

In November, protesting that it was a waste of time, he went into a nursing home for two days so that his eyes could be thoroughly examined by specialists. Their medical report filled two pages, but the essence of it was that in their opinion the optic nerves had atrophied due to unknown causes.

When I read it to Adam he laughed, shrugged, and said it was medical language for "We haven't the slightest idea."

As far as possible he simply ignored his blindness, and behaved as if he were not afflicted by it. This brought him some bumps, bruises, and falls, which he likewise ignored. When he fell, we learned not to help him up or sympathize, but to pretend nothing had happened. We also learned to wait patiently for him at table while he labored to cut up his own food by feel alone, and I think we could all have wept for him as we watched. but it was quite evident that he did not feel sorry for himself.

Only once did I hear him refer to his blindness. I had taken him out for a drive in the gig, and as we passed the barracks in Albany Street a military band marched out. Out little mare, a nervous creature, was startled and tried to bolt, but I held her and called out quickly to soothe and reassure her, speaking in the tongue of the Lo-bas. When she was trotting on quietly again Adam said thoughtfully, "That felt like a rather hazardous few moments. I'm very glad it was you driving." Then, after a pause, "Lord, I do wish I could see you, Jani."

In December I had a very official letter from a Mr. R. G. Milner, a Parliamentary Under-Secretary of State at the Foreign Office. It had been written on a typewriting machine, and in it Mr. Milner said that certain matters concerning myself and the State of Jahanapur had been brought to his attention, and he would be grateful if I would find it convenient to call upon him at his Whitehall office at eleven o'clock on the morning of Friday, 11th December, in order to discuss the matter.

I read it out to Adam as we took a short stroll in the park before breakfast, and he said, "Show it to my father and take his advice, Jani. He's been a diplomat all his life, and he knows exactly how to deal with this sort of thing."

Sir Charles read the letter at breakfast, then looked up with a gleam in his eye. "So that's their little game, eh? Well, let's teach them a lesson. May I have your permission to deal with this, Jani?"

"Oh yes, of course, Sir Charles, I'd be very grateful."

"And you confirm to me now that you have no wish whatsoever to assert your rights as Maharani of Jahanapur?"

"No wish at all, truly."

"Very well. But please do not say that, or anything else on this matter, to anyone at all without first consulting me."

I agreed wonderingly. Lady Gascoyne said, "You look as if you are girding yourself for battle, Charles."

"I am, my dear, I am." He gave a rather menacing chuckle, drained his coffee cup, excused himself, and went briskly from the room.

Adam said, "Father sounds as if he's got blood in his eye. Somebody had better look out for squalls."

Half an hour later Sir Charles came to the long balcony overlooking the park, where I was reading to Adam as he worked on a set of chessmen. In his hand was a sheet of writing paper. "Would you cast your eye over that, Jani, my dear?" He sat down beside me, smiling.

I said. "Adam, it's a letter addressed to Mr. Milner. I'll read it out.

> 'Dear Sir,
>
> I am in receipt of your letter offensively addressed to Miss Jani Burr instead of to Miss Jani Saxon, Her Highness the Maharani of Jahanapur, whose private secretary I have the honor to be.   —
>
> I now inform you that Her Highness will not attend upon you at your office on the day suggested or indeed at any other time. If you have matters to discuss with her you may call upon her at this address at half past four o'clock on Tuesday, 15th December.
>
> Her Highness graciously permits me to inform you that she will postpone the initiation of the legal action she intends taking until after your audience on the above-mentioned date.
>
> I have the honor to remain, Sir,
>
> Your obedient servant,
>
>   Charles Gascoyne, Bart., K.C.V.O., G.C.S.I., C.B.E., F.Z.S.
>   Private Secretary to Her Highness
>   The Maharani of Jahanapur.' "

I looked up from the letter, awed and breathless. Adam gave a shout of laughter and said, "Splendid, Father! But do please explain."

"Certainly, my dear boy. It's quite clear from Milner's letter that the India Office or Foreign Office or both simply don't want all the upheaval of Jani making a claim to Jahanapur. No doubt they're well pleased with the present

237

ruler, Mohan Sudraka, and as they have a stable political situation there they don't want to disturb it. So they're trying to play down the tremendous strength of Jani's claim, to bluff her out of making it, in fact. That's why Milner addressed her as Miss Jani Burr and asked her to go trotting along to see him. She would be at an enormous disadvantage on his own territory in Whitehall. So what I've done is to make the blighter wait, and give him something to think about."

Sir Charles chuckled, but he looked like a leopard preparing to pounce on its prey. "They will have a fall-back position, of course. I mean, they will have some sort of offer to make Jani, but once they see my name on that letter they'll know they have a fight on their hands, and they'll have to start thinking on a different scale."

I said, "Perhaps they'll just . . . well, ignore me now."

"Oh no." He smiled, and his eyes narrowed. "They're worried, Jani. Fortunately the law stands above the executive, and the last thing they want is for a judge to declare that you are the rightful ruler of Jahanapur. Now we'll wait and see what happens next. We shan't have to wait long, I promise you."

He was right, for his letter was answered by return of post. The new letter was addressed to Miss Jani Saxon, and Sir Charles gave a crow of gleeful delight when I showed him. "Got the beggar!" he exclaimed. "By addressing you as Jani Saxon he acknowledges that Francis Saxon was your father, and all the rest follows."

The letter said that Mr. Milner had received the communication from my private secretary and would be happy to oblige me by calling at the suggested time. Adam said, "Father, do please allow me to be present with you and Jani when you deal with this fellow. Oh, wait though—might it weaken your position?"

"Not at all, my boy." Sir Charles rubbed his hands briskly. "You could help by disconcerting him. Would it trouble you to wear dark spectacles? No? Then we'll place you a little to one side of him, so that you can simply appear to be gazing at him in silence. A mystery man. We won't even introduce you."

Adam grinned. "Father, you're an old fox. Jani shall take me out to buy some dark spectacles today, the most sinister pair we can find."

Mr. Milner proved to be a man with scanty fair hair in his early forties, very soberly dressed, and carrying a black briefcase, which he rested on his knees and seemed about to open at any minute, though he never did so. His manner was pleasant but rather languid, as if this whole matter was a trivial affair and hardly worth troubling about.

The "audience," as Sir Charles insisted on calling it, was held in the drawing room. Mr. Milner was invited to sit on a rather low chair in the middle of the room. Sir Charles and I sat one on each side of the big fireplace, our chairs half turned so that our gazes converged on Mr. Milner. Adam sat unmoving on an upright chair with his back to the window, so that he was on the edge of Mr. Milner's vision, an ominous figure in wire-framed dark blue spectacles which transformed his face and made it look artificial, mask-like.

Mr. Milner spoke rather vaguely for a few minutes, saying that His Majesty's Government had studied a certain letter alleged to have been written by an alleged criminal, an ex-soldier by the name of R.S.M. George Burr. Often he paused as if expecting some comment, but we simply looked at him, and gave him no help whatever. His languid manner became rather forced as he summed up what he called the Government's view of this matter. When he finally came to a halt, we sat looking at him and said nothing.

After a long pause Mr. Milner gave me a wintry smile and said, "I am authorized to give consideration to any comment you may wish to make, Miss Saxon."

As instructed, I gazed stonily over the top of Mr. Milner's head. Sir Charles said, "Comment on what, sir? You have wasted ten minutes saying that the Government may deny the claim of Her Highness to be the issue of Colonel Saxon and his wife, the Maharani of Jahanapur, and therefore may deny that she is now herself the rightful Maharani. If that is the Government's view, then let us proceed to test it in the courts, as we have been preparing to do." He rose to his feet and made a slight bow in my direction. "I see no purpose in prolonging this audience, Your Highness."

I inclined my head. Mr. Milner said, "Ah, now, one moment please, Sir Charles. I was about to inform Miss Saxon that the prime concern of the Government is to avoid possible division and dissension in Jahanapur and the neighboring states. We have therefore discussed Miss Saxon's pretensions to the throne of Jahanapur with the present ruler—"

"The present illegal ruler," said Sir Charles, "but pray continue."

"With Prince Mohan Sudraka," said Mr. Milner. "He is a good ruler, very cooperative, and also a generous man. In fact, he is willing to make substantial recognition of Miss Saxon's services, if she will use her good offices to avoid creating problems which will assuredly arise in Jahanapur should there be any dispute over the throne. This offer is made without prejudice, of course."

Sir Charles said stiffly, "Are you being deliberately insulting, sir?"

"Not at all." Mr. Milner was beginning to glance ever more often and with growing unease at the grim, silent figure of Adam. "I would hardly feel that the recognition in the sum of fifty thousand pounds could be deemed an insult."

I smothered a gulp of alarm. Until now my problem had been to look haughty and keep a straight face. Now I was suddenly afraid and out of my depth. Sir Charles's face grew slowly red. I learned later that he achieved this by holding his breath and contracting his stomach muscles. "Fifty thousand?" he echoed incredulously. "My dear sir, as you and I are both well aware, the annual income of the ruler of Jahanapur is in the order of one and one-quarter million pounds. Is he seriously attempting to—forgive me, Your Highness—to *buy* her off with two weeks' wages?"

For a while I lost track of the conversation. I could hear the words spoken, but could not make sense of them, and felt the dream-like sensation which I had sometimes known in the thin air of the high mountain passes. When I collected my wits again Sir Charles was saying, "Very well, sir. It may be that for the sake of her people in Jahanapur, and to avoid dissension, Her Highness will disregard my advice. But allow me to declare in plain terms that I shall urge her *not* to make this great sacrifice which is now being asked of her, and *not* to renounce her rights on the terms we have just agreed."

"Not agreed, sir, discussed," Mr. Milner said hastily. "I must secure final authority from the Minister."

"Do so," said Sir Charles coldly. "And pray do not hurry him. The longer you give me to persuade Her Highness as to her own best interests, the better pleased I shall be."

"Ah . . . quite so. And when may I expect her decision, Sir Charles?"

"When your Minister has made his, sir. Permit me to recapitulate what is required. First, that the sum of two hundred thousand pounds sterling be paid to the order of Her Highness within thirty days from this day, for her absolute benefit, payment to be guaranteed by the British Government in the event of default by the present and illegal ruler of Jahanapur. Second, that the Government recognizes the legitimacy of Her Highness's claim. Third, that the Government shall ensure that the innocence of Regimental Sergeant Major George Burr be officially declared in the London *Gazette*, that a suitable posthumous award be made for his devotion to duty, and that his remains be brought to such miltary cemetery as the Colonel of the Regiment shall approve, there to be interred with military honors. Fourth, that in renouncing all rights and authority in and over the State of Jahanapur, Her Highness shall retain her title, and shall, if she so wishes, have the official right to be known as Princess Jani of Jahanapur, and to be addressed as Your Highness."

Mr. Milner suppressed a sigh and stood up. "You have put it very succinctly, Sir Charles. I have little doubt the agreement will be drafted within the next day or two."

Sir Charles permitted himself a tigerish smile. "I have little doubt of that myself, sir."

When Mr. Milner had said his formal goodbyes and been shown from the room, I jumped up and ran to Sir Charles in panic. "Oh, I can't, I can't! All that money—I wouldn't know what to do. I had no idea you were going to say all those things . . ." Quite suddenly I began to weep.

Sir Charles put his arms round me, patting my shoulder as he held me. "Now, now, child, there's nothing to be afraid of. Having a great deal of money and a title won't change you. Not you, Jani. Now listen, my dear, all I have done is to ensure that you receive a little of what is your due. The money is there, and you can use it or throw it away. The title is yours, to be used or not. I think there may be times when you will find it to be a blessing, since you are half-Indian and we are a nation of snobs. Adam for heaven's sake take those dreadful spectacles off, my boy. I don't know what effect they had on Milner, but by God they terrify me."

From across the room Adam said wonderingly, "Do you really think the Foreign Office will swallow it?"

"No question." Sir Charles spoke over the top of my head. "I could have got twice the money, if I hadn't been afraid Jani was going to burst into tears at any moment. But it's better this way, because the fellow thinks he's done very well on the financial side, so they won't jibe at the ancillary demands."

"Ah, now that's very good," said Adam. "The demand
241

concerning Sembur is more important to Jani than anything else. Father, you're a man after my own heart." He gave that rich buoyant laugh I loved to hear from him. "Oh, and you can stop your sniffling, Jani. You're only doing it from wounded pride at losing your place as the champion haggler of the family."

Christmas was a time of sunshine and shadow for me. I had no greeting from Eleanor, and thought about her with aching heart, but was happy almost beyond words to sit at table with the Gascoynes now, and hear them talk easily and affectionately together. Of late Adam had been going out with his father more often, sometimes to a club in Pall Mall, sometimes to the City on business. There were also days when he would go off on his own in a hansom cab and be absent for several hours. I realized, with a pang of jealousy, that he might have taken a mistress, and if that were so I wished it could have been me. This was quite shocking of me, but I had discovered that where Adam was concerned I seemed to be entirely lacking in modesty, and unashamedly longed for him.

Despite this, it especially pleased me to see Adam go out and about with his father, partly because it showed how truly they had both buried the past, and partly because it gave me more time to spend with Lady Gascoyne, who sorely needed companionship. I had often felt guilty that both Sir Charles and Adam acted towards me as if I were really one of the family, yet they seemed not quite able to behave in the same easy way with Lady Gascoyne.

I spoke to her about it once, during Christmas, when I was in her room, hastily stitching the gown she was wearing, where a few inches of the hem had come loose. To my relief she smiled without resentment and said, "Don't worry about it, Jani. I'm just so happy to see how you've brought Adam and Charles together."

I stretched the next inch or two of hem across my knuckles ready for sewing, and said slowly, "When you came to Withy Cottage, you told me about Sir Charles being ill. I know we never speak about it, but . . . is he really as ill as you believed? I mean, he looks a little tired sometimes, but never seriously ill."

"I know." Her voice was quiet but steady, and she reached down to touch a hand to my cheek. "But there is no cure,

Jani. The doctors say that the diabetic condition is long established in Charles. We"—just for a moment she faltered, then went on calmly—"we hope for as long as two years, but it could be a matter of months only."

It was a little while before I could continue sewing, for my eyes were blurred with tears and my throat seemed to have closed. At last I whispered, "I want to cry, but you shame me. You're very brave."

"Not brave," she said a little wearily, "just resigned, Jani. I've spent my life learning to resign myself to the inevitable. A very comfortable life, but not an especially happy one, which I'm sure is as much my own faults as that of anyone else. It's so strange to think that in these last few months I've been happier with Charles than ever before. Such a waste, Jani. Are you in love with Adam, dear?"

Though the question came unexpectedly it did not take me completely by surprise, for Lady Gascoyne was a woman and must often have noticed the way I looked at Adam. I said, "Yes. Yes, I am in love with him. I think I may have been for a long time, but I only really knew it when I found him in that tavern in Wapping." I bit the end of the cotton and stood up.

She hugged me for a moment, then stood back with tears shining in her eyes. "Oh, I'm so glad, darling. And is Adam in love with you? Will he ask you to marry him?"

I smiled a rather forced smile. "I think he's quite fond of me, but no more than that. Anyway, it wouldn't do, Lady Gascoyne. I'm not really free."

"Not free?" She gazed at me incredulously.

"Because of Eleanor. I know it's hard for you to understand, but she *must* come first. She gave me everything. Oh please, please don't say anything of this to Adam."

She shook her head, her still beautiful face troubled. "Of course not. But, Jani, don't spoil your life to no purpose, child. Be a little selfish."

I busied myself putting away the needle, cotton, and thimble, almost angry with her in that moment, for I was only too ready to be selfish and needed no encouragement. I said, "You must be thinking that one day Adam will want me, Lady Gascoyne, but he won't. He'll always see me as a rather ugly little girl with chopped off hair, and ribs like a washboard from sickness."

There was a little silence, then Lady Gascoyne said, "I promise I won't say a word to Adam. But I know one thing. I want you for my daughter, Jani, so please don't forbid me to hope."

Christmas Day was on a Friday. On the following Sunday evening, by arrangement, Adam and I drove down to Wapping. There we met Molly and her fiancé of recent date, a cheerful but slow-witted giant called Sid, and took them to a nearby shop which served eel-pie suppers. As a wedding gift, Adam presented them with fifty sovereigns neatly fitted into a groove running round a horshoe of gold-painted wood.

The occasion was not a success. We were dressed in our plainest clothes, but we were still quite out of place. Molly called over several people to greet their old friend Buff, but they were ill at ease and did not linger. When we parted Molly said, "Well, ta very much for everything, an' God bless all here, but don't be comin' again, Buff." She gave a friendly wink. "Not without you're flat broke like before, an' even so you'd not be needing me now."

Two days later, in the big drawing room of the house in Chester Gardens, in the presence of Sir Charles, Mr. Milner, a Government lawyer, Sir Charles's solicitor, a legal representative of His Highness Prince Mohan Sudraka, Lady Gascoyne, and Adam, I signed an impressive legal document renouncing all claim to the State of Jahanapur. In the same moment I became possessed of a huge fortune.

Next day I went with Sir Charles to Coutts Bank, to authorize their Trustee Department to invest the money on my behalf. The following day, the last day of the year, the whole family drove with me to the other side of the river, to the Adelaide Crocker Home for orphan girls. There we saw Miss Callender, who recognized me at once, somewhat to my astonishment, and whose excitement at this unexpected visit from titled gentry completely overwhelmed her usual calm.

She showed us round the home, and though Adam could see nothing he seemed to sense the dreadful poverty of it from the strained silences and occasional murmurs of his mother and father. As we returned to her office I told Miss Callnder that I had arranged to endow the home with the sum of one thousand pounds a year. To my alarm she leaned against the peeling wall, put her hands over her face, and began to weep. I quickly shooed Sir Charles and Adam away, then helped Lady Gascoyne soothe and cheer her.

When we left, twenty minutes later, she was full of gratitude, but I felt a great humbug. It seemed to me that what I had done was costing me nothing at all, far less than it had cost me, on a summer's day in the New Forest long ago, to offer a stale bacon sandwich to a fainting man.

That night, at midnight, we saw the New Year in, standing on the long balcony which looked out upon the park, well wrapped against the cold, straining to hear the distant chimes of Big Ben at Westminster. As we embraced one another in turn, I had the joy of being held in Adam's arms for a moment, the first time since that day in the back room of the Grapes, at Wapping. It did not occur to me then that we were entering the year spoken of by the Oracle, as she stood before Rild in the monastery of Galdong, more than six long years ago.

This was the Year of the Wood Dragon. I was soon to have cause to remember it.

CHAPTER FIFTEEN

In the second week of January, by David Hayward's invitation, Adam and I took the train to Bournemouth to spend a few days in Larkfield. It was arranged that I should stay in the Stafford farmhouse, as my cottage was cold and unaired, and Adam would stay with David. The two men had not met before, but from the moment they greeted each other I sensed an immediate harmony. They were of very different natures, yet each seemed to take to the other in an easy, unforced way which did my heart good to see.

One of our first duties was to pay a call on Major Elliot, so I could tell him all that had passed between me and the Foreign Office, and thank him for the great help he had given me in the beginning. We also visited the Wheelers at the vicarage and several other old friends of mine, but on David's advice we did not attempt to call upon Eleanor. "You'll simply be told she's not at home," he said bleakly. "Eleanor has received no callers for months, and hasn't been out of the house for months. If it wasn't for Mrs. Burke, I'd almost wonder if she's still alive."

We were all at table in Mrs. Stafford's kitchen when he said this, and the food in my stomach seemed to turn to stone. David glanced at me quickly and said, "It's no use, Jani. I've given up hope, and so will you, if you stay long in Larkfield. When you pass Merlin's Keep every day, when you see it across the valley, when you run into that pasty-faced slug of a man every now and again . . . you can't stop thinking about Eleanor, and you know there's no help for her."

Adam said, "Will you go away, David?"

"I think I shall have to. I don't feel I could face the spring in Larkfield. Perhaps I shall go back to Lincolnshire."

Adam nodded thoughtfully.

During our stay we made one or two trips into Bournemouth, to enjoy the sea air and because it was a pleasure for Adam to listen to the sounds of the sea, but on most days we took to accompanying David on his rounds. Soon I was dressed in my riding breeches again and wearing the thick calico pinafore I had taken to wearing when helping him before. Adam would stand in a cowshed or stable, beside a pigsty or out in a cold field, waiting and listening patiently. David might be attending to a sick animal and I might be soothing it, lending a hand to hold, cut, sew, or swab if David called upon me to do so. But Adam never seemed to grow bored.

When added muscle was required, he could not be prevented from taking part, and on one such occasion a strange incident occurred. We were working on a small farm belonging to Mrs. Fennel, a widow who was trying to run it almost single-handed since the death of her husband.

Several of her cows had found and eaten some wet turnips, and were suffering from bloat, their left flanks distended. It was necessary to keep them on the move and prevent them lying down while David contrived to get a tube down each in turn to vent the gas. Mrs. Fennel and her one farmhand were pushing and pulling the creatures about when we arrived, and I at once joined in.

Adam stood by the gate, wearing old flannel trousers and a tweed jacket beneath a short covert coat. He was about to light one of the cigars he occasionally smoked, an unusual kind with a short tube-like piece of cane set in one end. I was tugging at one of the cows by its nose, using my most flattering persuasion in honorific Tibetan, when Adam took the unlit cigar from his mouth and called, "Anything I can do, Jani?"

"Yes," I called back a little breathlessly, "you can keep this one on her feet while I give Mrs. Fennel a hand. But you'd better take your coat off. It's a long, hot job."

He laid the cigar down carefully on top of the gatepost, quickly removed his coat, cap, and jacket, placed them on the top rail, then stood listening. I began to talk, saying something to the cow, to give Adam my direction without making it obvious. When he was close, I put his hand on one of its horns.

"You're sure you don't mind, Adam?"

"Mind? You can't imagine how good it is to be of a little

247

use sometimes, Jani. Come on now, just tell me exactly what to do."

We had to haul the reluctant cows about for another hour before David had dealt with them all and was satisfied. I took Adam's arm and walked across the pasture with him to recover his clothes, only to find that the cigar and his cap had vanished. When I told him, he thought at first that I was joking, and then that some creature had made off with them. "There must be a goat about, Jani," he said, highly amused.

"No, Mrs. Fennel hasn't got a goat."

"Then we'll have to look out for a dog or a horse wearing a cap and smoking a cigar."

I was holding his jacket, staring at it. "Adam, a little triangle of cloth has been torn from the lining of your jacket, just inside the collar! Who on earth could have done such a thing?"

"Well, it certainly destroys my goat theory. Perhaps the lining was already torn."

"No, before I packed them I went over all the clothes you brought away with you, to see if anything needed mending."

"I didn't know that. You spoil me, Jani."

"I suppose you must have caught it on a nail, or something like that, since we've been here."

"It's not important, anyway. Come on, I can hear David yelling for you." He laughed as he pulled on his short top-coat. "It's very entertaining to hear you two at work together. Anyone who didn't know you would imagine you hated the sight of each other."

That was certainly true at times when we had a difficult case, for we tended to discharge our anxieties upon one another and to save all our sympathy for the animal. I remembered how it had been two days earlier in the stables at the manor, dealing with a hunter.

"Dammit, Jani, don't let her move now!"

"Oh, stop grumbling at me! I can only tell her not to move, I can't stop her."

"Well, tell her, then. She's likely to kick my ribs in, any minute."

"If I were her, I'd feel like kicking your ribs in! You go at that stitching like a cobbler at a pair of boots." Then, in the language of the Lo-bas, "Gently, my princess, gently. Soon there will be no more hurting. Listen now and I will tell you of one called Pulki. She was not highborn, as you are, but a

248

little pony of the mountains who carried me when I was small . . ."

"A cobbler?" David's voice rose indignantly over mine as he tied the last suture, crawled out from beneath the mare, and flung out an appealing hand. "Did you hear that, Adam? Would you ever believe I once asked that vinegar-tongued shrew to marry me?"

We returned to London in the last week of January, and with our return a cold black shadow fell swiftly upon me, for within a week or two everything had changed. At first Adam seemed a little withdrawn from me, then there were times when I felt he was hard put to suppress his irritation, and finally he began to avoid me. I say everything changed. In truth only Adam changed, but he was everything to me.

I was hurt, bewildered, and increasingly nervous, for I had no idea what I was doing to upset him. With his father and mother he was as amiable as before, and for this I was thankful, but the easy friendship which had grown between the two of us seemed no more than a memory now. He took to staying late at his club, and those unexplained absences when I enviously believed he might be visiting a mistress became more frequent. Very politely he made it clear that he did not wish me to read to him any more, and I think this politeness was the worst thing of all, for suddenly it was as if we had no past together but were strangers.

The end came one evening as I was making my way downstairs to the drawing room, where the family always met and chatted for ten minutes or until the butler, Laing, entered to announce that dinner was served. On this occasion the door was half open, and as I was coming to the foot of the stairs I suddenly heard Adam's voice, speaking rather tautly and as if in answer to something said by his mother or father: "I am not being unkind or ungrateful. I have spend the last few months being as pleasant and amiable as possible to Jani, but I've quite run out of steam now. Oh, she's a nice enough little chatterbox, and good-hearted no doubt, but hardly my choice for a daily companion. I'm sorry if my boredom shows, but I really can't help it."

I had stopped at the bottom of the stairs. Now I turned and went up again as quietly as I could, my face hot with shame and hurt. What a conceited fool I had been to imagine he enjoyed my company. To him, I was still the child he had once known, and that would be the picture of me he carried in his mind. In all we had done together over the past weeks he had often smiled, laughed, seemed amused by me and interested in me. But now I saw clearly that he had simply humored me . . . and that he had come to the end of his tether.

By the time I reached my room my face was pale. I slapped and pinched my cheeks to bring some color to them, held a damp handkerchief over my eyelids for a few moments, then drew a deep breath and went downstairs again. Sir Charles and Lady Gascoyne greeted me perhaps a little too warmly, while Adam said politely, "Good evening, Jani, I hope the day has been enjoyable one for you."

The last thing I wanted was for anyone to guess that I had overheard what Adam had said about me, so I waited until we had almost finished dinner before I said apologetically, "You know, since visiting Larkfield I've felt rather guilty about being away for so long. I really think I must go back soon."

Sir Charles and his wife exchanged a troubled glance, then she said rather uncertainly, being careful not to look at Adam, "Oh, we hadn't thought about your leaving us, Jani. We felt you were one of the family."

"You have certainly made me feel like one of the family," I said, smiling from one to the other, "that's why I've stayed longer than I should have." I managed a little laugh. "It was Adam who foisted me on you to begin with, because he wanted a nursemaid, but he certainly doesn't need one any longer, and now I feel I must begin to put some of my plans into practice."

Sir Charles said, "What plans, my dear?"

"Well, David Hayward told me that Catling's Farm, adjoining the grounds of Merlin's Keep on the southern side, is coming up for sale later this year. It's a mixed farm of about seventy acres, and I know that sounds quite small, but in the New Forest area nobody needs much land for pasture because there are common grazing rights. There's a very nice residence as well as the farmhouse and three cottages. The Catlings are selling up and going to join their son in Canada, so I thought I'd buy it. I can't think of anything I'd like to do better than run a mixed farm. I shall have a terrible lot to learn, of course, but I'm sure Mr. Stafford will give me all the help I need."

There was little silence. Adam concentrated on stirring his coffee. Sir Charles, looking very miserable, said, "But, Jani—"

His wife interrupted, and as she looked at me I saw in her

eyes that she had understood. It was not necessary for her to know that I had overheard Adam's crushing words. She already knew I loved him, but that I was not free even if he had returned my feeling. Now his indifference was plain, and she would realize how painful it must be for me to continue living at Chester Gardens.

"Yes, you've been unselfish for far too long, Jani," she said gently. "We shall miss you dreadfully, but it's high time you thought about your own future."

Three days later Sir Charles and Lady Gascoyne drove with me in their carriage to Waterloo station, to see me off. We were all very miserable while pretending to be jolly, and I longed for the train to leave so that I could be on my own. Adam did not come with us. I had last seen him soon after breakfast, when he had shaken hands with me, wished me well in the future, and then sent for a cab to take him to his club.

By the time I had been back in Larkfield for two weeks it was almost as if I had never been away, except that I had forever to keep myself busy, to prevent the aching emptiness I felt within me whenever I thought of Adam. Mr. Stafford came with me to see Mr. Catling about the farm I planned to buy, and after some slow Hampshire bargaining between the two men it was agreed that when the farm was put up for sale I would be offered first refusal at twenty pounds an acre.

The Catlings had always lived in the farmhouse. The residence stood apart in its own grounds, a house smaller than Merlin's Keep but very well appointed, and leased for the past sixteen years to a very rich South African gentleman who owned a number of diamond mines, so it was said. He had houses in several different countries, and had leased Kimberley, as this and indeed all his houses were called, on impulse while visiting the district for a few days to seek records of his Hampshire ancestors.

Kimberley was looked after by an agent and was maintained by a staff of two, which expanded to eight whenever its owner and his wife took up residence. This had happened only twice since he had bought it, and then for not more than six weeks on each occasion. Mr. Catling had already spoken with the local agent, who felt that there would be little difficulty in persuading the South African gentleman to terminate, for a modest sum, the twenty-one-year lease he held. I could then buy the freehold for two thousand eight hundred pounds.

David Hayward said, "What are you going to do with the place, Jani? You can't very well live there alone. Or in the farmhouse alone, for that matter."

We were on Mrs. Fennel's small farm again, having trouble delivering a calf. I said, "I don't know yet. Oh, do stop pestering me with questions and get that calf out. I'm freezing, David."

"Well, I'm not." He thrust with his arm, grunting, eyes closed as he concentrated on getting a noose round the unborn calf's head. "Wipe some of this sweat off me, will you, Jani?" Then, as I picked up the towel to obey, "And you'd be a lot more help if you told this wretched cow to cooperate with me instead of trying to crush my arm."

"I *was* telling her, then you started to go on at me about the farm. You're always doing things and blaming me for them." I scrubbed irritably at his back, chest, and face with the towel, then went round to the cow's head and began to talk to her again.

After a few moments David said, "Good . . . good. Keep her relaxed. Look, why don't you marry me, Jani? Then we could make use of that mad South African's house."

"No."

"What?"

"No, I won't marry you."

"Why not?"

I winked at the cow and said, "Because you're just after my money, David Hayward, that's why not."

"*What?*" It was a cry of incredulous wrath, and David's head popped up above the cow's rump, his eyes and mouth round *o*'s of shocked indignation. In the same moment I felt her give a sudden heave, and I called, "Look out!" but David had no time to move before the calf he had been trying to lasso for the past half hour was suddenly ejected, tumbling out of its mother so that David staggered back and fell with the calf on top of him.

I dropped slowly to my knees, racked by helpless laughter, and watched as the cow turned placidly and began to lick her young. David crawled away, stood up, rinsed his arms in the bucket of soapy water, then came and lifted me to my feet. I was still helpless.

"You know, we could do a lot worse," he said quietly.

I stopped laughing, felt a sudden sadness sweep through

me, and rested my head a little wearily on his chest. "Yes. I suppose we could, David." I tilted my head to look up at him, and did not move to avoid him as he bent slowly to kiss me. It was very sweet and good, and I tried hard not to pretend it was Adam kissing me.

After a few moments he straightened up and said, "Will you think about it, Jani?"

"There's Eleanor."

"Eleanor's gone. I can't remain in love with a ghost for the rest of my life."

"I'm not sure any of us have a choice about who we love, David. But yes, I'll think about it in a little while, when I'm more settled."

It was a week later that I woke suddenly in the night, roused by an urgent banging on the door of Withy Cottage. I struck a match, lit my bedside candle, and looked at the small clock on the cabinet. It was half past midnight. I pulled on a dressing gown and went sleepily to the window. David had never called me out in the night before, but I supposed he might do so if he had an emergency involving a very difficult animal. I knew he had been attending a fine hunter of Major Elliot's suffering from a suspected torsion, and that he might have to put the animal down to save it from dreadful pain at the last, but I could not imagine he would need to call me out on a winter's night for this.

Drawing back the curtain, I opened the window a few inches, shivering at the touch of cold air. There had been a fall of snow, but so thin that it looked more like frost on the ground. "Who is it?" I called.

"Me. David." His voice was strained. "I'm hurt. Jani. Can you help me?"

"I'm coming down." By the time I reached the front door I was wide awake with alarm and puzzlement. I dragged the bolts back, turned the key, and as I threw open the door David stumbled against me. I glimpsed his gig on the verge close to the cottage. "Sorry," he mumbled, "sorry, Jani."

"It's all right," I gasped, bracing myself. "Now, lean on me and let's get you to a chair." As he slumped in an armchair I saw there was a cut and a swelling bruise on his temple, while blood was seeping through a gash in the side of his left Wellington boot.

I ran out to the gig and snatched the bag of instruments

from the seat, for I knew there would be disinfectant and bandages in it. Inside the room again I paused only to throw a log on the dying fire, then brought a bowl from the kitchen, put it under David's hurt leg, and carefully eased his boot off. His trouser leg was soaked in blood. The candle did not give enough light, and I hurried to put a match to the big lamp on the table.

"David dear, what on earth have you done?"

"Tried to shoot Quayle," he said thickly. "Didn't work . . . he just laughed . . . devil looks after his own."

I felt the blood drain from my face. "David, you didn't!"

He put a hand to his temple. "Didn't what, Jani? Can't think properly."

"Never mind you can tell me later." I was kneeling again, turning back his trouser leg to find the wound. There was a gouge several inches long in his calf, the flesh torn rather than cut. He would certainly limp for a few weeks, but providing the wound was prevented from turning septic it was not dangerous. I gave a sigh of relief and said, "Hold this tea towel against it to stop the bleeding while I heat some water and get everything ready. Can you manage that?" He nodded, leaned forward, and grasped the folded linen I held pressed against the wound.

For the next twenty minutes I was busy cleaning the gash thoroughly with antiseptic lotion, packing it with gauze, and making a neat bandage. I was glad to remember that for two or three years now David had had regular injections of something he called tetanus antitoxin, a new discovery which was said to make a person resistant to tetanus. All the time I was working he lay back as if half asleep, and we did not speak. I bathed the bruise on his head, washed the cut with the same antiseptic solution, a mixture David made up himself, then cleared everything away and made a jug of coffee, lacing it with brandy from the flask David carried to sustain him when working for long hours on a winter's night.

The fire was burning well now, and the little room was beautifully warm. I had been barefoot since hanging my bed socks over the fire after running out to the gig in them. Now they were dry, and I put them on before settling myself in the other armchair.

"David, wake up and drink your coffee."

"M'mmm?" He opened his eyes, blinked about him, and sat up slowly, touching his head, then looking down at his bandaged leg. "Thank you," he said slowly. "Thank you, Jani. Lord, what a good girl you are."

I thought to myself that his opinion would not be shared by anybody who saw his gig outside my cottage at one o'clock in the morning, but I did not voice my thought. The last thing I wanted was for him to go rushing out into the night. So far I had held my worries at bay by keeping busy, but now I was desperately anxious to know what had happened. I said, "How is your head, David? Do you feel up to telling me what happened?"

He sipped the coffee and nodded. "Yes. Ahhh, that's good." He stretched out his bare foot toward the fire. "Beginning to feel . . . almost human again." He looked at me, eyes dark and distressed in a troubled face. "That man Quayle. He's . . . protected in some way, Jani. He must be."

"Oh, David, please don't just ramble when I'm sick with worry. *Tell* me."

"Sorry. Well, old Elliot sent a boy round at about half past eleven. He said the horse was in agony, would I come along and put him down. So I drove over to Carlings and helped the poor creature out of its pain with a bullet from that Webley I use for such jobs." He looked at me a little awkwardly, then looked away as he went on, "I . . . well, I came back by the track behind Merlin's Keep. I know it's a longer way round, but I sometimes use it at night. I suppose because that's the nearest I can ever be to Eleanor these days." He stared into the fire, and I saw his face grow taut. "You can see over the wall at one point, and look along that broad path through the fruit trees to the house. And that's when I saw Eleanor."

"Eleanor? In the garden at midnight?"

He nodded, his hands shaking as they cradled the cup of coffee. "It was very dark. There's almost no moon tonight, but a light was blazing from that one big window of the Round Room. It seemed to be shining down on the lawn, and the window must have been masked in a special way, because the great patch of light thrown on the grass made the outline of a huge star. A star with five points . . . and with peculiar black shapes in each point." He stared into the fire. "Eleanor was kneeling there in the middle of it, Jani, with her arms lifted, and her hair loose, and she was naked . . ."

"What?" I came out of my chair, spilling some of my coffee, a huge and murderous rage sweeping through me, so that I babbled rather than spoke. "He what? He did what,

David? Eleanor . . . ? Out there on a freezing night, *naked?*"

David nodded wearily. "Perhaps she's not affected by such things any more, I don't know. But I know what you're feeling now, Jani, because it was just the same for me. I wanted to get my hands on Quayle's throat . . . and squeeze the life out of him. Then I saw him. He was standing at the other end of the path, with his back toward me, watching her. One point of the star was almost touching his feet. He wore . . . I'm not sure, but it seemed to be a short, silvery cloak, and in each hand he had something like a thin sword blade, or a wand. One was pointing to the sky, the other toward Eleanor." David looked at me from a drawn face. "Jani, I could swear I saw a kind of . . . black light streaming from the tip of the thing he was pointing at Eleanor."

My heart was still pounding, and it was an effort to make myself sit down. I whispered, "What did you do?"

He shrugged. "I don't remember scrambling over the wall, I just remember storming up that path toward Quayle. Then I . . . I must have run into a tree branch in the dark."

"But there aren't any branches low enough over that path, David."

"Well . . . perhaps I fell down and hit my head. Or perhaps it was something else. I could believe almost anything now. I was dazed for a few moments, then I got to my knees. Quayle still had his back to me. You know how I carry the Webley, in a little knapsack with a few cartridges. The knapsack was still hanging from my shoulder, so I got the gun out, and put a cartridge in the chamber. And, Jani, I wasn't out of my mind then. I was ice-cold."

He shivered as if with a fever, then took a long drink of the coffee and brandy before going on rapidly. "I got up. I started walking toward him, walking this time, with the gun in my hand, the trigger cocked. I was no more than four or five paces away when it . . . it seemed to go off of its own accord. I'll swear I didn't fire. I must have just taken a pace forward with my left foot, and the bullet seemed to rip down my calf. I fell again, and I heard Quayle making a horrible hiccuping sound. Just as I passed out, I realized he was laughing."

I had once heard that sound myself, and I shuddered at the memory. David put down the mug and rubbed his eyes with both hands. "When I came round I was lying in the darkness with the Webley beside me. No sign of Quayle, no sign of Eleanor, no light from the Round Room." He leaned back and closed his eyes. "So I came here. I was overwrought at first, Jani, talking of Quayle as if he were some sort of wonder-worker. His mumbo jumbo had nothing to do with what happened to me. I was beside myself, so first I fell down . . . and then I shot myself in the leg. Dear God, what an exhibition."

Despite the warmth of the room I was cold inside, and I hugged myself, feeling close to tears as I said, "Oh, David, what are we going to do? I mean, how can we stop him doing these dreadful things with Eleanor? Could we go to the police? Isn't there some old law against witchcraft?"

David looked at me heavy-eyed. "I'm too tired to think, Jani. But I'm terribly afraid that Eleanor will be the one to suffer if we make any move at all against the swine." He stared blankly at the clock on the mantelpiece for a few seconds, then gave a start of alarm. "Oh my God, it's the early hours, and I've left the gig outside your cottage." He struggled to pull on his sock and the torn Wellington. "Give me a hand to get up into the gig, I'll be all right."

"No, David, don't be silly. I'll get dressed and fetch Dr. Porter. You can say you dropped the gun and shot yourself by accident—"

"No, no, no, Jani!" he broke in angrily. "I've caused you enough trouble, and I don't need a doctor." He tried his injured leg cautiously, limping across the room. "Ahh, well it's stiffening up, but that's nothing. I'll rest it for two or three days. If there's any emergency work, perhaps you'll come and drive me." He took my hand and pressed it hard, looking at me with a twisted and rather feverish smile. "Bless you, Jani. Now pull on your boots and topcoat, and give me a leg-up into the gig. We'll talk about Eleanor again when I can think of her without wanting to do murder. Pray God there's something that somebody can do."

When I returned to my bed at last I lay awake for a long time, my mind in tumbling confusion. The more I thought about it, the more I felt that David had spoken truly when he said we were powerless against Vernon Quayle, and always would be while he had Eleanor as a hostage. Toward dawn the thought came to my tired brain that perhaps the best thing for David and myself would be if I were to marry him and go away to his home county of Lincolnshire, where we could try to forget our heartaches and anxieties. I was wondering if we would find it possible to turn our backs in this way, when sleep overtook me at last.

For all that the night was short, I woke at six and was making myself breakfast in the kitchen when the postman brought me a letter from Lady Gascoyne. She had written to me twice since my return, no more than a page or two of news and gossip, but warm and friendly letters. I scarcely knew whether I was pleased to have them or not, for though I treasured any scrap of news about Adam, I knew it would be far better for me to let my friendship with the Gascoyne family fade quietly away.

The very first words of this latest letter startled me.

Dearest Jani,

That dreadful man you told us about, Vernon Quayle, actually called here yesterday. Ugh! He made my flesh creep. I would never have received him if I had not thought his visit might in some way be concerned with you. As it was, Charles and I received him, and then he asked if he might speak with Adam. I have never, never known a man who at once appeared so indifferent and so sure of himself.

My dear, from the moment Adam came in I could almost see his hackles rise in the presence of this man, even though he could not see him, of course. In a voice that really frightened me Adam said: "Is Jani all right?" The unhealthy-looking wretch simply stared back at him in a strange, blank-eyed sort of way, without responding, and continued to do so even when Adam, and then Charles, asked him his business. At last those horrid eyes seemed to focus once more, and he murmured: "So my dear wife's perception was quite correct. You made an enemy in Haiti, Mr. Gasoyne."

Wasn't that an extraordinary thing to say? I felt sure the fellow must be quite mad. After a moment or two Adam snapped: "What do you want, Quayle?" The man smiled and answered: "Why, to restore your sight, Mr. Gascoyne. The moon is new now. You will see before it is full." Then he wished us all good day, and walked from the room without waiting to be shown out.

Adam and Charles dismissed the whole thing as a piece of nonsense, and of course it must be. But, oh, Jani, is it wrong of me to cling to a tiny hope that my son's blindness might be cured? Even if it were brought about by a creature who makes my blood run cold? But

I am being quite absurd now. Do please forgive my silly ramblings.

How are you progressing with your notion of purchasing the Catling farm? I do hope it goes well . . .

The rest of the letter was made up of comment on my own letter of the week before, and general gossip. I scanned it quickly, then turned back to the beginning again. Throughout the day I must have read that letter a dozen times, and it was on my mind every moment, even when I called to see David in case he needed my help. Rosie was there, on guard, and told me that Mr. Hayward had hurt his leg and was in bed, but that if he needed me to help him on an emergency call she would send word at once.

It was a relief that I did not have to see David, for I shrank from telling him about Lady Gascoyne's letter. The truth was that I felt a thread of guilty excitement, a seed of hope that I was ashamed of because it seemed to spring from dark and unnatural soil. Last night, when David had brought me his tale of Eleanor's dreadful humiliation, I could have wished for a thunderbolt to strike Vernon Quayle down. Now I still hated and feared him, but tiny and tempting hopes kept nibbling like mice at my mind.

I knew that Vernon Quayle had knowledge, powers, and abilities which few in the Western world would credit, and even fewer would understand. I had seen him in the Round Room, when he had sought and found Adam Gascoyne, working at his strange arts as prosaically as an engineer or chemist, contemptuous of the notion that the forces he used were in any way supernatural. Perhaps . . . perhaps he could give back to Adam the blessing of sight.

The thought made me feel weak with joy, yet at the same time it terrified me. Vernon Quayle was no man's benefactor. What would the price be? What would it cost Adam? Or Eleanor? Or me?

Three days later, when David was about again and called to see me, I said nothing of the letter, neither did we speak of what had happened to him at Merlin's Keep that night when he had come to me injured. He thanked me, a little awkwardly, for helping him, but no more was said. It was almost as if we both wanted to pretend that nothing had happened, perhaps because we could not bear to dwell upon Eleanor's degradation.

Next day, at about five o'clock in the afternoon, a boy

came to the cottage with a note for me. My throat turned dry as I saw Eleanor's handwriting:

> Dear Jani,
>   I should be grateful if you would call to see me at half past eight o'clock this evening.
>
>   Eleanor

The writing was Eleanor's, but the words were those of her husband, Vernon Quayle. I scribbled a hasty line:

> Dearest Eleanor,
>   Yes, of course. I long to see you.
>
>   With my love always,
>
>   Jani

I gave the boy a penny, sent him off with my reply, and decided that I must keep my mind occupied for the next two hours, for if I began to wonder and speculate I would be jumpy as a grasshopper by the time I left for Merlin's Keep.

I took out writing paper and pen, settled down at the table, and wrote a long letter to Miss Callender at the Adelaide Crocker Home for Orphan Girls. In it I mentioned a number of small ways in which I felt that the life of the girls under her charge could be made easier, basing my notions on my own experience as a girl at the orphanage. I made it plain that I was only putting forward suggestions for her to consider, and thanked her warmly for the kindness she had shown me during my years under her care.

I wrote a chatty letter to Sir Charles and Lady Gascoyne. and then, on sudden impulse, wrote a letter which no eye would ever read. It was to Sembur, telling all too briefly that the greatest of good fortune had come to me during my years in England, and that soon he would lie with honor in a military cemetery among his comrades. I thanked him with all my heart, both for myself and for the parents I had never known, praising his courage and devotion in all he had done for me, and I said finally that I would arrange for this letter to be buried with him when he was laid to rest at last. I knew this could not happen till late spring, for the regiment would have to send soldiers to the cairn at the top of the Chak Pass, and this was impossible in winter. I decided that I would give the letter to Major Elliot and ask him to arrange the matter, for I felt it would please him very much to do so.

It may have been a foolish thing to do, writing a letter to Sembur, but I did not feel foolish. Perhaps he lived on in another world, as the Reverend Hubert Wheeler taught, or perhaps he lived on in another incarnation, as Rild would have taught. I only knew that he surely lived on in my memory, and would do so until I died. The letter was simply my tribute to him.

At eight o'clock I laid down my pen, stretched my stiff fingers, and went up to my bedroom. I washed, tidied my hair, changed my dress, and at twenty past eight I was jogging along the lane in Mr. Stafford's dogcart, a waxing moon glinting on the well-polished harness. I saw nobody on the short journey to Merlin's Keep. Even if I had passed any of the Larkfield folk, I think they would have shown no surprise. Young ladies did not drive about the countryside alone after dark—except Jani Burr. She was different, of course, having been schooled by Miss Eleanor, and nobody ever quite knew what she might do next. Strangely, Larkfield seemed not to mind, and even to enjoy owning an eccentric Indian princess who had grown up in the village.

As I mounted the familiar steps to the porch of Merlin's Keep, I found that without knowing it I had taken off my glove, drawn out Adam's medallion from beneath the bodice of my dress, and was clutching it tightly in my hand, just as I had clutched it for comfort years ago as I lay half-delirious in the cave on the Chak Pass.

It was then I knew I was afraid.

CHAPTER SIXTEEN

It was very quiet in the Round Room. Vernon Quayle had received me and conducted me there at once. Eleanor, in a
plain white dress and sitting in the same chair as before, had
given me a small, tentative smile and whispered, "Hello,
Jani." She looked pale, almost waxen, and her once lovely
hair was dull and lifeless.

Now I sat watching Vernon Quayle, trying to contain the
hatred which had flared up anew as I saw him inject a color-
less liquid into Eleanor's forearm with a hypodermic syringe.
Her eyes had closed as if in sleep, but she still sat upright
without slumping. Vernon Quayle was weighing small
amounts of what looked like a variety of dried herbs, mixing
them, then putting a little of the mixture in each of five small
copper bowls standing on tripods above spirit lamps which
were not yet lit.

I said huskily from a dry throat. "Will you please tell me
why Eleanor asked me to come here?"

"Certainly. I required her to do so because your presence
will be of help to her in the somewhat exacting task which
lies before us this evening."

"What task?"

"I think you must have more than an inkling of that. I'm
about to perform an operation to restore Adam Gascoyne's
sight."

My heart lurched. "An operation?"

He spared me a glance of scorn from dull gray eyes. "Not
a surgical operation, but one which is equally subject to the
laws of cause and effect, and to natural laws."

"I . . . I don't understand."

"It is very simple. My wife is an instrument of remarkable

penetration. Through her, I have traced back certain intangible lines which link a sequence of events, and have discovered that Adam Gascoyne's blindness was caused in a particular way. In fairy-tale terms, a spell was cast upon him by an obeah he offended in Haiti. In realistic terms, the explanation is still simple but requires more detail." Vernon Qualyle consulted a scroll but continued without pausing. "There are primitive peoples who have faculties and abilities which they are able to exert even though they have little or no understanding of the laws and principles they are using. Witch doctor, shaman, obeah, houngan, there are many names for these practitioners of so-called magic. Gascoyne offended one such person in Haiti, who then performed an ancient West African ritual of which at least half is mere mumbo jumbo. However, the rest encompassed the use of the Law of Correspondence, which applies to interaction between the material and non-material planes of being, and which same law we shall call upon this evening in order to reverse the process which made Adam Gascoyne blind."

Suddenly Vernon Quayle seemed a stupid old man, talking gibberish. How could anyone be struck blind at a distance? How could any combination of herbs and potions, spells, chanting, mesmerism, or ritual of any kind, affect the physical parts of the eye, or the optic nerves connected to the brain?

As if reading my thoughts Vernon Quayle said, "Such operations take place upon the etheric plane, where distance does not exist as we know it. The operation of the Haitian obeah produced an effect upon Gascoyne's etheric body, and this was mirrored in due time by the physical body. I do not expect you to understand this. You would first require a basic intelligence considerably larger than you possess, and then after ten years of serious study you would still have only a small grasp of the subject. It is composed of many elements, and they do not yield to verbal explanation or analysis. I know of no more than a dozen men in the world today who could fully comprehend the operation I shall perform this evening. Of those twelve, only two would dare to perform it."

He put aside the scroll, adjusted the position of the five small tripods very carefully, and began to light the spirit lamps with a black taper. I cleared my throat and said, "Do you mean it is dangerous?"

"Not in my hands. I have total control of the energies to be used. There is no fear of any damaging reaction."

"Are you . . . are you one of those people you spoke of? Like an obeah?"

Again came that contemptuous look as he poured heavy red drops from a small phial into one of the copper bowls. "I am a scientist. I am adept in an area of science which few men understand and which most men do not believe to exist. No more questions, please."

Threads of heavy smoke rose lazily from the five copper bowls on their tripods, which stood a little way from where Eleanor sat in what I took to be a deep trance. In the center of the five bowls stood a slender, ornately carved pillar of black wood on three splayed feet. Its top was a round brass disk with something engraved on it in a script unknown to me.

Vernon Quayle was wearing white gloves now, and held something in his hands. It was a small doll, very crudely carved from soft wood. He opened a little round casket on his desk, picked up a pair of tweezers, and lifted from the casket a scrap of black cloth which he deftly twisted about the doll's neck. Again he probed in the casket with the tweezers. At first when he raised them they seemed to hold nothing, but when he lifted them up to the light, peering, I glimpsed a long curly black hair. This he pressed into a split in the softwood head of the doll. When he brought a third item from the casket I caught my breath and a chill ran through me, for I saw that the tweezers held a piece cut from a cigar, the kind I had sometimes seen Adam smoke, with a short piece of cane tube inserted in the butt.

As Vernon Quayle teased a few splinters from the cane, and pressed them into the tiny hole representing the doll's mouth, he said, "The Law of Correspondence. For the operation I shall perform, this manikin corresponds to Adam Gascoyne, and through it we shall produce effects on the etheric plane."

I remembered the winter's day when David and Adam and I had been dealing with Mrs. Fennel's cows, suffering from bloat. Adam had taken off his cap and jacket, and put aside his cigar to help us. The cigar and cap had vanished, and a scrap of cloth had been ripped from inside the collar of his coat. No doubt a black curly hair from his head could later have been found in the cap.

Vernon Quayle was doing something I could not see to the doll's face. He said musingly, "A hair, a scrap of cloth with body perspiration, a shred of cane touched with saliva. Few items of correspondence, but each one very potent. And I will have the medallion now, if you please."

My mind seemed to have stopped working and I felt sick. As I took off the medallion and handed it to Vernon Quayle I saw that the two places where the doll's eyes should have been were covered with blobs of what looked like black wax. He wound the chain round and round the neck until the medallion rested on the chest, then laid the doll down on the brass-topped pedestal of black wood.

"Listen to me carefully," he said. "Gascoyne preserved your life when you were a child coming to maturity, the time of life in a female when certain energies are at their strongest. The correspondence between you is therefore very powerful and will assist this present operation." He pointed. "Stand here, please, facing Eleanor across the pedestal. So. And now place the middle finger of your right hand on the body of the manikin."

I obeyed. Vernon Quayle no longer seemed a stupid old man, talking gibberish. He moved to stand behind Eleanor, took off his gloves, placed his fingertips on her temples, and said to me, "You will not speak again until I say that you may do so. You will remain as you are until I say that you may move. To the best of your ability, simply direct your thoughts toward remembering the occasion when Adam Gascoyne was nursing you through your sickness. Intense concentration is not called for. Simply hold the memory in your mind, as in a daydream."

I thought my mind would be too busy and distracted to do as he had bidden me, but I was wrong. I stood there remembering, gazing down at the ugly little doll beneath my finger yet not seeing it. I was a child again, lying in the cave, sheltered from the icy wind that skimmed the deep snow and blew it into drifts. Adam knelt over me, bathing the sweat from my face, my arms, my body, sucking away through a quill the filth that clogged my throat. The medallion hung from his neck. The fire threw flickering light on the dark roof of the cave. I heard the horses, Flint and Job, munching on their scanty feed.

From time to time I drifted back to the Round Room. The powders burned in the copper bowls. There was total silence. Eleanor sat like a waxen statue. Beads of sweat had gathered on her brow. Vernon Quayle stood with fingers on her temples as before, motionless, his gray blank gaze upon the doll beneath my finger. Nothing seemed to happen, but the air in the room felt heavy and brooding, as the air feels before a great thunderstorm.

I do not know how long it lasted. I only know there came a time when I was distantly aware that the blobs of black wax covering the eyes of the doll were melting, becoming liquid, running down the coarse wooden cheeks to spatter drip by tiny drip on the brass disk where the doll lay. There came a time when Vernon Quayle moved, and broke the silence, saying, "It is finished now."

I know that I tried to say goodbye to Eleanor, but she looked at me from a totally drained face, with eyes that did not recognize me. I know that Vernon Quayle put the medallion in my hands and walked with me down from the Round Room and out to where the dogcart stood. No word was spoken between us.

I do not recall driving home. I know that Mr. Stafford came out of the farmhouse and insisted that he would see to the horses and put the dogcart away. And I know that when I took off my hat and coat and set down limply in front of the glowing fire in my little room, the clock on the mantlepiece told me that I had left this room no more than seventy minutes ago.

I did not want to think. I did not know what to think about. I fell asleep in the chair, woke much later to find the fire almost dead, and with a great effort made my way up to my bedroom. There I undressed, fell into bed, and slept heavily until well past dawn.

In daylight I found it hard to believe that the events of the night before had truly happened. They seemed more like an unpleasant dream, and one I did not wish to dwell upon. I told myself that if I believed Adam would suddenly be able to see again, I was a fool. The best thing for me to do was to keep very busy, to avoid all speculation, and to expect nothing. But when a letter from Lady Gascoyne came for me by the morning post two days later. I found my hands were trembling as I opened it, and my heart grew heavy with disappointment as I discovered that it was her usual letter, with no startling news.

The only thing she said about Adam was that he still continued to go about, indoors and out, as if he were not afflicted by blindness, and that he still continued to collect bumps and bruises. He had actually fallen downstairs and half stunned himself the day before, much to her alarm. Over his protests she had insisted on fetching the doctor to him, and was happy to say that there was no damage. He was up and about again today.

She also said that Sir Charles's diabetic condition seemed suddenly to have become worse. She hoped I would come to London again soon, to visit them, because they were both very fond of me and often talked of me.

Reading between the lines, I felt she knew that the time left to her husband was now much shorter than they had once hoped. I wept a little, both for her and for him, then sat down to reply, saying I would come to visit them for a day as soon as I was able to, and certainly by the end of the month.

So much for Vernon Quayle's boasts. Adam was still blind.

That morning I went to see David Hayward, quarreled with him, rode home in high dudgeon, immediately turned round and rode back to apologize, and found myself accompanying him on his rounds for the rest of the day. This was the best medicine I could have wished for to cure the black mood which had settled upon me.

Two days later, on an afternoon surprisingly mild and sunny for late February, I rode up to Goose Hill and turned Sandy loose while I wandered slowly about the grassy crest, trying to decide where my future lay.

The Catling farm would soon be up for sale. Did I really want it? Did I want to live in that big house on my own? Would I be happy if I married David? Or would I always regard him as second-best to Adam, while he regarded me as second-best to Eleanor? And would this matter, if we were warm friends and truly cared for each other?

My eye was caught by a horse and rider coming down the far slope across the valley at a gallop, and going much too fast, I thought with a touch of annoyance. Only the Lo-bas and Jani Burr could safely ride like that. Then, with a little start of surprise, I recognized the horse. It was Bruno, the red roan with a white sock on his nearside foreleg, who belonged to Major Elliot. But he was not carrying the Major, or anyone I knew in Larkfield.

For a few moments horse and rider were lost behind a line of chestnuts, then they came into view again, starting up Goose Hill. I narrowed my eyes. A man with black hair, hatless, not in riding clothes but wearing a dark gray suit. What on earth . . . ? He rode as one with the horse, body moving to the stride of his mount with a kind of careless arrogance. There was something familiar here, something known to me long ago . . .

Mister! My mind shrieked the name, and it was the old name that came to me first.

Adam? Adam riding up Goose Hill toward me? As if . . . as if he could *see*? It could not be. Yet no blind man could have ridden as he was riding.

I stood rooted, my mind blank, not daring to think. He came to the crest and was swinging down from the saddle even as Bruno slowed to a canter and then a walk. The dark hair was tousled by wind, the deep blue eyes ablaze with a kind of wild joy. He came toward me with great strides, both hands outstretched.

"Jani!"

Tears blurred my eyes, and began to trickle down my cheeks. To speak was impossible, for my throat was numb.

"Oh, Jani!" His hands gripped my shoulders so tightly it hurt, and I reveled in the good pain of it. Holding me at arm's length, he looked me up and down, his face full of wonder. His hands moved, and he touched my brow, my hair, a teardrop on my cheek, my lips, and my neck. It was the gentle touch of a blind man, but he was now no longer blind. His eager gaze was almost devouring as he stood there, seeking with all his senses to know me. And as he stood, looking, touching, wondering, he spoke quickly, words tumbling from him.

"I went to your cottage, and the Staffords sent me to David's place, and Rosie said he was up at Major Elliot's stables, but she didn't know if you were with him, Jani, and when I got there, you weren't, and I thought I'd go mad if I didn't find you soon, and David said he thought you might be up here, and the Major said, 'Here, boy, take Bruno.' So here I am, and—oh, Jani, is this really you? Really that funny little girl I found in Smon T'ang and could never get out of my mind? But of course it is, I can see her in you. Oh yes, by God, I can *see* you. Jani! I fell downstairs a few days ago and got a touch of concussion. Last night I went to bed blind and woke up able to see!"

His hands slid down to grip my own and hold them tightly. "Jani. Beautiful Jani. Why did I call you a funny little girl? You were beautiful then, if I'd had eyes to see. I've been blind for longer than I knew. Lord, but it's good to look at you, Jani. Did you know I lost my heart to you from the moment you came to me out of the past, and put your arms round my neck, and wept because you found me blind? Or perhaps it was longer ago I lost my heart to you, as Molly thought. She said you were the one, didn't she? And sometimes, sometimes during all these past months together, I've felt that you cared for me. Do you Jani? Will you marry me? Please?"

I knew that if I tried to speak I would only weep more tears of happiness. I looked up at Adam, remembering the many times during his blindness when I had been close to him, as I was now, and had longed to put my arms about his neck and draw his head down and press my lips against his in a long wonderful kiss. Now I did it, standing there with him on the crest of Goose Hill, where we could be seen for half a mile around. But I did not care about that.

After a little while, when I was getting my breath back and he was holding me with my cheek against his chest, I said in a wobbly voice, "I thought you didn't much like me. I heard you say to your parents that I . . . bored you."

I felt him give a great sigh. "Jani, sweetheart, I meant you to hear. I knew exactly where you were on the stairs when I said those words. I have a blind man's hearing, and I spent most of my time listening for your footstep about the house."

I lifted my head. "But why did you say it, Adam?"

"Because I wanted you to be happy, and I was sure you could be happily married to David Hayward, but I knew that if you and I were together much longer I'd break down and tell you I loved you. And I was afraid you'd take pity on me and marry me. Me, a blind man. I couldn't have that, Jani."

I stood on tiptoe to kiss him again, then reached back into the past and said in the funny Cockney accent I had spoken in Smon T'ang, "Sometimes you don't 'alf say daft things, Mister."

David Hayward leaned back in his chair and looked at us as we sat side by side on the couch in his small living room, holding hands. An hour had gone by since Adam held me in his arms on Goose Hill. David had congratulated Adam, kissed me heartily, and claimed that he must either be best man or give the bride away.

For a little while there had been much excitement, but now we were quiet and serious, for I had just finished telling them all that had happened in the Round Room at Merlin's Keep on the night before Adam had taken the fall which brought back his sight. I had known this was a bad moment to tell my story, and that it would cast a shadow over us, but I also knew that there would never be a good moment to tell it.

David had gone pale when I told how Eleanor had been injected with what could only be some kind of drug to aid her trance. Now he said, "I've no doubt you'll think the man is a charlatan, Adam. I thought so once myself, but since then I'm less sure. Is it a coincidence that he conducted his operation shortly before the fall which apparently brought back your sight? Or is it a coincidence that you happened to fall shortly after his operation? Or did his operation cause you to fall?"

Adam said quietly, and to my utter surprise, "I'm inclined to take the last alternative. Ever since Jani first told me of Quayle I've been busy finding out as much as I could about the fellow, and also learning a little about his strange occupation from an old friend of my father's, who is very knowledgeable about such matters. I've never seen Quayle, of course, but I met him when he came to Chester Gardens and told me he was going to restore my sight before the moon was full." He shrugged and gave a wry smile. "Perhaps Quayle's science, as he calls it, consists of causing coincidences to happen."

I pressed Adam's hand and said, "Just after that night when he . . . did it, I kept wondering why. I mean, why should he want to give you back your sight?"

Adam lifted my hand and touched the fingers to his lips. "Because, my darling," he said slowly, "Quayle needs me for a purpose of his own, and all the threads of the past and present, mine and yours, his and Eleanor's, are converging toward that future purpose. At least, that's the view of my knowledgeable friend, Professor Manson."

Faintly in the depths of my mind I heard the voice of the girl in the monastery at Galdong as she gazed into the bowl of liquid jet: ". . . He is young, this demon. Black hair, tight-twisted, and eyes like a clear sky at dusk. Proud . . . too proud. But his pride will be broken . . . He will go down into blackness, and then will come the bloodless one, the Silver Man, the Eater of Souls . . . And there is the debt to pay, and in the Year of the Wood Dragon they will come to the land of Bod, to seize the teardrop that fell from the eye of the Enlightened One—"

Adam Gascoyne had indeed gone down into the blackness of the blind, where his youthful arrogance had been stripped from him, leaving the amiable, unself-pitying man with the ready laugh I had found in the back room of a dingy tavern in Wapping. And the Oracle had truly described Vernon Quayle as the Eater of Souls, for it was as if he were slowly draining my beloved Eleanor not only of life but of the inner flame of spirit.

I heard the voice of Rild, as he looked beyond the veil and spoke of the Silver Man who would be my enemy, recoiling at what his vision told him: "... *Within the bounds of earth and incarnation I had never thought to feel such power ... With the turning of the stars you will come to us again, child. Till then, go with my blessing.*"

I came back to the little living room of the cottage, to hear David Hayward saying, "It makes me shudder to think of Jani going to see Quayle on her own that night. She might have been . . . trapped. As my poor Eleanor was. I'd have stopped her if I'd known, Adam."

I shook my head. "Nobody could stop me," I said a little tiredly. "Eleanor asked me to see her, and I didn't care if she was only doing it on Vernon Quayle's orders. I shall always answer a call from Eleanor." I looked at Adam anxiously. "You do know that? You do understand, dearest Adam?"

He touched his fingers to my brow, then to his own, in a strange little gesture of belonging. "We're as one now, Jani. Your debt to Eleanor is mine, and somehow we'll pay it."

David got up, paced across to the window, and gazed out on the garden with a troubled air. "How knowledgeable is your friend Professor Manson?" he asked.

Adam said, "He's considered the leading European authority on occultism and allied subjects. Thirty-six published books. He knows of Quayle, and says that he's possibly the most dangerous individual in the world. From what I've discovered about Quayle's past from an international inquiry agency, I'm inclined to accept that opinion. I've spent a great deal of time talking with Manson and investigating Quayle, believe me."

In a faraway corner of my mind I realized that when Adam had gone out alone from Chester Gardens, and I had thought he might be visiting a mistress, he had in face been occupying himself on my behalf.

David turned to look at us. "Is Eleanor lost beyond hope?" he said in a strained voice.

Adam ran a hand through his hair, and spoke slowly, yet with an undercurrent of eagerness. "Manson said it would depend on her psychic strength, which must be very great, for otherwise Quayle would never have been interested in her. He thinks she can recover, if we can get her free from Quayle."

"And . . . can that be done?"

Adam said gently, "It can be tried, David. I can't see into the future, so I don't know what the outcome will be. But I propose to see Quayle this very day. According to Manson, he restored my sight because he needs me in some way. That gives me something to bargain with. What I intend to do now is find out exactly what he wants of me."

I said in a small voice which did not sound like my own, "I know what he wants, Adam. I didn't know till just now, and then I remembered what I learned from the High Lama and the girl who was the Oracle. They have powers, too, and they told me. They called Quayle the Eater of Souls. They said you would go to the land of Bod with him, Adam. And I shall be there, too. It was to happen in the Year of the Wood Dragon. This year. And Quayle will want you to seize the teardrop that fell from the Eye of the Enlightened One."

There was a long silence, both men staring at me in wonder, and at last Adam said, "The teardrop of the Buddha? Do you know what it is, Jani?"

"I'm not sure, but I think it's some kind of jewel in the Great Monastery at Choma La. We used to pass the monastery on our trade route to Magyari. Vernon Quayle asked me a lot of questions about it one day, but I didn't know what he was driving at. Now I remember Old Tashi telling me about a jewel, a very precious one that was in a special place in the monastery. He said that every minute of every day and night for the last three hundred years there had always been seven monks praying in front of this jewel. I expect they believe it was a teardrop shed by the Buddha, which turned into a precious stone."

"A teardrop isn't very big," Adam said slowly. "It seems unlikely the jewel could have enormous intrinsic value."

"I don't think Vernon Quayle would steal if for its worth in money."

"Then why, darling?"

"I don't know, Adam. But it must be . . . a potent talisman."

He stood up and drew me to my feet, full of restless energy, his eyes flaring with challenge. "Let's not stand on ceremony. We'll go to see Quayle at once, just as we are. The sooner we know where we stand, the better. All right, Jani?"

I nodded, forcing a smile, but I was suddenly very frightened of all that lay ahead, frightened that the Silver Man would destroy our newfound happiness. That I would lose Adam, lose myself . . . everything.

The surly manservant showed us into the drawing room of Merlin's Keep. Vernon Quayle wore his usual ill-fitting silver-gray suit. I had long ago concluded that all his suits were of the same material, except the tweeds he wore when riding. He stood with his back to the fire, lifeless grey eyes looking upon us without interest as we entered.

"Good afternoon, Jani. Good afternoon, Mr. Gascoyne." The shadow of a wintry smile touched his mouth and was gone. "I do not imagine, Mr. Gascoyne, that you have come to thank me for restoring your sight?"

Adam said curtly, "That's a large claim you make, Quayle."

The man shrugged. "Will you be seated?"

"I think not. We've come to ask your price."

"Price for what, pray?"

"Eleanor's freedom. Your wife's freedom. Her freedom from you, Quayle."

I was shaken by the savage bluntness of Adam's words, and for a fraction of a second I saw something I had never seen before—Vernon Quayle taken aback. He recovered in an instant and said, "Do you know what you are saying, Mr. Gascoyne?"

"Perfectly. Do you intend to waste time fencing with words?"

There was a long silence. At last Quayle said slowly, "I am able to read most people as if their thoughts were laid bare. I find it surprisingly difficult to do so with you, Mr. Gascoyne. Have you been receiving advice or instruction of some kind?"

"I've talked a great deal with Professor Manson over the past months, if that means anything to you."

Vernon Quayle's eyes narrowed. "I have his books on my shelves. He is a competent theorist, no more."

Adam smiled, and it was like a snow leopard showing its teeth. Suddenly I sensed in him that surging power I had seen in the days when he had fought the might of the mountain snows, burdened by a sick child.

He said, "The inquiry agents I employed many weeks ago now were competent practitioners, Quayle. You have had

273

three wives before Eleanor. The Italian lady and the Belgian lady both died by suicide. The first, a young English widow living in Hong Kong, was married to you for five years before she went into a decline and died in hospital. All three became recluses after marriage, as Eleanor has. All three were believed by their friends to have been human tools, used by you in your occult practices. You're a spiritual vampire, Quayle, you live on the life-force of others. Now you're doing the same thing with your latest human tool, Eleanor, and I'll ask you again—what's your price for her freedom?"

Vernon Quayle had listened without a flicker of expression. He said, "What do you mean by freedom, Mr. Gascoyne?"

Adam's answer was immediate. "Annulment of the marriage. Manson tells me it will not have been consummated, so there will be no problem. Then you clear off to wherever you damn well please, and never see or communicate with Eleanor again."

"On what grounds does Professor Manson assert that the marriage will not have been consummated?"

"On the grounds that if it were, you would be unable to use the poor woman in the way you have done. It would infringe the Third Law of the Etheric, whatever that may mean."

Vernon Quayle's eyes stared fixedly. "Manson is cleverer than I thought," he said at last. "I believed myself to be the only man to have deciphered that fact from the Hermetica. However, it is neither here nor there. You have asked me to name a price for Eleanor's freedom. Suppose I decline to make any kind of bargain?"

Again Adam smiled. Then he said very softly, "In that event, Quayle, I shall kill you, with no more scruple than I would have in killing a rabid dog. You have destroyed three lives, perhaps more, for all I know. I'll not allow you to destroy Eleanor, for she is Jani's friend, which makes her my friend."

I felt no shock. When I turned my head to look at Adam, and saw the cold dark flame in his gaze, I knew he had not spoken empty words, yet still I felt no shock, for now I saw clearly what I should have seen long ago. Vernon Quayle was killing my beloved Eleanor as surely as if his hands were about her neck and he were slowly strangling her.

I heard the horrid hiccuping sound which was Vernon Quayle's laughter. He said, "I have lived a long time, Mr. Gascoyne, much longer than you would think, and more than one person has attempted what you now threaten, much to their subsequent distress. Mr. David Hayward might have some advice to offer you in this matter."

"I am someone else, Quayle." Adam continued to stare unblinkingly at the Silver Man with a curiously brooding intensity. "You cannot turn my own hand against me, for I am a man who has lived in the long darkness, and my senses are too keen for you to play your vicious games with them."

Vernon Quayle half closed his eyes. "Your friend Professor Manson has given you a little learning, which is notoriously dangerous."

Adam gave a small shrug and took my arm as if preparing to go. "You wish to leave it there, then? You will not bargain?"

"I did not say that, Mr. Gascoyne.

"Well?"

There was a silence, then Vernon Quayle spoke in a voice that was slightly singsong, as if he were chanting. "The Great Monastery of Choma La stands on the trail which runs from Galdong to Magyari. It is built against the mountain whose name is never spoken. Seven times seven times seven steps rise to the Temple of Prayer, which lies beneath the topmost spire. Within the temple stands an altar of white marble. Upon the altar, a Buddha of gold. In the cupped hand of the Buddha lies the teardrop that was shed in the moment when the Enlightened One turned back from the peace of Nirvana to teach mankind the True Way."

Vernon Quayle's voice changed. He said in a matter-of-fact manner, "The story is rubbish, of course, and I think it likely that the teardrop is a semiprecious stone, perhaps only a pretty pebble. But if you will bring it to me, Mr. Gascoyne, I will meet your terms regarding Eleanor."

I felt Adam's hand tighten on my arm as he said, "What you ask is not entirely unexpected." Quayle's eyes widened for a moment, than he gave a shrug. Adam went on, "How many monks occupy the monastery?"

"Nine times nine times nine, plus those who serve them in menial duties."

"You cannot imagine that the will permit me to penetrate to the heart of their monastery and take the teardrop?"

"On the contrary, Mr. Gascoyne. It is their belief that in the Year of the Wood Dragon, two *trulku* will come to Choma La to take the teardrop and restore it to the Buddha."

"*Trulku?*"

"In crude terms, spirits in human form. I am sure Jani can explain further, if you so require. She is familiar with the religion of the area. The two expected *trulku* are a male and female. The female will have the tongue of Bod and will chant the seven times seven mantras of Galdong. I believe you will find that Jani knows them."

Adam looked at me. I nodded and said, "We used to chant them on the trail. Sembur wouldn't let me, but I used to do it under my breath."

Vernon Quayle went on, "The *trulku* may be true or false. If they are the true envoys of the Buddha, they will come on one particular day which is known only to the High Lama of Choma La and his Council of Nine. And to me."

"You?"

"Yes, Mr. Gascoyne. I performed a truly major operation to secure that piece of knowledge only a few days ago, with Mr. Hayward as an uninvited witness, I believe. It was a considerable feat, I assure you. Eleanor is quite the most remarkable source of energy I have ever used."

I think I would have flung myself at that hideous man and clawed his face if Adam had not held me back. Vernon Quayle gazed distantly through us and said, "I shall require you and Jani to meet me in the village of Shekhar, north of the Chak Pass, on the thirty-first day of May. Jani will know the place."

I knew it only from a distance. It lay a mile from the trail, and some five mile north of the pass, a huddle of tiny hovels occupied by Khamba tribesmen. They had often followed our caravans for days, hoping for the chance to make a sudden swoop and carry off a few of our bales and animals. I had sometimes wondered how my old friends were faring now against the Khambas, without Sembur and his rifle.

I heard the tinge of surprise in Adam's voice as he said, "You intend to make the journey yourself, Quayle?"

"Certainly. You need have no concern as to my physical capabilities, Mr. Gascoyne. I do not propose to travel in your company, however, for I have come to the conclusion that you may be a more dangerous enemy than most. I shall travel on the *Calabria*, which leaves Southhampton on the fifth day of April. You will make whatever other arrangements you please, providing you leave England before me. Agreed?"

"Agreed."

"I think there is no more to be said until we meet in Shekhar, Mr. Gascoyne."

"Will you answer one question?"

"You are curious to know why I seek to possess this bauble from the Great Monastery of Choma La. I will tell you. For three hundred and forty-three years, seven times seven times seven years, the prayer wheels of seven lamas have spun as the lamas chanted prayers before the teardrop of the Buddha, continuously, without ceasing, night and day alike. The potency of that jewel in the Buddha's cupped hand is therefore enormous. I note your disbelief, Mr. Gascoyne. Indeed few can believe that an inanimate object may be imbued with virtue or vice, benevolence or malevolence, the power to heal or destroy. I am not concerned to argue. I simply state that the teardrop had been the focus of fervent prayer for centuries without cease, and is unique on this planet. That is why I will have it."

There was a heavy silence in the room, then Adam said slowly, "What will you do with it?"

"That is a second question, but I will answer you." Vernon Quayle's mouth stretched in a smile which showed very small white teeth. "When the teardrop is mine, then with due ceremony and full ritual I shall proceed to destroy it. Good day to you, Mr. Gascoyne."

I scarcely remember leaving Merlin's Keep, and only came to myself as Adam and I rode side by side down the long curving drive towards the gates.

Too much had happened to me too quickly. Less than three hours ago I had known the wonder and joy of Adam coming to me with his sight restored, and then the glory of finding that he loved me. I could have wished for the world to stop still for a long, long while at that moment on Goose Hill, but we had been given no time to savor our happiness. Eleanor lay under the hand of the creature who ruled in Merlin's Keep, slowly draining the life from her. I loved Adam the more, if that were possible, for the fierce urgency with which he had taken up my cause as if it were his own, the cause of saving a woman he had never set eyes upon.

As he rode beside me, taut with a loathing I knew only too well in myself, he said, "Destroy it? Why in the devil's name would he do that? I must ask Manson."

I said, "He believes that by destroying something potent, like the teardrop, he can use the . . . the forces in it for his own purposes. I saw him use such things when he made Eleanor find you."

Adam made a wordless sound of disgust. We rode on in

silence for a while, and I saw that he was lost in thought. At last he roused himself and said quietly, "I wish to God I could go alone, but that won't do. It's in the lap of destiny now, my darling. I don't trust Quayle an inch, but all we can do is to follow his orders until we have the teardrop, and then watch each other's back."

I put out a hand. "I wouldn't let you go alone, Adam, I couldn't bear it. And you needn't worry about me, you know I'm very good on the trail. Remember how you used to rely on me to say what the weather would be, and to talk to the animals?"

He took my hand. "I remember every moment, Jani. These last months since you found me, I've often lain awake at night, remembering." He drew a long breath. "Now, let's think. We have to leave England before Quayle, but since *Calabria* is a fast mail ship he'll probably arrive before us. Never mind. If we leave only a day or two before, we shall have five weeks in hand here."

Adam's fingers tightened on mine, and he looked at me with such love and longing that my heart felt close to bursting as he said, "Marry me before we go, Jani, my love. Please. Whatever lies ahead, I want us to face it completely together, joined as one."

Four weeks later I became Adam Gascoyne's wife in the church of St. Mark, on the northern edge of Regent's Park. I was married in the name of Miss Jani Saxon, Her Highness the Princess Jani of Jahanapur. David Hayward was best man. Major Elliot, enormously proud that I had asked him to do so, escorted me to the church and gave me away. There were few guests. Mrs. Elliot and the Staffords had come up from Larkfield with the Major, and on Adam's side there was a brother of Lady Gascoyne, Lady Gascoyne, Sir Charles himself, now looking frail and gray-faced, a captain from a Gurkha regiment, and a small plump man with almost white hair, Professor Manson.

At the small reception later, at Chester Gardens, Professor Manson drew me aside with Adam and said quietly to us, "I am very glad you decided to be united before facing the great hazard you have taken upon yourselves. Quayle would of course mock at the notion that there is strength, great strength, in the power of love made complete in the union of body and spirit. Here, perhaps, is his one weak point, a failure to realize that his cold doctrine of objectivity does not embrace all powers and energies. Let us hope this weakness will defeat any treachery he may be planning."

Before we left the reception I brought David Hayward to the library for a final word with Adam, who took him by the shoulders and said forcefully, "Now listen, David. Get a locum for your practice at once, because you have a job to do."

David smiled from a rather strained face. "All right. What is it?"

"As soon as Quayle leaves Larkfield, you must get Eleanor out of Merlin's Keep. You may have trouble with Quayle's manservant, but don't let that stop you. Enlist Major Elliot's help, and the squire's if need be. Jani says there's not a soul in Larkfield who wouldn't back you up. So . . . get her out!"

David nodded, and a spark sprang to life in his eyes. "Right. And then?"

"Bring her here to my parents. Get hold of Professor Masson, and get hold of a doctor who's flexible enough to understand that there are some things beyond the scope of pills and scalpels. Better still, have Manson choose the doctor—I know he has a medical friend who practices hypnosis. Between them they can start getting Eleanor free from Quayle's influence. But you must stay here with her, David. Talk to her, talk of Larkfield before Quayle came, talk of Jani and the good times, and tell her a hundred times a day that you love her and that she's going to be herself again. Manson says that will be the biggest factor in her cure."

Adam smiled, and punched David gently on the shoulder. "Just one more thing. Jani has something for you."

I went to David, put the silver medallion in his hand, and kissed his cheek. "When the moment's right, give it to Eleanor with my love, David. I know she'll wear it, once Quayle has gone. And ask her to say a little prayer for us."

During the month before the wedding I had lived at Sir Charles's house in Chester Gardens, occupying my old room there. After the wedding Adam and I spent a three-day honeymoon at a small hotel in the Surrey countryside.

I had been a little afraid that what lay ahead might spoil these few precious days for us, but it was not so. We were truly and gloriously happy, and perhaps our joy was the more intense because we both realized in our hearts that it might

279

be short-lived. We were going into danger, and not only from Vernon Quayle. In Tibet, British soldiers under Colonel Younghusband were marching north to Lhasa, and there had been fighting. They were on a route far from the route we would be taking, but any stranger in Tibet at this time would be regarded as an enemy. I wondered how Vernon Quayle hoped to travel safely, and to stay unharmed in the village of Shekhar among the Khamba tribesmen there, but I had little doubt he would be fully in control of the situation.

We sailed from the Royal Albert Docks on a ship named *Satara*, and during the twenty-seven-day voyage to Bombay our joy in each other continued to grow, for now we were cut off from the world, in a golden limbo between what had been and what was to come, both of which seemed far away and unreal. By night we lay in each other's arms, having set the narrow mattresses from our two beds together on the cabin floor so that we should not be apart when we slept. Often we laughed together like mischievous children, the future forgotten.

Once I said to Adam as I lay with his dark head cradled on my shoulder, "Were you shy of me when I was little? I mean, during those days in the cave and afterwards."

I felt him chuckle, his breath warm on my flesh. "You guessed, then?"

"Not at first. When you had to nurse me and wash me, you used to scowl like thunder, and I thought you were angry, but when I could think more clearly, I realized it was mostly embarrassment."

"My darling, I simply didn't know what to do with that funny, skinny, brave little girl. She was something quite outside my experience."

"I'm not skinny now, am I?"

"Not at all."

"And I'm not outside your experience, either?"

"Definitely not. Oh, Jani, I ache with loving you."

"You only say that because I'm a rich princess." We burst into laughter, and turned to kiss each other again.

They were most wonderful days. We sailed through the Mediterranean through the Suez Canal and the Red Sea, then turned east for the last two thousand miles to Bombay. There we left the haven of the little world of the *Satara* and braced ourselves to face the future again, to travel by train across endless plains in relentless heat for another thousand miles. For three days and nights we moved steadily northeast,
280

through Bhopal and Jhansi, across the Ganges to Lucknow, then turned east to come at last to Gorakhpur, the garrison town where long ago I had lain weeping in my hospital bed because I had lost my only friend in the world.

During the third day our train spent two hours passing through the southeastern corner of Jahanapur. Like all India, it held a mixture of beauty and ugliness. Once, in the distance, we glimpsed the spires of the palace which stood in the capital town, also called Jahanapur. This was the palace where I had been born, yet I had no feeling of belonging, no wish to stay and explore the past. I was a stranger here, and content to remain so.

In Gorakhpur we bought horses, panniers, supplies, clothing, and a yak we immediately named Neb Two. Much time was spent selecting our horses. Mine was a gray, Adam's a dark bay. They had Indian names, but I renamed the gray Nimrod, after my favorite horse at Merlin's Keep, and Adam called his Preacher, because it had a curious white band across the throat, like a vicar's collar. Twenty-four hours after reaching Gorakhpur we set off north, retracing the long journey we had made together as man and child just under seven years ago, in the Year of the Fire Bird.

Once again we seemed to be cut off from the world as we made our way through the narrow strip of the Terai, so much like the English downs but of unhealthy climate, on through the great forest, and ever northward into the hills and mountain country beyond. We were happy together in the quietness, both by day and by night.

Twenty days brought us into Smon T'ang, and again I had no sense of homecoming. I saw the country now for what it was, bleak and poor, its people bowed under centuries of superstition, fearful of a thousand demons.

Since we were intending to seize the teardrop of the Buddha from the monastery at Choma La, we skirted Galdong by night, not wanting to be seen. I was quite sure Rild would be aware of our passing, for he had foretold it seven years before, but he would not act to stop us, because any action would bind him more closely to the Wheel of Life. However, I was content to pass quietly by night, for I had no wish to renew acquaintance with any I had known in the old days. We could have nothing to say to one another now.

There was a little time in hand, and as we did not propose arriving at Shekhar until the appointed day, we camped for three nights in the high valley which lay halfway up the Chak

Pass. Here, when we moved, we cached most of our supplies and equipment, and turned Neb Two loose, before riding on very lightly laden toward the summit of the pass.

We were now in the season of summer, and though the nights were cold it was very warm by day, even at this altitude. The cairn where Sembur lay buried was untouched, as I had guessed it would be. I felt no sadness as we walked our horses up the slope to it, only a warm gratitude. I said a prayer, laid on the cairn a posy of wildflowers I had picked in the valley below, and then we mounted again for the last few miles of our long journey to Shekhar.

We knew the *Calabria* had brought Vernon Quayle to Bombay only three days ahead of us, and marveled that a man of his age could have made the exacting journey we had just made. But I had no doubt he would be there in Shekhar, waiting for us, and I knew that our time of peace was ended now. From today, in ways yet unknown to us, we would be fighting for Eleanor's life, and perhaps for our own.

CHAPTER SEVENTEEN

A mile from the village a dozen Khambas came riding down upon us, sweeping round to form a close horseshoe about us and head us on our way into Shekhar. Most of them carried muzzle-loading rifles, the rest were armed with clubs and long-bladed knives.

I gave them a formal greeting in Tibetan, but they did not respond, only stared with hostile and envious eyes at the Lee Metford carbine in Adam's saddle holster. We continued at an easy trot, and I saw that Adam was smiling as if without a care in the world. One of the Kambas edged close and reached out to touch the rifle. Adam looked at him, and the man swerved away as if from the bared talons of a snow leopard. In a few minutes we came to a cluster of stone dwellings, and I was engulfed in the old familiar smells of *tsampa,* rancid butter, greasy smoke, sweat-soaked leather, and unwashed bodies.

Vernon Quayle emerged from a doorway and came walking toward us, hatless, his silver hair stirring in the light breeze. Incredibly, he wore collar and tie and the same tweed clothes I had seen him wear when riding out on his expeditions to collect herbs and insects. To come to this place he must have traveled as we had, living in the open for days on end, exposed to sun and weather, yet that heavy face was as white and pasty as ever. I felt a stab of superstitious awe, for it seemed as if the elements had no effect on him and human weariness could not touch him.

Vernon Quayle looked from one to the other of us with empty gray eyes. The silence grew, and at last he said, "I perceive you have married. If I had known your intention I would have made it a condition precedent of our agreement that you should not marry until this matter was finished."

Adam said, "If you didn't know our intention, then perhaps you're not quite as infallible as you like to think, Quayle."

For a moment something dark and menacing stirred in the man's eyes, but his voice remained flat as he said, I have also perceived of recent days that your friend Professor Manson has turned from theory to practice. My wife is hedged by an etheric barrier which only a handful of men in the world would have the knowledge to establish, Manson among them. At present I require all my resources for the matter in hand, but when I am free to turn them elsewhere, you may be sure I shall deal with Professor Manson."

Adam said, "Since Eleanor's freedom is part of the bargain, why should you still seek to control her?"

"You have yet to complete your own side of the bargain, Mr. Gascoyne."

"We're here to do so, and the sooner the better."

"Tomorrow is the day. We shall leave here at dawn, and reach the Great Monastery of Choma La by noon. Tomorrow the nine times nine times nine monks of Choma La will accept you two as the true *trulku* of the prophecy. You will ride to the great doors, which will be open. You will climb to the Temple of Prayer, and take the teardrop from the hand of the Buddha. Then you will return to the point on the trail where I shall be waiting with these men." He indicated the Khambas who were still grouped about us.

I saw Adam glance round at the fierce grimy faces. He said, "I'm surprised they haven't killed you, Quayle. These are wild people, and you're a lone stranger here, without the language."

Quayle flickered a glance of disdain at him. "You make false assumptions, Mr. Gascoyne. I have a sufficiency of the language. Also, I am not a stranger to them, since the coming of a silver *trulku* bearing gold is also part of the prophetic legend. I brought fifty gold sovereigns to them, which they found most satisfactory." He looked at the saddle holster on Adam's horse. "You will give me that rifle, please."

Adam smiled and shook his head.

Quayle said, "When you approach Choma La tomorrow, it is essential that neither you nor Jani carry any metal object with you. You may not take your rifle, nor the sheath knife

284

which you wear strapped to your calf beneath your breeches, Mr. Gascoyne."

Adam rubbed his chin. "I wonder how much of this story you're making up as you go along," he said thoughtfully.

Quayle shrugged. "Jani can question the men as to the details of the legend."

"All right," Adam nodded. "But I see no hurry about handing you the rifle and the knife. We'll wait till the time comes, tomorrow."

"As you please. I will instruct you fully before our departure."

We slept in our clothes in a tiny room of one of the hovels that night, eating and drinking from our own supplies, for as Adam said grimly, "Quayle's a herbalist, among many other things. I've no fancy to be in a drugged state when we go walking into that monastery tomorrow." Later, as we lay side by side in our sleeping bags, holding hands, he said softly, "Are you frightened, Jani darling?"

"No . . . not really. I feel as if I ought to be, because I know that horrible man means us harm, but I . . . I think I'll be all right as long as we're together, Adam."

"We" be together all the way." He pressed my hand. "It's wonderful that Manson has been able to block Quayle's influence over Eleanor. You could tell how that had set the swine back on his heels."

"Yes. And the longer he can't reach her, the better she'll be," I whispered in the darkness. "She's tremendously strong in spirit, Adam. It's strange, though, I haven't thought about Eleanor all day. That seems an awful thing to confess, but all through the pass today, I was thinking of your father. I hated it that we had to go away when he was so ill."

"He understood, Jani. And besides, you can do no wrong in his eyes. I believe he felt that he wouldn't live to see our return, and in a way he was glad for you to be spared the last days and weeks of his going."

"Yes. I expect he would think that way. I'm so happy you made friends with him when you came home at last, my darling."

"So am I, Jani." Adam leaned across to kiss me gently on the mouth. "Go to sleep now, sweetheart. Tomorrow is going to be a long day."

A mile or so beyond Shekhar the trail split three ways,

only to converge some ten miles further north, where the Magyari trade route passed along the ridge from which the Great Monastery could be seen on the far side of a shallow valley.

Where the trail divided, the center way was the shortest but most difficult. The left-hand fork swung to the west, and was a mile or so longer but much easier going, especially for a large caravan of pack animals. The remaining fork was known as the Way of the Pilgrim, for legend held that in the distant past a very holy man had traveled this way to found the Great Monastery at Choma La. The route he had taken was broken by a ravine, some forty paces wide, and of measureless depth. The ravine ran north, at first more than doubling in width, then gradually narrowing to a small fissure and disappearing completely before it reached the point where the trails converged. According to legend, the holy man had crossed the ravine by floating through the air.

A wooden bridge had been built at the crossing place, and renewed over the centuries, for this third trail had ever since been used mainly by men making a pilgrimage to Choma La. Most ordinary travelers avoided it, because the ground on the eastern side of the ravine sloped up steeply to the snow line and was covered with scattered rocks and boulders. I had never heard of an avalanche there during my years in Smon T'ang, but Old Tashi could remember one long ago.

We took the short trail. Two Khambas were acting as guides. Vernon Quayle rode immediately behind them. Adam and I followed, and the remaining ten Khambas brought up the rear. As the sun rose higher, the air grew warm. The Khambas took off their leather coats. Adam and I stripped off our jackets and tied them to our saddle rolls. I knotted a thin cotton scarf about my neck to prevent my shirt collar becoming damp with sweat and chafing me. Vernon Quayle ignored the change of temperature and rode steadily on, a grotesque yet frightening figure.

We came in sight of the Great Monastery half an hour before noon. As we halted, looking across the valley, I caught my breath in amazement, and heard Adam do the same. The sun was at its peak, and the spires were like great halberds of gold pointing to the sky. Prayer flags fluttered in rows on every terrace. A murmurous chanting filled the broad shallow valley which lay between the rocky trail and the monastery a thousand paces away. The monks were awaiting the coming of the *trulku*. Some seven hundred of them, red-robed and in tall red hats, each spinning a prayer wheel, stood little more than an arm's length apart, forming two inward-facing lines, and these lines extended right across the valley in a broad corridor leading to the massive red-and-gold gates which stood open on the far side.

We had halted by a crag at a turn of the trail a long stone's throw from the place where the red corridor began. Quayle said very quietly in his beautiful voice, "The rest of us must go no closer. I have given you full instructions, Mr. Gascoyne. Proceed now with Jani, if you please, but be sure you bear no metal upon you."

I said from a suddenly dry mouth, "I won't take my wedding ring off. I won't."

"God will produce no adverse effect. You may not take the silver medallion."

"I'm not wearing it." I twisted my head to glare at him, and said through my teeth, "But Eleanor is!"

His eyes flickered. He said, "The rifle and knife if you please, Mr. Gascoyne."

Adam drew the rifle from its holster, passed it to Quayle, then reached down and pulled up his trouser leg to reach the knife. Two minutes later we were riding at a walk, knee to knee, along the trail to the place where the twin lines of monks began. We were both hatless, both wearing shirts of khaki drill, trousers of cavalry twill with leather thigh patches, and stout boots. Turning together between the first two monks, we halted for a moment, looking along the two red lines which sloped down and then up, narrowing in perspective for a thousand yards to the monastery. As we paused, the soft chanting which had filled the air like the sound of distant thunder ceased abruptly, and a huge silence pressed down upon the valley.

Adam murmured, "Now, Jani, my love."

I lifted my rather poor voice, and began to chant the seven times seven mantras of Galdong which I had so often chanted under my breath with my companions of the caravans from Namkhara, to make the weary miles pass more quickly. A nudge of our heels, and together we began to pass slowly between the living red lines towards the Great Monastery of Choma La.

The sun was warm on our heads, and no breath of wind stirred in the valley. Apart from the soft slow pad of Nimrod's and Preacher's hooves on the thin coarse grass, no whisper of sound broke the silence. It was as if even the insects slept. For a time it seemed I was dreaming, and that the red lines grew longer as we progressed, so that though we rode forever we should never reach the distant gates.

My voice grew hoarse, and sudden fear that it would fail altogether roused me from my stupor. I saw that we had crossed the shallow bottom and were mounting the gentle slope beyond. The monastery loomed ever more immense before us. I snatched a brief glance at Adam. He was looking straight ahead, his face an unreadable mask.

We came to the red-and-gold gates at last, and as we passed through I saw that the human corridor continued across the courtyard to seven stone steps beneath great iron-bound doors which stood open, but the men were no longer monks. I guessed that these were the lowest of the monastery servants, the smiths, butchers, and cleaners, who had resigned themselves to little hope of progress in their present incarnation. Every man wore black, and every man carried a drawn sword. If the monks had decided that we were false *trulku*, then this was the moment when we would die.

We came to the monastery steps as I completed the last of the forty-nine mantras. Two white-robed novices moved to hold our horses as we dismounted. A narrow carpet, dull gold in color, ran up the steps and disappeared into the gloom of the lamplit hall beyond the doors. Vernon Quayle had told us to expect this. How he knew, I could not guess, but I wondered briefly if at some time in the past he had used his strange arts to cause Eleanor to "see" all that was happening now.

Side by side we mounted the steps. In the lofty hall, a hundred butter lamps flickered, and the smell of incense hung heavily in the air. Gods and devils looked down upon us from niches on all sides. We followed the gold carpet through an archway and on down the length of a hall where the painted effigies of seventeen High Lamas were ranged along the walls, between pillars draped with prayer flags, the seventeen who had ruled successively in Choma La since its founding.

Beyond the hall, the carpet ended at a stairway of stone which rose and turned, rose and turned. I began to count, for I knew that we must now have reached the seven times seven times seven steps which would bring us to the Temple of Prayer beneath the topmost spire.

I felt Adam's hand take mine. We mounted steadily, almost ploddingly, and again it seemed to me that I was in a dream. Neither of us spoke, neither of us gave any sign of wanting to stop and rest. For what must have been almost six minutes we climbed and turned, climbed and turned. In my mind I was counting, ". . . three hundred and thirty-four . . . thirty-five . . . thirty-six . . ."

There came the murmur of chanting voices. Seven more steps and we stood in an archway looking directly into the Temple of Prayer. It was a small temple, no more than a dozen paces square. We were standing behind a row of seven lamas who knelt before the Buddha. From their robes, I took the one in the middle to be the High Lama of Choma La, and the others to be of the next-highest rank. Each man seemed to be kneeling in the hollow of the broad stone step before the dais bearing the Buddha. The golden effigy was of life size, the right hand held close to the body, just below the heart, and cupped with palm upwards.

Still softly chanting, the High Lama shuffled back on his knees, stood up, and moved to one side, hands pressed together as he turned to bow toward us. Then I saw that what I had taken to be hollows in the stone were not simple hollows but twin grooves, six inches deep and more, worn in the rock by the knees of the thousands of monks who had prayed unceasingly before the Buddha for centuries past.

Adam pressed my hand. I recalled Vernon Quayle's instructions, and together we moved forward, mounting the high step where the lamas knelt, passing on each side of the empty space where the High Lama had been, and stepping up to the dais.

In the golden palm lay a milky-white stone, slightly pear-shaped and about the size of my little fingertip. I swallowed hard as a numbing reluctance gripped me. To make myself reach out and pick up the stone was one of the hardest things I have ever done. No doubt my nerves were stretched to a thrumming tautness and my imagination was running a little wild, but as my fingers closed upon it, the first human touch it had known in centuries, I felt a shock that tingled like fire throughout every part of my body.

Adam put out his hand. I placed the teardrop in his palm, and saw his eyes flicker suddenly. His fingers closed, and together we turned away. The chanting ceased. The High Lama bowed again as we moved past. Then we were on the steps once more, beginning the long journey down. Adam held his tightly closed hand in front of him, and I saw sweat on his

289

brow. Because I had become part of him I knew he was feeling as I felt myself at this moment. We were fulfilling a prophecy, long foretold and accepted by the lamas of Choma La, but we felt like thieves.

It was a relief to emerge at last into a dazzle of sunlight, where the white-robed novices held Nimrod and Preacher for us to mount. The servants in black had disappeared. When we rode out of the great gates, the valley was again filled with chanting. It continued throughout long minutes as we rode slowly down between the red lines of monks, then up the slope of the valley side to the Magyari trail. This was the moment when we emerged at last from the human corridor. As we did so, all the red-clad figures turned to face the Great Monastery of Choma La, and began to move toward it in two snake-like files, chanting to the rhythm of their slow pacing.

Adam whispered, "Wait, Jani." Those were the first words to pass between us since we had started out across the valley to the monastery. I asked no question, but sat watching as the two red snakes wound their way gradually through the distant gates. When the last of them had vanished, and we saw the gates swing to, Adam looked down at his closed fist with a strange, wary gaze.

"Jani," he said softly, "if anything happens . . . if anything goes wrong and we're separated, make for the cave. Sembur's cave. We'll meet there."

I felt a chill touch me, but again I asked no question, for it seemed to me that for the moment we were in a world where instinct ruled and logic was suspended. I said, "Yes, Adam." Then we turned together and began to ride south along the trail at a steady walk, toward the low crag where the trail turned and Vernon Quayle waited.

We halted facing him, his band of Khambas behind him. For the first time I saw two high spots of color in his dough-like cheeks, and the normally expressionless eyes were alive with a kind of horrid yearning. He said, "Show me, Gascoyne."

There was a silence, then Adam said in a curiously strained voice, "I can't open my hand."

Quayle's face seemed to clench with fury. "It is unwise to play games with me!"

Adam gave a short hard laugh. "Don't be a damn fool. Look at my hand." He held out his fist, and it was like white marble, with the veins standing out in cords.

Quayle drew a deep breath. His normal pallor returned, and with it his gray dispassion. He sat with lips pursed as if in thought, then said without emotion, "Proximity to the Temple of Prayer may be exerting some measure of influence. We will ride a little way." He said a word to the Khambas, who turned their horses to take up the same positions they had occupied on the ride north from Shekhar, with two Khambas leading and the rest behind us. But now Vernon Quayle had fallen back to ride level with us, on Adam's other side.

A mile passed, then another, and I saw the color coming slowly back into Adam's tightly clenched fist. He kept looking down at it, and as time went on he was able to flex the knuckles a little. After an hour, at the point where the track broadened and the trail forked three ways, Vernon Quayle gave the order to halt. "Are you able to open you hand now, Mr. Gascoyne?"

Adam stretched out his arm. Slowly, quivering a little, his fingers uncurled. Sunlight glinted from the milky-white teardrop in his palm. I heard Quayle draw in a hissing breath, but he made no attempt to touch the stone. Fumbling inside his jacket, he brought out a small box, about as big as the palm of my hand. It appeared to be made of stiff black leather, and was in the shape of a star with five points. On the ten vertical sides there were hieroglyphs in silver. Quayle snapped open the lid and held the box out toward Adam.

"Place the stone inside, if you please."

Adam tilted his palm, the teardrop fell with a tiny sound, and the box snapped shut. Adam let out a long breath and said, "That concludes our agreement, Quayle. My rifle and knife, please. Jani and I will make our own way back from here."

Quayle sat like a statue, unmoving, his eyes on the small black box he held. His lips scarcely seemed to move as he said in a thin, distant voice, "I have no further use for you or your wife, Mr. Gascoyne, and no intention of permitting two such potent enemies to disturb my future."

For a moment, still bemused by the dream-like happenings of the past hour, I did not grasp the import of his words. He went on, "I have caused these gullible Khambas to believe that the two *trulku* who carry away the teardrop from the Temple of Prayer are merely minions of the *silver trulku*, who is myself. It is he who will restore the teardrop to the Buddha in the halls of Nirvana, while his minions will put off

291

the bodies in which they have clad themselves, and return to their home in the sky."

Vernon Quayle took his eyes from the black star-shaped box and glanced at the Khambas. "That is what these men believe, Mr. Gascoyne. As the *silver trulku*, I have warned them that my minions may need persuasion to divest themselves of their earthly bodies."

In the instant I realized Vernon Quayle intended us to die. I was swept by a rage that overwhelmed fear, and I acted by instinct rather than thought. Nimrod felt my heels, felt my hands, heard my voice call to him sharply, and responded in a flash, muscles bunching as he lunged forward. I snatched the box from Quayle's hand, spun Nimrod round, sent him forward again, then spun once more so that his hindquarters hit the shoulder of one of the two horses ridden by the leading Khambas, knocking it into the other.

I saw one of the other Khambas, the first to gather his wits, lift Adam's carbine from under the blanket draped over his saddle, where it had been hidden. Even as he did so, Preacher's powerful body surged across the trail, with Adam freeing a foot from the stirrup and half rising from the saddle to smash a boot into the man's chest, knocking him from his horse.

I had Nimrod rearing on his hind legs now, hooves pawing the air, threatening a Khamba who had drawn a long knife. I saw Adam swerve, but he could not get to me, for there were men and horses between us. Quayle was shouting orders. Adam's hand leapt out, pointing to the middle one of the three trails, just behind me now, He cried, *"Go, Jani, go!"* and in the same moment swung Preacher toward the eastern trail, the Way of the Pilgrim, and drove heels into his flanks.

I turned Nimrod, and touched his ribs. He went as if flung from a catapult, flowing into a gallop along the short but difficult middle trail. For a moment I saw Adam's head and shoulders over a rounded hump or rock as our ways diverged, then he was gone. No more than five seconds had passed since the moment I lifted Nimrod into action and snatched the box containing the teardrop of the Buddha from Quayle's hand. Before another five had sped, I was out of sight along the twisting trail.

In Gorakhpur we had spent hours selecting the finest horses to be found, and we paid a good price for them. We were far better mounted than Quayle or any of his followers, and for this I now sent up a fervent prayer of thankfulness.

The Khambas were fine horsemen, as I knew from the days when they had harassed our caravans, but I was their equal, and so was Adam. They would not catch us now.

I tucked the small black box inside my shirt, low down near my waist for safety, and settled down to ride, putting everything else from my mind, for this was no easy trail, and if I took a tumble now it would mean disaster.

Nimrod carried me unflaggingly, like the great-hearted creature he was, and an hour later we came down a narrow and pebble-strewn track toward the ravine. On the far side lay the Way of the Pilgrim, for here the two trails ran one on each side of the ravine for a mile or two before my own swung away to the west again, well before the bridge. As we moved down the track I shaded my eyes to scan the far side eagerly. Adam could well have reached this point by now, and might even be ahead of me, for the long loop which the Way of the Pilgrim made before reaching the wooden bridge had yet to come.

I slowed Nimrod to a walk as we turned parallel to the ravine, to let him rest a little. I was glad to take a brief rest myself, for suddenly I felt very tired, as if I were moving in a dream. With an effort I collected my thoughts. Quayle would have sent some of his men in pursuit of Adam, perhaps, but I was the important quarry, for I was the one who had the precious teardrop. Yet still I held Nimrod to a steady walk, for I was sure the Khambas were far behind. My horse was not only better than any of theirs, but also carried far less weight. I judged that I must have a lead of at least a quarter of an hour.

I felt a sharp little pain under my heart, as if some part of Quayle's black box had pricked my skin. Easing it to another position under my shirt, I gazed up the great slope on the other side of the ravine to the dazzling whiteness above the snow line. For a moment my head swam and a cloudy darkness seemed to engulf me. I told myself I had grown unused to great exertion at such altitudes, and waited for the dizziness to depart.

My sight cleared quickly, but I knew I was still affected by the mountains, for the sky held an unnatural pinkish glow and my hearing seemed to be dulled, as if my ears were partly plugged with cotton wool. I looked across the ravine again, and my heart leapt as I saw Adam. He was coming from behind me on the far side, moving at a steady canter around a great shoulder of rock where the ravine twisted. The strange pink glow seemed now to have spread to the slope of the mountain, so that horse and rider were silhouetted against it. I rubbed my eyes to clear the trick of vision, but it continued. Adam's arm swept up in a greeting, and I wave joyously in reply. As he came level with me, a hundred paces away across the abyss, I touched heels to Nimrod so that we matched the Preacher's pace.

I kept looking across the gap, watching the man who had filled my life, longing to feel his arms about me again, and to know an end to fear and danger. Beneath my shirt the little black box was still pricking me, and I decided that I would be rid of it as soon as I could find a moment to remove the jewel. I wanted nothing of Vernon Quayle's near me.

A sound penetrated my dulled hearing, and for a moment I thought it was thunder, but the pink-blue sky was cloudless. The sound came again, a soft tremulous rumbling. My mind spun wildly, and an icy spear of terror pierced my heart, for high on the towering slope above Adam I saw vast slabs of snow breaking free, slithering down, gathering rocks, boulders, scree, spreading wider in a jostling surge, a monstrous wave of tumbling stone.

Avalanche!

Old Tashi had known of only one that swept the Way of the Pilgrim in all his years, but I was looking upon one now, in the moment when my Adam rode the trail that lay in its path. I saw him glance up, and next moment he had urged Preacher to a furious gallop. I cried out to Nimrod, and we thundered along the trail, keeping level.

My heart had stopped, my breathing had stopped, I was in a nightmare. The sound came to me in a muted roar. The pink wave of snow and ice and rock moved faster, faster, and I felt dreadful sob break from me as I saw that it extended far along the slope, that Adam could not hope to outflank it.

He was still crouched in the saddle, riding like a demon, when the avalanche took him. I saw the foremost edge of it leap out over the brink, and to my half-crazed mind it seemed to move slowly, slowly, carrying horse and man as if they were dead leaves, tossing them into the great chasm. I saw them separate as they fell, rocks and rubble and mighty slabs of frozen snow all about them, going down, down, down, out of my sight at last into the measureless depths far below.

I had reined Nimrod in, and was screaming Adam's name with shock and horror, yet I could not hear my own screams, for they were drowned by the dull, awful roaring that went on and on in my ears as the avalanche continued pouring its thousands of tons into the abyss.

I fell forward, my face against Nimrod's mane, my hands pressed to my ears to shut out the sound, helpless in the racking agony of a grief so terrible I did not know how it could be borne.

There were no thoughts in my head. None at all. I was sitting in the saddle, staring blankly across the ravine. My hearing was sharp again. I could hear Nimrod breathing. My vision had returned to normal, for the unnatural pink tinge to the world about me had gone. There was no movement. All was quiet again, as if nothing had happened. I did not know how long had passed. I did not care. If the Khambas came and killed me it would be a relief.

Without knowing why I did so, I took the cotton scarf from my neck and the black box from under my shirt. I opened the box, took out the milky-white stone, placed it in the middle of the scarf and made a knot to hold it securely there. Then I tied the ends of the scarf behind my neck, so that the knot holding the stone hung inside my shirt, on my breast.

I took the black box and flung it as far from me as I could, away over the seamed and creviced rocks beside the trail . . . not into the ravine, for my Adam lay there.

Something stirred in my mind. If I let the Khambas catch me and kill me, I would be failing Adam. I would be failing all the people I loved most . . . Adam, Eleanor, Sembur, Mr. Lambert. Somehow I must summon the strength to move.

I pressed my palms to my eyes and said in a whisper, *"I'll take the teardrop to Rild. He'll keep it safe from Quayle. And then . . . I don't know—I can't think yet. But I'll try to do . . . whatever you would have wanted, Adam . . ."*

Two minutes later, where the trail swung away from the ravine and into the hills, I set Nimrod to an easy canter and then shrank back into a dark cavern in my mind, hiding from the raw memory of those hideous moments by the ravine, when my heart had died within me.

Time passed, but I had no awareness of it. We came to the junction where the three trails merged, and moved steadily on past the track which led off to Shekhar. Some time later, Nimrod went lame on his offside foreleg. I found a small sharp stone in the foot, but had nothing with which to get it out. After I had been leading him for a while, the thought came slowly to my numbed mind that I might find something which would serve the purpose in the cave where Sembur and I had taken shelter from the blizzard, and where Adam had found us later. Between us we had carried a lot of equipment, and we might well have left something which would serve me as a tool.

The cave. Adam had said that if we were separated we should meet at the cave . . . but he would never come to me there now. My mouth opened and the muscles of my throat strained in a great dry sob which tore at my chest. I fought it away and plodded steadily on.

We were nearing the crest of the Chak Pass now, the point where the walls of the pass fell back to become slopes, with the cave a little way up the eastern slope. I realized that Nimrod had been pricking up his ears, and I halted for a moment to listen. From behind me the sound of hooves echoed along the walls of the pass, and they were not far distant. I should have heard them before, if I had not been moving in a daze of grief and shock.

I turned Nimrod, bade him farewell, and gave him a little slap to send him limping back down the trail toward the Khambas. Vaguely I hoped that when they came upon him they would stop for a few precious seconds to secure him and to debate what might have occurred. I knew Quayle would not be there to give orders, for he was no more than an adequate horseman, and could not have kept up with the pursuit.

I broke into a run, knowing I would need every moment if I were to reach the cave and be hidden within it by the time the Khambas came into view. What I hoped to achieve by this, I scarcely knew, for I was too broken and bemused to think clearly. It was unlikely that they would dare enter the cave to see if I were there, and I hoped they might think I had been thrown somewhere along the trail beyond the pass. But I was almost certain that Vernon Quayle would not fail to search the cave when he arrived, and I had little hope of final escape.

My legs were leaden, and the breath rasped in my throat as I went on at a stumbling run. I heard myself sob despairingly, "I'm trying, Adam, I'm trying . . ." and then I heard the thud of hooves, much closer now.

I looked back over my shoulder to see two Khambas come round a twist in the pass only a hundred yards behind me.

Both had drawn the long-bladed knives they carried, and were holding them high as they rode. The walls fell back and I was on the open crest, driving my weary legs to carry me at an angle up the slope toward the cave. It offered no haven now, yet I struggled on toward it, for I still doubted that the Khambas would enter, and perhaps before Vernon Quayle arrived I would have time to bury the teardrop deep in some crevice where he could never hope to find it.

But the horsemen were closing behind me. The flesh of my back crawled in anticipation of their knives, and I realized I would never gain the cave, that I could not even win the small victory of denying Quayle the teardrop.

Something cracked in the air like a whip, a little to one side of me, and I head a cry from behind. I knew that whipcrack sound. It was a passing bullet, and with it had come another sharp sound, different, yet still familiar from of old, the sound of a cartridge being detonated in the breech of a rifle. But not an ancient Khamba rifle, I would have sworn to that.

From above me a voice roared, "Jani!"

Through blurred eyes I saw the head and shoulders of a figure kneeling behind Sembur's cairn, rifle to shoulder in the aiming position. I flung a glance over my shoulder as the weapon cracked again, and saw the Khamba only twenty paces behind me suddenly knocked from his horse as if struck by an invisible giant. His companion had turned and was riding for the safety of the pass, swaying in the saddle, a hand clutched to his shoulder where the first shot had struck.

I plodded forward, lungs heaving, bending to the slope, my eyes on the ground, my mind in chaos, dazedly wondering if mountain demons had raised up an apparition of Sembur and his rifle to drive the Khambas away. At this moment I could have believed anything. I even dreaded that when I lifted my head it might be the face of Vernon Quayle that I should see before me.

Two hands gripped my arms above the elbows and shook me. A voice said, "Jani!"

I looked up into Adam's face.

Adam. Black hair streaked with dust. Blue eyes staring anxiously down into mine. Strong, solid hands gripping my arms. A rifle slung on one shoulder. A Lee Metford .303 rifle, the only kind I could have named.

Adam?

Slowly I put up a hand, a quivering hand, and pressed it to his cheek, his lips. He said, "Jani, are you hurt?"

Then my knees gave way, and I felt him pick me up in his arms as a great blackness swept down upon me.

CHAPTER EIGHTEEN

I was looking at a booted foot. Adam's boot. His hand was holding mine, our fingers linked in the special way we used when we lay talking in bed together, before we went to sleep I was lying on the ground, a pile of rocks beside me, my head resting on Adam's thigh.

I turned my head and looked up. I was lying by Sembur's cairn. Adam sat crouched against it, gazing over the top toward the pass. As I stirred he looked down and said, "What happened, Jani? I thought you'd be here before me, and I was worried out of my mind."

I stared at his upside-down face and whispered, "Adam . . . I saw you die. We were riding level . . . you were on the Way of the Pilgrim. And the avalanche came, and swept you away . . . I *saw!*"

Tears came at last, and my whole body shook with an agony of weeping. Adam drew me up with one arm to hold me close against his chest, alarm and bewilderment in his voice. "Jani darling, I'm here, I'm real! It truly didn't happen. Don't be afraid . . . oh, my God, it was Quayle's doing!" He held me closer. "Wait, wait! Let me think. How the devil could he reach you with such a monstrous hallucination?"

Then I knew. Then I understood the dream-like sensation which had come upon me as I rode Nimrod at a quiet walk beside the ravine. Then I knew how Quayle had been able to use his powers to breach my mind, and create a hallucination so totally real.

"The black box," I whispered. "It was under my shirt, touching me, hurting me a little . . . an evil thing. That's how he reached me, Adam. He did it to hold me, delay me . . ."

"Dear God," Adam said huskily, "what you must have

299

gone through, Jani." His voice sharpened. "Where's that damned box now?"

I clutched him with all my strength, and felt weak with joy as I heard the heart beating within him. "It's all right, my darling," I croaked. "I threw the box away. Something made me take out the teardrop and hang it round my neck, tied in my scarf. I threw Quayle's horrible little box away." My voice was wavering up and down. "If I hadn't, I think I would still be there by the ravine, frozen in a nightmare. And they would have caught me. Oh, Adam, Adam . . ." Tears came anew as I wept with thankfulness that he had been given back to me. I wanted to say his name again and again, to keep touching, holding him, assuring myself that he was truly alive and I was in his arms.

He stiffened suddenly and said, "Steady, Jani."

I set my teeth hard, pulled myself together, and moved away a little, kneeling to peer over the top of the cairn. Two Khambas had emerged from the pass on foot. As I watched they dropped out of sight behind a fold of rock, then appeared briefly again as they began to crawl up the slope, carrying their rifles before them. I said, "I'm sorry, my darling, I won't make any more fuss. It was just that I felt so . . ." I could find no words to say what I had felt.

Adam said, "I've been making myself think how it would have been for me, if I'd seen you go down into the ravine." His hand touched mine, and his voice broke for a moment. "Thank God you're safe."

I watched the Khambas wriggle forward another few yards, and said, "Nimrod went lame, and they caught up with me. Those first two would have killed me if you hadn't been here with the rifle. Is it Sembur's?"

"Yes. I buried it beside him, well-greased and in its case. I thought of it as soon as I got here." Adam took his eyes from the slope to look at me for a brief second. "I only had to move a few of the rocks, Jani. I didn't disturb him."

"Sembur wouldn't have minded." I looked down the slope, measuring distances with my eye. "How close will you let them get, Adam?"

"Until I have a sure target. There's a problem of ammunition. I found four rounds in the magazine, all in perfect condition, but there are no spare clips. So now we have only two rounds left."

Another pair of armed Khambas darted from the shelter of the pass and vanished amid the ridges and hollows of the
300

rocky slope. One was carrying Adam's carbine. The first two were no longer moving now. I said, "They'll work into position in pairs, keeping under cover until they're in a half-circle round us. Then they'll all attack at once."

"There speaks an old campaigner."

"Sembur told me. They almost pinned him once, just like that, when he was scouting ahead."

Two more Khambas ran from the pass and took cover. Adam said, "I can't afford to waste bullets on snap shots. Now listen, Jani. Preacher is in the cave, I haven't unsaddled him. Go in and get mounted. When I give the word, start down the slope, angling away from the Khambas. They can't get a shot at you without showing themselves, and I'll be ready to pick off anyone who tries. You just keep going on the Galdong trail."

I put my hand on his arm, and heard the faltering of my voice as I said, "Please don't make me, Adam. Please. I haven't the courage. I've lost you once. I . . . I simply haven't the courage to bear losing you again."

He sighted the rifle on a fold of rock which hid the Khamba with the carbine, and after a little while he said gently, "All right, my sweetheart. Remember how Flint carried the two of us? Let's see if Preacher can do the same."

I began to turn, to crawl back under the overhang and into the cave, but even as I moved there came a shrill whistle from somewhere on the slope. Six Khambas rose from hiding, well spread out, and began to run at us. At the same moment four more appeared from the pass, each man dropping to one knee and lifting his rifle. Some shots passed above our heads. Adam fired once . . . twice. Two charging Khambas went down, one of them the man with Adam's carbine. The other four came on. Adam spun the rifle in his hands, to hold the barrel and use the butt like a club. As he did so a third Khamba dropped, and began to roll limply down the slope.

For a moment I thought the Khambas below had shot one of their own men by accident, but then came a rattle of fire from our left, from the Smon T'ang side of the crest. Two Khambas firing from below went down, the other two darted back out of sight into the pass. Only three now remained on the slope, and they turned to run. I heard an English voice shout, *"Cease fire!"* A silence fell upon the pass. Adam stood up and drew a bare forearm across his brow, staring down to our left. I rose beside him.

Small dark men on ponies were pursuing the fleeing Khambas. They wore dark green uniforms with round pillbox caps. In their hands swung great curved knives. I knew only one nation in all the world who carried such knives. The Gurkhas, the wonderful little soldiers from Nepal who served in the British Army, were here with their *kukris.*

A few had dismounted to fire the volley which had driven the Khambas off, and they were still in firing position, waiting for the next order. More were coming up from the south side of the pass, behind the vanguard. Thirty men, I judged. A white officer in a freshly pressed shirt, looking as if he had just stepped onto a parade ground, began to move up the slope toward us on a beautiful gray horse. To one side and a little to his rear came a Gurkha wearing the three stripes of a havildar and mounted on a sturdy pony.

I watched blankly, with only a flicker of curiosity. In the past hour or so, fear had been wiped away by grief, and grief by joy, and joy by the seeming certainty that Adam and I were about to die together. Now I was spent, and could feel no more. The officer halted a few paces from the cairn, leaned forward on his saddle, and gazed down at us with a puzzled air. He was very fair, with blue eyes and a small mustache, wearing on his shoulder the three pips of a captain.

"Hello, old man," he said in a drawling voice. "Gascoyne, isn't it? Third Battalion? Remember you in Peshawar, back in ninety-six. Thought you'd left the regiment years ago. What are you doing up here, old man?"

"Well . . . that's a long story." Adam reversed Sembur's rifle and tucked it under his arm, squinting up at the newcomer in the sunlight. "You're George Plunkett. I won five pounds from you in the mess one night, jumping Flint over the long table."

"Absolutely right, old man." George Plunkett studied me with a baffled air. "Who is the young lady, if one may ask? Not Tibetan, I'll wager. Can't quite place her, actually."

Adam turned to me, his face very straight, and made a slight bow. "Your Highness, please allow me to present to you Captain George Plunkett of the First Battalion, 2nd Queen Victoria's Own Gurkha Rifles." Captain Plunkett's naturally blank face became even blanker as Adam turned to him and said formally, "Captain Plunkett, I have the honor to present Her Highness the Princess Jani of Jahanapur."

"Her—? Of Jahanapur? Oh, I *say!*" Captain Plunkett swung down from his horse. "Then she's the lady who—? But

302

that's why we're here, of course! The whole regiment knows the story. Oh, I say, ma'am, Your Highness, I'm vastly honored, deeply privileged indeed." He took my grimy hand and bowed over it.

A tremor of laughter stirred deep within me, and it seemed to bring with it a little return of strength and feeling. I smiled at the Captain and said, "Thank you, Captain Plunkett. My husband introduced me formally, but I am also Mrs. Adam Gascoyne."

"Really? Oh, I *say!* Well, my felicitations, ma'am. And my congratulations to you, Gascoyne, my dear chap." He pushed back his cap and scratched his brow. "I still can't imagine what you're doing here with Her Highness, being shot at by these Khamba fellows."

"Ah, well, I'm afraid that's something you would have to ask of the diplomats, old man," said Adam, lowering his voice a little. "You take my meaning?"

"Eh? Oh-ho, so it's like that, h'mm? Well, I certainly shan't bother to ask those fellows. Diplomats don't like soldiers asking 'em their secrets." His eyes turned to me. "Enough said, ma'am, what?"

I gave Captain Plunkett another smile, and said, "We're very grateful, Captain, not only for your discretion, but for appearing at such an opportune moment. Is it in order to ask what brings you to the Chak Pass?"

"Oh, beg pardon, ma'am, I thought you'd guessed. It's—as—well, I'm in charge of this party sent to bring back the remains of R.S.M. Burr, for burial with military honors in the regimental cemetery at Gorakhpur, do you see."

I took hold of Adam's arm and held it tightly. A few seconds passed before I could speak, and then I said, "Thank you, Captain Plunkett. Of course I should have guessed, since I was responsible for you mission, but . . . my husband and I have suffered a number of distractions today, and perhaps we are a little slow of wit."

"Not at all, ma'am, not at all," Captain Plunkett protested.

He spent the next ten minutes ensuring that I would be as comfortable as possible during the hour or so that we expected to remain here on the crest of the pass. His Gurkhas made a kind of armchair for me from boxes which had contained food supplies, and padded the seat with blankets. His batman brought me fruit, cheese, bread, and even wine. I made myself eat a few mouthfuls and drink a little wine, but could manage no more. Adam hovered about me until I told him not to make a fuss of me lest I wept again, and then he let me be and began to chat happily with the Gurkhas.

Six men were sent north along the pass for half a mile, to keep watch and make sure no Khambas approached. Others were detailed to remove the dead Khambas and give first aid to the one who was wounded. When Captain Plunkett was giving orders for men to be posted down the pass, Adam said, "If they find an Englishman dressed in tweeds and looking like a ghoul, please have your men arrest him. When we reach Gorakhpur he can be transferred to the custody of the civil authorities and charged with the attempted murder of Her Highness and myself."

Captain Plunkett fingered his little mustache. "Right, old man," he said. "But don't let my chaps know the last part, or they'll have the fellow's head off. They think rather a lot of Her Highness, you see."

As a small group of Gurkhas began to take apart the cairn, preparing to move Sembur into the plain coffin they had brought with them, Adam said to me, "Go and wait down below, my darling."

"It won't be horrible, Adam. Up here it's either freezing or very dry, and a body stays preserved, just a little shriveled, perhaps."

"Even so, Jani . . ."

"I know. I'd rather remember him as he was, but I can't bear for him not to have a friend here with him when he's moved."

"I'm his friend, Jani. He trusted you to my care. And these are Gurkha soldiers, of his own regiment, come to honor him. He has a score of friends here."

"All right. And thank you, Adam dear." I rested my cheek against his shoulder for a moment. "I'll go down and try to find Nimrod. Perhaps he's somewhere in the pass."

"Don't go beyond the Gurkha sentries."

"I promise."

They had set up a temporary post half a mile along the pass, where the riven and twisting walls fell back as the trail began the long descent to Shekhar and beyond. I found six stocky dark men with white teeth and big smiles . . . and with them was Nimrod. They had prized the stone from his hoof and were giving him water to drink from a mess tin when I arrived.

I made much of Nimrod, speaking to him in honorific Tibetan, then said a few words to the Gurkhas in their own tongue, thanking them warmly for all they had done. It became clear that their havildar had told them I was the great princess who had wiped the stain from the honor of their regiment by clearing the name of R.S.M. Burr. They were almost childlike in their shyness, and I did not embarrass them by staying to talk too long.

As I walked back along the pass, leading Nimrod, I thought about Vernon Quayle, and felt a fiery stab of satisfaction at his downfall. If ever he came within reach of the law, he would face charges of attempted murder. For my own part, I hoped he would end his days here, living as the Khamba nomads lived, and that we would never see or hear of him again—

The sky seemed to splinter, and I was lying face down on the ground, sick and dizzy, feeling the tremor of Nimrod's hooves through the rock as he skittered nervously away. A hand gripped my collar, lifting me slightly and I felt myself being dragged along with my toes trailing on the ground. Now I was in shadow. I was dropped, and a foot turned me onto my back. I tried to move, but the blow to my head from behind had left me half stunned, and my limbs would not respond.

I lay dazed and frightened, my cheek on cold rock, slowly working out that I had been dragged into one of the short blind crevices in the seamed and broken walls of the pass. With a painful effort I turned my head a little and lifted my eyes.

Vernon Quayle stood astride me, bending to stare down, pale jowls streaked with dust. The gray eyes held nothing at all, no hate, no fear, no passion, yet in his very coldness there was a devouring quality which made the words of the Oracle ring in my head . . . *Eater of Souls*.

He said a musing whisper, "You and Gascoyne have seriously endangered the most important operation I have yet undertaken. You must both be destroyed, of course. Without you, there can be no witness to accuse me."

He bent his spidery legs and sank down, straddling me, his knees pinning my arms. I tried to scream, but he jabbed a thumb into the hollow of my throat, and I was voiceless. With a cold methodical movement he unbuttoned my shirt. The knot in my scarf holding the teardrop of the Buddha lay on my breast.

Vernon Quayle remarked in a dispassionate tone. "For the moment I have depleted my resources in the very consider-

305

able feat of projecting a major and detailed hallucination. To deal with Gascoyne, I shall require a substantial renewal of energies. It is most fitting that the destruction of your life should provide them."

He drew from under his jacket a red cord, curiously plaited, about the thickness of a finger and less than a yard in length. Again I tried to scream as I felt his dreadful hands at my neck, passing the cord beneath the nape, but I seemed unable to draw breath, and only the tiniest sound came from my open mouth. A little time ago I had thought myself to have passed beyond fear, but now it leapt within me, raw and burning and terrible. Yet even the huge surge of terror brought no flow of strength into my limbs. I tried to struggle, but felt puny as a butterfly. My throat was closed, my lungs airless, and it was as if life itself were already draining from me, even before I felt the clutch of that vile red cord.

As I arched my neck back in a last futile attempt to avoid it, my blurring vision glimpsed what could not be real . . . a yellow-eyed mountain demon, crouching above us on the crag which hid the sun. I saw the haughty stare, the lift of lip to reveal the great teeth, the glint of light on the dappled fur, the flick of a long tail, almost as long as the body.

No demon. A snow leopard.

In the far reaches of my fading mind I cried out desperately, wordlessly, "*Help me, little brother!*"

Then darkness seized me, bearing me down into an abyss where no agony could follow, and as I fell, before the final moment of nothingness, I felt a faraway impact, heard a faraway sound . . . .

I was floating face down, being borne up through a dark sea to a world of pain. The flesh of my throat burned as if flicked with a fiery whip. Something was digging into my chest. Somebody was pressing on my back, crushing me. The pressure was released, and air rushed into my lungs. The pressure came again, forcing it out.

A plummy voice said, "I think she's breathing better now, old man."

Then Adam's voice, close above me, like a saw on steel: "What in the name of God were your men doing to let it happen?"

I moved a hand, tried to lift my head, anything to make him stop pumping at my lungs. He called out my name, and snatched me up in his arms, turning me to lie face up, holding me close, staring down into my face with ravaged eyes. The sun dazzled me, and I realized I was no longer in the dark crevice leading off the pass.

At the third attempt I managed a croaky whisper. "It . . . wasn't their fault . . . he was hiding . . . but you came in time."

Adam shook his head. "We didn't. Oh, dear God, I thought you were gone. All the blood . . ." I looked down and saw the great dark patches on my shirt. Adam said quickly, "It's not yours, Jani." He glanced away and I followed his gaze. Three Gurkhas stood by a blanket which had been thrown over a shapeless something on the ground. A smeared trail of blood led from the shadowy crevice to the thing which lay beneath the blanket.

"Quayle," said Adam. "It must have been a snow leopard. Half his skull was ripped away by the blow of a taloned claw. Then the creature took him by the throat and dragged him out here."

I closed my eyes and whispered, "I saw the leopard . . . I remember now, I tried to call out to him."

From somewhere behind me Captain Plunkett said, "Fellow's as dead as a doornail. Leopard did a dashed good job in my view."

Adam wiped my face gently with a wet handkerchief. "I knew something must have happened when Nimrod came out of the pass at such a pace," he said in a voice not quite steady. "We found Quayle lying dead in the pass, and then we found you, Jani, with that loathsome . . . thing lying across your neck."

I croaked, "He was going to kill us both, Adam. He . . . he needed more energies to destroy you, and he was going to get them . . . by killing me first . . . with that crimson cord."

Captain Plunkett said in a loud whisper, "Energies? Crimson? Bit delirious, what? Not to be wondered at, actually."

"My wife is not delirious," Adam said quietly.

I felt under my shirt and found the scarf with the teardrop knotted in it. This was the lump which had been digging into my chest as Adam worked to pump air into my lungs. A little strength was seeping back into my body. I whispered, "Help me stand, Adam. I'll be all right now."

He lifted me to my feet, steadying me with my back to Captain Plunkett and the soldiers, then fastened the buttons of my shirt. On the ground nearby lay a length of curiously plaited cord, but it was no longer crimson. My flesh crawled as I saw that the cord was now a gray, sluglike color, and when I put my hand to my throat I felt a fiery weal there.

I pointed with my foot and said huskily, "Burn it, Adam, burn it where it lies."

Nobody asked any questions. Captain Plunkett gave an order, and a soldier ran off, to return two minutes later with a small container of paraffin oil. He soaked the cord where it lay, then dropped a lighted match on it. The cord writhed and twisted like a live thing as it burned, and when the flame died at last there was no ash. Nothing remained but some thin wisps of foul-smelling smoke which were slowly dispersing.

Captain Plunkett said, "Extraordinary. In point of fact, this whole business is pretty strange, wouldn't you say?"

Adam, his arm about my waist to support me, did not reply. Looking at the blanket-covered shape on the ground, he said in a voice of granite, "I will not have that carrion travel in the same company as my wife. I will not tolerate his presence, living or dead."

"Quite agree, old man. My orders don't include bringing back chaps who've been killed by leopards. I'll have him buried somewhere here." Captain Plunkett turned away, lifting his voice. "Havildar!"

In seven years Rild seemed not to have changed in the slightest degree. I stood in the sunlit chamber with Adam beside me. Mudok, surly as ever, had tried to insist that Adam should remain outside the monastery, but I carried the teardrop of the Buddha and was more than a match for Mudok.

Rild said, "Destiny is wiser than man. You would have made a poor nun, had you remained as I suggested, child."

"I think it was not the way for me, Highborn."

"Truly." He looked down at the milky-white stone which lay on a small cushion of red silk before him. "We have held you in our prayers since the Year of the Iron Mouse, for then it was foretold that you would return, perhaps to save the teardrop of the Enlightened One from the grasp of the Eater of Souls . . . perhaps to die." His gaze turned upon Adam, and became blank, unseeing. After a long silence he continued in a singsong voice, "The Old One has passed, and in the moment of passing there came a reaching out of his inner flame, to touch the spirit of one who alone could destroy the Silver Man without penalty of heavy karma."

When I was sure Rild had finished speaking I said, "I have not understood, Highborn."

His half-closed eyes opened. "Nor I, child, yet. I speak only as I must. Dwell on my words and understanding will come." He looked down at the jewel again, and lifted a hand in blessing. "For seven times seven years, and beyond, to the Year of the Fire Monkey, your names will be spoken daily in the prayers that rise from Choma La."

"We shall remember and be grateful, Highborn."

"The term of these prayers is not the term of your lives, but the end of Choma La. It is then that the Yellow Men will come, and all the land of Bod will die."

I managed to hide my look of disbelief, and said politely, "That is a grievous prophecy, Highborn."

"All things die, all are reborn, until they acquire the merit which brings release from the Wheel. Go now with my blessing."

Later, as we rode from the courtyard to rejoin the platoon of Gurkhas awaiting us on the outskirts of Galdong, Adam asked. "What was he saying, Jani?"

"Oh . . . well, the teardrop will go back to Choma La, and they're very grateful. The lamas there are going to pray for us for the next fifty-odd years, so I suppose that means we'll live to be quite old. And he said it's just as well I didn't stay here to become a nun, because I wouldn't have made a very good one."

Adam chuckled. "I'm sure you wouldn't."

A pattern fell into place in my mind, and I reached out to hold his hand as I said, "Adam, there was something else. I didn't understand at first, but . . . I think Rild said your father had died."

Adam stared. "It's what we've expected," he said slowly, "but why would Rild see such a thing? It's surely of no interest to him?"

"He said . . . no, wait while I try to translate it properly." I thought for a while, then went on, "He said that the Old One had passed, and that when it happened there was a reaching out of his inner flame to touch . . . well, to touch the spirit of the snow leopard, I think. To save me, Rild was looking at you all the time, so I think he must have meant your father when he said 'the Old One.' Oh, I know it sounds silly, I think Rild must be getting very old. He was even saying that one day the Yellow Men would come and destroy all the land of Bod."

Adam shook his head. "That's nonsense. We'd never let them." After riding on a little way he said, "I expect the rest is nonsense, too. But you know, Jani, if Father has died, I'd be glad to think he had something to do with saving you and finishing off Quayle. There's nothing would have pleased him more."

On our second day out from Galdong, the monsoon came, flooding the gorges of the Kali Gandaki, blocking the trail with small landslides, and making every mile of our journey a punishing struggle. The Gurkhas did not care; these little soldiers were the happiest of men. Adam and I did not care. In the space of a few hours, each of us had thought the other dead. Compared with that, the harshest of journeys was a joy to us, for we were alive, together, and full of love for each other. And the truly deadly struggle, the struggle against Vernon Quayle, was behind us.

Each day Adam spent some of our rest time with pencil and a thick pad, writing down a full account of all that had happened to us from the moment we rode into Shekhar to join Quayle. "George Plunkett's report on Quayle's death will satisfy the authorities," he said, "but David Hayward will want to know the whole story. So will Eleanor, I hope, if David's done what I told him to."

I saw the wisdom of what he said. Eleanor's greatest need would be to cast Vernon Quayle out of her mind forever. She could never do so if we left her wondering about his end by making a mystery of it.

Because of the weather, our journey to Gorakhpur took four and a half weeks. There we found awaiting us a telegram and a letter, both from David Hayward and both dated June 2, the day after Adam and I had ridden out of Choma La with the teardrop. The telegram said: *Sir Charles died while in a coma yesterday. Your mother bearing her grief calmly and bravely. Deepest sympathy. Letter follows. Hayward.*

The letter was several pages long. In the first part David spoke more fully about the death of Adam's father, repeating his condolences and saying that Lady Gascoyne had asked to tell us that we were not to be worried about her, and that her love and prayers were with us. David went on to say that he watched the *Calabria* depart from London with Quayle aboard, then had journeyed immediately to Merlin's Keep and virtually carried Eleanor off.

The manservant, Thorpe, had followed them to David's cottage, threatening to fetch the police, whereupon Rosie, the blacksmith's sister, had kicked him into the stream and threatened him with broken bones if he did not mind his own business. That same evening David brought Eleanor to Chester Gardens, where they had been staying with Adam's parents ever since. A doctor and Professor Manson had attended her daily.

At first Eleanor had been like a sleepwalker, but as the days passed she had gradually awakened from the trance-like condition which gripped her. A marked change had come about after three weeks, when Professor Manson decided that she had roused sufficiently for David to tell her all that was happening, and to give her the silver medallion I had left for her.

Then she became distraught, weeping, crying out my name, praying for my safety. And she began to talk at last, never speaking Quayle's name, but saying that *He* had wanted to trap me as she had been trapped, and that in all those months of horror she had used the tiny scrap of will left in her to withstand *Him* in this one thing.

Next day she was very controlled, but almost gaunt with anxiety, saying again and again that as soon as Adam and I had served Quayle's purpose he would turn upon us and do his utmost to destroy us. David had tried to reassure her that we would be ready for treachery, and had worried about her acute distress, but Professor Manson had been delighted by it, since it meant that she was beginning to feel, to experience emotion, and to come to life again.

David's letter ended:

> . . . Over the past two weeks Eleanor has steadily improved, and with our help she has begun to have faith that you will return safely. This small spark of hope and confidence flared up in a most astonishing way only today, for she took me aside and with great composure told me she was certain Vernon Quayle was dead. "His hand has been lifted from me, David," she said, "I know it. Pray God my Jani will be safe now, and her dear husband also."

In closing this letter I echo those words of Eleanor's.

I realize, as I write that if you read this you will indeed have returned safely to Gorakhpur. Please send a telegram at once to relieve our anxieties.

Your ever-grateful friend,

David

Within an hour we had sent a telegram, and when the train for Bombay left later that day it carried a letter addressed to David, with the story which Adam had written during our journey from Tibet.

Ten days after our return to Gorakhpur, and two days after the arrival from England of Lord Kearsey, the Colonel of the Regiment, I stood watching a battalion of Gurkhas as they formed up on the great parade ground. From the four dresses brought with me from England I had selected one in pale gray, removing some maroon trimmings and stitching a black armband on the sleeve.

Adam stood beside me on a large dais at one end of the parade ground. With us were the Commanding Officer of the battalion, his senior officers, and Lord Kearsey, a small man with a face like a gnome and an amazingly loud voice. When the parade was ready he made a short speech in simple Gurkhali, and then Adam led me forward to receive the Distinguished Conduct Medal which had been awarded to Sembur.

Later we were driven to the military cemetery, to see Sembur's coffin brought on a gun carriage, with an escort of a hundred men slow-marching to the sound of a single measured drumbeat. Beneath his name and rank on the headstone was the Gurkha motto, *I will keep faith*.

I was very tired by the time it was all over, and thankful to be alone with Adam in the bungalow which had been provided for us in the married quarters. A little before dusk, as we sat quietly on the veranda, a servant came to say that Lord Kearsey had called and would be grateful if we could spare him a few moments.

We went to the small drawing room to greet him, and when he had bowed over my hand he produced a small flat box of sandalwood, intricately carved.

"One of these days," he said, "I would greatly enjoy hearing what you and this husband of yours were doing up in Tibet, ma'am. But this isn't the time, so I'll not trouble you now, except to give you this." He placed the box in my hands. "I stopped in Jahanapur for a day on my way here, and talked with Prince Mohan Sudraka. He's an educated man, and readily saw the justice of my suggestion."

I lifted the carved lid. The interior was lined with black velvet, and I looked down upon an emerald ring, two gold-set ruby earrings, and a peacock-tail gold brooch with two of its six diamonds missing. My mother's jewels.

Adam said softly, "Of course. What a fool I am to have forgotten. I delivered everything of Sembur's to Colonel Hanley in Calcutta. Eventually the jewels must have been returned to Jahanapur."

Lord Kearsey nodded. "I thought it proper to restore them to your wife."

I said, "Thank you, my lord. You are a very kind and thoughtful man. I . . . I wish I could find words to tell you how much this means to me."

"I forbid you to try, my dear," he said sternly. The gnomish face turned to Adam. "Take very good care of her, young fellow. She's battle-weary. I've seen that look in men's eyes, and I know it."

When Lord Kearsey had gone, Adam held my face gently between his hands and studied me. "I know it, too," he said. "This is the second time I've seen it in you, Jani, my little love. Once long ago . . . and now. But never again, Jani, never again. We're going home."

By the time our ship entered the Mediterranean I was myself again, and our happiness was even greater than we had known on the outward journey, for now the long black shadow of Vernon Quayle no longer fell across our path. When we reached Malta, and anchored for a day in Grand Harbour to refuel and take on fresh stores, a letter from David Hayward was delivered aboard with the mail. It had been posted only ten days before.

Dear Jani and Adam,

We received your telegram from Gorakhpur three weeks ago, to our infinite joy and relief. Early last week your telegram from Bombay arrived, giving details of your sailing for home, and this morning came the long letter you posted in Gorakhpur with all details of that terrible day when Quayle tried to destroy you both. I am writing to you at once, hoping to catch you in Malta on your way home.

What you have endured is horrifying beyond words, and we can only thank God that you have come through safely. Since reading your letter this morning, Eleanor has looked like a ghost, and yet I am glad, for the shock will pass, and we have above all the knowledge that this is the end of the long nightmare, and we need never speak of Quayle again. I am sure that is Eleanor's wish. In case what I have said of her so far may have given a false impression as to her present state of health, let me hasten to reassure you by bringing you up to date with our news.

First, Adam, your mother is well and in good heart. She is now staying with Eleanor—at Merlin's Keep! I am in my cottage again, as you see from the address. Every trace of Quayle's existence has been removed from Merlin's Keep, and by this you will guess that Eleanor is very much her old self again, for it must have called for great courage to return as she has done. Larkfield is very pleased, I can assure you, and has shown marked approval of the fact that Eleanor refused to go into mourning for "the owd devil," as they used to call Quayle.

It is my great happiness to tell you that Eleanor has agreed to marry me in September. We hope very much that you two will take the Catling farm, so that our lands adjoin and we can farm together.

Now, Jani, please know that Eleanor has tried to write you a letter to enclose with this, but finds it impossible. She says words are not enough, and is sure you will understand. She longs to see you, and to meet Adam, of course. I will not pretend that all is as if nothing happened to her during the year when that monstrous creature controlled her life, but I believe that with Professor Manson's help, and above all with Quayle's death, she has been able to detach herself from the long and terrifying experience, so that it has become a steadily fading dream.

As Eleanor says, words are not enough, and as you both know, I am not one to wear my heart on my sleeve. So let me simply say that I know Eleanor would have been lost forever but for you, and you have my undying gratitude.

In only a few days after reading this you will be home, and how wonderful that will be. I long to squabble with Jani once more as we deal with a bad-tempered patient! We have the date of your ship's arrival, and we shall wait for you that day at Merlin's Keep, for Eleanor holds her reunion with Jani too precious for a railway station or dockside.

Until that joyous moment, we send you both our full-hearted love.

Ever,

David

We were standing on deck under the golden ramparts of Grand Harbour as I read the letter, and for me this was a golden moment indeed. I could not speak for happiness as I passed the letter to Adam. He read it through, folded it, then said quietly, "Come down to the cabin, Jani."

I took his arm, a little puzzled. When the cabin door had closed behind us I said, "What is it, Adam dear?"

"Three things," he said soberly. "First, I was watching your face while you read that letter, and I'm sure you get more beautiful all the time."

"Oh, my darling, I do love your nonsense."

"Second, I'm much in favor of us taking the Catling farm."

"That's wonderful. But couldn't you have said all this on deck?"

"Ah. But the third thing is that it's at least two hours since you last kissed me, Jani Gascoyne."

I reached out, and he gathered me into his arms.

On a hot August afternoon we descended from the landau which young William had brought to the station to meet us. Young William was seven years older than he had been on the day I first came to Merlin's Keep, when he had looked upon me in my shabby, much-mended clothes and said, "Well, there's a noice 'at!"

Now he grinned shyly, shuffled his large feet, knuckled his brow, and said, "You'll foind 'em by the back terrace, Miss Jani."

"Thank you, William."

I was flushed and almost dancing with excitement as Adam tucked my arm through his. We made our way along the

315

curving drive to the stables and on round to the main lawn at the back of the house. Even as we came in sight of the terrace I saw a tall figure hurry down the steps and come running across the grass toward us, the skirts of her summer dress flying; a red dress, wine-colored, like the one in which I had first set eyes on her.

"Jani!"

Adam gave me a little pat on the shoulder, and I started toward her, but my eyes blurred so much that I faltered, groping as we came together, and then she caught me in her arms.

"Jani, Jani, Jani!"

She whispered my name again and again as I hugged her, and we were both crying. When at last I could master my voice I stepped back, took her hands, and croaked, "Let me look at you."

She was not unmarked. A tress of hair curved back in a half-inch pure-white band from her temple, and there were little crow's-foot lines at the corners of her eyes and mouth. But the glorious auburn hair gleamed as richly as ever now, the brimming gray-green eyes were full of life and feeling, and I could sense in her the surging vigor I had known of old.

"Oh, my faithful, faithful Jani . . ." She rubbed tears from her eyes and gave a shaky laugh. I put my arm about her and we began a pace slowly across the lawn, talking in half sentences, interrupting each other, near to laughter, near to tears.

"Will you take Catling's . . .?"

"Yes, of course, Eleanor dear! So exciting—but when is the wedding?"

"The twenty-fifth. Oh, Jani, I just can't believe . . ."

"I'm so happy for you. Is Adam's mother still—?"

"Yes, and she's very well. Waiting to greet you after the first wild excitement, she said—"

"And Nimrod?"

Eleanor laughed in the way I remembered. "Oh, darling, you haven't changed a bit. I'm sure Nimrod is longing to have one of your interesting talks together."

I saw Adam and David by the foot of the terrace steps, talking quietly together, and clapped a hand to my lips as I exclaimed, "Oh, I'm awful! I haven't greeted David yet, or let you meet Adam. Has David told you all about him? Oh, he must have done. He's not truly handsome, Eleanor, I mean

Adam isn't, because of his nose and eyebrows, but I love them anyway, and when you get used to them he's really very nice-looking, and oh, he's so wonderful, and I'm so proud of him. Adam! Adam!"

He came toward us, and Eleanor waited for him with both hands outstretched. He took them in his own, and they stood looking at each other in smiling silence, without embarrassment, almost as if in unspoken communion. David came up beside me. I kissed him and held his hand, but neither of us spoke. We stood watching Adam and Eleanor.

At last she said, "You have traveled a long way and taken grave risks for a woman unknown to you, Mr. Gascoyne. I am greatly in your debt."

Adam shook his head, still smiling. "No, Miss Lambert. The debt will always be mine. I have you to thank for Jani."

Eleanor turned her head to look at me. "I have always thought it was I who had you to thank for her, Adam."

He followed her gaze. "Shall we agree that you and I are fortunate people, Eleanor?"

"Wonderfully so."

They continued to look at me in silence, as if waiting. David took my arm and began to lead me firmly away. "Come to the stables and talk to Sarah," he said.

"No, wait, what on earth are you thinking of?" I protested. "For goodness' sake, let me go, David, we've only just arrived, and—"

"Don't be dense, Jani," he said amiably, and hustled me along a little faster. "Those two can't wait to talk about you and to wallow in saying all manner of ridiculously nice things about you. I refuse to join in such songs of praise, or allow you to listen and become conceited. Doting husbands should be seen and not heard."

"You'll be one yourself soon."

He laughed. "Yes. And bless you for bringing it about, Jani Gascoyne."

The little rise of grass before the stables brought us to a point from which we could see over the ivy-colored wall bounding the southern side of the grounds. There, by unspoken accord, we halted to look out across some acres of pasture to the green-and-gold patchwork which marked the Catling farm. I could see the white-walled farmhouse, the outbuildings, and the chimneys of the house, Kimberley, half a mile beyond.

A soft, glowing contentment enfolded me. This would be

317

our home. Adam's and mine and our children's. His baby was growing within me, and before the last leaves of autumn were shed I would feel it stir. Here on this land we would live and work through whatever life might bring, our love tempered in the fires we had passed through together, blessed with friends whose very heartbeats chimed with our own.

Beside me David said, "Welcome home, Jani. Now come and talk to Sarah. She's carrying her first foal."

I took his arm again, and laughed. "Then we have a lot in common," I said.

W0101-W

Mary Stewart

"Mary Stewart is magic" is the way Anthony Boucher puts it. Each and every one of her novels is a kind of enchantment, a spellbinding experience that has won acclaim from the critics, millions of fans, and a permanent place at the top.

☐	AIRS ABOVE THE GROUND	23868-7	$1.95
☐	THE CRYSTAL CAVE	23315-4	$1.95
☐	THE GABRIEL HOUNDS	23946-2	$1.95
☐	THE HOLLOW HILLS	23316-2	$1.95
☐	THE IVY TREE	23251-4	$1.75
☐	MADAM, WILL YOU TALK	23250-6	$1.75
☐	THE MOON-SPINNERS	23941-4	$1.95
☐	MY BROTHER MICHAEL	22974-2	$1.75
☐	NINE COACHES WAITING	23121-6	$1.75
☐	THIS ROUGH MAGIC	22846-0	$1.75
☐	THUNDER ON THE RIGHT	23940-3	$1.95
☐	TOUCH NOT THE CAT	23201-8	$1.95

Buy them at your local bookstores or use this handy coupon for ordering:

FAWCETT BOOKS GROUP
P.O. Box C730, 524 Myrtle Ave., Pratt Station, Brooklyn, N.Y. 11205

Please send me the books I have checked above. Orders for less than 5 books must include 75¢ for the first book and 25¢ for each additional book to cover mailing and handling. I enclose $_____ in check or money order.

Name_____
Address_____
City_____State/Zip_____

Please allow 4 to 5 weeks for delivery.

Victoria Holt

Here are the stories you love best. Tales about love, intrigue, wealth, power and of course romance. Books that will keep you turning the pages deep into the night.

☐ BRIDE OF PENDORRIC	23280-8	$1.95
☐ THE CURSE OF THE KINGS	23284-0	$1.95
☐ THE HOUSE OF A THOUSAND LANTERNS	23685-4	$1.95
☐ THE KING OF THE CASTLE	23587-4	$1.95
☐ KIRKLAND REVELS	23920-9	$1.95
☐ LEGEND OF THE SEVENTH VIRGIN	23281-6	$1.95
☐ LORD OF THE FAR ISLAND	22874-6	$1.95
☐ MENFREYA IN THE MORNING	23757-5	$1.95
☐ MISTRESS OF MELLYN	23924-1	$1.95
☐ ON THE NIGHT OF THE SEVENTH MOON	23568-0	$1.95
☐ THE PRIDE OF THE PEACOCK	23198-4	$1.95
☐ THE QUEEN'S CONFESSION	23213-1	$1.95
☐ THE SECRET WOMAN	23283-2	$1.95
☐ SHADOW OF THE LYNX	23278-6	$1.95
☐ THE SHIVERING SANDS	23282-4	$1.95